OTHER NOVELS BY

ITALO SVEVO

The Confessions of Zeno

As a Man Grows Older

A LIFE

A LIFE

BY

ITALO SVEVO

TRANSLATED FROM THE ITALIAN BY

ARCHIBALD COLQUHOUN

NEW YORK ALFRED·A·KNOPF

1963

L. C. catalog card number: 62–15565

THIS IS A BORZOI BOOK,
PUBLISHED BY ALFRED A. KNOPF, INC.

FIRST AMERICAN EDITION

Translated from *Una Vita* as published in *Opere di
Italo Svevo* by dall'Oglio Editore (Milan, 1954).
This text reproduces the Morreale edition (Milan,
1930), corrected from the first edition published by
Vram (Trieste, 1892).

A LIFE

CHAPTER

I

Mother dear,

Your sweet letter reached me only last night.

Don't worry about your handwriting; it has no secrets for me. Even when there's some word that's un-
clear, I can make out what you mean when your pen
runs on so, or think I do. I re-read your letters again
and again; they are so simple, so good; just like you.

I even love that paper you use! I recognize it, it's
sold by old Creglingi, and brings back the main street
of our village back home, twisty but clean. I can picture where it broadens into an open space, with Creg-

lingi's shop in the middle, a low little place with a roof like a Calabrian hat. He is inside, busy selling paper, nails, grog, cigars, or stamps, slow but flustered, like a man in a hurry, serving ten customers, or really only serving one while keeping a wary eye on the other nine.

Do give him my regards, please. Whoever would have thought I'd ever want to see that crusty old miser again?

Now Mother, you mustn't think it's bad here; I just feel bad here myself! I can't get used to being away from you so long. What makes it worse is the thought of you being lonely in that big place so far out of the village where you will insist on staying just because it belongs to us. And I feel such a need to breathe some of our good pure air coming straight from its Maker. Here the air is thick and smoky. On my arrival I saw it hanging over the city like a huge cone, like winter smoke in our fireplace at home, but we know it's purer there at least. The other men here are all or nearly all quite content, not realizing one can live so much better elsewhere.

I felt happier here as a student, because my father was still alive and took much better care of me than I ever realized! Of course he had more money. My room is so tiny it makes me miserable. At home it could be a chicken coop!

Mother, wouldn't I do better at home? I can't send money because I have none. On the first of the month I was given a hundred francs; that may seem a lot to you, but here it doesn't get you anywhere. I try as hard as I can, but the money won't do.

I'm beginning to realize, too, how hard it is to get on in business, just as hard as it is in study, as our notary Mascotti says. Very hard, indeed! My pay may be envied and I realize I don't earn it. My roommate gets 120 francs a month, he's been at Maller's for about four years and does work which I could only take on in a year or two. I've no hope or chance of a raise before.

Wouldn't I be better at home? I could help you, work in the fields myself even, and get a chance to read poetry in peace under an oak tree, breathing that good undefiled air of ours.

I want to tell you all about everything here! My troubles are made worse by the way my colleagues and superiors treat me. Maybe they look down on me because I dress less well. They're just coxcombs, the lot of them, who spend half their day in front of their mirrors. An ignorant bunch! Why, if someone handed me any Latin classic, I could comment on it all; but they wouldn't even be able to identify it.

There, those are my troubles, and one word from you can cancel them all. Say it, and I'll be with you in a few hours.

After writing this letter I feel calmer, as if you'd already given me permission to leave and I were about to pack.

A hug from your affectionate son,

Alfonso

CHAPTER

II

As six o'clock finished striking, Luigi Miceni put down
his pen and slipped on his overcoat, short and smart.
On his desk something seemed out of order. He arranged the edges of a pile of papers exactly in line with
the rim of the desk. Then he glanced at the order again
and found it perfect. Papers were arranged so neatly in
every pigeonhole that they looked like booklets; pens
were all at the same level alongside the inkpots.

Alfonso had done nothing but sit at his own place
for half an hour and gaze at Miceni with admiration.
He could not manage to get his own papers in order.

There were a few obvious attempts at arranging them in piles, but the pigeonholes were in disorder; one was too full and untidy, the other empty. Miceni had explained how to divide papers by content or destination and Alfonso had understood, but, from inertia after the day's work, he was incapable of making any more effort than was absolutely necessary.

Miceni, just as he was about to go, asked him: "Haven't you been invited around by Signor Maller yet?"

Alfonso shook his head. After his outburst in the letter to his mother such an invitation would have been a nuisance, nothing more.

Miceni was the reason Alfonso had alluded in his letter to the haughtiness of his superiors, for this invitation was often mentioned by Miceni. It was customary for every new employee to be invited to the Mallers' home, and Miceni was sorry Alfonso had not been asked, as this first omission might mean the end of a custom to which he was attached.

Miceni was a frail young man with an unusually small head covered with very short, curly black hair. He dressed as if he could allow himself a few luxuries, and was as neatly groomed as his desk.

It was not only in dress that Alfonso differed from his colleague. He was clean, yet everything he wore, from his freshly ironed but yellowish collar to his gray waistcoat, betrayed untutored taste and a wish to avoid spending. Miceni, who was vain, would twit him by saying that his only luxuries were bright blue eyes, their effect spoiled, according to Miceni, by a thick, ill-kept, chestnut-colored beard. Though tall and strong, he seemed too tall when standing, and since he held his body bent slightly forward as if to ensure balance, he looked weak and rather vague.

Sanneo, the head of the correspondence department,

now hurried in. He was about thirty, tall and thin, with light, faded hair. Every part of his long body was in constant movement; behind his glasses moved pale restless eyes.

He asked Alfonso for an address book and, as the word did not occur to him at once, tried to show the shape of the book with his hands, trembling with impatience. On getting it, as he was nervously flicking over the pages, he gave Miceni a polite smile and asked him to stay on, as he had more work for him. Miceni at once took off his overcoat, carefully hung it up, sat down, took his pen, and awaited instructions.

Alfonso did not like Signor Sanneo, because of his brusqueness, but had to admire him. Very active though physically weak, Sanneo had an iron memory and knew the tiniest detail of every little business deal, however long ago. Always alert, he wielded his pen with speed and ability. On some days he would work ten hours non-stop, indefatigably organizing and registering. He would discuss some petty detail intensely, as Alfonso knew from copies of letters he happened to see.

"Why does he put so much into it?" Alfonso would ask himself, not understanding the other's passion for his work.

Sanneo had a defect which Alfonso learned of from Miceni. He was inclined to pick favorites capriciously and persecuted those out of favor. He seemed quite incapable of liking more than one person in the office at a time. Just then his favorite was Miceni.

Signor Maller opened the door and entered the room after making sure Sanneo was there. Alfonso had never seen him before. He was thickset, rather tall. His breathing could be heard at times, though he did not suffer from shortness of breath. He was almost bald, with a thick beard trimmed short, fair to red. He wore gold-rimmed glasses. Red skin gave his head a rather coarse look.

He did not glance at the two clerks, who had got to their feet, or answer their greeting. Handing a telegram to Sanneo with a smile, he said: "The Mortgage Bank! We're in on it!"

This message from Rome had been expected for days, and meant that Maller & Company was entrusted with underwriting the issue for the new Mortgage Bank.

Sanneo understood and went pale. That message deprived him of the hours of rest on which he had counted. He controlled himself with a great effort and stood listening attentively to the instructions given him.

The issue was to take place two days later, but Maller & Company had to know the names of subscribers by the next evening. Signor Maller mentioned some companies to whom he particularly wanted offers sent. Others were to be addressed to clients to whom other similar offers had already been made. That very night some hundred telegrams were to be sent, which had been prepared many days in advance, with the address and the number of shares blank—shares that were to vary according to the importance of the company. But the work which would so prolong office hours consisted in letters of confirmation to be written out and dispatched at once.

"I'll be back at eleven," concluded Signor Maller. "Please leave on my desk the list of the companies you have telegraphed and a note of the number of shares offered them; and I'll sign the letters."

He went off with a polite greeting not directed at anyone in particular.

Sanneo, who had now had time to resign himself, said jovially to the two young men: "I hope we'll be done by ten o'clock or before, so that when Signor

Maller gets back he'll find the offices empty. Now to work."

He told Miceni to tell the other correspondence clerks and Alfonso the dispatch clerk about the new task, then hurried out.

Miceni reopened his inkpot, took a packet of writing paper from a drawer, and flung it on the table.

"If I'd gone off punctually on my own business, they'd never have laid hands on me, so that I have to spend the night here."

Alfonso walked off with a yawn. A dark narrow passage joined his room to the main corridor of offices, which was still blazing with lights, the doors were all alike, with black frames and frosted glass. Those of Signor Maller and Signor Cellani, the assistant manager, had their names in black on a gilt slip. In the harsh light the deserted corridor, its walls painted in imitation marble, the door jambs shadowless, looked like one of those complicated studies in perspective, yet made of only lines and light.

At the end of the passage was a door smaller than the others, and not double. Opening this and leaning against the door frame, Alfonso called: "Signor Sanneo says we're all staying till ten tonight."

"What?"

The question was equivalent to a reply. Alfonso entered the room and found himself facing a thickset youth with wavy chestnut hair and a low but well-shaped forehead, who had got to his feet and was leaning in a defiant attitude, with fists clenched, on a long table at which he wrote.

This was Starringer, who had rejected all other promotion to take a vacant post as dispatch manager, thus getting at once the higher pay he urgently needed.

"Till ten? When do we eat then? I've worked all day and have a right to leave. I'm not staying!"

"Shall I tell Signor Sanneo that?" asked Alfonso timidly, always timid with those who were not.

"Yes . . . no, I'll tell 'im myself!" That resolute "Yes" meant that he was off, whatever the consequences; the rest he said in a lower tone. Then suddenly he realized that he could not avoid staying and burst into a violent rage. He blamed the correspondence clerks, yelled that when he himself was a clerk (a time he often referred to) they all worked hard during the day but went home at regular hours in the evening. That day he had seen Miceni gossiping in the passage and twiddling at the lock on Ballina's door. Why did they waste time like that? Scarlet in the face, veins swelling on his forehead, he advanced on Alfonso. When he spoke of the clerks, he held out an arm and pointed at the correspondence department. Alfonso explained that they were not being asked to stay late for any normal work, but that a new job had been given them at the last minute. Starringer's rage did not lessen, but he stopped shouting. "Ah, so that's it!" and he shrugged his shoulders exaggeratedly.

Letters written during the day lay on the table, some already sealed. Taking no more notice of Alfonso, Signor Starringer seized one, sat down, and with a trembling hand copied the address into a book in front of him.

Sitting in the passage was a boy called Giacomo, who had entered the bank the day after Alfonso. He was fourteen, but his pink and white skin and shortness made him look no more than ten. Although he laughed and joked all day with the other messengers, Alfonso was sure he was homesick for his native village of Magnago, and felt fond of him.

"Till ten tonight," he said, touching his chin.

The boy smiled and looked flattered.

Signor Maller came out of his room. He had put on

his overcoat, and its cape hung from his shoulders. This
made him seem taller and slimmer. Alfonso said "Good
evening" and Signor Maller replied with a nod to him
and Giacomo. He had a way of making collective greetings.

Santo, Signor Maller's personal messenger, followed
his master along the length of the passage to open the
front door for him. He was a little old man, bald and
with a fair beard that was colorless in patches. People
said he led an idle life, as he had nothing to do but
look after Signor Maller, while other messengers served
the offices.

On returning to his own room, Alfonso found Miceni already writing away. Miceni was rather short-
sighted and almost touched the paper with his nose as
he wrote.

The telegrams, written out but unaddressed, were on
Alfonso's desk; so was a confirming letter in Signor
Sanneo's handwriting that had to be copied, and finally
there was a list of five companies to whom offers were
to be sent.

"Only five?"

"Yes," replied Miceni. "The pay clerks are writing
some out, too. We'll be finished by half past nine or
so."

He had not raised his head; his pen continued moving across the paper.

Alfonso put an address on a telegram, then transcribed it onto a letter. He began reading the telegram;
it gave a brief account of why the Mortgage Bank was
founded, hinted discreetly at a promise of government
support, and mentioned how difficult it was to become
a member of the syndicate. "We offer you priority. . ."
and a blank space followed, which Alfonso filled in
with the number of shares offered. The letter was more
detailed. It went into the need for new, large banks in

Italy, and how the new bank was therefore certain to flourish.

Miceni told him to jot the first letter down fast as it was to be copied by the other clerks, but Alfonso was incapable of writing fast. He had to re-read every phrase a number of times before transcribing it. Between words he would let his thoughts run on and then find himself with pen in hand, forced to cancel some part in which he had absentmindedly deviated from the original. Even when he managed to concentrate his whole attention on his work, it did not proceed with the speed of Miceni's because he could not get the knack of copying mechanically. When attentive, his thoughts were always on the meaning of what he was copying and that held him up. For a quarter of an hour nothing was heard but the squeak of pens and from time to time the sound of Miceni turning pages.

Suddenly the door opened with a crash. On the threshold, standing rigid for an instant or two, appeared Ballina, the clerk who was waiting for Alfonso to hand over Sanneo's letter so as to make other copies from it.

"What about that letter?"

He was a handsome fellow, with a clever, rather sly look, a Victor Emmanuel mustache, but an untrimmed beard. He was smoking, and the smoke he did not blow away—he would gladly have absorbed it to relish it the more—filled his mustache and covered his face to the eyes. His working jacket must have been white once but was now dirty yellow, except for cuffs which were quite black from cleaning nibs. He worked in a little room with a door onto the small passage, like Miceni's.

Miceni raised his head with a friendly smile. Ballina was always popular, as he was a jester, the bank jester. But that evening he was not in form, and was complaining. He had been working in his information office till then, and now he found he had to do other work; he did not even know if there would be any supper left for him that night. He was pretending to be more miserable than he really was. He once amazed Alfonso, whom Ballina called a *sponge*, by telling him that toward the end of the month he lived on Scott's Emulsion given him by a relative who was a doctor. He had well-to-do relatives who must have been a help because he was always speaking well of them.

Sanneo came in, rushed as ever; he was followed by the serious adolescent's face of Giacomo, who was carrying a big pile of paper at which he was staring with an excess of zeal.

Sanneo asked Ballina rather roughly why he was not yet writing.

"Well. . ." exclaimed Ballina, with a shrug, "I'm waiting for the letter to copy out."

"You've not had it yet?" Then, remembering that Alfonso was supposed to hand it over, he went on: "Hasn't he done even one yet?"

Alfonso, shaken by the other's angry look, rose to his feet. Miceni, still sitting, observed that he had not yet finished one either. Sanneo turned his back on Alfonso, looked at Miceni's letter, and asked him to give it to Ballina as soon as it was finished. He went out in the same rush, preceded by Ballina, who wanted to show that he had gone straight back to his own room, and followed by Giacomo strutting and banging his feet on the floor to make himself sound important.

A few minutes later Miceni handed Ballina the letter for copying. Alfonso from next door heard Ballina's curses in a voice thick with rage at seeing that the letter covered four pages.

In an hour or so Miceni had finished his work. Very calmly he smoothed out his clothes, put on his hat with as much care as if he would never take it off again, picked up the letters and telegrams which he wanted to hand over to Signor Sanneo as he passed, together with two letters written by Alfonso, and left humming.

In the complete quiet, work went faster. Alfonso, to keep his attention on his work, was in the habit, when alone, of declaiming aloud the letter he was writing in default of anything more interesting. This one was particularly suitable for declamation as it was full of reverberating words and big figures. By reading out a phrase and repeating it as he transcribed it, he reduced the effort of writing because he needed only the memory of the sound to direct his pen.

Suddenly to his surprise he found that he had finished, and went straight off to Sanneo, fearing he was already late. Sanneo kept the telegrams and told him to put the letters on Signor Maller's desk.

The floor of Signor Maller's room was covered with gray carpeting in winter. The furniture was also dark gray, with arms and legs of black wood. Of the three gas brackets only one was lit, and at half pressure. In the dimness the room looked gloomier than ever. Alfonso always felt ill at ease there. He put down the letters on top of another pile already on the desk for signature and went out cautiously, without making a sound, as if his chief were present.

He could have left now, but was held back by exhaustion. He thought of putting his desk in order, but sat there inert, daydreaming. Since he had become a clerk, and missed the physical exercise of a countryman, at the same time finding insufficient mental outlet in work, he had with his great vitality taken to producing inner worlds. The center of these dreams was himself, a self-mastery, wealth, and happiness. Only when daydreaming was he aware of the extent of his ambitions. To make himself into someone overwhelmingly clever and rich was not enough. He changed his father. Unable to raise him to life, he turned him into a rich nobleman who had married his mother for love, though Alfonso loved her so that even in his dreams she was left as she was. Actually he had almost entirely forgotten his father, which he turned to account in giving himself the blue blood needed for his daydreams. He would picture himself meeting Maller, Sanneo, Cellani with that blood and those riches. Then of course roles were entirely reversed. It was no longer he, but they, who were timid! But he treated them graciously, with true nobility, not as they had treated him.

Santo came to warn him that Signor Maller was asking for him. Surprised and rather alarmed, Alfonso returned to the room where he had been shortly before. Now it was all lit up; his chief's bare head and red beard glistened in the glare.

Signor Maller was sitting with both hands on his desk.

"I'm glad to see you're still here, a proof of diligence, which anyway I'd never doubted."

Remembering Sanneo's outburst a short time before, Alfonso glanced at him, fearing that he was being ironic, but his chief's red face was serious, blue eyes staring at a far corner of the desk.

"Thanks," muttered Alfonso.

"I'd be pleased if you could come to my home tomorrow evening for some tea."

"Thanks!" repeated Alfonso.

Suddenly Maller, as if he'd had difficulty making up his mind, looked at him and spoke less carelessly.

"Why do you upset your mother by writing her that you're not content with me or I with you? Don't look so surprised! I've seen a letter from your mother to our housekeeper. The good lady complains a lot about me, but about you, too. Read it and see!"

He proffered a piece of paper which Alfonso recognized as coming from Creglingi's shop. A glance told him it really was in his mother's handwriting. He blushed, ashamed of the ugly writing and bad style. In some vague way he felt offended at that letter's being made public.

"I've changed my mind now," he stuttered. "I'm quite content! You know how it is . . . distance . . . homesickness. . ."

"I understand, I understand! But we're men, you know!" He repeated the phrase a number of times, then warmly assured Alfonso that he was well-liked in the office not only by himself and Signor Cellani but by the head of the correspondence department, Signor Sanneo, and by everyone else, and they all hoped to see him make rapid progress. In dismissing him, Signor Maller repeated: "We're men, you know!" and gave him a friendly nod. Alfonso went out, feeling confused.

He had to admit that Signor Maller seemed decent enough, and being easily impressionable, he felt his position in the bank had improved; at last someone was taking notice of him!

But he regretted not having behaved more frankly and sincerely; why had he denied truths confessed to his mother? He should have reciprocated his chief's kindness by telling him frankly of his hopes, and so had had some chance of seeing one of them satisfied; anyway, he would have got on friendlier terms, since no one is ever offended by being asked for protection. He told himself he would be franker on some other occasion, which was bound to arise soon.

Meanwhile, to avoid contradictions between what he had told Signor Maller and what he had written his mother, he wrote to her again saying that his prospects at the bank were improving and that for the moment he renounced open air, oak trees, and repose. He would return home rich or never return at all.

CHAPTER

III

The Lanuccis, with whom Alfonso lodged, lived in a small apartment in a house in the old town near San Giusto. So from there he had more than a quarter of an hour's walk to the office.

Just before her marriage, Signora Lucinda Lanucci had spent a summer in Alfonso's village as housekeeper to a family. She had then made the acquaintance of Alfonso's mother, who had recommended her son. This introduction from Signora Carolina might have been worthless, had the Lanuccis not been looking for someone to rent a small extra room in their home. So Alfonso came along at the right moment and was welcomed.

A few years before, seduced by a longing for independence, Signor Lanucci had left a job which was not particularly good but did keep his family adequately, and begun acting as agent for a variety of companies representing almost every conceivable article. But though the poor man wrote off every day to companies whose addresses he took from the back pages of newspapers, he still earned less than he had before as a clerk. So now the family's finances were so precarious that the prevailing mood there was one of sadness.

This had increased Alfonso's homesickness, for sad people make places sad.

They treated him affectionately, but Signor Lanucci aroused Alfonso's pity, particularly when he saw the poor man making an effort to be polite, to smile and show interest in his affairs, although Alfonso realized himself to be only a source of revenue.

Signora Lanucci, long accustomed to consoling her husband for fruitless efforts, soon assumed a similar attitude to Alfonso and came to take such an intense interest in the young man's affairs that she spoke of them as if they were her own. Signor Maller's invitation, which Alfonso mentioned, aroused a most flattering reaction in her; she spoke of it as if it would make the clerk's fortune; so little was she used to good fortune that it took her by surprise.

Lucinda was about forty but, being small and plump, with thick gray hair, looked older. She had never been beautiful. The small dowry she had brought her husband had melted away in some speculation in Turkish shares. She was bright and lively, and loved a conversation; her pale suffering face had won Alfonso's sympathy at once.

She seemed devoted to her husband; not so devoted,

apparently, to her son Gustavo, aged eighteen, whom she called a rough diamond; her chief affection went to her daughter Lucia, aged sixteen, who did dressmaking in private houses. The mother earned more than them all as a teacher in an elementary school, but they could not have made ends meet without Lucia's earnings. Signora Lucinda was desperate at seeing her daughter forced to spend her youth at a sewing machine while hers had been spent better, for she came of well-to-do people and had studied and amused herself. Their means now were so narrow that she had been unable to do anything about Lucia's education; but this she did not complain of, not realizing that the results corresponded to the outlay. Intelligent though she was, she did not notice how insipid her daughter's prattle was. She saw her as beautiful, while actually Lucia was thin and anemic like the rest of the family, with fair reddish coloring and, because of her thinness, a mouth that seemed to reach her ears. The mother's behavior was like that of a woman of the people, and she even swore, all quite deliberately, for she was extremely democratic; her daughter had quickly picked up lady-like mannerisms in the middle-class homes which she frequented, but these were quite out of place in her own home. Gustavo, rough and simple, often jeered at her for them, earning his mother's dislike more by that than by his wastefulness.

Alfonso found his black suit laid out on the bed and carefully folded. Signora Lanucci had thought of everything, from tie to gleaming boots ready at the foot of the bed. Alfonso, too, felt excited by the visit he was about to make. Though he had not Signora Lanucci's illusions about it, they were contagious and he was more agitated than seemed necessary. He took off his everyday suit and flung it on the bed as if he would never have to put it on again.

As he entered the small living room where the family ate, he almost imagined himself to be really well dressed. Signora Lanucci looked at him and admired his appearance. Gustavo, filthy, came up to him trying to smile benevolently with his mouth full. This young gentleman aroused no envy in him, for his own desires were quite different; a few coins in his pocket for an evening at a tavern, no more. Gustavo was then attached to a copying office and was apt to criticize his new job, where there was little pay but a lot of work.

With his clean shirt, high collar, well-brushed, thick hair, and black suit, Alfonso looked quite handsome. He was holding in one hand some light-colored gloves bought that day on Miceni's advice. A more expert eye would have noticed shiny patches on the black suit, that its cut was not up-to-date, its collar too open and not of good enough material, so that it yielded to the stiff shirt. But the Lanuccis were not trained to such details.

Lucia had now stopped eating and moved a little away from the table, leaning on the back of a chair with crossed hands. She gave no sign that she had noticed Alfonso's special get-up. They were on good terms, and when he was at home she served him willingly. She liked to make herself useful to him because he always thanked her so pleasantly for all she did. Their exchange of courtesies verged on the excessive now that she had at last found someone whom she could treat in the way she had noticed people treating one another in the homes where she worked. Her mother encouraged her. Gustavo would say that she was letting off steam on Alfonso.

Signor Lanucci must have been over fifty. He dyed his hair, because he had free samples of dye sent by companies he had offered to represent; his hair was black where it was not whitened by age, and yellowish where it would have been white without dye. He wore a long, full beard, its color blending with his hair. To read in the evenings, he put on a clumsy pair of spectacles, so wide between his small gray eyes that they almost fell off his nose.

He complimented Alfonso and asked him to sit next to him, an honor no longer granted to Gustavo since the boy had lost a decent job they had obtained for him with great effort. This was the only punishment the father could inflict, having neither brain nor energy for any other.

Gustavo, without a word—he had a grudge against his father for having one against him—handed Alfonso a letter. Alfonso did not open it very eagerly. So preoccupied was he that he had not the patience to decipher his mother's shaky handwriting and put the letter back into his pocket after a quick glance.

"That didn't take long!" said Signora Lanucci with a hint of reproval.

"It's very short!" replied Alfonso flushing. "She sends you lots of good wishes."

The old man had begun describing his day's work. It was the same tale every evening. To justify himself to his wife, he would describe how much he had canvassed for business. That day he had earned, all told, a big package of needles sent by a small factory as agent's fee for some business he had arranged for them. In the morning he had called at a few private houses, with a letter of recommendation from a friend who was a merchant and whom he considered to have influence in the town, trying to sell cognac, but without results. The sample made a show on the table. At midday he had got some mail, consisting of that package of needles and a letter from an insurance company making him their representative. That very afternoon the old man had set off in search of people willing to

be insured, going around town with a list of acquaintances which he always carried with him. Friends had
explained that they did not want to be, already were,
or could not afford insurance: others either did not see
him—Lanucci liked calling on people who kept servants to open their front doors—or sent him off with
a few dry words as to a beggar. This comment was not
Lanucci's, who told his tale with the calm of perse-
verance, ready to begin all over again next day. But
later that day he had written to the insurance company
telling them that though he had not actually fixed
anything yet, he had good hopes, and that meanwhile
the agent's fee was too low in view of the difficulties
of doing business.

"Oh dear, that postage!" murmured Signora Lanucci,
with a wink at Alfonso, to whom she had already spoken
of her husband's hopes and manias.

But she had followed the account with close attention and her eyes shone with indignation at all his vain
efforts. Signor Lanucci spoke slowly, talking continu-
ally as he ate, putting his fork down after every mouth-
ful, and emphasizing each syllable to make his own
activity and astuteness clearer. He repeated all the
arguments he had used. To one person he had talked
of the advantages of insurance in general and how
wrong it was not to be insured; to another—some friend
or a known philanthropist—of his own need for encouragement. To all he had praised the company he
represented. Signora Lanucci listened to him, sitting
slightly back from the table, chewing little bits of bread
very fast in her front teeth.

Any remark by his family was apt to provoke Signor
Lanucci to dispute.

" 'Oh dear, that postage,' did you say? Why? You've
a strange way of looking at things! Why, I couldn't do
any business at all. . ."

The resentment that had accumulated during the day now burst loose. He sat stock still in his chair, but his lips were trembling. Gustavo grinned into his plate.

Alfonso soothed the old man; he understood his anguish since he, too, found himself in financial straits from time to time. He told him that his wife was only joking and he must not take offense, and that she really longed to see his affairs prosper more than anyone.

Alfonso's words started Lanucci on a completely different train of thought: for it now occurred to him that the comforter might become a client, and he began asking if Alfonso had ever had any idea of taking out insurance, against accidents, say?

Signora Lanucci protested.

"Oh! Can't you leave him in peace?"

Lanucci looked very put out: Alfonso was both embarrassed himself and distressed at the embarrassment of Lanucci, whom he supposed to be already regretting his tactless question.

"Do let him go on talking," he said to Signora Lanucci. "He's so interesting, and, after all, it costs nothing."

He thus managed to reduce the matter to something purely academic.

"Yes, indeed!" emphasized Lanucci. "I'll make him take out insurance either through me or somewhere else! He can do it wherever he likes. But anyone in a position to have insurance is wrong not to have it. Suppose a tile falls on his head? If he's not insured, he earns nothing while in bed, but if he is he's in clover."

To get out of it, Alfonso now gave a frank account of his own finances. Signora Lanucci protested, and the old man calmly put up objections while still denying that a refusal needed any explanation.

Every evening the Lanuccis went out after supper

to take some air. This was not the sole aim of the outing. Signora Lanucci had introduced the custom to
compensate Lucia for the hour's parade on the Corso
with other young dressmakers which she had made her
give up. Gustavo accompanied them but did not come
home with them. Sometimes Alfonso went too, bored
but making such a good pretense of being amused that
in the end he believed it himself.

Signora Lanucci got up from the table, put on a
threadbare but heavy cloak, and stood waiting for Lucia
to finish her far more complicated toilet. The old man,
in an overcoat too small for him, which his wife had
helped him don, went on talking, still hoping to do
some business before the day ended. But Alfonso, who
had been on the point of giving way for an instant,
now gave his exact salary and expenses in a slightly
irritated tone, finally saying that he could not dream
of spending more. He expressed himself crisply to avoid
finding himself in worse financial straits; and, distrust-
ing his own firmness, refused to hear any more arguments. It seemed to him that Signor and even Signora
Lanucci then said good-bye more coldly than usual,
although the Signora did not omit wishing him good
luck. Lucia bowed to him, wished him a pleasant evening, and held out her flaccid hand with a studied
gesture.

Once alone, to let a little more time pass before going to the Mallers', who might not have finished dinner
yet, Alfonso re-read his mother's letter.

Old Signora Nitti wrote of her hopes for Alfonso,
and told him that she had written to Signorina Francesca Barrini, the Mallers' housekeeper, to recommend
him. The whole letter was sprinkled with greetings
from friends in the village, patiently set down by the
old lady with Christian name, surname, and message:
"—— sends lots of greetings." Finally, there were two

lines of kisses and the signature: "Your mother, Carolina."

Beneath this, in a P.S., was the phrase: "I've not
been very well for the last two days, but am better
today."

CHAPTER

IV

Alfonso considered himself to have poise. In his soliloquies he certainly had. Having never had a chance of displaying this quality to people whom he considered worthwhile, now, on his way to the Mallers', he felt as if a dream was about to come true. He had thought a lot about how to behave in society and prepared a number of safe maxims to take the place of long practice. Speak little, concisely, and if possible well; let others talk, never interrupt, in fact be at ease without appearing to make any effort. He intended to show that a man could be born and bred in a village and by natural good sense behave like a poised and civilized townsman.

Signor Maller's home was in the Via dei Forni, a street in the new town, whose houses lacked any external charm. They were gray, had five floors, with warehouses at the street level. The street was badly lit and little frequented at night, after the traffic of carts carrying merchandise ceased.

It had rained during the day, and Alfonso walked close by the walls to avoid the mud. On finding the house, he was somewhat surprised by its hallway. This was lit up like broad daylight. Wide, divided into two parts separated by a staircase, it looked like a miniature amphitheater. It was deserted, and as Alfonso went up the stairs, hearing nothing but the sound and echo of his own footsteps, he imagined himself the hero of a fairy story.

The first person to appear was a hale-looking old man with a well-trimmed white beard, who was humming as he came downstairs. "Who do you want?" he asked, in a tone which was enough to show Alfonso that in spite of his black suit he could be recognized in that house as a poor man at first glance.

"Does Signor Maller live here?" he asked timidly.

The old man's face became grimmer. Every decent person must know where Signor Maller lived. Could this be a beggar?

They were now on the last steps before the first floor. On the landing appeared Santo's head, shaggy as a thistle.

"It's one of our employees," he called. "Come on up, Signor Nitti."

"Oh Santo!" exclaimed Alfonso, pleased to see a face he knew, and went up the stairs faster. The porter stroked his beard.

"Ah! So that's who he is, is it?" and the old man

went on downstairs without any greeting, humming again after a few steps.

Santo, leaning negligently on the balustrade, waited for Alfonso without changing position, and when he was near remarked, still motionless: "I'll take you in." Then he asked, after a moment's reflection: "Did Signor Maller invite you?" a question which made Alfonso think there must be a room set aside for employees invited by Signor Maller. Suddenly Santo began walking swiftly toward a door on the right.

"Excuse me a minute," he called and, leaving Alfonso on the threshold, hurried into a passage, opened the first door he came to, and banged it shut behind him. Alfonso was left alone in a half-dark passage carpeted in muted colors with two doors on each side and one at the end, all small and made of shiny black wood. To the right he heard an outburst from Santo answered by a woman's voice and laughter; he could not make out the words, which rang as if in an empty space.

Then Santo came out, roaring with laughter; his mouth was full. Through the half-shut door Alfonso glimpsed a kitchen with gleaming copper pots, a cooking stove, and next to it a blond fat woman lit by a reddish glow from the stove; she was threatening Santo with a spoon. Santo went on laughing into his mustache for a time, as he moved toward the door at the end.

They reached a square room with minute pieces of furniture made for creatures who had surely never existed. Small and soft as a nest, it was covered with blue stuff which Alfonso thought satin, and had carpets so thick and soft that he felt he wanted to lie down on them.

"This is Signorina Annetta's little reception room," Santo said, "but it's not entered from this end. This is the servants' entrance. I brought you this way to show you a few rooms; it's the best part of the house."

He looked at Alfonso with a patronizing smile, expecting thanks.

Various Chinese objects were laid out on a little table. Signorina Annetta's taste was oriental, it seemed. By the light of Santo's candle Alfonso saw a curtain with two small Chinese men painted on a blue ground; one was sitting on a rope attached to two poles but slack and dangling as if the Chinaman had no weight, and the other was in the act of climbing an invisible cliff.

"The Signorina sleeps here," Santo said when he reached the next room, holding his candle high to spread the light.

Alfonso asked, in some disquiet: "Is one allowed to come straight in here like this?"

"No!" Santo replied grandly. "No one's allowed but me."

His face was agleam with pride at all this finery. He made Alfonso admire the velvet curtains; and even moved toward the bed and was about to open the dainty pink hangings around the four-poster, when Alfonso stopped him.

"Oh!" exclaimed Santo, with a gesture intended to show contempt for his employer's wishes but belying his words. "Giovanna told me they're all still in the living room."

But, slightly shaken by Alfonso's alarm, he moved toward the door. Alfonso, despite his agitation, found the bed touching, and kept his eye on it until he reached the door. Enclosed like that, it looked truly virginal. Next to it was a *prie-dieu* in dark wood.

In the next room he was surprised to find a library. Big shelves full of books covered the walls. The furniture was simple: in the middle a big table covered with green cloth and around the room comfortable chairs and two sofas.

Suddenly in came Signor Maller.

They had not heard his steps. He asked Santo brusquely what he was doing in that room.

"I wanted to show Signor Nitti the library," stuttered Santo.

He had lost his easy, masterful bearing and stood rigidly at attention, holding his candle very low. Then he added, obviously lying: "We came in that way," and pointed to a door in the middle.

Alfonso moved forward.

"I was on my way to disturb you. . ." and he interrupted himself, thinking he had already expressed all he wanted to.

"Signor Nitti!" Signor Maller held out a hand with a polite gentlemanly gesture. "Welcome!" He spoke affably but with no great vivacity. "I'm sorry not to be able to remain with you as I would have wished; I have to see about a matter here and then leave. You'll find my daughter and the Signorina, whom you already know, there in the living room. Good-bye for the moment." Half-turned toward the table already, he shook Alfonso's hand.

Santo, rigid at the middle door, asked: "Shall I leave my candle here?"

"No, light the gas!"

Signor Maller lay down on the nearest ottoman and took up a newspaper.

Alfonso found himself in the passage by which he had entered. Helped by Santo, he took off his overcoat. While showing him into the living room, Santo found time to exclaim: "What a pity we met Signor Maller; his bedroom's worth seeing. Another time, anyway," and he gave a protective wink.

The living room was lit by a gas bracket with three flames. There was no one in it. Santo entered with cautious step, glanced around with a look of comical surprise, ran to a table, raised a corner of its covering, looked beneath: "No one here!"

Then, seeing Alfonso bored by this and not smiling at his jokes, he moved away.

"The ladies must have gone up to the second floor. I'll go and tell them. Make yourself at home meanwhile."

Knowing the worth of Santo's invitation, Alfonso remained standing. He was overawed by the wealth around him and had forgotten all about behaving like someone with poise. He longed to be outside and did not feel at all happy, sensing he must have the modest bearing of an underling in this house. A more trained eye would have noticed something excessive in the décor, but it was the first time Alfonso had seen such riches and he was dazzled.

The living room bore more traces of use than Annetta's rooms. A little piano was open, with some music laid on it; sheets of music also lay on a chair near the instrument. The furniture was varied: some chairs were wicker, some stuffed. He even sniffed a faint smell of food.

A large number of photographs were arranged like open fans on the walls above the piano; the four or five pictures were hung too high, to make room for the tall furniture.

Alfonso knew nothing at all about painting, but he had read a volume or two of art criticism and at least had an idea what the modern school meant in theory. He was struck by a painting representing nothing but a long road winding across a rocky landscape. There were no figures: just rocks and rocks. The color was cold and the road seemed to lose itself in the horizon. Its lack of life was disconcerting.

Lost in contemplation, more surprised than admiring, he did not hear the door open; then out of embarrassment he hesitated a little before turning when he realized that someone had entered the room.

"Signor Nitti!" said a gentle voice.

Red as if he had been standing on his head, Alfonso turned. It was the Signorina, as she was called, his mother's friend—not Signorina Maller, who must be younger, but Signorina Francesca, whom he guessed to be about thirty, although he could not tell why he thought her as old as that. She had a pale complexion, not healthy but anyway young, and clear blue eyes; pale golden hair lent sweetness to her rather irregular features. In stature she was rather short, too short had her figure not been in perfect proportion and so removed any wish to modify it.

She held out a plump white hand.

"You're Signora Carolina's son, are you not? And so a good friend of mine, eh?"

Alfonso bowed.

"Is everyone well in the village?"

She asked about a dozen people there, friends whom she had not heard mentioned for years, calling one or two by their nicknames, and mentioning some special characteristic of each. Then she asked about places, naming them with regret and citing happy hours spent there. She asked about a hill at the far end of the village and listened anxiously to his reply as if fearing to hear that it had collapsed.

Alfonso found Signorina Francesca charming. No one had revived memories of his home in that way before; Signora Lanucci's distant lifeless memories had revived nothing. He lived, dreaming sadly of his home,

by himself, and transforming it by his very thoughts.
The Signorina's talk corrected his memories and seemed
to give them a fresh impression. She was moved by
them, too.

As Alfonso soon learned, that had been the happiest
year of her life. She had been ill and the poor family
from which she came had made great sacrifices to carry
out a doctor's orders and send her to the country. There
she had enjoyed a year's complete freedom.

She took his hat from his hand and made him sit
down.

"Signorina Annetta will be here at once. Have you
been waiting long?"

"Half an hour!" said Alfonso frankly.

"Who let you in?" asked the Signorina with a frown.

"Signor Santo."

He said "Signor" out of respect for the person he
was speaking to.

Signorina Annetta came in and Alfonso rose to his
feet in confusion, flustered by the long preparation.

She was a pretty girl, although, as he told Miceni
later, he did not find her wide pink face attractive.
Tall, in a light dress which showed her pronounced
curves to advantage, she was not a type to please a sen-
timentalist. With all her perfection of form, Alfonso
found her eyes not black enough and her hair not curly
enough. He did not know why but wished they had
been.

Francesca introduced Alfonso. Annetta bowed slightly
as she was about to sit down. Obviously she had no
intention of saying a word to him. She began reading
a newspaper that she had brought with her. Alfonso
sensed that she was not reading and that her eyes were
fixed on the same point of the sheet. He flattered himself that she was as embarrassed as he was and wanted

to avoid showing it by this pretense of reading. But her face was calm and smiling.

Francesca, less relaxed, tried to start up the interrupted conversation.

"And does your family still live in that house so far out of the village?"

Alfonso scarcely had time to say "Yes." Annetta, with a little gurgle of pleasure which she had been holding back with difficulty till then, said to Francesca: "I was with Papa. We're leaving the day after tomorrow; he's promised."

Francesca seemed pleasantly surprised. Annetta's voice amazed Alfonso; he had expected one less soft in so strong a frame.

The two women were talking in low voices. Alfonso guessed that Annetta must have used guile to get some consent out of Signor Maller. Being quite in the dark about it all, he felt rather embarrassed. He looked at a picture to his right; a portrait of an old man with gross features, tiny eyes, and a bald head.

Francesca seemed to sense that he was ill at ease and tried to make up for the discourtesy of Annetta, who had been the first to whisper. She told him how they had planned a trip to Paris and now, after refusing for a long time, Signor Maller had finally agreed to go with them and leave his office for eight to ten days at the height of the business season. She turned back to Annetta.

"Did he definitely say I was to go with you?"

She must have been longing for that journey, too.

"Of course," replied Annetta, with a smile which Alfonso had to admit looked good.

For a space of time which seemed at least an hour he had to listen passively to the two women chatter, at times pretending to pay attention and at others turning modest eyes elsewhere when Annetta lowered her voice and leaned toward Francesca's ear. When Santo entered and announced Avvocato Macario, he felt relieved.

"Let him in, let him in!" cried Annetta joyously. "He'll give us a laugh."

Avvocato Macario was a good-looking man of about forty, dressed with great care, tall and strong, with a brown face full of life, and he greeted Annetta in imitation of Serravilla: "Even lovelier than usual today . . . ahi!" He shook hands with Francesca, who at once introduced Alfonso and, instead of giving the lawyer's name, said: "The finest mustache in town!"

"If you knew what a bother it is to keep it like this; I must say that before the Signorina says it!"

Alfonso tried to smile; he felt worse than before. Macario's ease did not relax his embarrassment or make him feel any better.

Annetta had put down the newspaper. She leaned both elbows lazily on the table.

"There's some news, my dear cousin! It'll surprise you!"

She seemed to be deriding him.

Macario pretended to look put out.

"I know it already. In fact I'd never have believed it. Uncle leaving town at the height of the business season! Are these walls so solid that they don't fall down from surprise? I met him on the stairs and he told me the news, though with quite a different expression than yours just now."

He gesticulated as he spoke; every now and then he would put his hands up close to his ears, as if hinting with an outstretched finger at things which Alfonso knew nothing of.

"I can understand your not being pleased about it," said Annetta. "Once you get it in your head, though," and she touched her forehead with her forefinger, "that's enough."

Macario asserted that Paris was even more boring in winter than in summer. He seemed to be taking revenge for some little defeat; obviously he had tried to prevent this journey.

"In winter the Parisians always have their heads abuzz with something that makes them unbearable. Each year everyone in Paris, every single person, fastens onto one subject. One day it's the fall of the Ministry, another a Deputy's speech, a third a murder. Always a bore!" he added.

Annetta recognized a novelist's Paris in this description and exclaimed: "Always charming!"

On an earlier visit she had searched in vain for that side of Paris.

"Each to his taste. If one visits a friend, he'll talk about nothing but a pistol shot fired at Gambetta; you try to arrange some business deal and the client is worrying about the pistol shot and Gambetta; even the shoemaker talks of nothing but Gambetta. Maybe that's all for the better."

At this joke Alfonso guffawed because he could find no word to put into the conversation but thought it his duty to show he was taking part.

"The Paris theater's all right in winter; a good *première* is worth the journey."

Now Macario had set aside any attempt to diminish Annetta's triumph and spoke seriously, turning to Alfonso, perhaps in thanks for the laughter.

"We'll go to the *première* of *Odette*," cried Francesca delightedly.

They would telegraph next day for seats.

Macario asked Alfonso if he was employed by his uncle and for how long. On receiving a reply, he explained that on the stairs his uncle had told him he

would find with Annetta one of his employees who
dealt with correspondence in any number of languages.
Alfonso replied in monosyllables, and when told of
Maller's praise bowed in surprise, attributing it to a
misunderstanding. Yet it must have been of him Maller
spoke. Macario knew Alfonso's home village and asked
if he suffered from homesickness.

"A little," replied Alfonso. He tried to complete the
dry little word by the expression on his face, and succeeded.

"You'll get over it, you'll see!" said Macario. "One
gets used to everything; very easily, I think, to living
in town after the country."

Annetta did not find this conversation amusing and
interrupted it without ado. At the sound of her voice
Alfonso raised his head, thinking that she wanted to
ask him a question too, but was at once disappointed
and so tried to hide the reason for his movement by
pretending to look attentive.

"Do you know I've learned some songs which are
popular in Paris so as to act the Gavroche in the streets
with Federico?"

Federico was Annetta's brother. Miceni, who knew
him, had described him to Alfonso as a very haughty
man. He was in the consular service and was vice-consul
at a French port.

"Could we hear one of these songs?" asked Macario.

"Why not?" and she got up. "Would you care to
accompany me?" she said to Francesca. "Come on!
Macario's such a bore this evening that this is the best
way of passing the time, I think."

"That's for us to judge, don't you think?" replied
Macario impertinently.

Alfonso forced a smile. The continual effort to appear at ease tired him. If he could have found a way,
he would have left at once.

Francesca, sitting at the piano, had taken a bundle of music on her knees and was reading off song titles to Annetta. Annetta rejected each with a shake of the head, keeping a hand to her cheek in reflection. Finally she cried, with a burst of laughter: "That one! That one!"

After a few introductory notes, the Signorina started up rudimentary but lively accompaniment.

Annetta began to sing in a sweet level voice, then to Alfonso's great surprise she started to sway to the rhythm and pretend to run. Francesca roared with laughter, Macario laughed too, and even the singer could not contain herself, to the grave damage of the song, which broke off again and again. Then she became serious, and so did Macario: Alfonso had only laughed in order to do as the others did.

As Annetta sang, she went into various acts, pretended to be tired, crossed her arms over her breast as if to run better, avoided an obstacle which she cleverly mimed, asked pardon of a person she had bumped into as she ran.

Alfonso knew French but his ear was not attuned, so he found it difficult to understand. Macario, staring fixedly at Annetta and speaking in one phrase at a time in order to interrupt the song less, said:

"It's a song sung . . . by a man . . . running after a bus." He interrupted himself and murmured admiringly: "You're doing it splendidly!"

Now Annetta really was tired; she was still pretending to run but jerking around less. She put a hand to her breast and her voice broke into gasps.

"I can't do any more," she said, and stopped.

Francesca, laughing, started the accompaniment again. After a few instants of standing still, Annetta began to sing once more. Her voice sounded fresh and sweet. She was now singing less vivaciously and pausing on a note or two, prolonging it with such feeling that Alfonso, who had not understood the words, began to find the song sad.

Those sweet notes showed him why he felt so miserable. They made him long to hear a friendly word from the superb creature with such a fine voice, and to realize that so far he had not had one. She had greeted him brusquely, interrupted ruthlessly when he had begun to speak, and not addressed a word to him. Why? She had never seen him before. It must all be contempt for an inferior, someone badly dressed; now he knew how badly dressed he was by comparison with Macario.

When Annetta stopped, Macario clapped with enthusiasm and Alfonso joined in the applause. He rather overdid it, and soon became aware of this, but did not want them to know he was offended. The pretense made him suffer a lot and he realized that he had definitely lost all the small store of ease which he had brought with him. Macario in his enthusiasm held for a long time a hand which Annetta left in his.

"The Signorina speaks French very well!" said Alfonso as if asking a question.

No one bothered to reply, and he was silent, feeling himself a stupid bore.

Annetta served tea, helped by a maid. She insisted that Macario also take something, and told the maid to carry a cup over to Alfonso, whose eyes were agleam with anger. He began to feel he should react; what worried him most was the fear that Macario, seeing him put up so humbly with such impertinence, would despise him. He would have given his life's blood to hit on a suitably pungent phrase.

"I never take tea," he said then in courteous tones, as if asking to be excused, nettled at finding no other phrase and at being unable to give the words any other intonation.

"Would you care for some brandy?" asked Annetta, without looking at him.

"No," was all he said, but an involuntary bow made even this monosyllable sound courteous.

Macario now began addressing himself more and more to Alfonso, who thought that he might have noticed Annetta's odd behavior and wanted to make up for it by his own attentions. Alfonso answered Macario more calmly but still in monosyllables.

"Do you play an instrument?"

"No."

Macario congratulated him; there was nothing worse than a dilettante strummer.

"Singing, as my cousin does, is all right. One can't understand all her words but she has quite a pleasant voice. It pleases even me: my enthusiasm a short time ago was genuine."

Annetta thanked him ironically, but it was obvious that she was more offended by the reproof than she wished to appear. This was also realized by Alfonso with deep satisfaction. Now she, too, was searching, without finding, for an answer to wound with or defend herself by.

Her tone had been jesting for some time, but as Macario continued to pay compliments on her beauty and grace but did not withdraw what he had said, eventually she showed her annoyance openly. Looking serious and even a little pale, she cried: "Tell me definitely where I went wrong? As criticism," she was trying to be pungent, "a jibe's not enough."

Macario began laughing so heartily that Alfonso envied him.

"Do you set so much store by your reputation as a

performer? Forgive my comment, I withdraw it!"

Alfonso was the first to get up. Francesca also rose to her feet and asked him to give her good wishes to Signora Carolina. Annetta remained seated, arguing with her cousin. But the latter now also decided to go and called to Alfonso: "If you wait a moment, I'll come with you."

Flattered, Alfonso waited.

Macario, still very gay, said to Annetta, as he shook hands: "Another time, dear cousin, don't doubt it, I'll give my criticism in detail!"

Joking but haughty, Annetta replied: "I don't care; if I need correction I'll find a way to correct myself."

She offered her hand to Alfonso, too; their two hands touched, both inert, and fell. Seeing her go pale, Alfonso had a second's alarm, followed quickly by a sense of satisfaction at having found a way of showing indifference.

In the street the two men stopped.

"Are you going that way?" asked Macario, pointing toward the sea.

"No," replied Alfonso, "toward the Corso, actually."

"Do please give me the pleasure of your company for a little way."

He buttoned his fur coat slowly while Alfonso thrust his hands into the pockets of his flimsy overcoat with a shiver. Without waiting for a reply, Macario moved slowly toward the seashore.

"Is this the first time you have seen my cousin?" On hearing Alfonso's "Yes," he asked: "And the last time, too, eh?" with a little laugh, which in the dark supplemented his habitual gesture.

Alfonso thought he showed great courage by replying frankly: "I hope so!"

"It's not worth being put out by women's whims; my cousin's silly!"

"I didn't think so!" replied Alfonso with some emotion.

Obviously Macario wanted to lessen the bad impression produced in Alfonso by Annetta's behavior.

"Do you know why you were treated so coldly? One of my uncle's clerks recently began to pay court to Annetta almost as soon as he was introduced. Apparently he even boasted of correspondence between them. My uncle heard of it and for some time had a good laugh at his daughter's expense. That clerk was a dark little man with short curly hair, and no fool. Annetta always acts on general precepts, and will have nothing more to do with her father's employees."

They had reached the shore. The sea was rough and there was a sound of waves crashing on the quay. In the darkness of the moonless night, beyond buildings lined along the shore, the sea seemed a vast black emptiness. Only a revolving ray from the lighthouse was reflected in the water and lit its surface.

Macario drew Alfonso off to the right, toward the railway station.

"I wish I hadn't been invited. Anyway, you can be sure I won't complain to anyone."

He had a suspicion that Macario wanted this promise.

Macario began to laugh.

"Oh, you can tell everyone, for all I care. Do you think I'm so fond of my dear relatives? Didn't you see how I enjoyed making my little cousin writhe? Vain little thing!"

Obviously he was no longer thinking of Annetta's behavior toward Alfonso, but speaking on his own account, and with some agitation.

"How could I praise her after hearing her sing that Gavroche song as if it came from Tosti? Very soon I'll be able to lie about it, as I'll have forgotten the song and only remember her face looking so pretty in excitement. Don't you feel that my cousin's face isn't lively enough usually? Why! Just as Napoleon was only really lucid on a battlefield, so my cousin is only really beautiful when she's excited! It's difficult to excite her, though!"

By the light of a street lamp Alfonso noticed he had not made his usual gesture.

With pleasant frankness Alfonso then asked Macario if he was not really very fond of his cousin.

"As for loving her. . ." he stopped to show he regretted his joke, and went on very seriously: "I love a different kind of girl. My cousin isn't a girl, she's a woman, and what's more. . ."—he gave a little laugh—"with so many gifts that at times she seems not to have done enough about them. She knows mathematics and philosophy, reads serious books as a choice, and I wouldn't be surprised to hear she understands them all, really understands them! She's so scrupulously exact she might well be capable of giving me a complete course. But an artist she'll never be. . . Maybe during some instant of emotional disturbance. . ." Here he gesticulated so livelily that he might have been talking about some revolution. "She's her father's daughter . . . not her mother's, who was a weak-minded ignoramus, pretty and nearly always attractive even when saying silly things. Annetta has an iron memory and outstanding mathematical abilities, a mind for the concrete and solid, like her father. They don't understand character, they don't appreciate music, they can't tell an original picture from a bad copy. Now Annetta is interested in Chinese works of art, she was the first to introduce them into our city, but she knows just as much as the artists tell her and understands nothing about them because she has no feeling for them. The only good picture they have in the house was bought by myself, of a road across rocks."

"I saw it, superb!" exclaimed Alfonso, and to give himself importance he asked: "Who is it by?"

"I don't remember the painter's name, I remember the picture," replied Macario. "I'm my aunt's son."

Alfonso laughed, but Macario did not. Even when his remarks sounded joking they were uttered with a deep rancor, and Alfonso did not feel it was natural to speak like that to him, a stranger. He began wondering whether Macario could be drunk and had not shown it at the Maller's.

Worse came.

"Certainly no man worth his salt would marry Annetta. Do you know the tales of Franco Sacchetti? They're worth reading, or one unforgettable one anyway. A friar stays at a house where he finds his host a weak man maltreated by the wife. In his anger the friar makes a vow to punish that woman by marrying her if circumstances allow. A plague comes, the husband dies and so do all the other friars in the monastery, which is then dissolved. The friar carries out his vow, marries the woman, and as he had intended beats her. One would like to make a vow like that about Annetta, to destroy that rude and boring haughtiness of hers. One would get the worst of it, though, for in the end one would find oneself the person beaten."

Maybe Macario had decided to tell truths in a tone which made them appear to have been said in jest, and had unintentionally abandoned that tone. This occurred to Alfonso when he saw that Macario, perhaps regretful, now began to explain why he was so loquacious.

"Don't think I'm in the habit of making such confidences to the first person who comes along. I find you sympathetic; believe me or not, but I do."

Alfonso, confused, muttered his thanks. Macario went on.

"I'm glad you felt such a strong urge to revenge your-self on Annetta, and glad too that you didn't satisfy it. Oh! I'm observant, denial's useless! People aren't stupid because they're not ready with an offensive word. On the contrary!" Then, thinking he had justified himself, he added another rude comment—with a laugh, though: "When I come across women so active and aggressive, so disturbing in fact, I think of an Englishman telling some overeager woman that he paid to kiss, not to be kissed!"

On the station square he shook Alfonso's hand, mur-mured some amenities, then left him and moved off toward a café. Alfonso felt cold and set off for home at a run.

CHAPTER

V

That year there was a heat wave in May; for some weeks the sun radiated, from a cloudless sky, scorching beams that were anything but springlike.

"It's not right for us to be sweating in May on such wretched pay," said Ballina.

Work had not yet slackened off. From Signor Cellani's office, through Sanneo's, into the correspondence room flowed huge piles of incoming letters. Even Giacomo grumbled at carrying them about.

In June work began to lessen slightly and Miceni,

who had a methodical nature, explained to Alfonso
the laws regulating this decrease.

"In June the richest bankers, the brains of the banking world, the people who initiate speculations, withdraw to the country. Our daily work remains the same
because those people don't make that, but we haven't
the sudden rushes of work, the issues and conversations,
that torture subordinates so. In July work lessens, not
because of any change in the banks, but because the
richer merchants begin their holidays. In August, our
best month of the year, off go bank managers and the
like, even shopkeepers. Only the bare essential number
of clerks stays on."

Maller's did not correspond to the rules. In May and
June some clerks and department heads took their holi-
days; in July, Signor Cellani, the assistant manager; and
Signor Maller had a few days in August.

First to leave was Sanneo, who took a fortnight's
holiday although he was entitled to a month. The
clerks said that Signor Sanneo could not bear to be
deprived too long of his daily sustenance of mail and
polemics.

Alfonso happened to be present when Sanneo gave
his instructions to Miceni, who was to act for him in
his absence. Sanneo's office was next to Signor Cellani's, and darker because the light was cut off by a
building opposite. This room also had carpets in winter, but, except for a comfortable wide desk of black
wood handed on by the assistant manager, who had
taken another, the furniture was identical to that in
the other offices; two wooden cupboards with rough
yellow paint, a chair with a platted seat, and beside
the only window another desk from which a leaf had
been taken.

Sanneo, seated, was handing over to Miceni, who

was standing on his right, a big pile of letters one by
one, pointing out exactly what he was to do on a given
day or after receiving such and such a letter. Some letters he put back even after giving full instructions
about them, observing with a wry look that there was
no need for an immediate reply and he would do it in
his own time. Obviously he did not like handing over
all his work to Miceni.

Miceni returned to his room with head high, his
slight body tense, and a stiff step. He sat down and
muttered with a smile of contempt: "As many explanations as if I'd joined the bank yesterday!"

Then some details of his interview with Sanneo occurred to him and he laughed: "What'll you bet that
at the last moment he regrets going and stays?"

Alfonso longed to get away and could not imagine
others wanting to stay.

Soon after, Sanneo came in to say he was deferring
his departure till the following day. Miceni looked at
Alfonso, and when Sanneo went out exclaimed angrily:
"Was it worth keeping me there an hour and giving
me all those instructions I didn't need?"

"They'll be all right for tomorrow," replied Alfonso,
who could not understand anyone getting angry about
business.

"He'll no more leave tomorrow than he has today."

But Sanneo did leave. That evening he went around
the offices saying good-bye to the clerks. He shook
hands with Alfonso, who stuttered in wishing him a
pleasant holiday and was thanked with a really kindly
smile. In spite of what had been said, Alfonso thought
he could see in those restless eyes a gleam of joy at a
fortnight's freedom.

Miceni occupied Sanneo's room, so as to be on hand
for the directors. He received his orders straight from

Signor Maller and Signor Cellani, and Alfonso envied
the easy manner with which he treated these high per-
sonages.

For Alfonso this was an interval of rest from all the
copying he had to do for Sanneo, and he regretted that
fortnight later. Miceni did not care whether large num-
bers of offers were sent out; to carry out his responsi-
bilities, all he asked was that the necessary work be done
without errors. He had the sense to abandon Sanneo's
system at once. Sanneo had passed on current mail only
to Miceni and two other clerks; all the others merely
copied out letters and revised accounts. "One clerk
who knows his job is worth a dozen who are fools,"
Sanneo used to say. Miceni called on all of them for
help, and Alfonso was given the job of writing short
letters about contracts for Italy, less but more varied
work than he had done till then.

Alone in his room, he found time to read books
brought from home. He read no novels, still having a
boy's contempt for so-called "light" literature. What
he loved were his schooltexts, which reminded him of
the happiest time of his life. One of these, a treatise
on rhetoric containing a small anthology of classic
writers, he read and re-read constantly. There was a lot
in it about style flowing or not, and about language
pure or impure, and Alfonso absorbed all this theory
and dreamed of becoming a great writer who would
unite good qualities and be immune from bad ones.

Toward evening a number of correspondence clerks
would meet to gossip in Alfonso's room, which was the
most out of the way. When Signor Sanneo was there,
they had to be on the alert all the time, as he would
appear unexpectedly, always in a rush and shouting
as he came in, whatever the hour: "Don't waste time
now, don't waste time!" Nobody risked a reply and the

group melted away like a flock dispersed by an angry sheepdog.

Miceni, on the other hand, even now came to spend a quiet half hour some evenings in Alfonso's room. He would lie silently on an old sofa, tired but pleased by his day, rather worried by the importance of his work.

Ballina treated him with affected respect, but derided him. One day, in the stress of work, Miceni had rebuked him for slowness and Ballina could not forgive him. When Miceni tried to justify his outburst, Ballina laughed in his face.

"You seem to think the bank's business is your very own! I can understand Signor Maller or Signor Sanneo bossing us but not someone who's just head of the correspondence department for a fortnight."

Even Alfonso noticed that Ballina must be a happy man, for he obviously enjoyed his mechanical labor, although he was unwilling to admit it. Ballina called himself head of the information office out of vanity, though actually he was its only member. He himself asked for information, copied it out, and filed it away alphabetically inside a big cupboard. He had nothing pending, as his work did not require it, and had a habit of staying at the office many more hours than necessary. He would clean some of his many bone cigarette holders, mend locks, sharpen razors, and shave in the office when he did shave. A great smoker, he always had a big pile of tobacco wrapped in oiled paper in a drawer. It was a mixture of different kinds, scented by some root which gave his room a strong smell of resin. That room was his real home: he had introduced his own little comforts, even nailed a bit of leather over his straw seat for greater comfort. One drawer of his desk was set aside exclusively for food and drink; bread, sometimes butter, often a bottle of beer, always a little

flask of grog, which he offered to any friends who came
to visit. Obviously he was not very cozy in his other
home. The room where he slept was so small, he said,
that it was filled by his bed and a cupboard, and a chair
was in the way of the door. As he could not do without
the chair, he had thought up an ingenious mechanism.

"I tied the chair to a rope which I attached to the
top of the door jamb after passing it through a hook on
the wall. When the door opens, the chair goes up and
leaves the entrance clear; when the door's closed, I find
the chair beside me and can sit down without moving
a step."

There was perhaps some exaggeration in this, but
some truth as well. One day in front of Alfonso he
handed the keys of this room of his to one of the bank's
porters, telling him to find him a new room and take
his few belongings there. His real home, for which he
had a womanly affection, was his office.

For all his sedate aspect, Ballina had gone through
a small legacy, which had come to him, he said, before
he understood the value of money. For one short year
of pleasure, he had spent many in poverty and was to
spend many more, "probably till I die," he would say
—while if he had now had even a small sum he could
have done better for himself, being so ingenious. As
things were, he had always worked for others, in a factory for cigarette holders, another for vinegar, as sales-
man in an exhibition, in a shop that sold walking sticks
and so on, always for bad pay. Eventually he had landed
up at Maller's, where he had become so fond of the
work that he was resigned to a poor salary.

The clerk for French correspondence, White, usually
took the lead in conversation. He came from an Eng-
lish family transplanted to France and had been sent
away from Paris by relations who feared he would go
through his whole inheritance in gambling and soft

living. He had come into the bank as correspondence
clerk for French, first working under Sanneo, then independently after a violent quarrel with him. Maller
realized that the two would not get on and separated
them, not wanting to force the submission of White,
who was protected by an old banker friend; his work
dealt almost entirely with stocks and shares, about
which he seemed to know a great deal. Apart from that,
he was a good employee and a quick, though rather disordered worker. Always smartly dressed, he was squat,
with an uncertain gait and a bent back, and the com-
bination of dandy's clothes on an old man's figure gave
him an odd look. But he had very regular features; spectacles improved his brown face and made it look more
sedate. In Triste, which he considered provincial, he
had acquired a passion for shooting, and his skin bore
traces of many hours spent in the sun. He worked with
great speed, and when he had nothing to do would take
a liberty which no other employees dared to and not
come to the office.

An intelligent *blagueur*, he was a good talker; he read
all the new French novels and spoke of them in a way
that made his observations sound original. He liked few
modern novels; he realized their merits, as far as Alfonso could judge, but did not always take to them;
finding one thing too much or another too little, he
would end by criticizing. He shocked Alfonso's tendency to idolatry by speaking with contemptuous familiarity of the most famous authors. "So and so gave his
novel a certain title to attract sales, another wrote filth
for the same end, a third with a reputation for great
virtue, and much read by young ladies, was a rogue who
beat his mother."

He offered to lend Alfonso books, always forgot to
bring them, and then one evening took him home to
fetch them. He lived in the center of town in a spa-

cious first-floor apartment. Crossing a small entrance
hall, they entered a big room furnished only with a
table and a few chairs; the windows were curtainless.
With all that light and space, the room looked too
bare.

A woman dressed in a pink dressing gown, fair, with
features that were almost too regular, was sitting by the
window working at a loom.

"My wife," said White in French, making the intro-
ductions, then: "My friend, Monsieur Nitti."

The lady made a move to rise, impeded by the cloth
hanging from the loom. The two of them looked at
each other, Alfonso murmuring a complimentary word,
she waiting for him to go before settling back at her
work. White had hurried into a nearby room, and Alfonso, annoyed at finding himself mute with another
mute, gave a bow, which was returned slightly, and
followed.

The bedroom contained two beds next to each other,
a cupboard, and some chairs. White's books, about
twenty, were lying in disorder on the floor, under the
only window, also curtainless. There was not a picture
on the walls; nothing more than necessary; they looked
like two rooms furnished as a temporary shelter, not a
home.

As he went out with White, the same scene with the
woman was repeated. She got up just as carefully, her
face calmly indifferent, and again the piece of cloth
threatened to fall.

In surprise, Alfonso asked White: "How long have
you been married?"

White gave a roar of laughter.

"Married? For a long time, but with this hand!" and
he raised his left.

A woman holding a child now entered the room.

"My son!" cried White, touching the baby with his

stick. "He's rather like me, holds himself in the same way."

The baby was leaning his little forearms on the shoulders of the woman, who was holding him too high and so making him bend over.

"We're franker than you people. I do everything openly, so my relatives here loathe me, but I don't give a damn about them."

He spoke Italian with ease, though obviously translating from French.

One day, while White was in Alfonso's room, Annetta came in with a friend whom she was showing around the bank. She greeted White as if she knew him well, introduced him to her friend, and started up a lively chatter with him in French. As she made her farewells, she said to Alfonso with a polite smile: "You, too . . . it would give me great pleasure."

Alfonso bowed, without understanding.

Annetta was in mourning for the death of a distant relative whom she had not even known. She looked better in black than in light colors, as it made her slimmer; her eyes seemed even more expressive.

"What did she say to me?" Alfonso asked White.

"She invited me home and invited you, too," replied White carelessly. "I'm not going!"

"Nor am I!" affirmed Alfonso resolutely.

On Sanneo's return, he greeted the clerks more coldly than when he had left. As soon as he was back, he at once became the boss again, whereas on leaving he had bid them a leisurely good-bye as a colleague.

Miceni spent the first day in Sanneo's room, handing over work in progress. Then things went back to their usual routine, and Miceni was the only one unable to return to his. He kept walking stiffly around the bank, idle because he had so buried himself in Sanneo's work that he had neglected his own. He bemoaned his fort-

night of almost sovereign rule, and praised the directors' behavior to him; but what he praised more than
anything else was Sanneo's job.

"This is quite different," he would exclaim with contempt, pointing to his papers. "No variety, no initia-
tive!"

He was the only one in the room to complain of
leading a quill-driving life. Alfonso, idle because Sanneo had not yet given him any letters to do, was meanwhile enjoying Musset's poetry.

Very soon it got around that relations between Miceni and Sanneo had become strained, for which everyone blamed Miceni.

Sanneo had a habit of jotting the initials N.B. (*nota
bene*) on any letter about which he had special instructions, so that the clerk it went to had to ask him before
replying. Ballina, who was always making up special
words and phrases, laid down that "to N.B." meant
to visit Sanneo and ask him to explain what his sign
meant.

Now Miceni, either because he considered he did
not need all these explanations or just from laziness,
often omitted to do what Ballina called "to N.B."; and
even more often, after receiving instructions, he modified them, preferring his own ideas to Sanneo's. Sanneo
attributed all this to oversights and merely sent back
the letters with orders to change them; Miceni on his
side tried to avenge himself by writing out the letters
carelessly, muttering all the while: 'He'll have to redo
them altogether in the end!"

This enmity might have remained latent for a long
time had not Miceni in a moment of anger openly
shown Sanneo his feelings.

At a peak working hour in the evening, Sanneo came
across a letter written by Miceni which was quite dif-

ferent from what he had told him to do; he also remembered that Miceni had not responded to his "N.B." for that particular letter.

He rushed to Miceni's room, in great agitation, because he suspected the mistake to have been made on purpose.

"This letter can't go," and he shook it in a nervous hand. "I want it written differently, didn't you see my N.B.? Show me the original."

Seeing that Miceni was moving very slowly to gain time, he took the pile of letters, scattered them over the table, and drew out the offending sheet.

"Don't you see this N.B.?" he yelled in a fury.

It was difficult not to see it, in fact. In red pencil, the first leg of the N went diagonally across the front; the second was shorter but only because after it was detached, parallel to the first, there was not enough space; the B went right off the paper and lacked one of the humps.

"I saw it," shouted Miceni, annoyed at being rebuked in front of Alfonso and White. "I'd already asked for instructions about other letters, and when this came it was too much of a bother to go around to you and ask for explanations, which I expected to find superfluous, as usual."

His voice was going strident; once the rage long smoldering inside him burst out, it made him say everything that came into his head. "Ah! So it's like that, is it?" yelled Sanneo, after a second of surprise at this reaction. Then he tore up the letter. "Do you think I put those N.B.'s in for fun? Redo this letter at once."

In a voice trembling with emotion, he gave his instructions.

"As I can no longer trust you," he added then, yelling again, "in future you will always hand me the incoming letter together with your reply. And remember, if you behave like this again, I'll see Signor Maller and ask him to tell you what I think of you."

Miceni had already begun writing, but at this he shrugged his shoulders almost imperceptibly, with a smile of open provocation.

It was said of Sanneo that he shouted until he came against opposition; certainly he did not like quarrels and avoided them as much as he could. Pretending not to see Miceni's gesture, he left.

Miceni was so red in the face that flushed skin showed through his black mustache; his pen was heard squeaking over the paper more loudly than ever. On finishing the letter, he flung his pen violently onto the table and cried: "He wants me to do what White did!"

After delivering the letter to Sanneo, he explained to Alfonso how he could free himself of Sanneo; Sanneo had enough on his hands with correspondence for Vienna and Italy; he, Alfonso, could be left the correspondence with Germany.

"Signor Maller knows my worth."

On the succeeding days Sanneo was obviously acting with studied moderation, for he never rejected a single letter by Miceni, who on his side asked him for all instructions that he was supposed to according to Sanneo's few N.B.'s.

"So that's the way he should be treated to make him behave, is it?" Ballina cried.

White congratulated Miceni and said he must realize that all he'd done was imitate him weakly.

"The next stage won't be long now," replied Miceni triumphantly, after revealing his purpose.

Ballina protested in the name of justice.

"Now that he treats you decently you'd be wrong to make any more rows."

He had never had the courage to react against any superior for fear of losing his job; he was worst treated of all the clerks in the correspondence department and envied those who said what they thought. White tried to calm Miceni too, not much liking to see his own actions copied by others.

But Miceni would not listen to reason. In his impatience to carry his rebellion through, he was incapable of waiting for a propitious occasion, though he realized one could not be long in coming, since Sanneo had periodic days of great irritability when he easily let himself go and said things which even his directors had to criticize. If Sanneo gained an easy victory, it was Miceni's fault.

One Sunday another clerk in the correspondence department came with an order, in writing as usual, to write out a letter at once to a client firmly demanding payment for the deficit on some deal in stocks and shares. Although he knew that the order came from Sanneo, Miceni did not carry it out and wanted to leave, declaring that he did not work on Sundays. The clerk repeated this reply to Sanneo, who lost his temper. He rushed to Miceni, and without asking for any explanation, foaming at the mouth, yelled: "Write this out at once!" and flung the admonitory letter on the table.

"Today's Sunday," replied Miceni, livid and trembling. His courage was forced; he was a coward by nature. "I don't work on Sundays."

It was Sanneo who had first made the correspondence department work regularly on Sunday mornings, but even before he became head of it, urgent matters had been dealt with then, work which could not be delayed.

"Oh! So it's like that, is it?" asked Sanneo quietly.

He had gone calm again from one moment to the other, and strode quickly off as if not wanting to give Miceni time to modify that answer of his.

Shortly afterward he sent for Alfonso.

"Please, Signor Nitti, would you do this letter?"

He spoke with unusual gentleness and in a voice charged with emotion. For a letter of a few lines he kept Alfonso a full quarter of an hour; first he explained its purpose and then dictated it word by word.

"So now it's up to me!" said Alfonso to Miceni.

Miceni frowned.

"If he finds it so easy to get someone to work on Sundays, anyone who refuses is bound to be in the wrong."

And he left, in order to assert that he could not work as he had something urgent on elsewhere. After having done what he had so long promised himself to do, he was now obviously worried.

Sanneo re-read the letter written out by Alfonso, put in a few commas which he had not pointed out and which Alfonso, with his exactness as a copyist, had not dared add, and with a smile of approval said: "Excellent! Please be kind enough to put it on Signor Cellani's desk."

Never had he been so polite.

At nine on Monday morning Miceni was called in by Signor Maller. Alfonso learned what had taken place in the managing director's office, partly from White and partly from Miceni himself.

Miceni had entered with a loud greeting and a bow which also included Cellani, who was present. White, who was about to leave the room, stopped to listen.

"Signor Sanneo is complaining about you," said Maller very seriously. "Why did you refuse to write that short letter yesterday?"

"I thought it might be done on Monday," replied Miceni; at the last moment he had decided to give his reply a tone of doubt.

"But if Signor Sanneo ordered it to be done on Sunday," here Maller raised his voice, "it must be done on Sunday."

The partial repetition of Miceni's phrase made the reply sound harsher.

"Anyway," objected Miceni in the tone of one falling back on the other's goodness of heart, "it was wrong of Signor Sanneo to make me work on a feastday."

"I myself had given orders for that letter to be written and sent out yesterday," replied Signor Maller severely.

Miceni made inarticulate sounds; there was nothing more to reply.

White took pity on him and left the room.

The rest of the scene was reported by Miceni, who left Maller's room as gaily as if he was quite sure things would work out in his favor.

He tried to arouse admiration. He said that when the verdict went against him anyone else would have given the thing up as lost, while he had been able to change his ground. He had brought up old incidents already known to his employers for which Sanneo had been rebuked; then he had talked contemptuously—thinking additional disrespect for Sanneo could do him no more harm—of those N.B.'s which merely made a mess of letters and set the clerks on the run.

"Signor Sanneo's behavior to employees isn't right, and I just won't accept it."

He had gotten back all his self-confidence.

Then he was called to Signor Maller's room, and came out looking utterly different. Alfonso understood and asked nothing. Miceni gave a little laugh, which was intended to be sarcastic; then with a decisive movement put his hat and working jacket on his desk and said: "I didn't expect this at all."

White, who entered at that moment, looked at Miceni with cool curiosity.

The sight of someone more fortunate than himself made Miceni lose the little self-control he still had. There was nothing to laugh about, he said, although White had not laughed; if he had enjoyed the protection that White did, things would have taken quite a different turn. White did not defend himself, and replied with a very cold smile that he knew he was protected and was not sorry others should, too. This made Miceni more furious than ever. He seemed to be trying to revenge himself for the attack which had left him so indifferent.

"Try and embrace too much and you'll have nothing to squeeze," said White.

Then Miceni, from fury, broke down.

"Did I want too much? Is justice too much? To be treated decently? Is that too much?"

He did not actually cry, but his voice was tearful. White grew milder, but could not avoid loosing a last arrow.

"You said you wanted to be independent."

This Miceni resolutely denied; he wanted, he explained, to be independent only if Sanneo did not learn to behave better. He was just realizing the difficulties of the role he had taken on and feeling ashamed of such a defeat.

Later White explained to Alfonso how serious Miceni's position now was. He was being relegated to the cashier's department, an inferior spot because no amount of practice as a correspondence clerk was any help to being a good cashier.

"And think of the boredom for someone used to

more variety in his work! He'll have nothing to do all day long but sums, sums, and sums."

Ballina entered and congratulated Alfonso ironically; he had come from Sanneo's room, where he had heard that Alfonso had been appointed as Miceni's successor. Alfonso looked at him incredulously, terrified already; the thought of Miceni's work alarmed him as being too difficult and too much, so that it would take away the little time he still had for reading. White tried to calm him; what he did not know he would be taught, and if he did not manage to do all the work, it did not mean the end of the world. Certainly this was a step up in his career and if he had any sense he should be grateful for it.

"It's only lately that Miceni has been giving himself this air of importance," Ballina said to him, "he didn't before, when Signor Sanneo had to explain every single thing from A to Z."

He also mentioned having seen Miceni with eyes starting out of his head at the difficulties of some transaction which was quite simple and clear to others.

"Eyes starting out of his head?" asked Alfonso, who found the misfortune that had befallen his rival less enjoyable the more he thought of the suffering it might bring to him.

Ballina's announcement received official confirmation only at three that afternoon. Sanneo sent for him when he had finished his N.B.'s to other clerks. He told him in an offhand way that Signor Miceni had left the correspondence department and that he had decided to entrust him with part of the Italian correspondence connected with banking; just ledger work in fact, he added contemptuously. Alfonso had intended to plead ignorance but did not have the courage; he was ashamed to show any hesitation about accepting work that was so easy. In a few minutes Sanneo handed him fifteen letters with a few words of explanation for each. He spoke of transfers, deposits, and suspense accounts, all terms whose meanings were still vague to Alfonso.

Two or three of the letters he wrote out easily: these were the last Sanneo had given him, so that he could still remember the instructions; the others he could not manage to answer without White's help.

"Who will he give the rest of Miceni's work to?" asked White in surprise after giving Alfonso, with great kindness, a thorough lesson on banking terms. "The Stock Exchange letters aren't included here, or the half a dozen controversial letters that come in to him every day. He's capable of doing them all himself."

In fact, when Alfonso left the bank late that evening, he saw Sanneo's room still alight and a shadow thrown on the pavement of the chief of the correspondence department bent over his table.

White accompanied Alfonso to the cashier about a draft. It was a little room halved by a light wooden partition, behind which, reading a newspaper at his desk, sat Signor Jassy, an old man with a face covered with spots and a few whitish hairs.

Alfonso noted the details of the draft on a lined sheet of paper proffered by White; then he passed it to Jassy, who put it down beside his newspaper without a word.

Just then a youth appeared at the hatch and presented a bill of exchange. Jassy took up a list, looked at him, looked at the bill of exchange, then, still motionless, called out in a complaining tone: "This is the right one, it's just listed, but why didn't you have it countersigned in time by Signor Cellani? Now there's no one here who can leave the cash desk, and there are people waiting."

He flung down the piece of paper in front of White, who at once replied irritably: "I've not listed this draft, it doesn't concern me; in any case, drafts can't be listed before a letter of advice is received. Don't you think so?"

The old man turned to Alfonso and said to him more gently: "Please show this draft to Signor Cellani, will you. Do you know where his room is?"

"Come with me," said White, and moved off.

Alfonso followed him, no longer looking at Jassy. Jassy was still talking to the young man who had come to cash the bill of exchange and at the same time moving with a vacillating step toward the counter. His legs were as flabby as if they were made of cloth, and he was holding out his hands in front of him as if afraid of falling.

"Is that the cashier?" Alfonso asked White.

"Yes, a poor old man who'd be better adding up sums or retired."

Signor Cellani was a man who had achieved his position by hard work, step by step; he seemed about fifty, but his thin figure and dry unlined skin made him look no more than thirty.

"My best wishes!" he said very politely to Alfonso, who was coming to him for the first time on a matter of business. "Please be very careful how you lay out your letters. I wasn't very pleased with Signor Miceni's. You are intelligent and understand how important the form of a banking letter is."

He put his initial next to the total sum of the draft.

Meanwhile others had come to the cash desk, and Giuseppe, Signor Cellani's messenger, was helping Jassy as he moved slowly between cashbox and counter, indecisive as ever, incapable even of getting help, perhaps out of shyness. Alfonso, in his zeal aroused by Cellani's kind words, wanted to hand the chit to Jassy himself. The latter was moving toward the counter with bank notes in both hands; he gave Alfonso a sullen look and, without stopping, shouted to Giuseppe: "Here, take that bit of paper out of his hand, will you!"

Later Sanneo gave him another two or three letters to do, and as a last job he had to send off some bills of exchange. White helped him with these too, because Alfonso was frightened of handling papers which were so precious.

When his first zeal had died down, and he was copying big sums down in a letter, Alfonso would calculate how the tiniest fraction of each sum would be enough for him to live a serene life in the country.

CHAPTER

VI

By next day Alfonso's work had already increased. Sanneo, who knew nothing of White's help, found Alfonso's letters quite satisfactory and felt he could give him more and more serious work. But that day the settlement came from Paris which White had to check over, and Alfonso was left to his own devices. By midday there was a first outburst from Sanneo, and by evening Sanneo was going around the bank saying that two days' work had given Alfonso softening of the brain. He called him in and told him to redo half the letters, which he had corrected, and Alfonso was forced to confess that he had been helped out by White on the previous days. Sanneo calmed down, but grew brusquer from then on.

Then Alfonso's work became more unpleasant. He had been forbidden to ask help from White, with whom Sanneo was not on good terms; often, instead of giving instructions, Sanneo would point to the date on which an identical letter had been written, and tell him to find the right letter in the file and copy it out. It was not easy to find a file in the Maller bank. With so many clerks using the files, he had to go to and fro between accounts department and cash desk, more than once too, since no one helped; everyone was concentrating on his own business and he had to search through every drawer to make sure that what he sought was not there. At first Alfonso went around every room shouting: "Gentlemen, please, have you the file for such-and-such a day?" But he stopped this because he found it was wasted breath. No one answered, and one or two just smiled. By running from room to room Alfonso eventually found the file beside a clerk who could easily have told him and saved him a useless rush. Once he had laid hands on the file, there was still the labor of finding the letter he needed. If Sanneo had even mentioned who the writer was, it would have been a great help, for he would not have had to read all through to find it. Sanneo's big handwriting filled a whole sheet of copying paper; Miceni's was reproduced whole and clear as the original; White's big wide pen strokes made blotches in the file copy.

Alfonso would go and greet Miceni in the accounts department and sometimes stop to exchange a few words with him. He forced himself to do this against his will because he felt Miceni resented him. Miceni's new desk had already taken on the look of his old one;

inkpot, pen, pencil, big ledger set parallel to the edge of the desk. He would count up on tiny bits of paper, which he filled with microscopic figures.

Alfonso found he got no enjoyment out of his advancement. It was a real advancement, for even though everyone went out of his way to remind him that he was very far from having Miceni's position, he had stopped copying letters and offers, servile labor with a pen instead of a broom. But when in the evening Sanneo handed back half his letters with annotations, he felt desperate and longed to take the first train home and leave those letters to be redone by Signor Maller himself. It was true, though, that if a moment later Sanneo gave a nod of approval when signing a letter, Alfonso, however tired he was, took up his work again with renewed zest.

Tired? Nauseated, rather. From day to day his work slowly increased, but varied little. He only had to think up one or two paragraphs for himself in a day; but he also had to copy out endless figures, repeat the same phrase innumerable times. Toward evening his hand, the only part of his body really tired, would stop, and his attention would stray, for lack of stimulus; sometimes he was forced to fling down his pen and abandon work out of nausea, like someone who has eaten too much of one dish. He never quite caught up with this work, and worry was now added to his malaise.

White had told him that all contractual letters could be left for a few days or even weeks without a reply, and this had greatly eased his work in the first days; very soon, though, as pending letters increased, his work became more complicated because incoming letters joined others from the same client awaiting reply, and Alfonso, distracted and forgetful of names, did not remember which were which. In the evening the letters were sent back by Sanneo with annotations. "What about the letter before this one? Signor Nitti N.B." The poor culprit would go off to Sanneo and listen to a long sermon on disorder, which did nothing to improve the situation because he did not lack good will, only capacity; his defect was organic.

While urged along by zeal for his new job, he felt less bored. He needed to concentrate continuously to get through as many letters as possible in the least amount of time, but the very intensity of the work distracted and tired him more than something less mechanical. But this early zeal could only be rearoused by circumstances independent of his will, and his work proceeded so slowly that a good part of his day was spent in reading letters that had just arrived to find out which he could put aside, and in tidying papers left on his desk days before.

Sanneo said he was surprised that a young man who showed such a wish to work could not get more done. He would come into Alfonso's room unexpectedly, hoping to surprise him reading a newspaper or chattering with other clerks; but he always found him at his place, pen in hand and eyes fixed on paper. He even lessened his work out of kindness, but the fifteen or twenty short letters which he gave him to do were never done by evening, and his pending tray always stayed as high.

Alfonso came to the conclusion that he felt generally out of sorts because his organism needed something to tire itself out on, to exhaust itself. This organism of his now became a plastic concept which he reshaped to every new sensation. In the evening, after a day spent on sums or rushing about the bank or sitting with pen on paper and thoughts elsewhere, he would imagine matter flowing fast through his body in pliable tubes, impossible to regulate or resist. Whenever he could, he took long walks and his malaise vanished; his lungs expanded, he could feel his joints becoming more flexible, his body obeying more promptly; and he would imagine that flow of material as having been absorbed or regulated, as helping him now instead of impeding. If he settled down to study, he would drop his book and feel that his chin was tired and a strange sensation would come over his forehead as if the volume inside was trying to increase, to enlarge its content. He felt the same sort of calm as if he had tired himself out running; his brain was lucid and his daydreams either conscious or absent. Very soon even the time he had given to walking was taken up by study: it took less time to find calm in study than in walking. A single hour spent on some difficult work of criticism would soothe him for an entire day. He was growing ambitious, and study became a means to satisfy this. That blind obedience to Sanneo, the scenes he had to endure daily, disgusted him; study was his recreation. A well-written book gave him megalomaniac dreams, not due to the quality of his brain but to circumstances; finding himself at one extreme, he dreamed of another.

Every second of his time outside the office, or even in the office, where he kept a few books in a cupboard, he spent reading. Generally he read serious works of criticism and philosophy, which he found less tiring than poetry or art. He also wrote, but very little; his style was not formed and he felt foiled by inappropriate words which never quite hit the target. He thought study would improve this. He was in no hurry, and the little he did was in accordance with a timetable he had laid down for voluntary work. After being tired out by work at bank and library, he would jot down a few concepts or a romantic dialogue with himself which no one else would ever hear. The odd thing about these was that in them he seemed to be suffering from some world-wide disease: never a hint of his real sufferings, of the nostalgia still torturing him. These writings were in the nature of rudimentary jottings which he hoped to use in some distant future for major works, plays, novels, worse.

He had never yet read an Italian classic all the way through, and had only a haphazard knowledge of literary history and criticism. Later he plunged into German works of philosophy translated into French.

Then he discovered the city library, and all those centuries of culture at his free disposal there meant a saving on his meager budget. He tied himself down to the library at fixed hours, which gave his studies the regularity he needed. Another reason for going there often was that his room at the Lanuccis' was not good for study. It was small and half of it occupied by the bed; it was rarely touched by sun, and he found thinking neither pleasant nor easy at a small round table whose four legs never touched the floor at the same time.

When he had managed to get through a day of this program, he would go to the bank next day still tired and work less well than usual. Pending letters piled up, and by evening he found himself facing a huge mound of sheets from every town in Italy; the whole world seemed to be conspiring to impose that labor on him.

He made very few acquaintances in the library. He would enter the long reading room filled with tables in parallel lines, take any seat, and sit there for some time with his head in his hands, so absorbed in reading that he did not even see the people sitting beside him. After an hour at most, this concentrated reading began to repel him, but he still forced himself to go on for a time and stopped only when his mind could no longer grasp the words seen by his eyes; then he handed in his book at once and left. After an hour spent with the German idealists, everything in the street seemed to be calling a greeting.

CHAPTER

VII

Alfonso had come to the city with a great contempt for its inhabitants; townsmen, he considered, were bound to be physically weak and morally lax, and he despised what he considered to be their sexual mores, their womanizing and easy love affairs. He could never be like them, he thought, and felt and actually was very different. Sensuality he had known only as an exalted emotion. To him a woman was man's gentle companion, born to be adored rather than embraced, and in the solitude of the country village where his body had grown to maturity he had vowed to stay pure until he could lay all of himself at the feet of some goddess. In the city this ideal had very soon lost any influence on his life, though it still remained a vague objective which he felt no urge to struggle for.

He held to it as a theory even after realizing that it seemed ridiculous to those he explained it to. He had no idea what to replace it with; its abandonment would have created a void in his life. But he no longer spoke of it, and Miceni was quite wrong in boasting of having converted him.

At twenty-two his senses had the delicacy and weakness of an adolescent's. He had desires which it was torture for him to repress. The sight or even the thought of a skirt, harsh mockery of his dream, was enough to provoke these desires; and they were strong enough to drag him suddenly from reading he had settled into, and make him rush through the streets, prey to an agitation which would have seemed vague had he not known its origin. There was only one occupation that soothed this state; to follow some attractive figure for long stretches of street, admiring her, timid and ashamed. The thought of going further only came later. Till then he had waited for his ideal to come to him.

One evening he found himself hurrying along behind a woman who had glanced at him in passing. Dressed in black, she was holding her skirt very high and showing a small foot shod in elegant gleaming shoes, a black stocking, a trim ankle on a body agile and not too slim. Alfonso caught a glimpse of a very white neck; not of her face.

He followed her resolutely, overtook, then waited for her like a puppy dog. The lady seemed to laugh and glance at him, so he felt encouraged enough to think of approaching her. It was the first time he found himself in this embarrassment. He hesitated, and so was forced to hurry his pace. She crossed the Corso and

turned into Via Cavana; she would have to pass by the
library. "At worst I can go in there," thought Alfonso,
to give himself an out.

He went ahead and stopped at the door of the library.
She passed by; a headlamp lit up the whiteness of her
neck and made the polish on her shoes gleam, but she
did not look at him, which for a little time left Alfonso
without any desire to follow her. She went slowly up
the SS. Martiri slope and under the Law Courts, while
Alfonso merely followed her with his eyes from the
curb. Then, when she had almost got to the top of the
slope, he moved on up to the Law Courts. He saw her
figure outlined against the sky, its curves clear as if
seen at close range. Another instant of hesitation and
he would lose sight of her; there was no time to reflect;
his desire spoke openly and imperiously, urging him to
rush so that he came up to her before she had reached
level ground. He was flustered, but so tired that he
very nearly dropped the resolve he had made a short
time before. He neared her with the same idea in his
mind that had made him run up from the Law Courts.
"Signora. . ." he said, and raised his hat; but he was
panting so hard as he halted that he could not go on.
Blue eyes gazed at him with glacial chill, and, finding
himself unprepared for speech since he had been concentrating only on running after her, he moved aside
to let her pass; so he gathered breath again, as glad
now of being prevented as he had been afraid before.
The desire that had seized him so fast left him equally
fast; a stab of fear or strain had been enough to make
him forget them.

For some time he followed some woman every evening—only well-dressed ones, for the object of his
dreams was certainly not in rags; and on every street
corner he deceived himself that he had found her.
These compulsions always ended in the same way. His

firmest resolves were overcome by shyness, and a discouraging gesture on the woman's part, or even an indiscreet glance from a passer-by, was enough to make him desist.

But he came to realize from experience that what prevented him from finding love was not only his own shyness, but also his doubts and hesitations, and even that ideal brought in from the country and put away in a corner but never quite abandoned. It would suddenly appear when Alfonso had thought he had quite forgotten it, and its splendor would make him despise his miserable reality.

He had an amorous adventure or two, but this was no sooner begun than he had to abandon it abruptly due to an awakening of moral conscience or merely to wanting to avoid sacrificing his hours of study.

For some years he remembered with regret a girl called Maria, with pale hair of purest gold and a straight figure which seemed not to notice all the weight of gold she bore on her head. One evening he had accosted her and, bold like all timid people when forcing themselves to be brave, at once declared his love for her. Maria, who was, so she said, a companion to an old lady, must have been in a state similar to his own, for to his great surprise she listened seriously and with some emotion to his wordy though sincere outburst of accumulated emotion. She had to leave a few days later, but, as a result of his insistent begging, she granted him a rendezvous before that. Meanwhile, his evening study hours had become the most important thing in his day. The appointment was during those hours, and at the last moment he had decided not to go. Later he felt bitter regret, but could do nothing about it, as he never saw her again.

Not that he renounced his skirt-chasing because of it. His pursuits made him dream better. Then he grew

ashamed of the habit and suffered a lot one day when
he realized that Gustavo had guessed.

Till then he had been a kind of master to the boy.
Wanting to help the Lanuccis, he had tried to lead
Gustavo back onto the right path. The young man
had listened seriously to Alfonso's teaching, but opposed it with his own firm and simple objections: work
being usually hard and ill-paid, he preferred to live as
a poor man and be free rather than as a slightly richer
one and be a slave.

All of a sudden Alfonso found that he had become
the pupil and Gustavo the teacher.

"What fun do you get out of it?" asked Gustavo in
surprise, interrupting one of his chases after a woman.

Gross though Gustavo was, he spoke serenely of subjects that were deeply moving and disturbing to Alfonso, who envied him. Though more adult and more
intelligent, in this important aspect he was inferior.
There was weakness in his disordered strength, while
Gustavo's thin anemic face shone with health and
peace.

Yet Alfonso did not feel unhappy. He found happiness partly in study itself, partly in a swollen ambition, a hunger for glory. He felt himself superior to
others, and though he did not yet know how he would
gain this glory, fortified his hopes by a love of study
which had become a passion. To his hours in the library
were added as many more at home, and they were still
not enough. Study invaded his office, his dinner and
supper hours, and was robbing him of many hours'
sleep every night.

During a particularly active phase he suggested giving
Lucia lessons in Italian syntax. It would be pleasant to
learn while teaching.

The suggestion sent the elder Lanuccis into a flutter,
and the father told Gustavo to take these lessons, too.

Even he became enthusiastic. He tried to show great diligence, and made Alfonso dictate definitions of parts of speech which he intended learning by heart, sure that it was just lack of preparation and not of intelligence that prevented his understanding them. Then he never appeared again and only remembered to excuse himself the first two times, though in both cases with good grace and repeating how much he had enjoyed that first lesson.

Signora Lanucci formally handed Lucia over to Alfonso. The first lessons were given in the living room, the others in Alfonso's room, as the living room at some hours was not quiet enough.

Alfonso took his duties seriously, and Signora Lanucci's enthusiasm eventually persuaded him that he was also doing Lucia a real kindness in giving her these lessons.

They had started with Puoti, but soon changed the program, both bored to death. Lucia had not understood a thing and Alfonso knew it all.

For some time Alfonso had been reading Tommaseo's book of synonyms. He decided to have Lucia study those instead of grammar.

"At least one doesn't have any system to cope with," he told her, "though in fact there is. One would never realize one had not grasped it because it's disconnected, every page and article standing on its own. Study these and one fine day you'll find to your surprise that you've built up a whole building and conquered the Italian language. . ."

What he most loved in these lessons was giving introductory talks. After that, both Lucia's ignorance and the details of teaching bored and wearied him. Lucia managed to seem capable and clever for the first two lessons because she understood the many subtle differences between the words "abandon" and "leave." She took the huge volume with her and learned that paragraph by heart. In the third lesson, seeing that the girl had followed him so easily till then, Alfonso declared that they could proceed more rapidly; about a quarter of the work was already known to him and he was in a hurry to get to where he could begin learning himself. She wanted nothing better than to go a long way quickly. For she loved him, or at least thought he loved her, which stirred her deeply. On his side, Alfonso was quite fond of Lucia at that time; he had found no one to take Maria's place and Lucia acted as a substitute. He did not describe his longings but just taught her, and the dogmas and theories which he produced between synonyms were enough to relieve his bitterness. Lucia's little face, not intelligent but attentive in a way that seemed to come more from homage than self-interest, made him forget Sanneo's restless eyes and rough words.

Sometimes he was put out by Lucia's ignorance, and would get violent when he realized that his explanations were not understood or his previous ones forgotten. Subtle distinctions did penetrate now and again into that brain of hers, but it was no home for them and they left it again after a very short stay. If the same idea came up a second time, he had to introduce it formally all over again, and then the anger oozing from the teacher's every pore destroyed the calm needed by the pupil for thought. When he asked her to repeat his explanations, she would raise her little nose, then smiling but pale say the opposite of what Alfonso had said, or hastily produce some phrases that had stuck in her mind without worrying much about their meaning. Alfonso, so as not to lose patience, would silently repeat maxims of goodness and tell himself that he must not offend someone of lesser intelligence.

"Lesser intelligence is something to be pitied," he was shouting a week later. "But not lesser application!" In fact, the girl was no longer studying. With an immense effort her brain had reached a certain point, then stopped because it was tired, almost saturated. When the lessons began, her mother, being used to school systems, and in order to find her daughter enough time for this new occupation, had arranged a timetable by which an hour of the day was set aside for preparation. This hour the girl regularly spent, not studying in her room, but with the rest of the family at the table listening to her father's stories. There she would sit restlessly, nagged by her mother's calls for greater zeal, and by her own wish to make a good impression on Alfonso, and positively tortured by the fear that he might shout at her if she stayed there! She did stay, from inertia, resigned to enduring Alfonso's cutting observations and far preferring his blows, rather than try to struggle by herself with concepts which he had explained only briefly. She could have learned them by heart, but that was not enough; if she forgot one word, that was bound to be the essential one according to Alfonso.

Alfonso was not a good teacher because he failed to appreciate any efforts by his pupil. He very rarely praised her and then only when sorry for some harsh word and hoping to prevent her tears, but never because of some answer that was nearly correct. He had deluded himself about a vocation for teaching, which he enjoyed not from any fondness for his pupil. Lucia's progress was of little or no account to him. He was offended that she did not learn more, and on irksome days, after having had to put up with the anger of others himself, he would have an outburst.

It was surprising that Lucia did not lose patience and

suspend those lessons which caused her so much agony
and were of such little use. She did not want to! In
fact, at the end of every lesson, when Alfonso, saying
good-bye, became milder and treated her with his usual
respect, she promised herself to study really hard so as
to deserve such treatment during the lesson, too. How
lovely it would have been to spend that hour, too, as
friends, admiring each other, which she could so easily
do on her side. After that hour of forced effort, study
seemed easier and pleasanter to her than it had before
the lesson, which had helped to rub off the rust formed
on her brain during a day spent working at her needle.
She promised herself to get up earlier next morning to
begin studying again; but night plunged her back into
her usual lethargy.

No, she did not want the lessons suspended, but her
dislike of them showed by the fact that she would
snatch at any excuse to avoid one. On some evenings
she had to visit a friend, and on many others, for lack
of a better excuse, she felt unwell. One evening Gustavo, seeing her pretending to be gloomy and listless
since Alfonso's entry, and not realizing the purpose of
her indisposition, asked: "Been taken ill very sudden,
haven't you?"

There was no need of this warning to show Alfonso
the sort of love for study which he had managed to
inculcate in his pupil, but he found it not unpleasant
to be feared.

Once Lucia plucked up courage to refuse a lesson
without making any excuse. She went to open the door
for Alfonso and just announced, with a loud laugh
copied from a friend, that she would not be having her
lesson that evening.

"Why not?" asked Alfonso with a frown. He was
not laughing, but unpleasantly surprised.

"Let's spend the time having a laugh, not studying," replied Lucia bravely.

"Hadn't we better stop these lessons altogether, as you don't seem to like them much?"

Lucia blanched, terrified at once. Her mother came to her rescue and explained to Alfonso that Lucia had not found time to do her homework and so was having no lesson that evening lest they got too far ahead before she mastered what they had gone over together. Then he, too, spent a much pleasanter evening than if he had studied with Lucia. He chattered away and was listened to devoutly.

At their next lesson he was more brutal than usual and even called her an ignoramus. He had given her half an hour to find an answer which she could not give at once, and behaved as if she had committed a crime by being unable to think of it in that interval; he forgot that where there is no blood it cannot be made to flow. He declared, for lack of other pungent phrases, that it was time to suspend lessons that were producing no results, and got to his feet to terminate this one at once. The girl had not dared declare frankly till then that she could not say what she did not know. She looked up at the ceiling for a reply, made sounds of impatience to diminish Alfonso's own impatience, and gave a smile so forced that it was pitiable. At Alfonso's crude announcement she burst into tears, got up, left, banged the door violently, and flung herself into the arms of her mother, who was alone in the living room. Alfonso, alarmed by the effect he had produced, would willingly have stopped her and apologized.

He followed her and was struck by a look of intense fury flung across the room at him by Signora Lanucci, who was holding the girl tight to her breast. Lucia was sobbing so hard that she had been unable to explain anything so far. On seeing him, the Signora said grimly: "What have you done to the poor girl?"

Very embarrassed, Alfonso replied: "I shouted at her because she'd done no studying!"

"Of course she's studied! I saw her myself!"

Lucia's anger, like all weak people's, burst out violently because it had been long repressed. Between sobs she now yelled at Alfonso three clearly distinguishable insults: "Fool, idiot, donkey!"

In her emotion, the fine manners learned with difficulty during recent years left her, and she was reduced to the words, tone, and gestures of Gustavo. Alfonso was offended but speechless, and uncertain whether to defend or save himself from her anger by taking refuge in his room.

Signora Lanucci, pained at this break in the harmony she hoped to see between the two young people, turned on Lucia: "It's you who're the idiot and fool! Will you be silent?" And she pushed her away.

Lucia flopped into a chair, but did not seem to have had her say yet: "He thinks he's clever. . ."

"Will you be quiet?" interrupted Signora Lanucci threateningly.

Lucia went on sobbing for another half hour.

Signora Lanucci wanted to minimize the incident and laughed about it to Alfonso, who felt in no state to follow her lead.

"But I do want peace in my home and I realize that the only way to have it is to put an end to these lessons. Such a pity!"

She could show regret without fear of arousing Alfonso's suspicions, because at the start of the lessons she had explained how much she hoped Lucia would gain from his instruction. "Men, particularly those with a real enthusiasm for study," Signora Lanucci had said, with a flattering bow toward Alfonso, "are better teachers than women, who love petty things and get lost in useless details, so harmful to an understanding of the whole." But men, she was just realizing, had other defects that were just as damaging. In spite of these defects, she went on being surprisingly kind to Alfonso.

Lucia less so. For a week she did not address a word to him. She served him at the table as her mother ordered, but without pronouncing a word. Signora Lanucci, in consolation, would wink at him, laugh, and, turning to Lucia, say ironically: "Just hand that dish to Signor Alfonso, will you. Do you hate him so much you'll let him die of hunger?"

Lucia obeyed, looking very glum; Alfonso, just as glum, let himself be served with a cold word of thanks.

One evening, upon suddenly entering the living room with Gustavo, who had the keys to the house, he found the elder Lanucci and his wife looking angry and Lucia with eyes red from weeping. Evidently the two old people had been preaching at her. He sat down at the table, pretending that he had noticed nothing.

He regretted his behavior, but did not know how to ask her forgiveness. When he thought it over in the evening alone or in the office, the poor girl's mute attempts at excusing herself came back to him and he had to confess that his rage had been both stupid and brutal. He concluded that it was his duty to meet Lucia halfway, beg her pardon, and stop making her wretched. But when he saw that stupid, expressionless face again, with its projecting cheekbones and set sulk, the kind words he had ready turned in his throat.

Lucia, without looking him in the face, after some hesitation went up to him, held out her hand and said: "Excuse me, Signor Alfonso, I was wrong; let's make it up!"

Alfonso, touched, shook her hand warmly.

"The fault was mostly mine, it's you who must excuse me!"

Lucia gave him a grateful glance, which made her less ugly, and soon had the calm relaxed air of one who has forgotten any misunderstanding. She laughed often and quickly went back to her affected ways.

He was sorry to have been outdone in generosity and was less at ease. He, the person of culture, the teacher, should have been first to give way. This regret, slight as it was, continued to worry him even when he was lying in bed. There were always insignificant facts such as that disturbing his life, in which nothing important ever happened, and every night he would brood over some ill-considered remark made by himself or by someone else whose real meaning he had only just realized and would either regret not having revenged himself with a sharp answer or blame himself for having produced an answer that was unjustifiably brusque.

In the living room they were talking, and he listened mechanically. It was Signora Lanucci and her husband; he could distinguish nothing but the sound of their voices and only when they passed by his door on their way to their room did he clearly hear Lanucci exclaim with a good-humored little laugh, probably to end their discussion: "Real lovers' quarrels, these are!"

He already had suspicions about Signora Lanucci's designs on him, but had considered them till then not so much real designs as hopes which could flatter but not alarm. Those few words overheard by chance, the end of a longer conversation, seemed to prove that they not only had hopes of him but were plotting against him, against his liberty. The behavior of both mother and daughter fitted in with this. The mother had handed over to him, who in his simplicity had wanted to teach her daughter, not a pupil but a bride.

He remembered some words of advice from her

which could have had a double meaning. The daughter
had put up with everything rather than see the lessons
interrupted as he had threatened. Now making up the
quarrel must have revived their hopes.

Should he get indignant? Their attempt deserved it
because, had it succeeded, his situation would have
been very much worsened.

The Lanuccis were in a nasty situation themselves
though, with the two men in the family unable to
better their state! So safe did he feel from the nets
spread by Signora Lanucci that he could look at the
situation quite objectively, and realize that never again
would he ever have such a chance of doing a good deed
as marrying Lucia. What would her future be? Probably she would be an old maid, uselessly hanging on to
all those "society manners," as her mother called them,
till the end of her life. In his dreams he was capable
of heroic action; but next day his bearing toward her
was less affectionate. When alone, he saw the situation
quite differently than he did when he was with Lucia;
he found excuses, forgave her, even felt remorse at
being incapable of acting nobly enough, recalled the
love which Lucia had demonstrated by her patience
in putting up with his brutality and by the violence of
her misery on realizing she could not reach her goal.
But face to face with Lucia he noticed her jutting
cheekbones. No, he did not desire her! He was free and
wanted to remain so.

"I'm ill!"

This conclusion was reached after he had made a
series of observations about himself. The deep gloom
which turned everything gray and dull for him had
seemed till then a natural result of his discontent; his
insomnia he thought must be due to nervous tension
brought on by night study; and an abnormal restlessness he sometimes noticed in himself must come from

the fact that his muscles and lungs were insisting on exercise and pure air. At other times a few hours' freedom was enough to restore his vivacity and calm. But now he was constantly, monotonously, obsessed by one vision which made him incapable of taking part in the present, hearing and examining anything said by others. Sanneo, after giving very lengthy instructions, asked him in a changed tone: "Do you understand?" That change of tone tore Alfonso from his fantasies. He said "Yes" just in order to be left in peace and fall back into his dreams as soon as possible. But he had understood nothing, heard nothing, and was even incapable of worrying. He went slowly off to his place, taking short steps so as to gain time and interrupt his beloved visions as little as possible.

He still went on spending every evening in the library, though he came out as he had entered, with no new ideas, because his mind was shut to them. He could only re-evoke the past, complete some megalomaniac dream in which he saw himself showing off his knowledge before others. A vague sensation of madness weakened his nerves. He feared and avoided people whom he did not know, and a passer-by at night made him start with fright. He felt awful in the dark and quivered at the faintest sound. Crouching in bed, his head under the covers, he would lie for hours unable to conquer sleep. What a difficult conquest it was! How could he think of nothing? Sometimes he went to bed really tired, and felt he would only have to close his eyes to fall asleep. But as soon as he flung himself on the bed, sleep left him, and when hours later he managed to lie quiet on some part of the bed he had to be content with a sleep lacking density, in which his brain went on working dumbly and instinctively, and none the less tiringly for that.

"You're unwell, it seems to me," said Cellani, seeing

him pale, with eyes staring. "Take a couple of weeks off if you need them."

Alfonso did not accept at once, and had to go ask Cellani that evening for what he had refused in the morning.

Sanneo rather brusquely also granted him the required permission. For some time now he had had an assistant working with Alfonso, one Carlo Alchieri, an artillery lieutenant on half pay because of weak lungs. As the small pension granted him was not enough, he had joined Maller's. He was young, with an old man's face and a full drab beard: outwardly he looked strong enough. He was the only one to curse on hearing of Alfonso's holiday, because he knew he would have to bear all that burden of work alone. Sanneo was not one to take other clerks away from their usual jobs to help out someone temporarily overwhelmed by work—because the temporary clerk was officially a substitute for the clerk who was away.

All Alfonso needed to get rid of his inertia was to be out in the open air knowing he could stay there some time for the sake of his health. He longed to feel well again. Till then he had not felt any regret for his weakness, thinking of it as do holy men in India who find an increase of intelligence in annihilating matter. But his state of boredom, of grayness and monotony, was not that of an intelligent person.

The sun was just up when Alfonso jumped out of bed with a violent effort of will. He did not know where to go or where chance would take him; there were plenty of hills around the town.

First he thought of following a company of soldiers going out on maneuvers. But the sound of their heavy measured tread on the cobbles irritated him. He went up Via Stadion almost at a run to get away from them, as they were taking the same road. He wanted to reach a cliffside. The effort would have been enough for that first day. But before he was past the last houses of the city, low and rustic, some thatched and painted in bright muddy colors, he had already changed his mind. Now he wanted a green hillside lying on his right, not a grim cliff. He crossed a wooden bridge over the wide but nearly dry bed of a stream; a thread of water ran capriciously amid white stones. He crossed a wide avenue on the other side and at last felt bare earth beneath his feet, live grass giving to his weight. Already tired and panting, he flung himself on the ground. He was in a copse of young trees with slim trunks, with tufty tops murmuring in the morning breeze. This sound merged with the mutter of water trickling into a pool, near a low white house only a few steps away.

Again he was seized with a desire to run, a yearning to get a long way off. As he climbed, the trees became thicker and stronger. Here and there bushes held him up, and he forced his way with febrile impatience, without the strong man's calm step. He crossed another road and strode through another copse, still climbing aimlessly. The blood was churning in his head and his breath was failing, but this only stopped him for very short halts. Exhaustion only overwhelmed him when he came up against a high wall blocking his way. He had climbed for less than an hour before flinging himself on the ground exhausted; it seemed a well-deserved rest.

For a minute or two he was terrified by a violent beating in his heart and temples. He took off his jacket, put it under his head, and lay down on dry ground by an oak. Shortly after, though his blood was still agitated, his lungs opened and he took a deep breath, deeper than he had taken for a long time. He looked at the little field around him and enjoyed seeing it clear and green and smiling, as if it were his own and would one day be his home. A corner of the city was visible: some twenty close-packed houses, then others scattered one by one on the opposite hillside. Beyond was a patch of blue sea with motionless boats. The clear sky, cloudless to the horizon; the green of the country; those houses flung down haphazardly, reminded him of an oleograph in which colors had been leveled out by the machine, the painter's idea muted by reproduction, its light and movement gone.

Like a child, smiling, with closed fists, he fell asleep.

He had an absurd dream about Maria, whom he recognized by her bright colored dress. She told him that she knew that circumstances had prevented him from coming to that appointment. She forgave him and loved him.

CHAPTER

VIII

Alchieri, rushed and flustered, holding a bundle of papers, was hurrying toward the cash desk when he saw Alfonso, hat in hand, about to enter Sanneo's room to announce his return to the office. He gave a cry of delight, tried to stop Alfonso, who passed by without noticing him, then grew calmer and sat down next to Giacomo, on duty in the passage and intent on deciphering a newspaper, half aloud. Finding no one else to tell, Alchieri confided to Giacomo that this was the first time in a fortnight he had sat down to rest and not to write.

Sanneo greeted Alfonso cordially; then, turning back to a huge register on which he was writing in his big script, asked if he was well. Without waiting for a reply, in phrases interrupted by work, which at intervals called for all his attention, he spoke of some letters that were pending and needed to be answered as soon as possible. Then he handed him a few, to the accompaniment of explanations, which Alfonso only half understood, referring to things that had happened before he had left, a period which seemed to Alfonso much more than a fortnight away. Sanneo dismissed him with a piece of good news.

"Signor Alchieri will continue to help you, he works quite well . . . it seems."

Alchieri stopped him in the passage, and tried to hug him in thanks for returning on the exact date promised.

"I couldn't take much more!"

Then he, too, began to explain various business matters, and there and then in the passage handed over all the letters he had in his hand—statements of account or advice of drafts. He could not wait to be free of them.

With those letters in one hand, and his hat in the other, Alfonso went to pay his respects to Cellani.

He found him opening the mail. With one snip of his huge scissors he opened an envelope, took out the contents, which he threw on one side, and before putting down the envelope gave it a prudent glance against the light. He, too, went on working while talking to Alfonso; but when the latter, with his usual shyness, murmured thanks and reminded him that he owed his holiday to him, Cellani got up and went to shake Alfonso's hand with a friendly smile on his pale face. His long sportsman's body, elegant but weak, seemed borne along rather than self-propelled, so little energy was there in his movements and so exactly and unhesitatingly did he pass through the narrow space between desk and chair.

"You're looking fine," he said to Alfonso, glancing almost enviously at the latter's suntanned face. He was in a hurry to return to his own place. Shaking Alfonso's hand again, he said laughing: "Now. . ." and made a sign of writing very fast with the pen in his left hand.

Alfonso found that Alchieri had diminished his pending tray and, sitting in his place, he decided under the encouragement of Cellani's welcome to get it all done and allow no more to accumulate. Alchieri, coming from a barracks, had introduced in only a fortnight a system of work far preferable to Alfonso's, who found it easy, at least at first, to keep to it. His improved serenity, reinforced by the open air, made him capable of greater concentration, effort though it always was.

Even when back at work he continued his open-air cure, as he called it. Every morning he walked for an hour or two, usually toward the plateau, because he needed the climb. Up he went with his measured pace, and tramped along the whole of the wide Opicina Road, whose enormous length took him up to the plateau in a single, wide, gently sloping semicircle around the town. Alfonso would rest on this road where a lane branched off toward Longera.

From there he saw the vast silent deserted plateau, with its innumerable stone hillocks of all shapes, pointed, round, squat, heaps of stones fallen from above and arranged as haphazardly as was Monte Re on the horizon, with its wide back, gentle slope at one side, and almost perpendicular drop on the other.

Alfonso never passed that point, partly because he had no time. From there he could see the city, with its white houses, and the sea, usually in morning calm as if the few hours of light had not yet been enough to rouse it. The green of the promontories on the left of the city and the colors of the sea contrasted strangely with the gray stones of the plateau.

He descended into a city quieter than he ever knew it except when leaving the library. Near Longera he passed without entering, an oblong village halfway down the valley, hugging the mountain as if for refuge, its houses all clustered together, though it could easily have found air and space by encroaching on surrounding fields. People were already beginning to swarm onto the village streets at that hour, and from a distance all the outer forms of human activities and destinies seemed hinted at in those few figures moving about the narrow alleys of the little place. A boy's quick run, which Alfonso could follow from one side of the village to the other; a peasant leaving home, with his hat on, and then, before moving on, calmly examining the sky, maybe to see whether to take an umbrella; in a more remote lane a man and woman were chattering away, maybe of love already at that hour; in a courtyard grain was being beaten amid so much movement that from a distance it could be mistaken for gaiety. Then Alfonso passed prosperous San Giovanni, with its scattered houses, its little white church, empty during the week but so full on Sundays that not all the faithful could enter, so that peasant women, dressed in black wool edged with wide strips of blue or red silk, crowded the little square and made their devotions out in the open.

Alfonso's new way of life was damaging to his studies, because the first result of his frequent outings was a need for yet more air and an incapacity to stay shut up for long. Sometimes he would move toward the library on coming out of the office, but he could seldom stay there more than a half hour; he would be seized by an invincible restlessness, which took him

out into the open to stand riveted to some pier, with
no ideas or dreams in his head, his only preoccupation
to absorb that sea breeze whose beneficent effects he
thought he could feel at once.

Then he would go home, and at supper be still intent on spending the rest of the evening on a book,
but weariness would overcome him and he would go
off into ten hours of calm, beneficent, unregrettable
sleep.

Yet it was precisely then that his ambition took definite form. He had found his path! He would lay the
foundations of modern Italian philosophy by translating a good German work and at the same time
writing an original work of his own. The translation
remained purely an intention, but he did start on the
original work: a title, *The Moral Idea in the Modern
World*, and a preface in which he declared the aim
of his work. This aim was theoretic and without any
practical intention, which seemed to him quite new
for Italian philosophy. The idea briefly laid out in a
table of contents, beyond which Alfonso himself knew
no more, was to show that the only basis for a moral
idea in the world was the good of the community. The
idea was not particularly original but his development
of it could become so, if treated exclusively as a search
for truth, with no preoccupation about possible practical consequences. For this he lacked neither the courage nor the sincerity; when writing, he had all the
courage that he lacked in life, and studies undertaken
purely for the sake of learning would have no effect
on his sincerity. He did not know and cared less what
elements were needed for literary success. He wanted
to work, to work well, and success would come by itself.

He did work well, but very little. Too often his
thoughts were with the completed work, while phrases
actually written could be counted on his fingers. Thus,

he imagined more and more qualities in the book which, because so far more or less nonexistent, could not be damaged by his pen's resistance. After some months, seeing that the result of his efforts was three or four short pages of preface, which promised to do and attempt much while nothing was actually done or attempted at all, he felt very discouraged. Those pages represented the work of months, for he had done no other meanwhile. He had not been studying much, and those pages were the only progress he had made toward his goal; so small that it was equivalent to a tacit renunciation of all ambition.

With more reason he could persuade himself that this lack of progress was due to renunciation, for he really did find himself happier at the bank and hating less the work that was in fundamental antagonism, so he thought, to the intellectual labors he wanted to dedicate himself to. Alchieri had helped to make the bank less odious, but so, he considered, had the interruption of almost all his other more intelligent activities.

For some time he tried to get back to reading at the public library, even at the cost of leaving his philosophic writing aside for the moment. One evening Sanneo scolded him for a mistake. Although realizing that he deserved such rebukes, he was put out by the manner of their delivery, by an overbrusque word. At other times, he remembered, he had rid himself of the bitter mood aroused by these incidents in a clerk's life by applying himself more fervently to studies which would eventually pull him out of his position of inferiority. That was what took him back to the library after a long absence.

He plunged into reading an Italian bibliographical journal. He felt that language was not obeying him and that he must go in for reading more Italian. For about an hour he read spontaneously and attentively (due to Sanneo's brutality) a discussion about the authenticity of some of Petrarch's letters. When he paused he felt satisfied; but the tiring of his brain reminded him of past readings; he felt an overwhelming sense of regret and of how much his life had changed since.

On raising his head, he noticed that opposite him was sitting Macario, who was gazing at him indecisively.

"Signor Nitti!" he said almost questioningly; he must have had a bad memory. Then he held out his hand in a friendly way.

They went out together.

"Do you often come here?" asked Macario, busy straightening his overcoat, a long gray garment with large bone buttons.

Alfonso replied carelessly that he came every evening, and tacitly decided to make the lie into truth in the future.

"I've come for the last week, and it's a pity this is the first time we've met," said Macario kindly. He asked what he was studying.

"Literature," confessed Alfonso, hesitating.

He was glad to be able to say this to Macario, but hesitated because he knew and feared his malice. He explained that he was in the habit of doing an hour or two of studying every day as a distraction after the day's work.

"And what are you reading?" asked Macario, who was looking at him with surprise.

He found that Alfonso, apart from his bronzed face, seemed less rustic than in the previous months. He spoke more easily and, what was more, as Macario was sufficiently intelligent to understand, his decrying the importance of his regular studies denoted a certain superiority.

Knowing how much some despised philosophers and

philosophy, Alfonso abstained from naming his favorite authors and only mentioned a critic or two. But Macario must have realized that he was dealing with someone who could allow himself the luxury of his own opinions and was surprised to find him so cagey. Alfonso was enthusiastic about authors whom he did not mention to Macario.

On his own side, Alfonso very soon acquired some notion of Macario's culture. He was pleased to find himself highly enough esteemed for Macario to make ill-concealed efforts to bring subjects he knew about into the conversation. Macario spoke of contemporary realist writers. Alfonso had read some of their novels, and a review or two, and made up his mind about them with the calm of the disinterested student he then was. He admired some sections, criticized others. Macario was a resolute partisan and his enthusiasm made Alfonso sift his own opinions. While Macario was looking at him with a rather derisive smile which meant: "My flair makes my few studies worth your many," Alfonso's serious, attentive aspect, like a scholar at a lesson, hid his enjoyment of his own superiority. He avoided a discussion in which he had no hope of gaining a victory over Macario's facility with words. But with such a talker it was impossible to look indifferent, and almost involuntarily Alfonso began giving signs of assent, which, to calm his own conscience, he addressed to Macario's separate phrases and not to his concept. Some of these phrases were so fine that Alfonso suspected them to be stolen. He spoke of the creations of man which were quite up to the Biblical creation in results. These creations differed somewhat in method, but both had achieved the production of organisms which lived by themselves and bore no trace of having been created.

Macario told him he came to the library for some

calm reading of Balzac, whom the realists called their father. Balzac was not that at all, or at least Macario did not consider him as such. He classified Balzac as a writer of ordinary rhetoric, typical of the first half of the century.

They reached Piazza della Legna, walking so slowly that they took half an hour. On the way Macario found time to admire a pretty seamstress and make a young lady blush by staring straight into her eyes. Alfonso, though, had been unable to do anything but listen.

"Where do you live?" asked Macario, taking his arm.

"In that direction," and he pointed vaguely toward the old town.

"I'll walk part of the way with you."

How could he not be flattered by such kindness and how could he start to defend Balzac from the taint of rhetoric? In reply to the pleasant offer, Alfonso resolutely sacrificed Balzac.

"He's often rhetorical, of course!"

They did not enter the old town but returned to the Corso.

"Do you know, you ought to be very much at home now at my uncle's? It's quite a different place; Annetta is dedicating herself to literature. Would you like us to go call on her? She's been back from the country a week and receives friends almost every evening; she's even more emancipated than she was before."

"Really!" exclaimed Alfonso, showing surprise.

He tried to find some answer to refuse the invitation.

Macario behaved as if Alfonso had already accepted. Followed by him, he crossed the Corso and entered Via Ponte Rosso. Alfonso was still undecided.

"You'll see! She's at her prettiest! Half her day she spends at her desk. This new vocation doesn't worry anyone, by the way; in a few months she won't even mention it. I think what stirred her up is the fame being won by other women in Italy. Women! One begins and the others follow like geese. Man's example doesn't count at all. They imitate this, they imitate that, and never realize what they are imitating, because their tiny brains know so little about originality that they consider it equivalent to accuracy, accuracy in imitation. The really original woman is the one who first imitates a man."

Alfonso laughed.

"What about Signorina Annetta?"

"About Signorina Annetta as a writer I know nothing. She's so cautious that until she's imitated something very closely she'll show no one a thing; so one must wait before giving a definite opinion, as it's a matter of knowing who she's chosen to imitate. My opinion of Annetta you already know. Highly developed mathematical aptitudes. . ." and he made his usual gesture to accentuate the hint. "Anyway, now we'll go and pay her our homage."

They entered Via dei Forni; Alfonso stopped him.

"I'm not coming, I can't come. I'm expected at home, and then in this state. . ."

His face was flushed and he spoke with far more warmth than was needed to refuse Macario's invitation.

"I can't make you, of course. It's a pity, though! If someone is waiting for you, of course you're right to refuse, but if it's because of your clothes you're wrong. First, you're quite decent. Then, now that Annetta is a literary girl, she likes Bohemians. So come along, do!"

But Alfonso resisted. He had already realized from what Macario had said that Annetta would treat him pleasantly, but he wanted to be begged. He had been unable to obtain any other satisfaction for the offense done to him and intended to get at least that.

"You still remember Annetta's coldness months ago," and although Alfonso protested and asserted that he no longer remembered, Macario, as he went off, gave him a friendly scolding and treated him like a child.

Next evening they both met again at the library. Alfonso went there more willingly. He was amused by Macario's conversation and flattered by his company.

Macario's wit always triumphed over Alfonso's knowledge, and Macario was convinced that he was doing the teaching. He was mistaken. If Alfonso learned anything from him, it was by observing him as an object of study.

He had understood now the quality of Macario's wit. He noticed mistakes, he realized when Macario puffed up an idea to show it off more easily, and if he did sometimes show admiration, it was because he admired the ease with which Macario made denials or assertions where superior minds would hesitate.

Macario often fell into contradictions, but never on the same day. He was subject to moods. He would put on borrowed clothes and live in them as if they were his own, and he would never take them off. That was easy for him thanks to his superficial culture, which was extensive enough for him to create the image of a quickly civilized personality, and not deep enough to give him any firm convictions of the sort that are not renounced even in jest.

That second evening he attacked the press. He said that those who wrote for the press always had to pretend and could never be sincere. In public the old was called new, the blameworthy praised, and so on. All this was rather weak stuff so far, but then he got underway. What use was learning? Apart from those who dedicated themselves to original research on a certain subject, others were wrong to bother too much about it. They tired out their brains and got no advantage, because someone who understands one part of something well has educated his brain just as much as another who has studied more parts. Thus, printed paper damages the brain more than it develops it. That "thus" did not quite follow, but Alfonso gave no sign of noticing this and Macario was pleased at his own reasoning.

"This is good!" exclaimed Macario one evening at the library, putting in front of Alfonso a little book he had just finished reading: Balzac's *Louis Lambert*.

Alfonso also read it in two or three days with no less admiration. Apart from a love letter of such deep and sensual passion that it transcended love, he did not admire the book's artistic merits as much as the original way a whole philosophic system was explained briefly but completely, with every part indicated, and all handed over by the author to his hero with a grandee's generosity.

Macario asked Alfonso how he had liked it, and Alfonso was about to give him his sincere opinion. But Macario quickly imposed his own ideas, as if fearing they would be stolen.

"Do you know why it's such a fine book? It's the only one of Balzac's that is really impersonal, and it became so by chance. Louis Lambert is mad, all those around him are mad, and this time the author, to conform, makes himself mad, too. So it's a little world presented intact, by itself, without the slightest influence from outside."

Alfonso was amazed by this criticism, as original as it was false. It must have been made according to a method which Alfonso avoided mentioning only because he feared being also put into that "little world presented intact."

His company must have pleased Macario, who often sought him out, even some evenings going to fetch him from the office.

Alfonso soon guessed the reason for this sudden af-

fection. He owed it to his docility and, he thought, also
to his size. He was so small and insignificant that Macario felt fine beside him. The friendship pleased him
none the less for this. Courtesies, however expensive,
are pleasant. He did not esteem Macario the less. He
admired this young man for certain qualities; elegant,
an unconscious artist, intelligent even when speaking
of things he knew nothing about.

Macario owned a little sailing cutter and often invited Alfonso for morning trips in the bay. Alfonso's
life being so empty, those trips were a real joy. In the
boat it was also easier for him to agree with Macario's
assertions, most of which he did not even hear. He was
still trying hard to acquire the health necessary, he
considered, for the life of hard work he intended to
undertake, and sea air should help him find it.

One morning a gusty wind was blowing, and at the
end of the mole where they were standing waiting for
the boat to come to fetch them, Alfonso suggested to
Macario that they put off their sail that morning as
it seemed dangerous. Macario began to jeer and would
not hear of it.

The cutter approached. Heeling under white sails
swollen in the wind, it seemed about to turn over at
every instant but straightened up just before it was too
late. Alfonso, on land, was seized by those nervous
tremors which people get when they see others in danger of falling, and, had it not been for his fear of Macario, would have let him leave alone.

Ferdinando, a port worker who had been a sailor,
was in charge of the boat. He left his place at the helm
to Macario, who sat down after taking off his jacket
as if in preparation for great efforts.

"Let her go now!" he called to Ferdinando.

Ferdinando jumped on land and dragged the cutter
by the bowsprit from one corner of the mole to the

other; then he jumped back and with one foot on land and the other on the boat he gave it a push out to sea.

Alfonso looked at him, frightened of seeing him fall into the water; the imminence of danger, small as it was, startled him.

"How agile!" he said to Ferdinando.

He felt himself to be in the man's hands and had an unconscious desire to make friends. Ferdinando raised a head, youthful in spite of baldness and gray in his beard, and thanked him. As this was not his real job, he very much wanted to seem good at it. But he misunderstood the purpose of Alfonso's comment. He strained the sail toward himself and fixed it, putting all his weight into stretching it taut. Immediately wind which seemed to blow up that very moment swelled it out and the boat heeled right over on the very side where Alfonso was sitting.

He had intended making a great show of coolheadedness, but his intentions were no match for his sudden terror. He was just able to avoid shouting, but leaped to his feet and flung himself on to the other side hoping to straighten up the boat by his weight. Now that he felt farther from the water he grew a little calmer and sat down, gripping the gunwale.

Macario looked at him with a slight smile. He felt well and calm and to make the distance between himself and Alfonso more obvious he kept the cutter very close to the wind. Alfonso saw the smile and tried to look calm. He pointed out to Macario some white mountain tops on the horizon whose bases were not visible.

As they passed the lighthouse, he was able to measure the speed with which they were cutting the water; then started as the boat seemed about to crash against rocks.

"Can you swim?" asked Macario, all serene. "If the

worst comes to the worst, we can swim back. But," and he pretended to be very worried, "even if you feel you're drowning, don't grab me because then we shall both be lost. Ferdinando and I will see to you. Won't we, Nando?"

Ferdinando gave a roar of laughter, and promised.

Macario then began pensively discoursing on the effects of fear. Every ten words he raised and languidly waved an aristocratic hand, and all the hints in the hollowed hand Alfonso knew referred to him and to his fear.

"More people die from fear than from courage. For example, if they fall into the water, those who seize whatever is nearest to them are the ones who die," and he winked toward Alfonso's hands nervously clutching the gunwale.

They passed by green Sant'Andrea without Alfonso's being able to get hold of himself. He looked but did not enjoy.

The town, when he saw it on the return tack, had a gloomy look. He felt very unwell, and tired out as if he had come a long way some time ago and not had a good rest since. This must be seasickness, and he provoked Macario's laughter by telling him so.

"In this sea!"

In fact, the sea was lashed by an offshore wind and had no waves. Wide patches were crinkly, others beaten by wind, which seemed to have smoothed off the surface. In the dips there was a gay murmuring like that produced by innumerable washerwomen moving their washing about in running water.

Alfonso was so pale that Macario took pity on him and ordered Ferdinando to shorten sail.

They were inside the port but to reach the point of departure had to tack in front of it twice.

Little calls of sea gulls could be heard. To distract

Alfonso, Macario wanted him to observe the flight of these birds, as calm and straight as if on a highroad, and their rapid falls like bits of lead. They looked lonely, each flying on its own account, with great white wings outstretched and a disproportionately small body covered with light feathers.

"Made just for fishing and eating," philosophized Macario. "How little brain it takes to catch fish! Their bodies are small. Think what size their brain must be! Negligible! Those wings are the danger to the fish, who end up in a sea gull's beak because of them! What eyes and stomach, what an appetite, to satisfy which such a drop is nothing! But brain? What has brain to do with catching fish? You study, you spend hours at a desk nourishing your brain uselessly. Anyone who isn't born with the necessary wings will never grow them afterward. Anyone who can't drop like lead on prey at the right second by instinct will never learn, and there'll be no point in his watching others who can, as he'll never be able to imitate them. One dies in the precise state in which one is born, our hands mere organs for snatching or incapable of holding."

This speech impressed Alfonso. He felt miserable at having been seized with agitation about something so unimportant.

"And have I got wings?" he asked, sketching a smile.

"Yes, to make poetic flights!" replied Macario, waving a hollowed hand, though the phrase contained no underlying hint which needed a gesture of the kind in order to be understood.

CHAPTER

IX

Annetta had returned to town about a month before her father, who had gone straight from the country to Rome on business. In that month a number of Maller's telegrams passed through Alfonso's hands, carelessly jotted, higgledy-piggledy. They were about business, and Alfonso was loth to take the trouble to read them. The last was shown him by Starringer, the dispatch clerk, through whose hands all correspondence passed and who had to read it all. Maller's last telegram ended with the words: "Advise family of my arrival tomorrow, and arrange carriage to meet me at station."

Signor Maller must have been back twenty-four hours and Alfonso had not yet seen him. He expected at any moment to meet him face to face, and walked more timidly than usual along the passage.

Miceni came to tell him that he had just come from Maller's room, where he had been to welcome him. Maller had greeted him with great courtesy and shaken his hand twice. Miceni was usually acidly democratic when speaking of his superiors, but that day, under the impression of those two handshakes, he was gentler; they seemed to have made him forget his quarrel with Sanneo. Not only did he praise Signor Maller for his courtesy but was pleased as a loyal employee at finding him so well.

"Do you advise me to go and welcome him, too?"

"Nearly everyone is; do whatever you think best."

Alchieri had gone, but that was no precedent, for Sanneo had sent him to the manager's office on business and so he had welcomed Maller by chance. White could be used even less as an example for Alfonso because the managers' offices were like his own and he spent half his day in them.

Ballina did not want to go. He was firm.

"One doesn't jeer at Jesus, but one does at his vicars. When Sanneo returned, I went to welcome him because I knew he liked that and was not clever enough to understand that I only did it as a diplomatic gesture. But Signor Maller must have something in his head to be the master of us all, and I don't allow myself any jokes with him."

For a whole day Alfonso remained undecided. He had forgotten to ask the advice of Macario, who would have swept away all doubt with a single word. Anything at all doubtful eventually became important for

Alfonso. He feared that by going he would bore Maller, who might show it, but if he didn't, his absence would be taken as lack of respect.

He was about to leave the bank, putting off the difficult decision till next day, when it was made easier for him by the number of clerks he saw waiting in the passage to go into Maller's office and welcome him. Quickly he decided to join them.

Out of the manager's room came old Marlucci, a Tuscan who always spoke regretfully of the grand-ducal government. He was about sixty and, by sitting for twenty years or so behind a big ledger, had become a great friend of Jassy. They came and went together, linked by the same misfortune, weakness of the legs; but while Jassy had a vacillating brain and weak, twitching hands, the Tuscan had calm black eyes and limpid and precise speech. Daily in his ledger he lined up his given quota of neat ordered figures, and there were no corrections in his books apart from those made necessary by the mistakes of other sections.

Alfonso, following the impulse given by his preoccupation, asked him: "And what does one say to Signor Maller?"

"If you don't know, keep silent!" replied Marlucci laughing, and passed him by.

There was no other employee except White with Maller, who was giving him instructions. A woman was sitting at the window; without looking at her, Alfonso guessed this was Annetta and felt the blood rush to his heart.

Signor Maller interrupted his consultation with White for an instant. He held out his hand to Alfonso and with a cold smile asked him if he were well. Then he withdrew his hand and began talking to White again.

Alfonso was just leaving when he was stopped by a

sweet, feminine voice which sounded out of place in that room: "Signor Nitti!"

He stopped and turned around. It was Annetta. She was wearing a gray dress, with the gray veil of a little round hat raised over a white forehead. A chaste but matronly figure.

She held out her hand.

"Are you angry with me, that you refuse to see me?"

Alfonso protested that he really had not seen her. He was stuttering, but saying more than was strictly necessary.

"Not that I'm blaming you," she said in a lower voice and so confidentially that he gave a quiver of joyful surprise, worrying what the others present might think. "In fact, you're quite right. Now give me your hand, and in a more friendly way than last time."

She smiled and gazed at him, expecting to find her kindness answered. Alfonso made an effort and smiled with gratitude. He was flattered at her showing that she remembered the details of that evening.

She looked at her hand enclosed in Alfonso's. Alfonso opened his and looked, too. Her white plump hand, half-covered by a glove, lay in his rough one, whose third finger was black with ink.

"Do you often see my cousin?"

"Almost every evening!"

"He talks a lot of you!"

"Thanks!" muttered Alfonso.

These thanks were meant for Macario.

"Is there any chance of seeing you at our home some time? You'll be less bored than last time, you'll see."

Alfonso muttered some vague words. From their sound she understood that he was putting himself at her disposal.

"Come tomorrow evening. There may be a few friends. But don't bother about them, as you don't like people, they tell me. My home is always open to you."

Laughing, Maller got to his feet.

"Dear friends, this room is a business office. If you wish to chatter, go into Signor Nitti's room."

Annetta was not put out by this interruption. She answered her father by suggesting he should get his business over soon or she would go off without waiting for him any longer. Alfonso she dismised in a gentler tone and with a polite smile, maybe partly in pity at seeing him blushing to the roots of his hair.

Soon after, White came to see him and, as Alchieri was there, tactfully spoke in a low voice.

"Congratulations on the friendship you've struck up with Signorina Annetta. She's pretty but dangerous. Take care not to fall in love with her."

Next evening Macario took him along to Annetta's. On entering the hall, Alfonso remembered his state of mind when he had left it some months before, and that visit seemed to assume great importance in his life. In fact, Annetta had made him feel bitter at the very start of his life in town, and this bitterness had left its imprint on all he had done afterward. It had increased his natural shyness and made his relations with Maller, Sanneo, and all his superiors more difficult. Now at last he would have somewhere other than the Lanuccis' where he could allow himself to behave not just as a humble inferior.

On the way to Annetta's, Macario gave him a description of the people whom he would presumably meet there.

First Spalati, a teacher of languages and Italian literature from whom Annetta was taking lessons. To judge from the description, Macario did not like him much. He proclaimed himself a "realist" but would inveigh pedantically against any Italian writer who used words not legitimized by Petrarch. Macario admitted he was also a very handsome young man, and obviously it was this quality which deprived him of his biographer's sympathy.

In the desire to surround herself as soon as possible with people suitable to her new interests, Annetta had drawn on her most intelligent acquaintances. Among others Fumigi, a relative of Maller's, who was about forty. Macario said that he was known to be yearning to get free of his office work in order to dedicate himself wholly to his favorite study, mathematics. He was head of an important firm of merchants, and gossip had it that he could perfectly well be free if he wished to, which was Macario's opinion, too. It was quite natural that other desires had eventually been taken from Fumigi by hard, everyday work.

"I think his only real inclination now is toward the kind of mathematics whose results can actually be touched. He keeps up his mathematician's air because it must be pleasant to be looked upon as future discoverer of how to square the circle."

Annetta's evenings were also frequented by a young doctor called Prarchi who had recently left the university and was one of the few people in this world passionately attached to his own job and not to that of others, said Macario. "Annetta met him at a thermal establishment, and with the small amount of good taste she has, which she owes to me, she likes to hear real things talked about, including medicine. The young man has one big defect, a tendency to exaggerate his own qualities. He enjoys talking about medicine so much that he sometimes even talks about dosages. Actually, Annetta has confided to me, and this must remain between us, that all this company bores her. Last year, when she had genuine friendships with other people who were of lesser quality but lived better, I must confess the house was gayer."

As they reached the landing, they heard the sound of a piano. Macario asked Santo who was playing.

"Signorina Annetta!" Then replying as usual more than he was asked: "For the last hour or so!"

"Oh, the wonderful patience of these people!" exclaimed Macario, turning to Alfonso. He asked Santo who they were.

"There's no one here!"

"Isn't today Wednesday?" asked Macario, perplexed.

"Yes, sir. But the Signorina sent to tell Professor Spalati—I know because I went myself—not to come as she had a bad headache."

"Then ask the Signorina if she feels like receiving us, as her headache may be for us, too."

The sound of the piano stopped, and Annetta came to meet them at the living-room door.

"Do come on in!" she cried. "My headache's gone."

Macario had preceded Alfonso. He stopped firmly: "On condition you don't give it to us. Promise not to play any more!"

"You know quite well that you'd have to *beg* me to play."

They entered. Annetta concentrated on Alfonso and let Macario sit down alone.

Alfonso felt quite free of embarrassment, which must have been all melted by Annetta's cordiality. He found himself thinking up fine phrases in cold blood as if he were alone in the room; but when he tried to say them he lost his nerve and cut them short by stuttering.

He muttered that he would so much like to hear Annetta play, while what he intended to say, when stopped by Macario's taunt, was that if he'd had a headache the sound of the piano would have soothed it. Annetta thanked him, after helping him to complete the phrase, and he realized how very easy it was to cut a good figure with those who have no intention of making one cut a bad one.

It was actually her headache, said Annetta, that had driven her to the piano. Macario did not speak; and the pair, conversing for the first time, kept to the same subject as if fearing they would not find another if they left the first. Annetta said once more that she could understand music giving others a headache, but that the concentration needed to play would be a distraction from worry or sickness.

Alfonso admired the truth of this observation and would have liked to confirm it by quoting one of his philosophers who equated pains with worry and suggested distraction as a remedy for both. But he kept silent, and nodded with a smile of assent. At the last moment he had taken fright at those simple but well-linked phrases of his and heroically renounced saying them rather than expose himself to the danger of mixing them up.

What made him rather uneasy was a careful examination of his own feelings. He had begun to do this the moment he had crossed the threshold of that room. This woman was certainly not indifferent to him. But he had suffered for months from her ill-treatment. Now on the other hand he was behaving very coldly, stupidly coldly. He sensed that to keep Annetta's friendship he would have to show himself slightly infatuated with her, and could not manage to.

Annetta got up to hand Macario the piece of music she had been playing, and Alfonso was delighted to feel a quiver of sudden desire. She was so close to him that as she got up he could not see all of her, just a well-rounded bosom and a trim, though not slim waist, firmly enclosed in her favorite gray material.

She had been playing a Beethoven symphony arranged for the piano.

"How did you play it, I wonder?"

"Not well," said Annetta with a smile.

"It must be difficult," observed Alfonso, looking at a sheet full of notes.

"Impossible!" corrected Annetta. She described how she had heard it played by an orchestra a short time before. It would be no satisfaction performing it on the piano. "Anyway, I put up with far less than perfection. I leave out half these notes, for instance."

"But," exclaimed Alfonso, "it's a pleasure . . . particularly for a listener . . . one seems to hear the notes left out."

"Yes, indeed! In imagination!"

"When one's imagination is in tune with the player," observed Macario calmly.

"You're doing some studying, I'm told?" asked Annetta seriously.

"A little, what I can!"

"A lot, I'm told. I do wish I could do the same! Are you writing anything? Will you publish something soon?"

"Not for the moment."

The thought of his study on morality flashed into his mind, and if he had only finished the first chapter he would have spoken of it.

"Women want immediate results!" said Macario laughing.

He was defending him and treating him with more respect than when they were alone. He seemed to want Annetta to think highly of him, and only very much later did Alfonso realize that Macario had taken him to that house, not for Alfonso's advantage, but to amuse Annetta, whose gratitude he wanted to earn.

Now, from the direction which, as Alfonso knew from Santo's explanation, must be that of Maller's reception room, Francesca entered. Alfonso sprang to his feet. He wanted to show his thanks to his old friend, the only one who had at once received him well in the Maller home.

It was obvious from the Signorina's bearing that she did not intend to stay in the room. She returned Alfonso's greeting with a nod.

"Please don't get up." She did not greet Macario and, turning to Annetta, said: "I'm in my room if you need me."

She had quite a different bearing than usual, less free, more reserved; she was very pale and dressed more carelessly. Beside Annetta's, her figure lacked shape. Only the warm color of her fair hair gave light to her suffering face. She went out at once and Alfonso saw Macario looking with curiosity toward Annetta, who, when Francesca left, gave him a meaning look as if pointing out to him how badly the other had behaved.

"Why don't you publish some of your work as soon as possible to make a reputation? Some young men become pedants before their time from love of accuracy, they prefer finish above all, and end by doing nothing. I know that by accounts given to me. Polish needs not only talent but critical sense. One can be an artist when one writes, but when one polishes one has to be an artist and a scientist."

Her face, still very serious since Francesca's departure, cleared at this last idea. It must have given her some satisfaction to say it. Anyway, it was an idea of which Alfonso himself would have been proud. She managed those critical concepts with great ease.

"You are advising me to publish, and give me advice but no example." The phrase was short, very short, but it had been said without hesitation.

"We women have other things to consider. But," she added laughing, "I hope that you won't be able to reprove me like that in a few months' time."

Alfonso congratulated her. Macario gave a cry of surprise and wanted to know something about the writing Annetta was doing; she had not said a word to him about it till then. Knowing Annetta's literary character only by the facetious description given him by Macario, Alfonso thought that, as she had been silent about it till then, her book must be in an even more embryonic state than his own and that she had mentioned it only to soothe her wounded vanity.

Finally the subject changed, due to Annetta herself. They talked about the imminent theatrical season, but more of people in the boxes and orchestra than of those on the stage; and Alfonso kept silent. Macario and Annetta amused themselves naming and describing young men who frequented the orchestra, and from the moment when Annetta began joking about them and accompanying her jests by long trills of loud laughter which made her twist about and show her plump white neck, on which tension drew a few faint lines, Alfonso felt uncomfortable. He felt as if he were watching her sing that peculiar song again and prance about in front of him as shamelessly as a Roman matron before a slave.

They would speak of art again another time, as Annetta said smilingly at the moment of farewell. Alfonso, who, on his few visits to the theater, had soon noticed the harm done to the performance by the spectators' chatter, suggested introducing into theaters the German system of imposing silence and lowering the lights in the auditorium. He could no longer agree with Annetta for the simple reason that she took the opposite view after he had given his. In a theater Annetta cared less about the performance on the stage than about the audience. She said that she preferred watching people like herself rather than wretched creatures perform with other wretched creatures.

"One misses the art, I realize that, but is the art of the theater real art?"

She made a gesture of contempt which left Alfonso in admiration once again. He was incapable of embracing other people's ideas so blindly.

As he went out, Alfonso noticed, on the landing above, a woman who hurriedly withdrew on seeing Macario. She was Francesca's height, but Alfonso could not see her face.

He felt drawn closer to Macario by that visit than by months of their former relationship. At once he was indiscreet: "Odd that Signorina Francesca didn't stay and keep us company. The other time she seemed so expansive and gay. What could have made her so unsociable?"

"A headache probably," replied Macario briefly, and changed the subject. "So you see my cousin is better than her reputation or than the idea you had of her. You heard her invitation. From now on, you belong to what Spalati calls The Wednesday Club. Try to become a good friend of my cousin's because her friendship can be a help to you."

He was talking seriously. The help to which he alluded was Annetta's protection in the office. Alfonso found the allusion tactless, and flushed; but he did not protest, and in fact gave a very friendly handshake when he said good-bye. He might not like to be thought of as someone trying to achieve his own ends by unusual means; but he felt he should be all the more grateful to a man who apparently wanted to help him, even though thinking him unscrupulous.

CHAPTER

X

Signora Carolina wrote to Alfonso with great regularity. Her letters showed what a strain writing was for her and how only her high notion of motherly duty induced her to send her son those regular two pages in her spidery hand. Writing can take the place of talking only for the cultured. Usually these letters were filled with advice, or greetings on her own and others' account; and obviously the writer found her labor lightened when there was some big event in the village, a wedding or the death of people they knew. Then the two pages became three or four.

He received a letter from his mother the day after his visit to Annetta and, even in his state of agitation at the time, its contents aroused his lively interest. It was a letter of four sides, the first two of which were as usual because obviously written without the writer's thinking she would have to add the other two. In the last part Signora Carolina told how Signorina Francesca had written asking if there was enough space in the house to rent her a room. Signorina Francesca's letter must have been very warm; it also contained a sad phrase or two that had surprised Signora Carolina, who was not without acumen, and supposed Signorina Francesca must be feeling very miserable to write so affectionately to someone she scarcely knew. "She seems very sad about coming: I've given her the room she asks, but feel I'd prefer gayer company."

The reason why Signorina Francesca was leaving the Maller home must certainly be the same one which had made her bearing change so. There must have been a real quarrel with Annetta, after which the weaker side had to leave the field.

Perhaps when Macario found that Alfonso already knew so much, he would also tell him the rest. That evening Alfonso met him walking with an elderly man who was gesticulating as he described something which must have been most interesting, for Macario was listening attentively. Between the two Alfonso thought he noticed the same relationship as between himself and Macario.

He did not usually stop Macario in the street, for he often saw him with others or striding along absorbed in his own thoughts, but as he had something to tell him which would be of interest he had no scruples. He went up to him.

"I'd like a word with you."

Before hearing this remark, Macario was about to pass

him by with a polite greeting. As soon as he heard it, he turned to dismiss his companion, then asked Alfonso if the matter would take long.

"Only a second!" replied Alfonso, already regretting having stopped him.

The other man agreed to wait.

Now he must be concise, exposing himself to the risk of Macario's answering with a shrug in reproof for having stopped him about a futile matter. This did not happen, quite the opposite in fact. Macario stood listening attentively, making gestures of surprise. To increase the importance of the matter, Alfonso also mentioned Signora Carolina's observations about Signorina Francesca's sadness. Macario, supposing that this had all been told to get his advice, said Alfonso must ask Signora Carolina to help Signorina Francesca as much as she could. Then he returned to the man waiting for him, and Alfonso found that he had told all and learned nothing.

A few days later, he was called in by Maller. His chief had never been so pleasant; he spoke simply and without his glance moving from one side of his desk to the other as he did when he was trying not to look his interlocutor in the face. He asked that since Signorina Francesca could not write herself because she was unwell, would he, Alfonso, please write to Signora Carolina with the Signorina's excuses and cancel the request she had made a few days before. Alfonso promptly declared that he would write right away.

Maller smiled, bowed in thanks, and, taking him at his word, said that he wanted Signora Carolina to be told at once of Signorina Francesca's change of arrangements in order to avoid the bother of useless preparations. There must, however, have been another reason for his wanting things done in such haste, for he even lowered himself to repeating his request all over again, as if one single word from him was not enough to give Alfonso wings.

"Can I be sure then that you'll write today for certain?"

"Of course!" assured Alfonso in surprise.

In fact, he wrote at once to his mother to tell her that Signorina Francesca had given up the idea of retiring to the country. So absorbed was he on carrying out Maller's order as soon as possible that his letter became overly curt and he had to follow it up immediately afterward by another sending her his own news and those assurances of unchangeable affection which Signora Carolina expected to find in every letter from him.

He had taken his letter to Starringer for immediate mailing, and in the passage, on his way back to his room, he met Maller leaving. In his eagerness to show zeal and eliminate any preoccupation Maller might have about the order being carried out, he said smiling: "I've already sent that letter."

"Thanks!" said Maller, who stood in surprise for a second, as if he no longer remembered what this was about. His tone of voice was also much colder than that he had used half an hour before.

This was enough to throw Alfonso into agitation. He had been wrong to stop his chief with such familiarity in front of the messengers and still more wrong to speak to him about a service he had done him as if asking for thanks in return.

In his room he found only Alchieri, ready to leave. Agitation made Alfonso talkative. He could not bear his worry alone; a soothing word from an outsider could calm him. He told Alchieri about the letter from his mother and his interview with Signor Maller. Alchieri listened distractedly because he was worried about his own affairs. He was waiting impatiently for the result of a request for a raise in pay which he had sent to the managing director that day; he had threatened to leave his job, and hinted that he had another one in view, though actually he would be a ruined man if taken at his word.

"Was I very wrong to stop Signor Maller in the passage?"

At this question from Alfonso, Alchieri, who had been able to give his attention only to a part of what was told him, replied: "She's his mistress, I'll bet!"

This supposition seemed so likely to be correct that Alfonso was surprised at not having thought of it himself. Alchieri's own malice had suggested it, but in the light of circumstances known to Alfonso it was probably true. What else could have happened to change the relations between Annetta and Francesca so much, and the latter's bearing? However natural it was that Maller had been charged with speaking to him, his way of setting about it seemed unusual; his employees were accustomed to receiving only short and concise orders in official tones. Alfonso had been told that Maller was a woman-chaser, but Alchieri's supposition had never come into his head because Maller's home, even if he had known of his habits, had seemed enveloped in an aura which let no human passions penetrate except vanity and pride. It had been difficult for Alfonso to imagine love in those cold showrooms, most of which were unused, still less in Maller's bedroom, where, so Santo had told him, there still stood his young wife's bed, left intact since her death there. But the suspicion of Alchieri, a man who had never set foot in that house, was enough to melt that aura, and Alfonso's imagination populated it with criminal loves all the murkier for the surrounding luxury.

Francesca's seduction did seem criminal, made easy as it was by her inferior position. He felt something akin to jealousy in imagining that fair hair and white flesh thrown into the arms of that cold man Maller, an affair which would ruin her life but which would cost him nothing at all and have no more value to him than a pasttime.

He did not understand what part Annetta played in this affair. Probably she had tried to get Francesca away and not succeeded.

For the first time he dreamed of becoming Annetta's lover. It seemed less impossible now that he saw her amid love intrigues which no one bothered to hide from her. The dream became easier. He did not go so far as to dream of being loved though, because he could not imagine an expression of affection or desire on her calm marmoreal face. His was the dream of a vicious boy, in which she abandoned herself to him coldly, for pleasure, to revenge herself on a third person, or even out of ambition. His dreams always began with embroidering on reality and then detached themselves from it completely, so he easily imagined himself being of such value in Annetta's eyes that he was even loved out of ambition.

He could not think of any way of visiting Annetta alone. The invitation she had given him had not seemed definite enough and, having sought Macario all week in vain to accompany him, he did not go on the first Wednesday. Those dreams of his about Annetta probably made him even more timid, lest he let some hint of them slip out.

But he wanted to see Annetta again, more intensely now than the first time, when it had been just a matter of getting himself liked by his boss's daughter. Now he loved her! For this must be love, this desire for one person and for no one else. He drew his conclusions from his agitation, being unable to do so from feelings he lacked. In the few days when he had tried unsuccessfully to smother his desires and give them another

direction, he had felt himself become a man, an adult.
He desired a woman, that particular woman, and for
him, for his senses, no other women existed. He remembered some observations he had made about Annetta's
appearance, and was now amazed he had not realized
at once that the originality and beauty of her face
were made up precisely of what he had qualified as defects. Her eyes not dark enough! Her hair not curly
enough! Annetta had the face of Venus, and that head
of hers, with its calm blue eyes and almost modestly
smooth hair, was a head full of intelligence. A kiss
would have been all the more delicious on lips which
seemed incapacable of corresponding!

When on the following Wednesday he ran into Macario, who reproved him strongly on Annetta's behalf
for having failed to come the week before, Alfonso
quivered with joy. He was sought after, called.

Then Annetta, too, reproved him, gently. She said
that Macario had told her not to alarm him.

"Or I'd shout at you! Why should you be timid with
me? Do I frighten you?"

These blandishments, however, touched him less than
the ones she had sent by her messenger. With her before
his eyes he forgot his dreams. She was all intent on
forming her literary group, and her natural coldness,
which could take on in memory the air of some minor
quality, was now very apparent and colored everything
else. When she spoke of literature, she was not female. She was a male struggling for life, morally a being of muscle.

That afternoon her drawing room seemed very snug,
as outside the bora wind had broken off violently and
swept away every vestige of summer in a few hours.

Alfonso and Macario found Spalati there, arrived a
short time before; Fumigi and Doctor Prarchi came immediately afterward.

Doctor Prarchi turned the conversation away from literature by describing the suicide of a cashier whom they had known. He was a man who had lived very modestly and done nothing worse than people richer than himself frequently did. That had been enough to ruin him in spite of his moderation. Prarchi ended his description with a word of genuine compassion. He had also seen the suicide's body.

Annetta shrugged her shoulders with contempt. "Serve him right!" She had not liked the fellow much: perhaps she was afraid her father would come across someone similar.

Alfonso found himself too involved in a discussion with Fumigi to be able to turn his attention to the general conversation. The little man had plumped down beside him and was questioning him on his studies. These must have been much talked about because the mathematician was admiring and flattering him. He wanted to know how Alfonso had arranged his timetable to dedicate one or more hours daily to those studies. He said he had never been able to achieve such regularity himself and was worried because only systematic study brought profit, not study in fits and starts.

All Alfonso's attention was on Annetta. But he felt no desires in her presence, which worried him. He tried to provoke them, studied her face to see if he could find there any sign of the passion which was lacking in himself. The moment was badly chosen, just after that crude remark of hers about the cashier's suicide.

He felt a need, or thought he did, to define the respect which prevented his noticing the affectation of her behavior. When Macario had described her for the first time, he had felt like laughing at this little woman who had suddenly felt a vocation, even though this vocation was an advantage to himself. All this show, these pretensions to forming a literary society around her were ridiculous too, and if he did not laugh at them it was not because of any change in his feelings about them. He easily noticed the false or absurd side of others' actions, but often found he could not laugh at them because the shyness which he was apt to feel with people in other ways inferior made him doubt himself, his own feelings or judgments. And the same thing was true now. He was impressed by Annetta's lack of doubt, her self-confidence, her carelessness about the impression she made on others, the air she had, in fact, of a superior creature who feels she cannot be lessened by any inferiority even in the very thing in which she wishes to excel, where inferiority is usually most bitter.

Prarchi spoke of a realist novel he was writing.

"I'll remain a doctor," he said, "even as a novelist. In my novel I intend to make a thorough study of progressive paralysis. Doctors begin studying it when it's at its last stages; but I'll be just leaving it then, as I'll begin at its formation. The character of a paralytic, the organism of a paralytic, the ideas of a paralytic, what causes distress to people around them, and . . . the novel's done!"

"Yes," exclaimed Annetta, "the novel is, but what about its success?"

Alfonso, who had some experience in this field, felt a vague intuition from Prarchi's description that he had written nothing at all of the novel described and had actually got the first idea for it at that very moment.

Prarchi was sturdy without being fat. He was not good-looking, with a large, almost bald head, and a small, too fair mustache on his broad face.

Alfonso should have found Fumigi more sympathetic, particularly because he addressed him most of that evening. That was only because Fumigi disliked speaking aloud and was rather quiet, his thin little body leaning over the back of his chair, listening attentively and putting in a rare word in a low voice to his neighbor. The hair on his head was gray, his mustache and beard still black.

Alfonso tried hard to get his own words into the general discussion without succeeding. So far Annetta had only Macario's recommendation to go on about his being a literary man. He had been unable to give any proof of it.

Just when he was on the point of saying good-bye, Francesca appeared. She was pale but calm. She shook Alfonso's hand effusively and asked him for news of his home. With a smile, which seemed sad to Alfonso, she alluded to the letter he had written to Signora Carolina. So she knew about Maller's mediation.

Annetta addressed her formally and Alfonso tried to recall if he had not heard her treated with greater familiarity before.

On the stairs, at a question from Prarchi about what reason could have made Signorina Francesca want to leave the Maller home, Macario replied: "Women!" with great contempt.

CHAPTER

XI

From then on, Alfonso visited Annetta regularly every Wednesday. Macario had warned him that one Wednesday or another he might find Annetta with her opinions and tastes quite changed and literature abandoned, which would also mean the end of these meetings. Alfonso would go each time fearing to find Macario's predictions come true. He set great store by these meetings, both for the pleasure of seeing Annetta and for the satisfaction to his own vanity. It was known in the office that he frequented the managing director's house and he was treated with greater respect by his superiors. Cellani's behavior was modified, too. He could not become kinder, but he became more familiar.

Annetta did not seem at all close to fulfilling Macario's prophecy and was more and more immersed in her new studies. Every week she had a story to tell of some artistic thought, some book she had read, which, with a beginner's exaggeration, she declared to be the most important of its kind, or criticized capriciously, all in her usual competent tone, often with sharp or funny comments whose only defect was that they did not always suit the subject.

One evening an unusual guest came, Cellani. It was probably the first time he had ever appeared in that company, for Annetta had to introduce Spalati to him. He did not seem ill at ease, as far as Alfonso could judge. He listened with great attention, but did not say a word. Once his opinion was asked during a discussion, and he refused to give it, smiling and asserting that he had none. He seemed to be on very friendly terms with Annetta. That evening she devoted herself to him with an attention that showed affectionate respect.

Prarchi appeared less often at these evenings because he was very busy. Fumigi was rarely absent, but the most assiduous was Spalati. As Macario had said, Spalati was before all else a handsome man, a Herculean figure beside whom Alfonso, tall and quite well set up as he was, seemed of no account. Alfonso did not like him. He criticized Spalati for pedantry but hated him out of jealousy. For this he had some reason. Spalati was the furthest along in Annetta's confidence. For nearly a year he had been giving her lessons in Italian literature, and had attained the intimacy of a teacher without boring her with too much hard work. He let her talk, listened, approved, or modified, content to be treated as an equal.

Alfonso, feeling inferior with his difficulty in speaking, would feel violent fits of jealousy, storms in teacups. Outwardly he showed nothing because of his habitual reserve in expressing his feelings, a reserve which became greater as the feeling grew.

One evening he went off early, saying he was unwell. He wanted to show his bad humor, and was exasperated that no one realized it, believing him ill. He wandered around the streets, discontented with the others and with himself. Being in the habit of talking to himself when agitated, he soon realized how ridiculous his ill-humor was. Even in the most abstract daydreams, a word clearly pronounced can recall one to reality. He had reached the point of desiring, of loving, of being jealous of Annetta; she, on the other hand, scarcely knew the sound of his voice. Whom could he blame? What had offended him more than anything else was her farewell handshake, given so coldly, with eyes turned to Spalati, who went on talking! Would he have preferred her to brood on what had caused the sudden illness which he had used as an excuse? Nothing could be guessed about an illness, after all, when nothing had been said beforehand to explain it. Spalati, if that had happened to him, would have had nothing but good wishes for his health.

Looking into himself, he thought how petty and tiresome he was, with his disproportionate desires. He had actually dreamed of Annetta loving him!

He wanted to drop the whole game. It was the only way still open. He would pay no more of these visits. They were a waste, first of the time he spent at the Mallers', then of the time afterward, because of the agitation into which those visits plunged him. They were embittering. He had begun a struggle in which he was bound to succumb, he who was incapable of talking to please but only talked to make himself understood;

he was bound to succumb also because of his own position in life, which was unlikely to attract such an ambitious woman as this. With some excuse or other, in making which he would try not to sound too incredible, he would avoid ever setting foot in the Maller home again. It was those visits which had made him deviate from his determination to work continuously; without his realizing it, the ambition born in him shortly before was changing into vanity, a desire to be thought more than he was.

He felt he had already taken up again the serious intentions he had when he was an assiduous frequenter of the public library. But his thoughts kept on going back to the house from which he had come, imagining scenes in which he was implored to return.

He returned without being asked, simply because on Wednesday morning Macario had called out in passing: "Till this evening, eh?!"

The week had seemed very long, an interval of time full of incident, though actually nothing had really happened. He kept thinking that he had already carried out his intention and imagined a thousand consequences resulting from his energetic action. He was free to turn back, or rather to stay where he was, which pleased him. That week reminded him of his adventure with Maria, but this time it was only chance that prevented his taking some ill-considered step which would have broken off his relations with Annetta. If he had broken them, what would he be? Just a humble little clerk at Maller's, about whose bad temper no one would bother.

He presented himself at Annetta's half an hour before the usual time, and was rewarded for his resolution because for the first time he found her alone. Everyone had sent excuses except Macario, who was still expected. Annetta said that she supposed they did not want to give up some public celebration on that day, and showed Alfonso her gratitude by saying to him sweetly that he was wrong to come and shut himself up in a dreary room.

"Dreary? No, not at all!" assured Alfonso, looking at her ardently.

If she had never known she was beautiful, Alfonso's glance would have been enough to tell her so. He confessed frankly that it was the first he had heard of any public celebration that day.

"Do you lead such a solitary life, then?" asked Annetta in surprise.

They were sitting on a sofa next to the window, the brightest lit place in the room. Through the heavy curtains the colors of sunset entered mutedly.

In the street parallel to Via dei Forni the town band was passing. Nothing could be heard but the accompaniment and the rumble of a big drum. They listened in silence.

"I wonder what they're playing?" asked Annetta, and flung open the window. The breeze swelled the curtains and the clear ring of a trumpet brought the tune which had been lacking.

For an instant they also heard the murmur of the crowd behind the band.

Laughing, Annetta raised her face to Alfonso, who was still leaning on the window sill.

"I wonder if our serious friends are among those people, too?"

From the light side of the room, where she was standing, she could not make out Alfonso in the half darkness admiring her without restraint.

Her half mourning, her gray had vanished, too. She was dressed in soft white wool with a black cord around the waist. Annetta's figure, in spite of its curves, was chaste and virginal, with a straight back hollowed toward the neck, and a white face that looked clever and active.

She told him to come to the window, too, and feel the breeze which the strong bora of the week before had changed into.

The avenue was almost deserted; only on the corner was a group looking toward the next street.

"It almost makes me want to go down, too," said Annetta.

Alfonso was intent on sensing the contact of his arm with Annetta's, stirring his desire. He risked a movement to increase the pressure, and the blood rushed to his head from his own ardor and not from contact with Annetta's arm, which was like a lifeless body's.

Annetta had probably not noticed his daring. At first they were both a little embarrassed, because they had been too seldom alone together to find with ease a subject that could interest them both equally. But when the subject was found, Alfonso's voice echoed calmly and sonorously, for the first time in that room, and for the first time Annetta heard complete phrases from him. If he did not know how to converse with numerous people, Alfonso at least knew how to talk alone with one.

Smiling, Annetta asked him: "What about your homesickness? I've heard so much about it!"

"It no longer exists!" replied Alfonso.

His voice, to his surprise, was firm, calm. But that first phrase still remained truncated because he had wanted to pay a compliment and say that it did not exist at that precise moment. With all his ease, he had not enough to make a bold remark; though he might possibly have got away with one.

One of Annetta's affectations since she had taken to

literature was to make a show of finding everything interesting and wanting to know the reasons for it. She asked him to explain what homesickness was.

"It's difficult," began Alfonso, "but I think I can explain partly."

He described first of all how it was an organic illness, because the lungs suffered from change of air, the stomach from change of food, the feet from change to pavements. What he did not attempt to describe was the intensity of his longing to see again places he had left behind, a blank wall, a tortuous lane with a gutter in the middle of it, even an uncomfortable room which leaked in bad weather; without mentioning his loathing of the building in which he actually lived, he described his reaction to the bank, the big wide street, even the sea.

"And with people then . . . it's the same."

"Did you hate me so much?"

"Not hate you! But I felt I would like to be far away from you, far away at home, so as to be there, and not here."

Fearing that what he described with such sincerity did not seem sufficiently far back in the past, he added explanations. He hated all the people whom he felt obliged to treat with respect; he liked freedom, and he wanted to treat those who were not his equals as if they were.

Ah, how lovely it was to talk to Annetta as an equal! How sweet to confide in her as freely as if he were talking to himself! This sweetness flowed into his speech, till then tongue-tied, careful, literary.

Annetta listened in surprise. So this young man could talk as well as study, could he?

She explained to him that when one wants something in life one must know how to win it. Alfonso recognized this as a dominating idea of Macario's.

"It's not difficult to win my friendship. This is the first time you've talked to me. You may not have noticed it, but you're nearly always dumb. I felt, though, that it was not up to me to make you talk."

She laughed, thus taking from her words anything that might have been offensive. Alfonso also laughed, finding rather comic this idea of someone waiting to be made to talk.

It was those first thoughts that gave Annetta the idea of their writing a novel together. A character revealing itself so ingenuously seemed to her worth describing. She told him simply of the first idea which had suddenly come to her, and which was certainly better than any later modifications.

"A young man once comes from the country to the city with some very odd ideas about city life. He's worried at finding it different from what he had imagined. Then we'll put in a love affair. Have you ever been in love?"

"I . . ." and his heart beat more strongly, from fear. He had been on the point of making a declaration.

Annetta called Santo to light the gas, and Alfonso was both blinded by the light and made to realize how false the step was he had been about to take. Annetta was just the same; she was giving sharp orders to Santo, who, surprisingly, carried them out in silence.

She made Alfonso sit down at the table.

"Now we need pen and ink . . . but I prefer to leave first ideas to memory. We'll put black on white later. Now how would you develop this novel?"

"We must have a good think."

"Is it so difficult? We'll describe your life," and here she was still at her first idea. "Of course, instead of a clerk we'll make you rich and noble, or rather just noble. The riches we'll keep for the end of the book."

With one light jump she had abandoned her first idea altogether.

"We must allow time for the imagination to work."

"Ah yes!" said Annetta with the surprise of a young pupil reminded of a forgotten maxim. "Do you know what we'll do? Each of us on our own, quite independently of the other, will put his own ideas on paper; then we'll compare them and come to an agreement."

Alfonso liked this suggestion immensely and said so with ingenuous expressions of joy that made Annetta smile with pleasure. Some good ideas for the novel were occurring to him, and he imagined what it would be like fitting them to Annetta's. He was thinking only of minor details, not the whole. He did not worry at all about being published and read. For the moment his only aim was to cut a good figure with Annetta.

They spoke of the writing each of them had done before. Annetta described a novel she said she had written about a woman married to a man unworthy of her. In time her artist's soul affected her husband's and changed him, and eventually the two really understood each other and lived together in perfect happiness for many a year.

Alfonso did not much like this theme, but Annetta stressed that she could not describe all she had written; for instance, in one place she had a careful description of a landscape, in another of a house: so Alfonso ingenuously began admiring what did not exist.

Alfonso described his work on morals. As he spoke of it, he felt he had written it all, and taking a different tack from Annetta's he began describing what he had not done. He mentioned the kernel of his work, the negation of morality as everyone understood it, founded on religious law or individual good.

"If in a society founded on our moral ideas," said Alfonso, "there happened to be a person with enough energy to set himself above all these, he would be better off than anyone else, as he would of course have the superlative intelligence needed to act astutely and ably in the abnormal circumstances in which he would soon be."

Annetta looked at him, surprised at the ardor with which such an axiom was described by a voice which till a short time ago she had heard only in a timid and broken stutter. Then, less wordily and less energetically, he also spoke of a new foundation he wanted to give morality. The explanation of the first part of his work had made a striking impression and he could not hope to obtain an equal effect with this other part, which did not deal with destroying but with creating laws, a very different and boring matter.

Such was his delight at finding himself linked in some way to Annetta that he thought of hurrying home and jotting down the whole theme of the novel, even fixing the chapters. It was surprising to have become Annetta's collaborator all of a sudden, and when he thought of the feelings for him which he had attributed to her the preceding week it all seemed quite incredible. If he had run across Macario just then, he would have flung his arms around his neck to thank him for the great happiness which he owed him, and with the expansiveness due to happiness would have told him of Annetta's suggestion and of the value he attached to it.

But a part of his enthusiasm was cooled that same evening. He set the plot out as succinctly as possible: "An impoverished young noble comes to seek his fortune in the city . . . persecuted by his boss and his companions . . . loved by them because an intelligent action by him saves the company from serious loss . . . marries the boss's daughter." The plot was not very original in itself, but what he disliked most about it was the end, which had not actually been suggested by Annetta, though it naturally derived from the premises. To Annetta that marriage might seem like a proposal, and alarm her, make her suspect him of intentions similar to their hero's. He also realized, when he had pen in hand, that he did not know what Annetta really wanted. They had both been content with half hints: he because, in his happiness, he had not remembered the insignificant matter of the plot; Annetta perhaps because she was such a novice that she did not realize all that was needed to write a novel.

He went to Macario and asked him to tell Annetta his doubts. Macario had free access to the Maller home and could talk to her before Wednesday.

But Macario seemed to have little wish to do this. He did not hide his surprise at hearing that they intended to write a novel in collaboration. Alfonso was now subdued, realizing it was not dignified to show too much joy and thinking that he had even succeeded in seeming very cold. But Macario looked at him with a nasty ironic little smile and said: "Congratulations!"

Alfonso accompanied Macario to his office. Macario seemed very distracted, and when Alfonso told him with a serious air that he felt honored by Annetta's suggestion and wanted to return her trust by working hard and carefully, Macario covered his mouth with a hand as if to hide a yawn. Alfonso was a good enough observer not to believe in that yawn; under the hand he had seen a mouth open but inert, not contracted by any instinctive movement. Macario was jealous! Both the distraction and the yawn were affected, intended to hide anger or pain.

Alfonso went on talking with the same warmth, because, whenever he found himself wanting to hide something, his first instinct was to pretend he had not noticed it.

"Do please tell Signorina Annetta that I'm ready to

begin at once, but need to know a little more about what I'm to do."

"All right," said Macario, who seemed to Alfonso a little paler than usual, "when I happen to see her I'll tell her."

He regretted speaking to Macario, and was sure he could no longer count on the other's friendship. Perhaps Macario did not love Annetta—that Alfonso could not know—but was jealous of him only because he had a jealous nature. Alfonso had not understood this nature before because it was the first time Macario could have had any reason for jealousy. Macario's own cleverness or social position must always have made him feel superior, and it was probably just because he so often enjoyed feeling that superiority and making it felt that he had sought out Alfonso's company. Probably Macario had taken him to the Mallers' supposing him too timid ever to gain Annetta's friendship.

So he had confided in an enemy whom he had already given a chance to harm him, because it was likely that Annetta did not want their plan to be known. However much Alfonso wanted to appear cold, he must have shown his joy, and Macario was capable of describing it to Annetta with exaggeration. He saw him repeating some phrase of his, raising that hand which was sometimes more malicious than his tongue, and he imagined that would be enough to lose him Annetta's friendship, won with so much effort. He recalled the treatment of that clerk who had dared to pay court to Annetta.

That week had been disagreeable because the fear of being tactless took away the joy of Annetta's sudden friendship. He waited in vain from day to day for some communication from Macario in reply to the request which he had made. So the man did not even bother to hide his ill-will and seemed to be avoiding him, because

Alfonso did not manage to set eyes on him for the whole week.

He went to Annetta's, anxious to learn how Macario had behaved; he would know from the way she greeted him.

The whole company was gathered in the living room. Fumigi, Spalati, Prarchi, and Macario; even Maller stayed half an hour. Macario greeted Alfonso with a smile that was not malicious, and Annetta shook his hand warmly. Her friendship had not decreased since the Wednesday before. Alfonso suddenly felt other ideas open out, but could not even enjoy sloughing off his worries because he was disturbed by Maller's presence, in spite of the latter's friendly handshake.

Francesca was sitting apart on the sofa, holding some embroidery. Alfonso greeted her and went up to her, and she rose to her feet to give more warmth to her words, which were, as always, rather dry and brusque. Signorina Francesca was never embarrassed. He had heard her talk in friendly, gay, or annoyed tones, but always briefly and decisively like someone not to be imposed on. Maller was sitting on Annetta's right, Spalati on her left. Spalati always sat next to Annetta and seemed to set great store by it.

Alfonso, although more disturbed by Maller's presence than were the others, noticed how their behavior changed because of it.

At that period whenever literature was mentioned there was always a discussion about realism and romanticism; this was a cosy literary argument in which all could take part.

Maller was a partisan of "realism" but, as he always wanted to seem more witty than learned, he confessed that he liked the realists all the more because they were not moralists. He also pretended to despise them because he considered their methods made it easy for them to achieve popularity.

Spalati, whose ideas, as far as Alfonso knew, were not likely to conform to Maller's, immediately found a point of view with which he could agree.

"Yes, you who read only for pleasure are right to enjoy them."

Prarchi tried to go too far. He wanted to prove to Maller, who denied it, that the pleasure he found in reading those immoral authors derived from an unconscious artistic sense.

"You think you love them for that reason, but without your realizing it, surely it's the books' artistic merits that you enjoy?"

"May be," said Maller, who did not seem to perceive that these two literary men were doing their best to flatter him. "I don't understand, though, why some pages please me more than others. They're the most artistic, perhaps."

If he had perceived they were trying to flatter him, he was deriding the flatterers.

When Maller began making his literary confessions, Annetta said to Alfonso in a loud voice: "Just listen carefully and you'll hear some nonsense."

Alfonso was so flustered by this phrase, which came as an unexpected gift to him in that general discussion, that he actually listened less attentively.

Very soon Maller got up and bowed good-bye to everyone. He moved toward Francesca, followed by an attentive look from Alfonso. Francesca did not seem to notice his approach but, when he was near, raised her eyes from her work without pretending to affect surprise, looked at him calmly, and held out a little hand, which he, as calmly, took in his.

"Why do you ruin your eyesight with such work?"

She withdrew her hand, which he still wanted to hold: "It does me no harm."

As Maller passed once more before the table on his way out, the men rose to their feet in farewell. The only person who had neither tried to rise or changed her bearing at his departure was Annetta.

Only when saying good-bye did Annetta ask Alfonso in a whisper how far he had got with the novel.

"I've not been able to do anything because the trouble is I don't yet know what to do."

After reflecting for an instant, Annetta said, in a low voice: "Come tomorrow at seven, can you?"

"Of course!" and he felt his heart leap.

In such low voices do lovers, too, make lovers' appointments.

CHAPTER

XII

Alfonso was met by Santo on the stairs.

"I was waiting for you," Santo said, smiling at him in a most friendly way.

He treated Alfonso respectfully, letting him pass through doors first and bowing deeply after opening the library door for him. At the bank, also, he took every opportunity to show deference.

In the library were Annetta and Francesca, the older woman at her eternal embroidery, the other writing.

"I was doing the first draft," Annetta said to him. "Come on, help me, because I can't do it alone."

She put some paper in front of him, elegant little pieces of letter paper, and a pen.

"The space is a bit awkward for you, but there's room enough when two people want to work as much as we do."

The table was too low and there was no room on it because she had not bothered to remove some newspapers. Francesca remedied Annetta's forgetfulness.

"I see that without my help you'll never get down to work."

She took the bundle of newspapers and threw them in a corner.

The relations between the two women seemed improved. Francesca no longer looked so ill, though still pale; but her lips were less white, and Annetta was not avoiding speaking to her.

"Take care not to try and put your ideas into the novel too, as a novel might conceivably be written by two people, but not by three."

Annetta and Francesca had an urge to address each other often, like two people reminding themselves all the time that they were no longer on bad terms.

"A preliminary word or two," said Annetta to Alfonso with some gravity. "I'd like to explain the method which I consider should be followed in our work so as to avoid obvious signs of two minds or intentions. Of course we must first see that our intentions differ as little as possible. That will be the most difficult thing, but with a few concessions on each side I think we can achieve this. As to our method, we'll just have to divide the work."

With a nervous hand she traced some circles on the paper in front of her to make her idea of this division clear. But she had some hesitation, so she asserted, in explaining how the division should actually work in practice, since she feared he might find her allotting him too inferior a part.

"Don't hesitate to tell me," said Alfonso with a smile and a blush. "I want to do my part, but nothing that can make me forget what an honor it is to collaborate with you."

The compliment was not badly put. Annetta thanked him.

"Well, you have good ideas, that we know, so we'll allot you the part of suggesting and developing them. As I happen to move around town more, I'll do the dialogue and descriptions. You live among books the whole time."

This observation was intended to console him for the suggestion that he did not move around town. Alfonso, much flattered, accepted the suggestion. Every chapter would be drafted by him first and then redone by Annetta.

"I hope I'll at least be able to recognize your good ideas and leave them intact." She could not have been more modest. "Well, that's all settled!" and she gave a sigh of satisfaction, as if, with that settled, part of the novel was already finished.

"Now let's go on to settle the plot."

Here, too, some premises were needed. They must remember, warned Annetta, that they wanted a success. They would be publishing under a pseudonym, but there would be little pleasure in such a publication unless it was successful. They were not out for future glory or thinking at all of posterity. But they did want an immediate success.

"I know the way to get it. It's not so difficult, you know! For some years I've been noticing what goes best with theatergoers or readers, and I always find the same recipe of taming a shrew. It doesn't matter much if the shrew is male or female, but he or she must be tamed by the force of love."

Alfonso, too, admitted that he had sometimes found his interest aroused by such productions, though never enough to lessen his contempt for book and author. But this was not the moment to emphasize this contempt. Annetta had never attracted him so much. Bent over her writing, her smooth brown hair simply arranged, pen in delicate hand, he saw her for the first time wholly forgetful of her beauty, not bothering whether she pleased or not, with shut lips and frowning brow, her noble head nobly poised.

Alfonso agreed to everything. At top speed she jotted down the contents of the first ten chapters, then in a few words a general idea of the rest. He had not noticed a single original attitude or concept, but the slightest doubt would have seemed an offence to Annetta's first flight of enthusiasm. Anyway, it seemed premature to give opinions; the plot could improve in execution.

When alone with the work he had taken on, he had a stronger sense than ever of its vulgarity. The shrew this time was feminine. Annetta had sketched out a plot about a young lady of rank who was jilted by a duke and on the rebound agreed to marry a rich industrialist. She did not love him, and treated him with contempt. The industrialist, who was an excellent man with muscles as strong as his character was gentle, eventually triumphed over his wife's aversion and the two of them lived happily together for many a long year. Annetta's skeleton plot was marked with "scenes" at what she thought effective points, which made it all the more like the plot for a comedy, a very ordinary comedy.

But the first chapter, though it plunged right into the subject because Annetta said that long openings bored the public, was so vague that from it Alfonso could make up a chapter to his own taste.

"Clara, a young countess, learns that the duke is marrying a shopkeeper's daughter; her despair." The precedents of this situation needed describing, and this came to another plot in which Alfonso had a free hand. In a few words he described the state of mind of the girl's mother on receiving the announcement of the duke's marriage; she tells her daughter, not knowing the storm this news would arouse in the heart of the poor girl, who takes the blow with dignity and only gives vent to her feelings when alone again in her room. There she not only gives vent to them but muses sorrowfully over the past, her early childhood with the duke, who was a cousin, a wild lad who had often hit her, yet was very lovable. Down went what Alfonso thought a successful description, sweet as an idyll. Various touches showed that the author was someone with grave worries who had been unable to give all his attention to the narrative and so let his pen run on, putting it back on its path every now and again and not bothering much if it soon wandered again. He knew that the whole novel could not go like that, but anyway that chapter was done.

He handed it to Annetta the next Wednesday, when Annetta told the whole company about the work she and Alfonso had embarked upon. She then explained to Spalati and Prarchi why she had not chosen them instead of Alfonso. She said that she had not chosen Spalati because people are shy of working with their own teachers; Prarchi, on the other hand, she had excluded because he was too determinedly a "realist." Prarchi asserted that he was less of a "realist" than he said himself, and would sacrifice any exaggerated opinions for this chance. He spoke seriously, as if still in time to persuade Annetta to go back on her resolution. Then he began to laugh.

"For this chance I'd have collaborated in a really romantic romance."

Alfonso took this quip as a warning to himself.

Fumigi walked with Alfonso part of the way home, asked shyly about their method of work, and seemed very interested in the plot of the novel, but when, with an affectation of indifference and looking elsewhere, he asked how many times they met a week, Alfonso felt the same surprise as he had at Macario's yawn.

"Are they all in love with Annetta, then?"

He went to visit Annetta next evening as they had agreed. He found her writing in the library. On seeing him, she gave a movement of pleased impatience, then pushed aside the manuscript, and started to talk of other things, of the wonderfully mild weather for that time of year. Alfonso, who knew no motive for hesitation, asked her how she had liked his chapter, with a smile asking for clemency. It was rather unpromising that she had not mentioned the subject first.

"I don't like it!" Annetta said to him, giving him a friendly look to attenuate the crude phrase. "It's very fine of course, I recognize its merits, but it's dull."

She told him that she had begun correcting it but had not succeeded, and that he would definitely have to rewrite it, because she had to confess that even then she did not know just what was lacking in that chapter.

"It's all of a piece!"

At this critic's expression she became enthusiastic because she knew that things "all of a piece" are praiseworthy; and Alfonso's heart beat lighter.

"But it's dull, very dull. Who would you expect to read with any pleasure such a string of thoughts with no interruption or ornamentation? And then you do too little narrating; you're always describing, even when you think you're narrating. After an opening like that, how are we to go on? There are a thousand words of description to one of narrative. The other way around would have been better. It's more important to lay down the main theme, Clara's first reactions on her marriage to that industrialist and his long-standing love for her, rather than describe some drawing room which the reader is never going to see again, and give all these details about Clara's childhood."

She read her own version aloud to him. A few of Alfonso's words and phrases were kept, obviously out of kindness, but they were so unimportant that he could not feel grateful; the parts that meant most to him had been treated most summarily.

On finishing her reading, Annetta looked at him expecting enthusiastic approval; but Alfonso with a great effort just managed to mutter out some words of praise which were still too cold. He made things worse because he was unable to hide his disappointment at having worked so hard and uselessly; so, finding no immediate way of expressing disappointment without offending Annetta, when he did hit on a way, he used it without stopping to consider its consequences. Without speaking of his own work, he said that Annetta's would be more popular, and criticized her theories; it was quite true, he said, that they would have a sucess by using those theories but denied that it was worth while sacrificing every higher artistic aim to a hunger for ephemeral success.

"Excuse me!" interrupted Francesca, who had been silent till then and had not seemed to follow the conversation. "By the look on your face I'd have said you enjoyed Annetta's work. So it cannot be as inartistic as you say."

Alfonso thought that Francesca accompanied her phrase with a glance which might have been an invita-

tion for him to agree, and this was such a surprise that
for a time he could not take his eyes off her. Had Francesca also collaborated on that chapter she was defending? Now it was obvious that he had to admire it, and
he adapted himself with the best grace he could. He
said that he had liked the chapter but was only against
the theory. Actually the chapter had seemed to him
ugly, bare, and declamatory, and he was humiliated to
have to make that explicit declaration by which he ab-
dicated the right of giving his own opinion. He was
amazed to see that Annetta had no doubts about the
sincerity of his declaration. Then it was settled, she said,
that this chapter was to stay just as she had rewritten
it and they would agree about other chapters in the
same way.

In fact, about the second and third chapters they did
agree in the same way, but more easily. Alfonso wrote
them out trying to imitate Annetta, and Annetta re-
wrote them without bothering much about the first
version.

This situation had an agreeable side for Alfonso.
Having won her superiority and made it manifest, having probably noticed how much it cost Alfonso to submit, Annetta tried to make up for this by showing him
more friendship, at times even a protectiveness, a kind
of maternal affection. She derided him for his weakness,
described him as a little bear who lacked tact and did
not know how to pay a compliment; one evening she
said to the Wednesday group in his presence that there
might be greater philosophers than Alfonso, but none
who had taken philosophy so seriously or lived in such
conformity with its dictates. She gave him—but only
when they were alone together—the nickname of
"frog." A "frog" when he stuttered out half a phrase
and did not know how to complete it, a "frog" when
he said that literary success was worth little because it

was attained by the ignorant; she even called him a
"frog" when he brought her his drafts all ready to be
thrown aside. She would say the word to him with a
sweet smile, looking at him with admiration as if he
were some eccentric creature to be studied . . . but not
read, while he stood rigid, talking little and clipping his
words to deserve her nickname the more. She always
stuck firmly to her first opinion that although Alfonso
had many more superior ideas at his disposal he did not
know how to connect them and form a good novel. He
was too heavy, too dull. Sooner or later he would make
a fine name for himself by some excellent work of
philosophy, but not by novels, which were too light for
him.

But the tedium of the work was considerable. In the
second chapter there was a terrible scene between Clara
and her husband in their bedroom, but in the third,
and by Annetta's express wish, husband and wife both
realized they loved each other, although divided by immense pride. The whole of the rest of the novel was to
be about these two prides which had to be tamed, because such was the plot. But it did not even continue
about these two prides, for Annetta wanted to graft
into the novel a thousand other little tales which had
nothing to do with the main one. A former fiancé, a
shopkeeper, Clara's rival, the nobleman's wife, and also
a brother of Clara's and a sister of the industrialist, who
eventually married, were all brought in; so were various
other characters who took part in some political comedy,
an election put in to swell the novelette into a full-
scale novel. Alfonso proposed omitting all this useless
matter and leaving the two prides as Annetta wanted
them, facing each other to fight it out between them; a
good analysis of pride could still be made of that.
Annetta found this suggestion positively comical.
There was to be chapter after chapter of long talks

and struggles between the two women, Clara and the
nobleman's wife; every chapter was to be adorned by
one or more glances of love between husband and wife.
They got no further.

For Alfonso this work began to take on an odd re-
semblance to his work in the bank. In the evening he
would sit down to it with a yawn, struggling against
sleep, intent only on keeping closely to what Annetta
had told him to do, glad when he had finished. Sometimes the boredom of the work was such that he ended
by going to Annetta's without having done anything.
At the last moment he had not worked, resolving to
send her his excuses next day and renounce seeing her
that time rather than have to write such stuff. But he
could not renounce seeing her, found some other excuse, and went.

Annetta always greeted him kindly and never reproved him. She made him read what she had done
and then let him change the subject. She rather enjoyed hearing him talk. He was shy now only on purpose, because he had realized that it was wise to pre-
serve a certain shyness with Annetta. When about to
leave, he would remember Macario's warnings and
Francesca's little sign and even the bearing of Spalati,
Annetta's oldest friend, who when he took liberties did
so always with an air as respectful as his words were
free. Spalati was clever enough only to lack respect for
her when he flattered her. In this way his flattery took
on an aspect of frankness that made it seem sincere.
He was quite capable of telling her that she used too
many adjectives, like Victor Hugo. Alfonso understood
his method and his bearing, made easier by his capacity
to simulate the character attributed to him. By showing
contempt for exterior forms, he was allowed to trans-
gress some of them, but it was not such forms that Annetta demanded. The important thing for her was to

have admiration or enthusiasm shown at the proper time.

Their pleasantest evenings were when the novel was not mentioned at all, but Alfonso realized that in the long run Annetta might be displeased by the slow progress of the work. He was also warned of this by Francesca, who for a second time showed a wish to direct him in his relations with Annetta.

One evening she received him when Annetta was still in her room.

"Have you done nothing today either?" she asked him with a note of reproof. "Take care, as Annetta easily gets impatient."

That evening he did happen to have something done. He understood the importance of the warning and accepted it; from then on, and for some time, every evening he brought some proof of having worked on or thought about the novel.

He was finding this more and more difficult. There was a lot to do at the bank. Now he had nearly all Miceni's work on his shoulders, so that there were daily bouts of hard work which he and Alchieri could scarcely cope with. He felt the need for long walks and for rest more strongly than ever.

The first time since Francesca's warning that he happened to visit Annetta without bringing a single page of writing, Annetta greeted him with her usual sweet smile; but he, afraid she was hiding the anger mentioned by Francesca, and in no way reassured, expected to be dismissed suddenly and forever. In his fear he did not think one excuse enough but mentioned how busy he was, then said he'd had a headache and even some worrying news from home about his mother's health which had spoiled the calm he needed for work. Annetta listened to him with a deeply sympathetic air, very moving to Alfonso. He hated having to excuse himself like a little schoolboy when he longed to say something quite different, and this brought tears to his eyes, which Annetta attributed to worry about his mother's health.

That evening Annetta must have found Alfonso more agreeable than usual. After speaking of the many reasons which had prevented him from working at the novel, he had gone on to tell her that he longed to devote himself to it, and then to assert that his favorite occupation was meditating about that delightful work. For the first time his flattery was not forced, for it was a moment when he would have turned forger to ensure Annetta's friendship. He described his job at the bank and, not daring to complain to Signor Maller's daughter of banking work in general, he lamented that he was still not entrusted with the more intelligent and responsible work which he considered his due.

"Would you like me to talk to Papa?" asked Annetta, much touched. "Of course you have a right to more difficult work."

He had not foreseen this offer, which disconcerted him somewhat. He protested that he did not want to take advantage of Annetta's friendship to obtain protection. Anyway, influence was not enough to break through the bank's hierarchy, and the suggestion partly destroyed his illusions about these evenings with Annetta. She wanted to know what these illusions were.

"When I'm here," replied Alfonso, "I just want to remember that I'm your friend, and a writer. For the moment I'm nothing else."

Annetta thanked him.

"So you do like coming here, do you?"

She had switched to a much lighter tone, which Alfonso did not notice at once, so busy was he assuring her that he always enjoyed coming to her home.

Annetta had uttered that phrase in good faith, thinking it very polite, but it produced many hours of agitation in Alfonso. Yes, polite it certainly was, but had she so soon forgotten seeing him cry that she could only come out with that conventional phrase? It took him a long time to understand why the phrase seemed so offensive. Meanwhile, he felt very discontented with himself, as if remorseful for some bad or silly action. He had wept before her and she had thought it her duty to say a kind word! There was such a difference between the importance of the two facts that he was ashamed of having shed those tears. A woman with any gleam of affection for him would have wept with him.

It was a fine evening, the air cold but serene, and the sky clear but for a few stars. He stood in the street for a long time, feeling he could not achieve calm inside a room. For the second time he felt an urge to break off his relations with Annetta, again because of his uneasiness at the coldness and indifference that showed through her great guise of friendship. These painful recognitions jolted him out of his complacency, his living by habit rather than by his set purpose; then he analyzed that purpose, surprised at not having lived more in conformity with it, at not having at least viewed it under another light, and at being now as far from reaching his goal as he had seemed near it before. Was his passion the kind that needed many a pang before being satisfied? Now, more even than at the start of his relations with Annetta, he had a clear feeling that his love for her was increased by the riches surrounding her, embellishing a pretty face as a setting does a diamond. He remembered that before realizing Annetta's grace and charm he had been excited by knowing that she was Maller's daughter, and from that agitation and emotion had come the feeling he called love.

But what was the point of all this analysis? He had noticed a difference between his way of feeling and that of the people around him, and he thought this consisted in the fact that he took life too seriously. That was his misfortune! Was it worth racking his brains like this to find a way out of a tangle which should work out naturally by itself? If Annetta loved him, he certainly had a lot to gain; his life would be quite changed; yes, if she loved him, he had nothing to lose.

He wanted to be calm, but these were not thoughts to free him from either doubts or agitation. The indecisive situations to which he was prone tended to save him from analyzing his own instincts. Self-knowledge made him suffer.

The next day on the Corso he happened upon Macario going down to the sea. They had not seen each other for some weeks, for which Macario was kind enough to blame Alfonso.

"Are you so busy with the novel," he asked, "that you're not to be seen about any more?"

It was the first time Macario had even mentioned the novel to him, and his friendly, jesting tone gave Alfonso a pleasant surprise. He was again the good friend who enjoyed instructing, and Alfonso, on his side, did his best to put on his former submissive attitude again; but in vain. He was no longer able to hold back spontaneous comments completing or rectifying Macario's ideas. Macario invited him for a sail and Alfonso had to refuse because it was nearly time for him to be at the office. They walked some way along the mole together.

Macario greeted a lady who, though ponderous and hardly in her first youth, was still attractive.

"There's a woman," he said, "whose lover one can easily become, they say, and quite fun it would be, too." From this observation he went on to discourse about seduction in general. "To get a woman who wants to give herself may not seem difficult, but it can tax even an astute man's resources. One must know when to move, because even a woman who wants it doesn't want it all the time, and once one does know when, then one should pounce immediately, which is anything but easy, as that decision needs stronger nerves than a general does directing a battle. Even if the attack's expected and bound to be victorious, it gets no easier. With women who are indecisive and need to have one conviction given them and another taken away, it's so difficult that I've never gone for them, in spite of my considerable experience. I'm convinced, though, that there, too, it's more a question of action than of talk. Talk beforehand, a long time beforehand, but no speeches take a woman to the point of no return. With women one must act. A kiss for example, a kiss on a hand, a face, a neck, even a foot, whatever's nearest. Good talkers never have luck with women."

This speech seemed made especially for Alfonso, but on his way to the office he laughed. He imagined taking Macario's advice seriously and *acting* with Annetta. He saw her white hand raised threateningly to slap. Perhaps Macario had hoped Alfonso would follow his advice! Alfonso suspected him capable of anything. All the better! The kind of trap that Macario had set became a warning.

Very soon he had occasion to think over Macario's advice again. One evening Francesca left them alone. Annetta was writing calmly in her fine minute handwriting with its decisive strokes; her left arm was stretched out on the desk, against which her bosom was leaning; her hand was directly under Alfonso's mouth. It was impossible not to think of the action advised by Macario, and Alfonso quivered as he realized that the skin on the end of his chin had already touched that hand and that it was not withdrawn even so. He remembered Macario declaring that a man became ridiculous in a woman's eyes by risking less than she desired. The decision was not consciously taken before, with an almost involuntary movement, his lips were on that hand. He felt the contact of velvety skin and remembered it later; for the moment, terrified by his own ardor, not knowing how to make amends, he tried to put on the indifferent air of a child who hopes its own naughtiness will be blamed on others. The lightning he feared did not come! He saw Annetta's face change color and the pen pause on the paper. Perhaps she was undecided what attitude to take. Then the hand was withdrawn, slowly, with a natural movement as if she needed it to lean her head on. The silence lasted almost a minute, a century for Alfonso. Finally she spoke, and not of the kiss; she spoke with careless ease, looking at him more than once in a smiling friendly manner.

He was saved! More than saved, happy! The declaration was made! At least she would now realize herself to be no longer just with a clerk or a writer. From now on he could hope that she would in some way guess when he suffered from a cold word or from jealousy. He tried to be modest, to consider Annetta's silence due only to gentle forbearance, but it had already made him happy. He had made a gigantic step at the very start. That evening he had no doubts. He loved Annetta and wanted her for his own. That was his easy way to riches, but of that he did not think at all at the time. A smile from Annetta was happiness! Action had been demanded of him, and his action had been bold but not brutal; gentler, more respectful than any word.

For a number of evenings Francesca was present at their meetings, which did not displease Alfonso. Now

he spoke with his eyes; the language of the eyes is like
that of music; it makes nothing definite when no word
has been said, but when it has, says more and says it
better than do words themselves. His looks were not
bold, he did not try to make out her curves by gazing
indiscreetly at her soft clothes, or to squeeze her hand
or stroke it to get a thrill from the contact. That declaration, that outburst of solitary desire had fortified
his love, made him breathe pure air. He had been unable, though, to produce any addition to that kiss in
actual words.

One evening when they were in the library, Francesca tiptoed off in the very middle of the sitting so as
not to disturb them. Her absence lasted a quarter of an
hour, and when she returned she found them just where
she had left them. Alfonso had quivered on her departure, thinking, still according to Macario, that he
must now say something. He brooded over a few little
phrases, but Annetta prevented him from saying them
by speaking quite calmly about the novel. Apparently
she expected nothing and it was better not to do anything which she did not foresee. So he was silent; his
position was already excellent and for the moment he
wanted nothing more. He did not speak of love, but
everything he said to Annetta was colored by his feelings. He did nothing but make declarations of love!
When he spoke to Annetta, in a very different way
than did Macario, he hinted at it in every word and
smile or tone. When saying the simplest things, he felt
his voice infused with a sweetness of which he had not
thought himself capable, its tone so clear and bold that
it seemed possessive, making him quiver all over with
the excitement of a realized dream.

He ran into Macario again, who with suspicious insistence talked to him once more about ways of getting
a woman. Alfonso listened indifferently to the crudi-

ties suggested, because he now had a better idea what
to do in his own case. He was quite content at a pause
in his relations with Annetta and did not want it to
end before he knew what the next stage would be. Also,
he suffered less when away from her. Waiting for evening was a bore, but he did not daydream so much
because a smile from Annetta had dissipated fantasies
which she herself had created.

Alfonso figured that even if she did not love him, she
must be flattered by his love and respect. He exaggerated his shyness because that explained the strange situation and made it possible to prolong it.

Amid this love-making, literary work languished,
which flattered Alfonso because it seemed to have become secondary for Annetta, too. One evening Alfonso
happened to bring some work of his on the book and
Annetta forgot to ask if she could read it. As the book
proceeded, however, every single thing was done according to Annetta's suggestions and every day Alfonso felt
the plot becoming emptier and the novel sillier. He
thought that, as confidence between them increased, a
day would come when he could tell her his opinion,
but for the moment he did not even dare express the
slightest doubt. He did not want to expose himself to
the danger of seeing any dimming of the gleam in
Annetta's eyes when she looked at him. For him that
novel was of very slight importance, and he could not
bear to hear even a brusque word from his loved one
because of it.

He was torn from this idyll not by any wish of his
own or Annetta's; it had been created unknowingly by
Macario and was now destroyed by Miceni and Fumigi.

Miceni made it most obvious that he envied Alfonso
his familiarity in the Maller home. Of course he had
not said so, and as usual Alfonso refused to admit it
even when Miceni, with his bizarre character, made it

clear. Miceni's darts did not wound him even when the poor man began to speak of his love for Annetta and to pretend that it would have been returned had he been more insistent. From some words of Macario's Alfonso knew what to think of this. One day Miceni, as if feeling more intimate with Alfonso, told him why he had stopped paying court to Annetta; out of regard for Fumigi, whom he knew to be in love with her. Fumigi was an old friend of Miceni's, who had got him his job at Maller's, so he had a right to consideration in return.

This assertion left Alfonso less cold than the other. He, too, had noticed that Fumigi was in love with Annetta, and it was a love which, it had to be recognized, might quite probably achieve its aim. By the cold light of reason he realized that Fumigi was not too old and was in fact a suitable match for Annetta.

Noticing that it disturbed Alfonso to hear Fumigi spoken of, Miceni often had a dig, exorcising his own jealousy by the sight of Alfonso's.

It is more difficult to seem indifferent when one is not, than to seem impassioned when one is indifferent. Miceni usually began by speaking to him about business, a pretext to go to his room. When forced to name Annetta, Alfonso sifted every word before saying it, and with a carelessness which he felt to be obviously excessive and affected spoke of her as if he had seen her very few times in his life. He said she was beautiful, and topped his show of indifference by mentioning that he desired her as any man does any pretty woman. But when they spoke of Fumigi, he could not get out a word that sounded indifferent. He was not bothered if Miceni thought that Annetta loved him, but it hurt him deeply that any man could think her lover to be anyone but himself. He said with visibly forced calm that he knew Fumigi and did not think he could be in love with Annetta. Then Miceni lost his calm, too.

"Why do you think I'd come and tell you if it's not true? Ask around. Everyone in town knows it but you."

He was as heated in affirming as Alfonso in denying it; but when Alfonso noticed himself to be straying too far from his role of indifference, he cut short the discussion, declaring that either could be true and he really did not care. He spoke energetically, but too volubly, and the look on his face and the sound of his voice were anything but indifferent.

Pleased as if bringing good news, Miceni told him that Fumigi and Annetta were engaged. Alfonso began laughing, calmly and this time sincerely.

"I was at the Mallers' yesterday and would have been told if it had been true."

"It's not official yet; but probably as we're talking Fumigi is at Annetta's home for the first time as a future husband."

His voice had gone shrill, as if offended by Alfonso's tranquillity.

Alfonso did not deign to discuss the matter. The evening before, Annetta had treated him even better than usual. She had told him about her childhood, her life in a college where she had been sent after her mother's death. These were confidences, and, surprised and pleased, Alfonso saw another improvement in his position. For some time he had been admiring his own ability, and that evening, coming out of the Maller home, he murmured: "There's real art. Effortless advance."

He was not supposed to go to Annetta's that evening, but agitated by Miceni's words he walked for a long time up and down the Via dei Forni. The house looked just as usual, its long row of uninhabited rooms with windows hermetically closed and all blinds drawn; only the window of the living room was half open.

Coming out of Via dei Forni toward the sea, he ran into Fumigi. Having thought of him so much, Alfonso felt embarrassed at suddenly setting eyes on him, and the other seemed no less confused.

"Are you . . . leaving?" asked Fumigi, stuttering and making a sign toward the Mallers' house, from which direction Alfonso was coming.

"No!" said Alfonso rather sharply. Fumigi might have been accusing him of some crime. "I've been out taking exercise for nearly an hour. If you'd like to keep me company. . ."

Fumigi, usually such a dandy, looked rather disordered; his tie was not in place, the collar of his black overcoat, which was brand new, was turned up.

"Shall we go to the new quay?" he asked. He looked at the clock again and after a slight hesitation began to walk along beside Alfonso.

They were silent as they moved along under the pale rays of the setting sun. From the station square they turned toward the sea and stopped on the first mole, recently finished, with white irregular paving stones.

"Splendid!" said Alfonso, glad to be able to talk. He was looking at the sun. Half its incandescent ball was still showing out of the sea. The calm white light that illuminated the houses on the shore did not seem to come from that red object. It made pink reflections on the horizon and reddened half a little white cloud, motionless over the city where dark was already falling on inner streets.

Neither of the two really had eyes for the magnificent spectacle. Alfonso was observing Fumigi, who was so absorbed in his thoughts that he did not even bother to hide his preoccupation. He looked again at his watch and murmured a few words, which Alfonso did not understand; then he thrust his hands into his pockets, trembling with impatience and looking at the water at his feet. He had even forgotten he was in company.

"Are you in a hurry?" Alfonso asked him.

"No!" replied Fumigi. "I've got an appointment at half past seven."

So what Miceni had said was true, Alfonso thought, and the appointment which Fumigi was so keen to be in time for was with Maller. Fumigi was awaiting a decision, and Alfonso still felt so sure of himself that he pitied this feverish impatience of a poor man who he knew was about to suffer.

Fumigi's bearing was so abnormal that pretending not to know its cause made pretending not to notice it impossible.

"Aren't you well?"

"No . . . yes, a slight headache. But what disturbs me is having to stay outside to be sure of not missing my appointment. Anyway, what I'm worried about just doesn't really deserve it, I can assure you."

"It's unimportant, is it?" asked Alfonso in amazement.

"No, very important indeed, but. . ." and he gave a little shrug of the shoulders, which Alfonso took to mean utter certainty about his own position.

"Then why worry?"

Alfonso went on calming him, but he would have given much to destroy this trust Fumigi had, which stung him.

For a few instants Fumigi seemed calmer. Then he fell back into his meditations, heeding Alfonso so little that he suddenly bid him good-bye in the middle of another phrase which Alfonso was thinking up to calm him. He needed to be alone but wanted to make time pass, and he bid farewell while still having to say something in order to find relief; it was not the kind of thing he would have said spontaneously. He said good-bye rather wordily, telling about another appointment he had to go to even before that one.

Alfonso followed him with an attentive eye and no-

ticed a slight hesitation about his direction on reaching
the middle of the square. It was obvious! The poor
man was just wandering about with his agonizing
doubt, and had no other reason for moving.

That hesitation alone touched Alfonso's pity and
took away the anger aroused in him by Fumigi's stupid
certainty. This pity even went so far that he began
dreaming up ways in which he could reconcile his own
happiness with Fumigi's. There were none, but that did
not prevent him from making a story out of a situation in which he reserved for himself the not unpleasant
role of Fumigi's old friend. What he found unpalatable
was the feeling that he had co-operated in Fumigi's
unhappiness and knowingly deserved someone's hatred
for the first time in his life. This was enough to give
him a deep disgust at his own happiness.

Then he settled down to work on the novel in case
the nasty labor of it might make him feel he deserved
his good fortune more and he were placating the envy
of the gods by making himself miserable. A word of
Miceni's was enough to take away part of his security.

"Probably it's all settled by this time."

If that very second Alfonso had been suddenly told
that Fumigi had killed himself after being refused by
Annetta, he would not have been at all sorry.

He was fated to remain in that state of mind for a
number of days. That evening he did not see Annetta.
The maid stopped him on the stairs to say that Signorina Annetta could not receive him.

"Is there news, then?" asked Alfonso in alarm. Then,
seeing the woman's surprise, he added: "Is the Signorina unwell?"

"No!" replied the maid, oldish and rather preten-
tiously dressed, who had always treated Alfonso with
great indifference, maybe partly because he had forgotten to flirt with her. "She's quite well." And she hurried

off as if she was so busy she could not remain idle even for a few minutes.

That was enough to make Alfonso wonder whether Fumigi had received a different reply than he had supposed. Where had Fumigi derived that security in which he seemed lulled? Though Alfonso knew nothing new, he was beginning now to put together signs that Fumigi's question had been greeted favorably and no longer found indications of its rejection as he had done till then. Even the maid's state of hurry seemed to show that a serious change had taken place in Annetta's life.

Though he was still convinced that Fumigi must have been refused, now it was only because it seemed incredible that Annetta could ever consent to marry him; not out of love for anyone else, not out of love for him. He had nothing to do with that decision, he felt now. Threatened with a great disaster, even when the imminent danger had been avoided, he would not feel any the safer.

Next day Miceni told him that he had no news yet, but was in no hurry; his card of congratulations would still arrive in time. He hurried off without allowing Alfonso time to make a reply, which he must have expected to be sharp. They had never exchanged a single word about Alfonso's relations with Annetta, but Miceni acted as if he knew of them and Alfonso realized this.

That evening he went to Annetta's. On the way he felt hopeful; he would find her unchanged and awaiting him in that library where he would spend yet another unforgettable evening.

Just as he was about to put his hat down in the entrance hall, already reassured, Santo called him from the landing.

"The Signorina can't see you today; she's ill."

Alfonso went pale. Was Miceni right then?

"Very ill?" he asked Santo. He had to pretend even with him.

"Oh you know! Women!" explained Santo with the irreverence usual to him when speaking of his employers behind their backs.

She was not ill! In the drawing room, all lit up as on evenings when she was receiving, maybe she was sitting by Fumigi, who was enjoying the full joy of sweet emotion, the calm of uncontested possession, which Alfonso thought must be supreme happiness.

Santo had already turned his back. Until then, and since seeing him at the Mallers', Santo had treated him with almost irritating servility. His contempt now was an evident sign that he considered him a failure. Alfonso followed him for a step or two.

"Please tell Signorina Annetta that I've been here and am very sorry to hear she's unwell."

He went down the stairs looking straight ahead and without deigning to answer the greeting which Santo did actually give. His thoughts were still on the two who were perhaps kissing alone in the sitting room; but until he was in the next street he took care to show no sign on his face of the feelings agitating him; someone might be watching him from that house so as to enjoy his sorrow.

This was a silly idea, he thought then: nobody bothered about him any more, even to hurt him. It was drizzling and he was holding his umbrella closed in his hand. The thought of how he could tell Miceni had bothered him, imagining Miceni's atrocious and facile irony. But now he need be careful no longer. To hide from Miceni the stupid illusions he had nourished till that day was, he now realized, impossible. Yet, he might try to describe to him how these illusions had started and how they had been encouraged by Annetta.

If all was over, as he kept repeating to himself it was,

then he had lost a very great deal indeed. No less than the whole purpose of his life. What else remained to him? For that love he had forgotten his ambition, which he did not think he could ever revive now that there was no future for him in the Maller household. To be drawn from his squalor by a woman's kiss had been a dream, a splendid dream. Life for a time had lost its feeling of severity and injustice, had sent without a struggle fortune and happiness to one who deserved it; it sent forth its fiat from above, and he had got wealth and love.

Suddenly he realized he was soaked to the skin and far from home. Was it true then? He felt he would have been less agitated had he been in no doubt. He would have made up his mind how to behave, and maybe still got some satisfaction from his misfortune, carried his head high, repaid indifference by indifference, been hurt and hurt in his turn by showing himself unharmed. Annetta was capable of triumphing by the pain she brought him.

She was just as Macario had described her! Cold and vain, vain before all else. Was he not holding at that moment the proof of her vanity, that novel dictated by vanity in person, from its silly vacuous concepts to each of its emphatic phrases, attempts at flight by someone who did not know how to walk? No mere spirit of vengeance made him think of her like that now. Once she had fallen from the height on which his love had placed her, he thought he saw her as she was.

On reaching home, he found a note from Annetta asking him to call next day.

"Dear friend!" the opening alone should have been enough to change his mood and give him immense joy. Instead of which he read and re-read it, trying to find what was not there; an assurance that he was wrong in fearing Fumigi and doubting Annetta's love for himself. That note did not exclude disaster, or if it did momentarily, it was no destruction of the threat. He could not regain his calm or even enjoy being much happier than he had been just before. Sorrow, particularly when over, has its attractions, and those with weak ambitions find a satisfaction in dressing up in it. Could he get happiness from this situation when chance had revealed the disaster that this very situation could be to him? He could always be thrown aside like a useless object; as soon as Annetta neglected him, he would again become a poor little clerk without even a right to show his suffering.

Not that it was suffering which had sent him wandering over the streets of the city shortly before, but the great emotion of self-pity. If Fumigi had been rejected, his relationship with Annetta would continue apparently unchanged; while in reality his jealousy, his fears, the threat of change, made it unendurable. There was only one way to get out of such a situation. He could withdraw first and so, however painful such a renunciation, be able at least to think back over the whole adventure without blushing, without a feeling of offense. Even so, it would not be a pleasant memory. He would never be able to forget Annetta's hardness and vanity, discovered, it seemed, that very moment. The experience he had been through was harsh and would serve him for the whole of his life. Now he wanted to return to his plain habits, to the ideal of work and solitude contested by no one. That was happiness. Habit and regularity would give it.

But when he was with Annetta, when she shook his hand with the same sweet smile with which she had bade him farewell a few days ago as if there were nothing in the meantime to disturb their good relations, he forgot his intentions. There was another way of dealing with that situation, he now understood, apart from giving up the whole thing. His only regret was that he could not blurt out all that he had suspected in the last few days so as to provoke an explanation which might lose him Annetta's friendship but which could also reaffirm, reawaken it as love. Meanwhile, shyness allowed him only to express calmness and cordiality.

They were in the living room, and alone because Francesca was unwell. Annetta talked about a chapter of the novel, made some suggestions; Alfonso approved these and without any effort was able to make a show of admiration. It was not a moment for agitated criticism. Annetta needed advice because she was having difficulty in making headway with a plot that was now tending to the absurd. Her hero and heroine were still passionately in love with each other, and not saying so out of pride. This confession would end the novel, and Annetta's little head was beginning to fail in ideas as what to do next.

Suddenly Alfonso became talkative. He needed to talk, and began holding forth about the novel and his admiration for Annetta's ideas. When people shout, it does not matter what they are talking about; the voice provides the outlet. Alfonso was soothed by the flow of his own words, and such pauses as he made were prompted by calculation and by an idea that if he did not let Annetta talk he would learn nothing about her. Eventually, and with a cold calculation that got to the point at once, he began animatedly describing his life every day, coming to the conclusion that his happy hours had added up to no more than a few days in one whole year, counting among these all the hours he had spent at the Mallers'.

At his request, Annetta described how she had spent the last week. When she began, Alfonso flushed and stared, as mere listening did not seem enough. He wanted to guess at what point in her account she would think of Fumigi, and to see her expression when she did.

That week she had been to the theater twice. But she had also had a number of dull evenings, on one of which she had been on the point of sending for him to lift her from her boredom with philosophic talk and work together on the novel.

"I'd have loved to come!" murmured Alfonso in a voice suffocated with emotion.

"Yes?" asked Annetta, also blushing. "Another time then, we're agreed?"

This gave Alfonso a lion's courage.

"Nothing else?" he murmured when she had finished describing her week.

"Nothing else!" replied Annetta in surprise, suddenly going pale.

"I've spent a horrid week," said Alfonso in a deep voice.

He told how he had heard that a disaster was hanging over him and had at first not believed this; then he kept coming up against indications confirming the threat, so that when he heard this had been avoided he refused to believe it because he had so long considered the disaster inevitable. He still doubted that it had passed. But a series of facts had been described so truthfully that, on remembering his pain, tears came to his eyes and he had to stop talking.

It was his declaration; and when Alfonso thought it over later he had to smile because it was certainly not love which brought tears to his eyes but, as always with him, self-pity. Although he was no longer speaking, tears were pouring down his cheeks and he did not dry them because the gesture would show them to Annetta, who might not have noticed. This was the second time that he wept in front of her; the first time, results had not been very flattering.

"Tears!" exclaimed Annetta, moved. "Am I the cause?"

Wanting to soothe him, she took him warmly by the hand. The gesture, not the contact, not the pleasure of desire, made Alfonso happy. It destroyed his misery about the coldness of his relations with Annetta, and the change from his own idea of those relations to these real ones in which Annetta now acted as consoler was so sharp that he had to close his eyes. He kissed Annetta's hand without moving it, bending his head until his lips reached it, careful this time to make the bold gesture respectful. He just grazed the hand with his lips; it was a sketch of a kiss and he did not want to go further. Till then they had advanced very little, and if that kiss separated them he would be able to return to the almost ingenuous sweetness of their relationship.

"The explanation is sufficient," said Annetta with a smile, but in a voice broken with emotion, which surprised Alfonso. She withdrew her hand.

"Poor Fumigi!" exclaimed Alfonso, who could not manage to infuse his own voice with the emotion heard in Annetta's.

"Not so poor!"

She said that he was a strong and energetic man who would soon recover from this little blow. She had felt honored by his proposal and had not accepted because she did not wish to marry.

"It's partly our artistic ideal that makes me prefer my liberty." This phrase, with the first person plural, cancelled in Alfonso the impression of coldness given by the preceding one.

"Anyway, Fumigi remains a good friend of mine, he's promised! And now let's go back to our novel."

But they did not go back to it. There was too great a gulf between that cold, forced thing and the passion which they were talking to hide. Alfonso saw Annetta was now calm again, her voice steady and sure, her hand firm as it held the pen.

"Now what on earth does this fool of ours want?" asked Alfonso, alluding to their hero, who had been made to pass, in a dark corridor, his wife who loved him and who out of dignity was pretending not to see him. "Does such dignity exist?"

Speaking and acting with an air of spontaneity which was really calculated audacity, he knelt before Annetta and tried to take her hand again. She began to laugh, but put her own head close to Alfonso's dark one; neither could have said how they came to kiss each other on the lips for the first time. So little had he foreseen it that after the contact ceased he thought he had not felt all the happiness he should and tried to make up for this by a second kiss. But she had drawn back her head and risen to her feet in alarm, apparently not feeling quite safe when sitting. But her cheeks were brightly flushed, her eyes glistening and splendid, and she gave him a glance which did not seem angry, though it must have been intended to intimidate him. Like that she was really lovely.

"Enough, Signor Nitti!"

He got to his feet and, standing still, in a voice thick with emotion said, to calm her, that it was indeed enough, and he could live near her all his life and never ask for more.

Annetta smiled in thanks; she felt safe with this boy; it had been really this boyish quality which had taken him so far. What had she to fear from this personified shyness? She had been touched by the sweetness of his wordless love, by his shy silence even after his first daring had gone unpunished. He had never hinted in any way at that stolen kiss on her hand, never betrayed impatience, and she had ingenuously believed that he would ask for nothing more, considering that, because the little favor came from her, it would be enough.

They had now taken a huge step forward and there was no way back. They had spoken, and, what was more, Alfonso had seen Annetta's weakness, had suddenly discovered he was the stronger.

Annetta did not realize this and, with a smile intended to attenuate the despotism of her order, told him never to talk of love again. She was disobeyed at once. He asked if he could please talk about it just once more and then made a regular declaration of love, mingling memories of novels he had read with phrases which had long been going around in his brain and which were only awaiting a chance to be addressed to Annetta. He had been longing to talk about his love to her and had thought of this as his first poem; love could be ennobled, elevated, by intelligent wording, he had thought, and this could help to make their difference in status be forgotten. Now, though, he realized that desire is wordless. While he mouthed contrived sentimentalities as seemed his duty, he felt their bloodless and lifeless conventionality; this surprised him, for he did not know to what to attribute such coldness. Only when he spoke of his friendship with her did his voice fuse and tremble in an emotion which took his breath away. He had thought of this sweet intimacy ever since first nearing Annetta but now, speaking of it, a quite different desire was dressed out in the same words and made his head swim as it passed before him.

"I knew it," said Annetta with sincerity, "but it would have been better not to tell me."

She threatened him with a jesting finger, while a shadow of seriousness passed over her face. Anyway, as she had said, his words of love seemed colder because of what had preceded and provoked them. She did not fear them; they were a mere satisfaction to her vanity.

She interrupted him, saying with great sweetness: "Enough, enough!" so that, had he not been bored, Alfonso would have gone on.

This was enough for that evening, but not for the next. Till then timid partly on purpose, Alfonso realized how much happiness he could derive from the step he had taken. She had pointed out to him with some clarity how far he could go, and he wanted to be at least always at that point, if not beyond it. So every evening he said a word of love to Annetta; if he could not at first, he did it on leaving, when shaking hands in farewell.

Suddenly Francesca had become Annetta's indivisible companion again. She was always present at their meetings, and now that they were working very little or not at all on the novel, took an active part in their conversation. All strain in her relations with Annetta, first cold and then exaggeratedly friendly, had now vanished, and the two women chattered away of fashions, journeys, and people he did not know, leaving him silent and embarrassed. He remained mute even when they spoke of other things, because he did not feel like addressing banalities or critical remarks to Annetta. All that was too cold, empty, and aimless. Why, he thought, exchange words which he did not care to say, or she to hear? Some did occur to him, but of the kind that needed some bold and passionate action immediately after being spoken. Anyway, he did not care much. The kiss on Annetta's hand had given him a need to talk, that on her lips had taken it away.

He was always received in the living room because the stove was there, and every object in it reminded him of desires and joys obtained. Every single thing in that confusion of differing furniture, solid comfortable pieces, was indissolubly linked to his sensations, seemed part of Annetta, mirrors always reflecting her face.

When he had to wait for a long time in that room alone, these sensations lulled him, then became so strong, the closeness of Annetta so palpable, that if she had suddenly entered he would have taken her in his arms and treated her as his own, with one word which he thought could explain and justify all. But Francesca came in first and found Alfonso confused, stumbling over words which he had prepared and could not get out.

One evening Francesca came and told him that Annetta had had to go off with her father to visit relatives. They had been unable to let him know in time, Francesca said with a sly smile, but asked him to stay and keep her company. This disappointment was such a shock that Alfonso did not know how to react. He stood rigidly for a quarter of an hour replying in monosyllables to the questions which the Signorina kindly asked him, then, to avoid the bother of pretending, went off, saying that he had only looked in to excuse himself for not staying that evening as he was feeling unwell. Francesca gave him an ironic but benevolent bow of farewell.

Impatience made Alfonso lose the correctness of bearing admired by Annetta till then, and if she did not take offense, it was because every rudeness of his was explained and excused by his obvious suffering. Francesca only had to move up to a window and look out on the street for him to become suddenly active, though he had been completely absorbed till then in his own dreams and desires. He said his word of love to her in a low voice like a melodramatic broken cry.

In Annetta's eyes his worst crime was his inability to maintain his bearing before a third person. With others present, he became as mute as he had been before out of shyness, worse because he seemed discontented and irritated, too. One Wednesday Prarchi came and asked him if he felt unwell. This question finally opened Alfonso's mouth, because he could still talk about himself. He talked feelingly of an illness which he could not define, a disquiet which took away sleep, pleasure in study, joy in life; everything bored him.

Prarchi gave him serious advice as a doctor. He diagnosed the vague illness of course as nerves, and advised him to spend a month or so at home in the open air. Annetta understandingly and sweetly suggested her asking for this leave of his. The suggestion of this cure annoyed Alfonso, who let out: "I'd have to go a very long way to get any good from it."

Had Prarchi not been simple enough to try and diagnose the illness according to the accepted medical practice, Alfonso's reaction would surely have made him realize what the matter was.

One evening he found her alone, and when, deeply disturbed by this unhoped-for chance, he began putting a bold plan into action, she dropped a few brusque words which had the effect of a cold shower. She said that she had found an excuse to get Francesca away and have a private chat with him. She was displeased with him; she resented his expression, which looked haughty and careless to others. Did he want to compromise her? She gave him a suspicious glance. Alfonso guessed its meaning. She had thought that she was dealing with a shy man deeply, aimlessly in love. Now she was afraid of finding that he was an able deceiver who was trying to compromise her.

Alfonso was alarmed. He had no intention of compromising her, but he certainly did have in mind what she suspected him of, which she thought he intended to attain by compromising her. He now expected to be forbidden access to the house, which would have been a logical consequence of what she had said. He could not excuse himself; he had been bold, ill-behaved. His only defense was to turn pale and act as if he had not properly understood what he was being blamed for.

But his alarm was Annetta's best excuse. She went on reproving him, yet asking affectionately if her friendship was no longer enough for him and if he did not think that by his ways he was exposing himself to the risk of losing that, too.

"I'll do whatever you like!" exclaimed Alfonso, relieved at finding that she was not yet forbidding him the house. Obviously she only wanted to prevent him from going too far, to intimidate him. She herself had been caught unexpectedly, reached a point which she never would have in cold blood, and was now regretting the time when this strong clever young man had loved and admired her timidly.

Annetta felt her compassion growing. She came up to him, squeezed his hand, and asked: "Let's see, Signor Alfonso, if we can't live like good friends again, happy and contented as before? What's happened to make you always silent and showing people how wretched you are?"

"It's that I always have words here," and he pointed to his throat, "and am prevented from saying them." He was still calling what he had in his throat "words"! Annetta at once became gay; he had not seen her so for a month, not since that evening when they had last spoken of their love. The fact is that, due to the sharp lesson given him by Annetta, he was not for the moment at all troubled by desire. He kissed her hands when she left them in his; this gave him only the pleasure of reassurance, as well as the bother of having to pretend enthusiasm. She grew warmer, as the excitement of the evening brought back his quick original turn of speech, and this always stirred her.

He went off tired but quite calm, with a weariness like satiety. When Annetta had tried to intimidate him

and lead him back to his former show of respect, he had
suffered at finding her as Macario had described. That
evening he had first seen her cold and disdainful, obviously a calculated bearing due to fear of compromise in
an unsuitable love affair; then she had been stirred,
though her disdain had not lessened. Perhaps she loved
him, but self-interest had been struggling with this love
and been victorious, until her senses spoke. All that was
so clear, showed so obviously, that Alfonso noted it
even in his daydreams. For, as usual, he tried to annul
his discomfort by urging his fantasy to deviate from
reality. But this time his daydream was no help. He
could imagine Annetta giving way, feeling the same
desires as he did, but only for a few seconds. Coldness
preceded and followed her bursts of emotion; calculation marked the limits of the tiny whiffs of passion
which the young lady allowed herself. This struggle of
hers, once won, would always be starting all over again.

This was not the only distress brought by this evening. Till then, though conscious that the first impulse
for his love had come from Annetta's wealth, he had
never felt that others, even Annetta herself, knew and
perhaps exaggerated the importance of that element in
it. He loved her! Even in his soliloquies he defended
himself warmly from such a reproach. Now he loved
her! There was an enormous difference between him
and that able intriguer whom Annetta seemed to suspect him to be; what she had taken as means toward
achieving his ends, such as melancholy and disquiet,
had actually derived from desire and love. His was certainly not a respectful love, and the hardness of Annetta's character prevented it from being so, but he
loved her and wanted to convince himself that if her
circumstances changed he would love her all the same.
This he felt so vehemently that it seemed he had never
expressed what he felt then.

In spite of his love, he was still harsh, even unjust in judging her character. Why, if Annetta regretted her momentary defeats, did she not remove all possibility of them by forbidding him access to her home? That Annetta was promising herself a triumph over her own weakness he would not admit. No! She was simply pretending to escape those uncontrolled instants, though longing for them when calm. From this conclusion of his, Alfonso's contempt grew, as did his hopes.

From then on, he was able to follow part of Annetta's orders and control himself before others; but when alone with her he was calculatedly daring, forcing himself to be so in spite of the blood rushing to his heart and snatching at his words.

One evening when, after waiting in vain for Francesca to leave the room, Annetta accompanied him to the landing, he resolutely carried out a plan he had had in his mind for several evenings. In the full light, there before all those doors, any one of which could suddenly open, he drew her to him and kissed her on the lips. Annetta, terrified, broke away from his embrace but, shaken and not at all angry, murmured gently: "Leave me, Alfonso!"

He went off with drunken steps, though even in his agitation he had a clear idea why Annetta had not rebuked him. She liked such daring, and hesitations imposed by respect merely satisfied her vanity. When drawing her to him, he had muttered aloud: "If I'm killed for this, it would be a fine death!"

He had not needed to say the melodramatic phrase, as his action was already excused in Annetta's eyes—so Alfonso had grounds for believing.

Next evening she refused to accompany him beyond the living-room door, but laughingly, with an air of teasing. They had been laughing the whole evening, because Alfonso had firmly decided to make himself agreeable; certainly Annetta did not like glum discontented men around her, only gay faces.

It was not his only care for Annetta's wishes. He had been suspected of wanting to compromise her and wanted to avoid all hint of such baseness, particularly as he hoped not to have to fall back on it. He was particularly careful with Macario, whom he suspected of trying for his own purposes to find out what form their literary work took. Alfonso decided to show a great deal of interest in this work and to pretend, nevertheless, that only a spirit of duty made him continue to frequent the Maller home. "For really," he assured Macario, "I have to be so careful there that it bores me."

But he felt that Marcario did not believe him.

Partly to save himself from the machinations which he feared, and also to make a merit of his own discretion, he told Annetta about Macario's questions and his own replies. The latter did not entirely satisfy her, and she advised him to exaggerate less so as to be more easily believed. She said, quite rightly, as Alfonso recognized, that he had not used all his perspicacity in getting Macario to believe in the coldness of his relations with Annetta, his conscience being so delicate and honest. No! Once this conscience of his was smoothed, he had treated the matter as if it were of secondary importance. Deep down, he did not dislike making Macario jealous.

This weakness became obvious when he tried to deceive Miceni as well as Macario. It was easy, Miceni being far from suspecting anything, so far that Alfonso was piqued and often felt an urge to turn Miceni into a confidant and his contempt into envy; for it was more and more obvious that Miceni thought Alfonso loved Annetta and was not loved in return. He did not know of Annetta's rejection of Fumigi, and Fumigi must have told him a lie to explain why there had been no engagement. It was strange how easily Miceni, usually so sharp, believed the tales spun for him. Fumigi, he told Alfonso, was about to marry a girl richer and lovelier than Annetta, whom he had left because of her.

Alfonso found it easier to keep silent about himself and his relations with Annetta as soon as he realized that to avenge himself on Miceni and irritate him, he had only to deride Fumigi and his pretensions.

"The man dropped his idea of asking for Annetta's hand from one moment to the next, did he? Odd! I was told he'd dropped it only after trying to execute it!"

Miceni went red as a boiled prawn and answered furiously, as if to a personal offense, that Annetta was a vain little thing who wanted to see someone die of love for her, but had not succeeded so far.

Alfonso could feel angry with Fumigi for a short time only. One morning, on the way to the office, he saw the little man trotting along in the same direction. Alfonso passed, pretending not to see him, but Fumigi ran behind, calling him loudly. He turned and was surprised to find a very different figure from what he had expected. It was not the gauntness and pallor of the face that surprised him; it was the disquiet in the eyes, the strange chewing, or rather ruminating, movement of the mouth, and particularly his carelessness of dress: a jacket that was too long and did not seem made for him, light white trousers in spite of a temperature slightly below zero, and on his right knee a large ink mark at which Alfonso, out of politeness, tried not to stare.

"I've to announce that I'm marrying . . . marrying . . ." and he did not seem to remember the name of his fiancée. Alfonso congratulated him hesitatingly. He did not understand; the man looked more mad than happy.

But he talked more or less sense, though his tongue seemed out of control, as it rushed along at a great pace. Alfonso found it difficult to follow him, Fumigi's pronunciation being slurred and not at all clear. When Fumigi realized he was not understood, he began shouting to make himself clearer.

"I understand, I understand!" cried Alfonso in alarm.

Fumigi described his studies in mechanics. He had invented a traction engine which saved seventy-five per cent of fuel. He was not quite sure about it yet because he had no means so far of measuring the exact consumption of gas. It was an air-pressure machine.

"I've unfortunately no means . . . that is . . . for measuring. . . . In theory, I'm sure . . ."

Alfonso, who knew nothing about mechanics, asked him, just to show he was taking an interest in what was being said: "Why don't you use a gasometer?"

Fumigi looked at him in amazement.

"I'll try," he muttered. "Do you still go to Signorina Annetta's?"

He pronounced the name with utter indifference.

"Very rarely."

"I don't go any more because I've no time. So much . . . so much to do."

The clock in the square struck nine o'clock. Fumigi counted the nine strokes.

"Nine o'clock already? I must be off."

He put his right hand gently into Alfonso's, then quickly withdrew it and let it drop to his side. No farewell came from his mouth, still busy with that chewing movement, and his thoughts were obviously concentrated on where he was going next; he turned and trotted off toward the sea, crossing the Corso diagonally.

That day Miceni and Alfonso did not quarrel. Shaken, Alfonso asked Miceni what illness Fumigi was suffering from.

"Illness?" asked Miceni in an angry tone. "It's not illness, it's nervous tension from working too hard. He invents machines, as well as working all day long in his office."

"I'm so glad!" said Alfonso sincerely. "Has the doctor assured him he'll recover?"

He longed to be certain that Fumigi's illness was not serious.

"Oh yes, of course!" replied Miceni brusquely.

Reassured, Alfonso said he hoped to see Fumigi very soon again and in good health. He would be warm to him, and try to do all he could to alleviate the sorrows which he himself had helped to bring on the poor little man.

That evening he ran into Prarchi, rushing furiously down the Corso; he stopped him. "Sorry, I've no time!" said Prarchi, trying to pass.

"Just one question. How's Fumigi?"

Prarchi at once forgot he had no time.

"How do you know he's ill?"

"I spoke to him this morning and he seemed very odd."

Prarchi hesitated for a minute, then: "It's true," he confirmed, "I've noticed it too. But I can say nothing yet. He's been in the hands of his family doctor till now and I've only been called by Maller today. I heard some talk of nervous tension and that seems possible. A month ago he was just excited and no more. He'd gone back to his studies suddenly, and when I advised him to rest he answered with an energy I wouldn't have thought him capable of: 'Better die and achieve some result. I'm old and in a hurry.' Who can tell? Perhaps I'm mistaken and it's only a matter of tension, as it's called."

Again Prarchi hesitated. Then resolutely, in a deeply moved tone, he said: "To you I can talk. I wish I were mistaken, but I don't think so. It's progressive paralysis. Please don't mention this to anyone for the moment."

He shook the hand which Alfonso had held out to him before hearing the terrible verdict, and went off at a run.

CHAPTER

XIII

The financial position of the Lanuccis showed no signs of improvement. The old man's business affairs always came to the same end, and Gustavo was without a job for the second time. As poverty increased, so did ill humor, and Alfonso, who was now spending more time at the Mallers' than with the Lanuccis, suffered particularly in their company because he was unused to the asperities that came from need.

When Gustavo came home one day and announced that he had left his job because his boss had insulted him, there was an ugly scene. First the old man praised his son's self-respect and told him he was a real Lanucci. He only changed after his wife observed sadly that the family finances would be the worse for this. At the idea of any increase in poverty, the old man lost all logic and pride. He yelled and cursed, more and more put out by the pert replies of Gustavo, who was trying to protect his own dignity as best he could. In his fury, the old man said that he was sick and tired of bearing the expenses of the whole family all alone. Again and again his wife asked him not to shout. Being more educated, she realized how this scene must disgust Alfonso, and was ashamed of it; but she could find no better way of stopping him than by shouting him down herself. As she grew excited, she became insulting and gave free vent to the bitterness stored up in her heart because of the wretchedness of her life. When the old man, for lack of other arguments, repeated that he was tired of working alone for them all, she lost her temper and said it was not true that he was working for them all and that he scarcely earned enough to keep himself.

This was enough to silence Lanucci; mortified, with bloodless lips and glasses awry (being badly made, they hung over to the right when he forgot to prop them), after a long silence he said gently: "I wasn't saying that to you but to this slacker here. Is it right he should live off us when even Lucia earns her own living?"

Signora Lanucci was touched at once, and Alfonso thought she must be regretting her harsh remarks. But seeing that the old man would still not quiet down, she grew angry again and called imperiously; "Enough, enough!" with a glance towards Alfonso, whose silence she interpreted as ominous. But he was actually silent because, understanding the reasons for those quarrels, he felt touched. Taking the old man's part, he told Signora Lanucci that her husband should be allowed to defend himself. Assured by this that the sight of their

disputes aroused no anger or contempt in Alfonso, she
became gentler, as she would have been from the very
first had she not been more preoccupied about lessening the bad impression on Alfonso than about attack-
ing her husband.

"Enough now!" she repeated. "You, Gustavo, will, I
hope, deign to find yourself another job, so all arguments and quarrels between you and your father will
end. Maybe what is a misfortune for us today can
become luck for us tomorrow. You may be the person
who makes us a bit richer and so a bit nicer."

She shook her husband's hand, and the tears came to
her eyes.

At the beginning of the dispute, Lucia, shouting, had
ostentatiously stopped her ears with her hands, and
hers was the only behavior which disgusted Alfonso.
Had he shown this disgust, Signora Lanucci would
have got no pleasure from his indulgence about the
other matter, for her fear of disgusting him was due to
the fact that she had not abandoned all her hopes for
him and Lucia. She felt that if a young man like
Alfonso entered her family he would reform it, and,
what was more, however much Lucia denied it, she presumed the girl was, must be, in love with him. But
Lucia had different tastes. And she could not see in
Alfonso the virtues which her mother found.

Of course the old woman was not blind, and her
hopes had been diminishing for a long time, but they
were still alive. She had spoken about them to her
daughter just once, when Alfonso began to give her lessons, and her mother's explanations had been enough
to make Lucia put up with that fiend of a teacher
whom they had imposed on her. That showed her intelligence, as did her losing all hope long before her
mother. Struck by some act of indifference on Alfonso's
part, Signora Lanucci would sometimes declare to her

husband that she had lost hope, but even then these were outbursts of anger rather than of disappointment. It would have been so wonderful, and, according to common sense, it was something that not only could happen but should happen; for when two young people, both friendly, are thrown continuously together they inevitably fall in love sooner or later. So the Signora Lanucci's hopes always lived on, only communicated to her husband in low tones and in bed, before they closed their eyes in sleep to dream about them.

She was the first in the Lanucci family to discover that Alfonso was in love with Annetta. She did not know Annetta at all, and had even been ignorant of her existence before she became interested in her because of Alfonso's passion; but she had known of this love almost as soon as Alfonso himself. She noticed his restlessness, his variable moods, and drew conclusions which happened to be right: one that his agitation was due to love, the other that this love was inspired by Annetta Maller. Her hopes were not dashed by this discovery because she rightly thought that Alfonso's passion would bring him many sorrows from which he might take refuge in the ever open arms of Lucia. When Alfonso was still spending a good part of his time with them, she had amused herself by making sly hints in order to learn more, and Alfonso reacted so openly that on indications thus drawn from him she was even able to follow the phases through which the affair passed, the usual ups and downs of love, all strung together by her as: "Hot . . . cold . . . quarrel . . . peace . . . he loves her!"

He loved her, yes, he certainly loved her! She had read it on Alfonso's brow that evening when he returned beaming from a visit to the Mallers', after three days of despair following the Fumigi incident. In those three days she had high hopes; later she was on the verge of despair because Annetta's kiss was almost visible on Alfonso's lips; it had changed his features.

But the morning after, on seeing him sad at breakfast, she at once hoped she had been deceived. She sat down next to him and with an air of affectionate sympathy asked him the reason for his ill-humor and for the sorrows troubling him, to judge from his expression. He replied sadly that he was not well, but when Signora Lanucci, piqued, warned him that ladies of high society were not to be trusted because they enjoyed flattery and flirting but eventually dropped men without a thought, he replied that he had no idea to whom she was alluding because no one was flattering him at all. But he gave a sure, happy smile, like one who knows his own mind, so as she left him she was convinced she had judged right the night before. Annetta had told him she loved him, and perhaps she did. To draw her conclusions, she wanted to wait and hear what was the opinion of old Maller, whose opposition could restore Alfonso to Lucia. She passed on her observations to her husband, with a long preamble intended to prove to him, and at the same time to herself, that Maller would never consent to the marriage of his daughter with a petty clerk.

Lanucci, on the other hand, was delighted to hear of Alfonso's love affair. It was long since he had shared his wife's hopes, and he was now delighted at the idea of a friend of his becoming Maller's son-in-law. He would become the protégé of a highly placed personage, a protection which would be enough to make his business affairs prosper. So, while Signora Lanucci treated Alfonso more coldly, he began to show him deference, and when his wife examined Alfonso's words to try to reinforce her hopes, he would be inquiring what point Alfonso had reached, in the hopes of hearing the good news he was expecting.

Lucia became more friendly with Alfonso too, while before, offended by his complete indifference, she had treated him with affected contempt. Never pretty, she had recently become more attractive; now that the period of growth was over, her mouth seemed smaller and her features more regular; she had good hands and small feet always elegantly shod. A lady-killer or two on the Corso had paid her compliments, which made her resent Alfonso's indifference more strongly. When she was told—for her mother could not keep quiet about it even with her—that Alfonso was in love, she became gentler with him because this love seemed to excuse his behavior to her.

Gustavo was franker. He went straight to Alfonso and asked him, if he became Maller's son-in-law, to get him a job as commissionaire at the bank, where he guessed life was very snug. Gustavo was the only one of the Lanuccis whom Alfonso quite liked. Above all, he preferred his frankness to the falsity of the others, to their allusions, which were always self-interested in some way. He liked Gustavo as a character. Young Lanucci had long since ceased struggling against his own laziness, and to spare himself remorse elevated it to a theory. This had made him so serene that talking to him, and seeing him always calm and content, with no doubts, Alfonso found peace, too. In his long periods of idleness, Gustavo had used his imagination a great deal, and need of money had sparked in him some original and comic ideas. His good humor was unalterable and withstood both the shouting of his "dear parents" (he never omitted the adjective) and the rebukes of his various bosses, to whom he always attributed strange and unfortunate characteristics. "They don't know how to live!" he would say, really surprised at finding them angered by confusion in papers entrusted to him or by some impertinence of his.

"Such men die young" or *"There's* someone I'd never marry."

Macario was away for the whole month of March, and Alfonso took his morning walks with Gustavo, who was an early riser, the only good habit they had managed to instill in him. They took short trips to a hill about half an hour's walk from the town. On reaching it, Alfonso would seek shade and sit down, while Gustavo stretched out in the sun like a cat and, on some theories on hygiene of his own, opened his mouth to let in light and warmth. He was silent for hours, as was Alfonso for completely different reasons. He would keep his eyes shut and fall asleep, or drop off into a kind of nirvana in which he understood nothing, although still stuttering words without sense. When he had money, however little, he did not leave the town, for he preferred sleeping in some café or watching others playing billiards for days on end. He did not play himself, as he did not like to get agitated, and he rarely got drunk, as a night's binge made him feel unwell for a long time after. His friends were sober and hard-working, laborers from the various factories through which he had passed. They had a great liking for him, because he was a good sort and even more because he had never competed with any of them.

In his idleness the good idea occurred to him of taking on a voluntary job, which seemed at first neither difficult nor onerous: to find his sister a husband. He said that marriage was necessary at Lucia's age, and it was certain that if no one bothered she would never find a husband at all. He asked his parents for permission to look around the homes of the young men he knew. His father at once gave him permission, for Lucia's marriage would mean to him the elimination of a mouth at home. The mother, on the other hand, was opposed but could put up no reasons as she did not dare tell him of her hopes in Alfonso. She chewed her nails with impatience and spoke with contempt of Gustavo's workmen friends.

"You don't want her to go to a workman?" asked the old man in surprise. "Who to, then? Are you waiting for a prince?"

It was many years since father and son had got on so well; they leagued together against the poor woman, who, while defending herself as best she could, cursed Alfonso in her heart for not having yet fallen in love with the only girl of his class he had been close to. Eventually she came forth with a good suggestion. Instead of Gustavo's friends, workmen and worse, why not draw to the house Alfonso's friends, who were bank clerks and bookkeepers!

"Those, too!" said the old man approvingly. "But let's have both, so we're more certain of success."

He formally charged Gustavo to bring his friends, the richer the better, to the house.

Meanwhile, Signora Lanucci had occasion to bring up the subject with Alfonso and was somewhat hopeful after their discussion. If the poor wretch, as she called him, had betrayed doubt, disapproval, or the slightest hesitation, she would have found a way of saving Lucia from Gustavo's friends.

Alfonso had got into the habit of withdrawing to his room after lunch in order not to have to listen to the Lanuccis' empty chatter during the half hour he had before going to the office. One day she followed him there. On seeing her, Alfonso, who had already sat down at his desk, got up, and they stood facing each other between desk and bed.

More affectionate than she had been to him for a long time, she said that, as they were now used to considering him as a son, she was asking him a favor, one of those favors one only asks of intimates.

"Yes, tell me!" Alfonso encouraged her kindly.

"I can't just blurt it out but have to explain various things."

She liked talking and, while Alfonso made an effort to listen, began telling him the story of her family, which, she asserted, should have quite a different position from the one it occupied. It was impoverished due to errors on her father's part, a disaster which she exaggerated by describing their former state as higher than it had really been.

"And therefore"—the speech had been prepared and its opening and peroration were pat—"we just cannot resign ourselves to this position, but if we agree to Lucia's marrying a workman or some such"—her disdain seemed to help establish more right to superiority —"it would pin us down once and for all." She went on with another "therefore," while Alfonso had by now lost interest because he feared to find himself suddenly attacked with an offer of marriage. She guessed this from his embarrassed air, but, though she realized that it was really fear and not hope, the proof did not seem sufficient. From the living room came sounds of Gustavo and Lucia quarrelling, and she took a step toward the door to separate the two, but stopped, not wanting to leave Alfonso with any suspicion that she was trying to get him by force. She asked him to bring home some young men, poor or not, but belonging to an intelligent class. So intent was she on observing Alfonso's reaction that she did not even hear the sound of a slap which certainly landed on Lucia's cheek, for Lucia gave herself away by her sobbing and shouting.

"So you want me to bring friends to the house, do you?" Alfonso asked gaily. "But why take such a long way around to ask for such a simple thing? Aren't I, as you yourself say, like a member of the family, and oughtn't I to do as much as I can to help each of you to achieve a little happiness? As soon as I can I'll bring as many friends here as you like."

He was not thinking of any of his friends in particular, but the offer had been made spontaneously, and Signora Lanucci, though pained by his promptness, had to thank him. She would willingly have excused him from the task, but could not decently do so now. She tried at least to lessen his zeal: "There's no hurry. We've all the time we need to do things calmly."

This also induced the old woman to consent to Gustavo's plans too; in fact, she soon began persuading herself that her son's action would bring about Lucia's marriage at once.

"Now it's up to you to do something," she said to Gustavo, "and as soon as possible. That way we may still manage to make someone die of rage." This "someone" was Alfonso.

Gustavo's friends were pretty awful. First he brought along a hawker of secondhand books, rich though. Alfonso, not knowing that Gustavo had been asked to do the same as he, did not realize that this man was a candidate for Lucia's hand. He could never have guessed it. The candidate was about fifty, but looked even older; his skin was parchment-like from the sun and weather to which his job exposed him. His eyes were teary and, not knowing that he was making a fiancé's visit, he had omitted to shave the white and yellowish hairs growing all over his cheeks.

When he left, Signora Lanucci looked laughingly at her husband, and he smiled, too. Gustavo felt offended, and could not resist an urge to defend himself at once.

"He's loaded with money, though," he said. "One never knows a woman's tastes, and it would be a fine bit of luck if Lucia took to him."

The second friend whom Gustavo introduced to the family was the owner of a butcher shop. He was well-to-do and younger than the first one, but no less dirty. He had been a widower for some time and Gustavo thought he was looking for a wife. He was mistaken. The butcher drank too much of the wine on the Lanuccis' table, then, beaming to show gratitude to his new friends, exclaimed: "Ah, it's good here! If only one could always be with friends! Thank heavens, now that I'm a widower, I can allow myself that at last!"

Signora Lanucci declared that she did not want to see him again and even asked that the visits of Gustavo's friends stop. The young man defended himself.

"I can't very well tell my friends to come home with me in order to make them marry my sister. I must choose those who seem most suitable for marriage. A widower like the butcher, for example. He'd already married once!"

It seemed to Alfonso that the men next presented were invited by Gustavo more in order to make a show of having respectable friends than in the hope of seeing them fall in love with his sister. One of these was Signor Rorli, a rich macaroni manufacturer from Naples. Gustavo had long announced his visit, and induced his mother to prepare a copious meal.

Signor Rorli did not come the first evening he was expected and only appeared a week later, after having twice more thrown the little family into confusion by announcing his arrival. He was very young, very thin, with a little pale mustache which just showed against his dark skin. He was well dressed, but over-richly, with rings on his fingers and a gold chain on his chest, which Gustavo said was worth three hundred francs or more. He seemed to enjoy himself. He explained how his macaroni was made and when asked to make old Lanucci a representative of his factory refused, first telling him that they did not work through agents and then that they already had four, two good arguments which naturally destroyed all the old man's hopes. He ate a lot, which gave Signora Lanucci a high opinion of his health, for she said that thin people who eat a great deal are strongest. This appetite of his took up most of the supper, and when Rorli asked her why she did not eat more she answered, with an air of great distinction: "I never eat in the evening."

He took no notice of anything else, as he took no notice of Lucia, who was sitting next to him. He talked mostly with Alfonso, whom Signora Lanucci had introduced as an employee of the Maller bank and a man of letters. Grandeur aggrandizes the house it inhabits.

Rorli now began chatting about literature, and of course about French novels. He was enthusiastic about Alexander Dumas and Paul de Kock, whom Alfonso had forgotten ever admiring. Alfonso cut the worse figure of the two, for after declaring that he knew these writers, he had been unable to show he had read all their works, including some minor volumes which he heard named for the first time, while Rorli was able to describe the whole of their plots to Signora Lanucci, who was enjoying herself thoroughly.

He was, in fact, a great chatterbox and admired by all except Alfonso, who, though realizing the man's ignorance, was impressed by his facility with words. Late in the night, afterwards, he heard from his room the confabulations of the Lanuccis and the old woman declaring that she liked the manufacturer very much.

But Rorli did not appear again. Perhaps he had guessed what was in the air, and when invited by Gustavo excused himself, promised to come, and did not. But Gustavo had achieved a triumph which he boasted of for a long time.

Alfonso, to look as if he was also doing his part, one day brought Miceni with the excuse of showing him his room. Used to greater ease and elegance, Miceni could

not hold back his laughter before those bare walls, that
enormous iron bed, and the little bedside table with a
short leg.

Signora Lanucci made him sit down in the living
room and introduced him to her daughter, whom he
greeted seated, with a slight nod of the head, but in a
friendly manner, used as he was to dealing with seam-
stresses.

He paid her compliments, and chatted away about
things women like. He even admired Lucia's dress and
compared it to one he had seen worn by Signora Can-
cari, one of the richest ladies in town. He was a woman-
chaser for whom every woman was desirable and the
inspiring of desire always a pleasure.

"Shall I suggest he stay for supper?" Signora Lanucci
asked Alfonso in an anguished voice, seeing that the
party was going on too long.

"Do invite him! He won't accept."

Signora Lanucci embarrassedly invited him, warning him at once that the supper was modest but, as
there was enough for five, there would be enough for
six.

Miceni refused with thanks, and realizing that the
family was about to sit down to dinner said good-bye.
He went off accompanied by Alfonso, who was impatient to know what impression Lucia had made on him.
It was flattering, for he had been anything but indifferent.

On the dark wooden stairs that led up to the first
floor, Miceni leaned confidentially on Alfonso's arm
and asked: "Have you had her?"

Alfonso protested indignantly.

"Now don't get angry. If you've never really tried,
that's the only reason you haven't succeeded, in which
case you must admit you're even sillier than I thought
you. A girl of that class, put close to a young man who's

of better class, sooner or later throws herself at his head, unless he shows he rejects her."

It was impossible to be angry, and Alfonso ashamedly excused himself.

"She doesn't attract me!"

"Really?" asked Miceni in surprise. "Then I can only deplore that your taste is not better developed."

When Alfonso returned, the good comments about Miceni wasted by the Lanucci family made a painful impression on him. Lucia, too, let it be understood that she had quite taken to him. Alfonso looked at her to see if she was really so desirable as she had seemed to Miceni. Certainly she was not utterly ugly. Lounging on an armchair made her waist look trim, and her puffed starched skirt improved her thinness.

One evening in April, Alfonso left Annetta's house at ten o'clock and met a breath of winter, a wind sharp as an arrow which had risen only in the last hour or so. It whistled around the deserted streets of the old town and became frenzied where they narrowed. An unexpected guest, it fractured unfixed tiles, tore from roofs everything that was not firmly attached or did not belong there. Cold as Alfonso was, he took with him through the wind the happiness of a kiss stolen from Annetta.

He found the Lanucci family still at supper with a new guest, one Mario Gralli, foreman at a printer's. He was a dark young man with small eyes but a hard proud look which showed him to be quick-witted and tenacious. He was introduced with the usual phrases, and Alfonso, ill-pleased at having to make the acquaintance of the whole neighborhood, treated him coldly. Gralli got up to greet Alfonso, who was rather surprised to find him shorter than he had expected. He was dressed with care, though in cheap materials; the usual yellowish neckband fitted his neck closely, and his cravat, though threadbare, was not soiled and was knotted with a certain care.

He spoke little and evidently unwillingly. He would throw a monosyllable in reply here and there, contenting himself by staring in the face of whoever spoke to him with a fixed but vague look. It was not Alfonso's sort of embarrassment, that of one who wanted to speak and did not know how to, but calculated indifference. He went off shortly after Alfonso's arrival, perhaps bothered by a new face when he had just begun to feel at home with the others. On his getting up, Alfonso thought he saw him drop Lucia's hand, which he was holding under the tablecloth. Had he got so far so soon?

Then he was told that Mario Gralli was the first real aspirant for Lucia's hand. For some time he had been a close friend of Gustavo's, to whom he would give the job of distributing newspapers, which Gustavo liked because, of the five or six hours he spent at the printer's, only one or two were of work. Having so many hours for talking and nothing else to talk about, Gustavo spoke of his plans for his sister's future and of the wish of the family to see her married as soon as possible. One day Lucia was invited by her brother to the printer's to look at the machinery. She was dressed well as always, and Gralli seemed interested at once. He took her to see every machine. As they passed, the workmen rose respectfully to their feet; what Mario liked most about Lucia so far was her getup, while she liked to see him surrounded with such respect. So it was that the two found each other.

Gralli earned a good living and, as the girl was pleased, her parents could find no objection. Anyway, they had not been asked, because Gralli had declared to Gustavo that he could not formulate his request officially so soon, not within a year. He never in fact talked directly to the parents at all, but always through Gustavo. He got him to explain to them that his position was not yet secure enough because he had obtained it as a result of the sudden death of a superior and he did not know if he would be permanently appointed. Gustavo added on his own the observation that it did not seem decent to insist on Mario making his request at once.

All this was described to Alfonso by Signora Lanucci. That same evening, with a gay air, she told him how pleased they were with it, for she had always loved literature and a printer's seemed to her very close to it. She went up to him again in the morning as he was about to leave. At first, with the same air as the night before, and like a person really with happy news, she said: "It means some light for us at last."

Suddenly she changed. She spoke of the great care required in such a matter, and, once she began complaining, went on to say that she did not like having to trust herself to Gustavo's judgment. Eventually she began to sob desperately, declaring that she never thought she would have to hand over her daughter to someone she did not know. She had spent a bad night and her pale fat features were discomposed; tumbled white hair added to her suffering look.

Alfonso tried to calm her by saying that Gralli had made an excellent impression on him.

Still weeping, she assured him that she liked Lucia's future husband too, and added that she knew she was wrong to cry, as crying was a bad omen. But she was suffering too much and must confess the hopes she had nurtured in him since he had entered their home; she could tell him now because her confidence could not possibly be misunderstood. Her sincerity surprised Alfonso. But she lied, Alfonso suspected, when she went on to say that Lucia had known nothing of her hopes. With touching sincerity she explained the reasons why she had hoped to see him fall in love with Lucia.

"I knew you. I'd have felt sure that even if things went badly with you both, you yourself would always have found patience enough to treat your wife gently. And when there are two, I figured, one is never really unhappy!"

Alfonso was not embarrassed about his attitude. More than once he had felt a desire, a very platonic desire, to make this poor old woman happy, and now he thought it right to pretend that he was sorry to be no longer able to do what he would not have done anyway.

"A lovely dream, yes, indeed!" said Alfonso. "But it could never have been realized, as my position is even more wretched and uncertain than Gralli's. I'm penniless."

When he was alone, he thought of Signora Lanucci's sorrow. Amid her misfortunes, the poor woman had pinned all her hopes on her daughter's future, and this had made her meeker and happier. Now her hopes were dying. Her daughter was to have the same destiny as herself. She would be surrounded by a poverty-stricken family in no way better off than the one she was leaving.

"Signorina," said Alfonso seriously to Lucia that evening, "I want to be the first to congratulate you, and do so at once."

Lucia thanked him ceremoniously.

"There's nothing to congratulate me on yet, as Mario hasn't made his request officially." She was already calling him by his Christian name. "But from you I can accept congratulations beforehand."

In the evening Alfonso fell asleep unusually early, after enduring for two hours the mortal boredom of the

Lanuccis' and of Gralli's company. It pained him to see the future husband so lacking in wit or ideas; but he realized that the mother, too, suffered because of this, as he realized that Lucia did not notice and liked her future husband so, dignifiedly mute.

Alfonso drew the covers up to his chin and at the conclusion of a long reflection on human destiny murmured: "Man should be able to live twice; once for himself and once for others."

If he'd had two lives, he thought, he would dedicate one to the Lanuccis' happiness.

CHAPTER

XIV

One evening Annetta announced to Alfonso that her brother Federico was to arrive a few days later. She was warning him beforehand so that he should be ready to behave as prudently as possible. Federico was devoted to her and while he was in town would be unlikely ever to leave her side. So Alfonso was to be very careful, because to arouse the slightest suspicion in Federico would mean their having to stop seeing each other.

Alfonso promised all that she asked him. That evening she had allowed him much, and he wanted to be equally yielding; he even asked if she would prefer that he suspend his visits during that time and declared himself ready to agree. She did not ask as much as that, because such a sudden interruption might itself arouse suspicion. She did not find it necessary to say that she would be sorry not to see him all that time.

In a way, Alfonso and Annetta's relations had become less affectionate. She had never told him that she loved him. He had let himself say so, but even he no longer felt a need to repeat it, nor did she notice the omission. It seemed because of this that their bearing had become franker and that they had a tacit agreement which did not really exist; for Alfonso was still hoping for something else and had realized, regretfully, that the road he was taking could lead to the conquest of a paramour but not of a mistress or a wife.

In other people's presence he had an air of a suitor, launching glances, paying compliments, or asking to be alone with her for a second to say a word. When they were alone at last, she would tell him with a smile that he sometimes thought faintly ironical that he could speak. Without opening his mouth, he would draw her to him and kiss her frantically. She defended herself at a certain point, but with the calm energy of self-confidence. After Alfonso became more prudent in the presence of those whose suspicions Annetta feared, they never had a dispute. She almost seemed readier to become his mistress than his wife; his behavior angered her in public, not when they were alone.

When Alfonso was told in the office of Federico's arrival, the news produced in him a strange impression of alarm. Gradually he had won the friendship of all those who frequented the Mallers'. It had been a slow and difficult conquest, which seemed to have succeeded mainly by luck, through Macario's gift of his esteem, rather than through the respect accorded him by that little ignoramus Annetta. Now someone new inter-

vened, a person used to deciding according to
unknown criteria. He was to be feared since Annetta
feared him on Alfonso's account. Federico was certainly
a man of ambition who would start by despising him.

That evening he did not go to Annetta's; he did not
want to show himself too soon. By next evening it
seemed a century since he had seen her, and he went to
call at the Mallers', ingenuously thinking that it must
seem so to others, too.

He found only Francesca, and made a face, as if finding a liquid bitter after swallowing it. Francesca understood.

"For just one evening," she said to him with a smile,
"you must put up with talking to me about Annetta.
She's had to go out with Signor Federico. Now listen!
Tell me something about your relations with Annetta."
She waited in silence for him to speak, while he
remained mute, surprised by the strange preamble
which Francesca seemed to be hoping would draw confidences from him.

"I thought you'd like to talk about Annetta, and you
can with me, since, as I hope you've realized, I'm her
confidante." She tried to give him a proof that she
knew all. "But never do that on the landing again!" she
said with a laugh, threatening with a white hand, her
best feature. She was alluding to the embrace which
long ago Alfonso had stolen from Annetta on the landing.

This proof that she had given was enough, particularly because he felt a strong need to talk about Annetta and complain about her. So he said that he was
not at all satisfied with his relations with Annetta, as
Francesca called them: Annetta was not what he had
hoped.

"You've really no reason for complaining," observed

Francesca in a tone which sounded ironical to him. "You don't seem to appreciate your good luck as much as you should."

He did appreciate his good luck as he should, but it did not seem to him very great. He asked Francesca to tell him the exact terms used by Annetta in her confidences; he wanted to hear if she had spoken of love on that occasion at least. Francesca asserted that she could not remember and so could not do as he asked.

"Do you know," Alfonso said very seriously, "that she's never told me she loved me. I really don't know if Annetta loves me or scorns me."

Francesca seemed about to laugh at Alfonso's confidence, then became very serious and let drop a thought spoken aloud: "All the Mallers are like that. Coldness is a family characteristic."

Alfonso did not forget this phrase, which seemed to him a confirmation of the rumors about Francesca and her relations with Maller. Who else in the family could she have known to be cold in love?

"But this much is certain," went on Francesca, "Annetta is not making fun of you, and I can say that I've never seen her as she is now." Then she changed the subject, apparently wanting Alfonso, too, to consider her as a kind of attentive governess. "If I don't tell Maller all about it, as is my duty, it's because I trust your honesty of character, and Annetta's." But she warned him not to flatter himself too much about Annetta's love, which, she hinted, could suddenly die. It was the first love affair of the kind she had had, but its conclusion could be foreseen, and again Alfonso thought he noticed something bitter in her smile.

"I never flatter myself nowadays, I know it's only a joke." He was playing the strong man, but speaking with difficulty.

Francesca exclaimed with maternal compassion: "Is this not a moment for you to return home? Haven't you realized yet that this city is not for you?"

"Why?" asked Alfonso, touched at this sympathy.

"If you don't understand, I can't explain. I'd willingly live in the country too, and would give much, oh so much, never to have left your village, which is our village, isn't it?"

They looked at each other with sudden tenderness. The similarity of their fates drew them together and stirred them.

Francesca said she wanted to give him some advice and asked him to listen and follow it as if it came from his mother. This preamble made Alfonso very hopeful and he was greatly disappointed when she merely said that she could not understand why he went on worrying his head about Annetta, when he was bound to recognize in the end that it took quite other arts than his to infuse life and passion into such a statue. She advised him to behave exactly as Annetta asked him to, coldly.

Was this her great piece of advice? It was advice already given by Annetta herself though not in the same words; and he presumed it was being repeated by her desire. Perhaps Francesca took her duties as chaperone more seriously than he had thought till then, and was telling him this in order to lessen the danger threatening Annetta.

When saying good-bye, Francesca's language changed and she said two or three short phrases whose importance he did not at once understand.

"Can't you see that caresses not followed up destroy any influence over us women on the part of the men who give them? All that kissing! Just the way to get no further!"

She gave him a searching look to see if he had understood, and, winking to explain what she had said, sketched a smile; an accomplice's smile.

This was her advice! He had not fully grasped it yet, but already realized that his suppositions about Francesca's intentions were mistaken. This amazed him! Perhaps these last words had been pronounced thoughtlessly, but it was more likely that all her others had been said to mask these last and give the impression of a person only making a mistake in language. That had been betrayed by her diffident searching glance and sly smile. He had been given advice, and its purpose was obviously not to draw him away from Annetta but to show him a way of winning her.

He was not being advised to pursue a course entirely new to him; and this reminded him of a pretense of coldness which Annetta had wanted to give the hero of their novel, which she said would overcome their heroine's hesitations. It was just the sort of coldness suggested by Francesca. The advice was good. It would be pleasant to follow it because, even if it did not lead him to the victory foreseen by Francesca, he did at least hope to achieve what he wanted, the conquest of Annetta's affections. At once he began hoping to achieve more by the behavior suggested than by the aggressive one he had followed so far. For a long time the pleasure of being able to hug and kiss Annetta had not compared to his bitterness at her brusque word or cold greeting. The mere intention of his assuming such a bearing reduced his nervous tension and released him from the daily struggle in which he had been engaged for a year, a struggle always with the same result, neither victory nor definite defeat.

It was a long time before he could put his intention into action.

He was introduced to Federico Maller. He had al-

ready seen him at other times and from a distance, in
the street, and thought him a handsome and elegant
young man. Fair, tall, slim, with a thin oval face and
big, gentle, intensely blue eyes, he had an aristocratic
and slightly effeminate appearance. Close to, on the
other hand, his eyes lost their gentleness because they
were restless and set in dark parchment-like skin; wrin-
kles seemed already forming on the youthful face, its
feminine aspect now not unlike a virago's. Thin hair
was carefully arranged to seem thicker.

Alfonso's disillusion was increased by the brusque
way Federico treated him. After being introduced,
Federico asked if he was happy working at his father's
and, expecting a hymn in praise of the Maller bank,
was not too pleased at Alfonso's stuttered reply. Alfonso, realizing he had already made a blunder, lost his
power of speech, and because of Federico that evening
was very like his first evening at the Mallers'.

On his way out, he met Annetta in the passage.

"I'm very pleased with you," she said, with a warm
handshake. She wanted to reward him for his quiet
bearing, which she thought must be due to her instructions. He tried to draw her to him, but she escaped
with a cry of alarm and from safety threatened him
with a hand, saying: "Incorrigible!"

He went off feeling sore at not having shown ease
with Federico and strength of will with Annetta. She
had her own reasons to be pleased with him and those
had prevented her noticing how awkward he had been
that evening! As for the mistake with Federico, he
soothed himself by thinking it was not of much importance. Before meeting him, he had often thought of
those aristocratic features and imagined them intervening decisively in his favor. Now he realized that none
of the Mallers would take a step toward him of their

own accord; so he turned to considering Francesca's plan more keenly.

It was difficult to show more coldness than Annetta required of him during Federico's stay in town. When they were alone, there was no time for Alfonso to screw himself up to a pretense of coldness, and a look or a sweet word immediately led him to advances which it took time to regret.

In compensation, Alfonso had no reason to complain of Federico, who after that first evening treated him with aristocratic chill, but not brusquely. Shortly after his arrival, Annetta asked Alfonso to make her brother think they had stopped working on the novel. It had been mentioned to Federico, and he had apparently shown no pleasure at their collaboration.

One evening, with a smile intended to be friendly, he asked Alfonso: "And whyever isn't that novel finished yet?"

"It's not my fault. One fine day Signorina Annetta took a dislike to the plot and dropped it all. Maybe she will start again one day."

Federico spoke against collaboration. A book could not be good done in halves, and even if it did turn out well, that would be a sign that each of the two collaborators could do better by himself.

Alfonso did not feel up to a discussion.

"It all depends on circumstances and temperaments, I think," he said modestly.

The two never became friendly. Alfonso felt particularly irritated by the way Federico never listened and only took an interest in what concerned his own little self or might show it in a better light. It occurred to him that even this aristocratic personage must be little used to society and its effects, to accepting its yoke, for the first result of constantly rubbing shoulders with equals, particularly if they are intelligent, is learning to put up with the boring ideas of others. This defect of Federico's was alone enough to divide the two men, for Alfonso—due to his literary ambitions—expected to be listened to with attention at times. He suspected that Federico only behaved like that in his company out of contempt.

Even after recognizing that there was no possibility of making friends with Federico, from time to time he made attempts, whose only result was disappointment. On the last evening spent by Alfonso with Annetta's brother, in his joy at seeing him depart, he put himself out to be courteous and said sweetly as he shook hands: "*Au revoir*, Signor Federico!"

Federico gave him a look of impertinent surprise, not at all flattered by any courtesy from one of his father's clerks. Then he bowed politely back but only said "good night," which was too little not to be rude in reply to Alfonso's friendly remark.

Even after Federico's departure Alfonso could not act as coldly toward Annetta as he had intended. Free once again, alone with her, he felt so pleased at returning to their former relations that he was unable to renounce that happiness voluntarily. A warning hint by Francesca was not enough to fortify his resolution. She must have been quite put out at seeing him unchanged, for one day when he could not guess the answer to a conundrum, she said: "You're less intelligent than I thought."

She smiled at him to tone down her insolence; but her voice was trembling with anger or impatience, something violent, scarce restrained, so that he realized her real meaning to be quite apart from the conundrum. A short time before, she had surprised him very close to Annetta, his face scarlet while hers had been pink and calm; at the time he remembered thinking that Francesca would object to his attitude. He blushed and felt ashamed.

Francesca's insistence in reminding him of her advice eventually put him in fear of her as if she had a right to reprove him. He avoided her, and from weakness, not on purpose, in front of her he treated Annetta coldly as if to make Francesca believe he had finally taken her advice. But Francesca had considerable powers of observation, and the disdain did not leave her pale face.

When, however, he did happen by chance to adopt her system, she was the first to notice it, even before Annetta herself, and by her expression showed Alfonso her approval when he did not even know he deserved it.

Alfonso, grinding his teeth with rage, had sworn revenge on Annetta for some offensive remark. One evening she had been colder to him than usual, had concentrated only on Macario, who had been making some quite successful jokes, and taken no notice of him at all, which was enough to arouse jealousy in his lover's heart; he made some excuse to stay even after Macario had left, though Annetta always insisted on his being very careful before Macario. As soon as he was alone with her, he tried to pull her to him, but she resisted firmly and said contemptuously: "All this constant kissing's a bore."

It was a very offensive phrase. By it Annetta laid bare the ridiculous side of their relationship, which he had already felt, and was withdrawing from it, leaving all its weight on his shoulders. Thus he was faced with someone who could deride him, Annetta herself.

It was then that he decided to follow Francesca's advice, for revenge first of all. He wanted to thrust those words down Annetta's throat and show her that if there was anything ridiculous in their relationship it was not his fault alone. Oh, he was convinced she needed him, needed their relationship and in the very

form she had wanted to deride. Obviously Francesca
was of this opinion, too. This gave him great confidence; without her approval, though convinced himself,
he would never have had the confidence or resolution
necessary to act.

Then, once set on his line of action, he felt all right.
His anger had soon vanished, but he kept up the bearing dictated. Annetta, on noticing the effect produced
by her words, had at once become sweet and was trying, he thought, to make him forget them. The first evening she had no surprises. He was as she had wanted
him to be; and when he went off with a cold shake of
her hand, she merely gave an ironical smile. She did
not consider that the lesson she had given him would
last for long, and wanted him to think, or thought herself, that she was the first to hope she was wrong. He
had been pleasant with some difficulty; it was not
easy for him to recapture that tone of friendly courtesy
with Annetta which he had long ago exchanged for one
of passion, put on with an effort when it did not come
spontaneously.

Very soon he ran into greater difficulties. To pursue
his act he needed to find some subject of conversation
which would take him through an evening in Annetta's company without her feeling bored or his showing if (as he was resigned to being) he was bored himself. Till then he had relied on little snares laid for
Annetta to fill up all the time; the nervous tension they
produced excluded boredom. They had stopped working on the novel long since, and what they had told
Federico only remained a lie because, on being alone
together again, Annetta never omitted to lay out writing materials. Between them they always went on putting up a show of intending to continue the work.

"Shall we get to work?" he asked Annetta.

She approved, but as he wanted to begin writing at

once, she had to look for a pen. Their show of wanting to work needed paper and ink only, not pens. He
flung himself with great zeal into the novel because he
longed to distract himself with other ideas and not
have to make efforts at indifference. Once again, they
got a little done; further progress would have meant
their re-reading the whole novel, some parts of which
they had forgotten. It was so new for Alfonso to be
alone with her, and close without threatening to pounce,
that Annetta mistook one of his movements for an attack, and having made to defend herself, blushed on
finding it was a false alarm. He realized her embarrassment, and that time had to make a tremendous effort not to help her out of a humiliation which he felt
as if it were his own. But he resisted, and that whole
evening Annetta remained embarrassed, less at ease
than usual; Francesca, who sat down at her usual loom
shortly afterward gave a slight smile of satisfaction deliberately so that it might be seen by Alfonso.

Instead of wasting time uselessly re-reading the novel,
Alfonso suggested, and Annetta agreed, that they
should correct it together, examine it phrase by phrase
and then just bring it to a close. It was boring work,
but less dangerous for the literary relationship between
the two collaborators because neither had any very developed sense of language, and Alfonso, though he
would have preferred a slightly more sober tone, easily
adapted himself to Annetta's taste. Having already
made other concessions to it, he realized that a book
with such a plot could only be dressed up in clothes of
the same showy melodramatic taste.

Annetta must have given a good deal of thought to
Alfonso's unusual bearing, for the following evening he
found her calm and serene, still friendly, with a certain
air of smiling superiority which rather suited her. Anyone seeing them together then would have said they had

come to a tacit agreement to be good friends and nothing more, and even that Alfonso had become timid. Ah! Actually he was already experiencing tortures of despair, regretting those evenings prior to the advice to be astute. It was a bad sign that she bore him no grudge. He had not hoped to hear reproof, but neither had he thought that she could show such indifference so soon. The only thing that still made him doubt the sincerity of her coldness was the fact that she never gave him a word of praise for his finally behaving as she had said she wished. Praise for this was due him, and she showed a lack of her vaunted cold reasoning by not having given it. She never mentioned Alfonso's new bearing but tried to show she had not noticed it; and it was this silence which induced Alfonso to persevere.

One evening, a week later, she accompanied him as far as the living-room door and then hurriedly withdrew with a ceremonious little bow. He had behaved badly! Already cold and tired for lack of stimulus, he had not bothered to lavish on Annetta the many other attentions which he realized he should if he were not to alienate her completely. He had omitted to show himself in love! His part, as he had said from the very beginning (and it had only been from inertia that he had not made better use of it) his part should always be that of a sensible lover contented with a look or a handshake, yet always obviously in love.

He felt very troubled until he saw her again. He feared her giving him, in some form or other, the dismissal which he had once feared as a result of his daring; not having been dismissed for that reason, he might possibly be for this. He felt himself to be in a bad state, and in his mind blamed Francesca and her advice. He thought of going to Annetta and asking her forgiveness by telling her why he had been behaving this way. He did not feel he was to blame and would convince her that he was not; he might even make her sweeter and more yielding by telling her that he had merely imitated the astuteness of their own hero. It was an easy excuse and a way of gathering fruit from the coldness forced on himself for those few days.

He understood from Annetta's reserved but friendly manner that the danger he feared was more distant than he thought, and her reserve made him pursue in spite of himself, from timidity, the attitude he had decided to drop. He spent a very pleasant evening. As always, he only had to emerge from his uncertainty or fear in order to have the sight of Annetta be an immense happiness. The pleasantness of the evening staved off his agitation, always ready as he was to fling his arms around Annetta's neck and return to that subject position which had so many joys to offer. It took no effort to remember that Annetta always needed courting. He loved her, at least for that evening, as he had not loved her since the day he had dared to kiss her for the first time on the lips. Such trepidations increase desire. He spoke better than usual and hazarded allusions to his love as if he had not already made his declaration at other times. He found he had leaped back again to a freshness of impression as if to something entirely new, and Annetta listened and smiled. Never had she seemed so yielding. At other times she had let herself be embraced while now she accorded only words and looks, but before, when conceding these, she had always seemed to regret her own incapacity to resist, while now she gave promptly what was asked and more.

Of course, he was at once reconciled to Francesca's advice and regained the energy he had after Annetta took offense. Holding a monologue, as he always did when agitated, he told himself happily that in his able hands Annetta was becoming soft wax, which he could shape as he liked. At the thought, he moved his fingers as if he had the wax in his hands.

Annetta still had her air of superiority, and her frankness of speech, which at times sounded imperious. Actually, this superiority no longer existed, and the difference in her bearing now showed visibly before other people; he was always the one of whom she took most notice. Even in such discussions as they still had about the novel he was always victorious, though he cared so little about it.

He did not know if he could nourish any great hopes, from these changes, of bringing their relationship back to the point it had reached before, and this time with Annetta's explicit consent. From one day to another he put off that step which he had to take sooner or later and which would definitely show the results obtained; but a week later, he was no longer thinking of taking it because he felt all right as he was. He had hoped to speak words of love, but to ask for them would have been silly and equivalent to a retreat.

They spent whole hours side by side, never talking of love and yet both their voices and ways as sweet as if they were. She would even interrupt phrases she had begun, because she cared little about finishing them, and he had no curiosity to hear them now that he realized that really she had nothing to say to him. Eventually she found herself in the state of mind in which he had been so often himself. She loved, or at least desired, him.

Often, very often since intervening as adviser, Francesca was present at their meetings, which was the main reason why the two lovers stayed in their respective places.

In his happiness he wanted to show his gratitude to her to whom he thought this happiness was due. He forgot the way in which the advice had been given, and with the frankness of one carrying out a dutiful action he said to Francesca as he shook her hand: "Thank you, thank you."

"What for?" asked Francesca disdainfully. Then, when he withdrew in alarm, thinking that Francesca was annoyed because she took those thanks as an accusation of a complicity, which she did not want to admit, she burst out: "If you twitter away like doves, it's not my fault!"

Once again she was discontented with him and thought he had not understood her advice properly. This annoyed him because he did not feel like laying any traps for Annetta for the moment. He said to himself that Francesca was mistaken in thinking that he would dare anything new to please her when he felt so content as he was. In a matter of such importance he wanted to hold his own opinion.

His own opinion? Later on, he would not dare assert that things took the turn they did by his own wish.

The fact is that his coldness, calculated to stir Annetta, had reacted on himself. His senses had been agitated by promises never kept but repeated at each of their meetings. Before, in his attempts to steal a caress or a kiss, his mind had been kept constantly riveted toward a goal, and once this aim was reached, his senses were soothed in a satisfaction that, though relative, was what they sought. Now, on the other hand, he lacked both activity and satisfaction, and in his inertia he analyzed his own desires and made them more acute. These, of course, had become stronger for other reasons, too. He believed now that Annetta felt the same desire as himself, and when he thought that only will and daring were needed for their desires to meet, the idea of such happiness being so near made his head spin. His dreams were taking on more and more reality. He knew or thought he knew Annetta's look or

sound of voice when she was moved by love for him.
One evening he tried to pull her to him with a rough
gesture. She escaped from his embrace with a cry of
alarm. Why her sudden alarm? Did she know what he
wanted before he did himself?

When Francesca was present, Alfonso talked a lot
about matters indifferent to him. Annetta, he realized,
was following the sound of his voice with real vivacity;
Macario thought her incapable of that, and here she
was showing it to Alfonso. But this sensation did not
seem linked to his actual words.

And yet, though he was acting with a morbid sense
of exaltation which made him live in a continual dream
for days on end, he was calculating coldly, like someone conscious of what he wanted.

He waited impatiently for Francesca to be away,
but her leaving the library was not enough; she must
be outside the house. She was the only person who
could disturb him, and he wanted to feel reassured
about her. He controlled himself for one or two evenings and, red with impatience, observed every movement of Francesca's as she left the room frequently,
only to return at once. She was behind all this, he
thought afterward. Finding him incapable of being cold
as she had advised, she was forcing him to keep within
certain limits by her continual presence, and the behavior thus imposed on him had already been enough
to take him where she wanted.

One evening he appeared unexpectedly. They had
arranged not to see each other that day, but after a
long struggle he had been unable to stay away. The
two women had said they wanted to go out if the
weather were good, and now it had been overcast for
some hours, so they had probably given up their outing.

On the stairs he met Francesca going out alone. She
greeted him more politely than usual and, looking him

in the eyes with that scrutinizing gaze she used when she deigned to fix her eyes on anything, said that she was surprised to see him, and then with an air of frankness asked if Annetta had invited him when they had been left alone the evening before. The unexpected question embarrassed Alfonso, and he could think of no better way out than to pretend he could not remember arranging with Annetta for them not to see each other that day. So he let her think that Annetta had given him an appointment without her knowledge.

"Annetta's waiting for you in the library," said Francesca, more drily after learning what she wanted, and went on down the stairs. "I'll be back in half an hour," she said again.

Alfonso's legs trembled as he went up. Would he screw up courage to do what he intended in half an hour? The action itself agitated him less than the thought of compressing it into so short a time.

"Alone at last!" he said, and as soon as he entered, he drew her toward him, but not violently, rather as if he wanted to shake hands.

She dropped her head on his chest and, in rebuke for the position he put her in, said seriously but in a voice too calm and steady to be natural: "We were alone quite recently."

"Forgive me," stuttered Alfonso. He did not want to be stirred more and kissed her gently on the eyes, calculating how far this abandon of hers could take him.

The library was lit only by an oil lamp on the table, and its light, enclosed in its shade, projected itself around in a wide hoop on the green tablecloth and in a strip of light running down toward the floor. The austerity of that room made it a good place for love, amid simple black cupboards and serious books with broad backs and gold lettering. The contradiction spurred Alfonso's desire. Some large, roughly bound volumes, perhaps collections of newspapers, piled up in a corner emanated a strong smell of glue.

Holding her by a hand, he drew her out of the light. Seeing him so calm, she had no suspicions and sat down next to him on the ottoman. They had been like that at other times, sitting next to each other or embracing in the same place. He felt a regret that she was sitting by chance where the sofa had no back. But still he was uncertain. He pressed her backward, hugging her tightly. He wanted to find out how she would resist and seemed to be asking a timid but clear question; if Annetta did not react, he could then refer to that question as an excuse. Out of cowardice he also murmured: "May I . . . ?" but so faintly that he could not know if she had heard. It was this that warned Annetta of her danger. She begged and threatened him, but in gentle tones, and defended herself, though, with arms so loosely crossed on her breast that they prevented nothing. But he had expected no resistance at all and, weak as it was, it annoyed him. Brusquely, hurriedly, brutally, he forced her into what seemed a betrayal, a theft.

On coming to himself, he again noticed the strong smell of glue permeating that room, to which he seemed to be returning after a long absence. She said the first words: "My God, what have we done?" They rang of surprise and despair. She looked at the objects around him as if hoping they would call her back from what she hoped was a dream. The disorder of her dress, which she was only now trying to settle, confirmed that she was in her senses. She got up, not without dignity, called all her forces to her aid, but could find no refuge, or even a suitable attitude to adopt. Then she regained control of herself, silently dried her tears, and moved up to the table away from him.

It was his duty to try to console her, he realized. He went up to her and kissed her on the forehead. It was a duty, but apart from that action, he could think of nothing else. What was he to say?

She let him be, but again sorrow overwhelmed her, and once more she wept and repeated her desperate phrase. She did not say a word of reproof, which showed that in the circumstances she was relatively cool. He himself had nothing to regret, because he had done what he had aimed to do for a long time and which she knew to be his goal.

Finally Alfonso found words. He said he loved her, would have given his life for that moment, and so could not regret his action.

She, allowing herself to be embraced, cried: "Yes, but we'll never see each other again, never again!"

Then for a second his lucidity clouded. She did not understand that the step taken was irrevocable, and seemed to think it could be cancelled by that exclamation!

"As you wish!" cried Alfonso ingenuously.

He felt ill at ease with this weeping girl, and had he not feared to displease her would have left at once, maybe even promising never to return. He was surprised to feel so calm and so far from the desire which had led him to such risky action ten minutes before.

Francesca returned, and at once guessed what had happened, since Annetta was not yet in a state to hide it or even to try. Her eyes were red with weeping and she was staring obstinately into a void, forcing herself to think. On her side, Francesca asked nothing and gave no occasion for lies. Alfonso, in his embarrassment, tried to leave. Francesca said good-bye with a shake of the head and a friendly, even respectful bow.

"Virtue has its own reward!" she seemed to be saying.

On the landing he was stopped by Annetta, who had run after him on the spur of the moment.

"Here, here," she said harshly, "I must speak to you."

Certainly the tone of her voice did not reveal that these words were any invitation to a night of love, and he realized afterward that she had not intended them to be. In the utter darkness, motionless in the middle of the room, not daring even to sit down for fear of making a noise, he was assailed by strange thoughts. Some drama was being prepared for him, the scene of a penitent girl; he resolved to put up with it all resignedly. He knew he deserved all Annetta's possible reproofs.

Instead, she came toward him, her eyes without a trace of tears. She had paused at the door with a finger to her lips, listening for any movement in the passage, smiling like a boy hiding from someone as a game; and the sight of her thus was enough to take away all Alfonso's fears. He had already understood; once more her senses had won.

She was an obliging, passionate lover. She asked him to forgive the brusque words she had uttered a short time before.

"I did think all that, but realize now it was silly of me."

Without his being able to guess her thought processes she then gave him her definition of life. Life was when he kissed her; nothing else was worth a thing. She was expressly renouncing all else for his kiss, he thought. As he kissed her to show his gratitude, it occurred to him that she must despise him if she considered herself to have lost the right to all other happiness by giving herself to him. She repeated her declaration a number of times during the night, varying its form. "What, marry that logician, my cousin Macario, because he's rich!"

She smiled at such a notion, which somebody must have had.

Alfonso's happiness, if it existed, was diminished by a fear. Had this woman whose feelings and opinions had changed in a single hour maybe gone off her head? He felt himself reasoning as usual, calm, pulled along by his senses for short periods, then satiated, and he could not imagine that in others emotion could always be maintained with equal intensity.

Only once, with a quick change of mood, did she give an impression of sadness, even of despair, the way she had an hour before. She mentioned a noble family with whom the Mallers had recently come to be on visiting terms. It was only for a second, then she made every effort to forget it and make it stay forgotten.

The pink curtain on the window had become visible in the first ray of dawn and, although little light yet filtered from outside, it paled that of the candles they had left alight.

"Already!" exclaimed Annetta, snuggling closer.

Hypocritically he repeated the same word.

From the floor above was heard the sound of bare feet.

"Poor woman!" murmured Annetta. "I caused her such great distress."

"Is that Francesca?" asked Alfonso in disquiet.

"Yes," said Annetta smiling. "But it can all be put right!"

She embraced him to show that the good work she intended doing was due to him.

He had time for curiosity now, and Annetta told him that Francesca had been the mistress of Maller, who had intended to marry her. "When I heard, I laughed in Francesca's face and opposed it . . . of course . . . it seemed an offense to my mother's memory." Her father had managed never to exchange a word on this subject with his daughter. Only when Annetta advised Francesca to leave their house did Maller openly oppose it. Relations between father and daughter were cold for some time and only improved when Francesca swore to Annetta that there was no longer anything between her and Maller. Till that night Annetta had believed this. "I bet they're deceiving me," she thought aloud and quite calmly. "Of course in love there's no such thing as deceit."

At four in the morning she got up to accompany him to the door.

In the dark hall she flung her arms around his neck again and told him they would not see each other again until they could do so in the full light of day. That was to come about as soon as possible. She began to laugh, and with frank sensuality added: "We'll have lots of days and lots of nights together!"

He stood outside watching her efforts to turn the key in the lock; then he heard the slow heavy drag of her slippers on the stairs.

"Good-bye!" he cried, moved.

"Good-bye, good-bye!" replied Annetta in a low voice.

In that greeting she had put all the affection she could, and he guessed she had blown him kisses with her hand.

As he was moving hurriedly homeward, he heard himself called. He turned. A white figure from the window of Annetta's room was waving him greetings with a white handkerchief. He jerked his hat about in reply. The gesture was forced, but he lacked the corresponding sensation. The sight of Annetta at the window reminded him that that was the customary procedure in the game of love.

Then he tried to feel as happy as his good luck deserved, and hummed a tune which did not sound particularly gay in the empty streets faintly lit by an invisible sun in a lilac sky. Deep unease made him silent. His rationalization was that he still had doubts about his future relations with Annetta; even after that night such doubts had not left him. But Annetta was his! Was not that a great deal, so much that he should feel the happiest man on earth? He had long desired, loved Annetta. It must be lack of sleep and exhaustion that had taken away the enjoyment of his happiness, and as he went up the slope toward the Lanuccis' he tried to persuade himself that next day he would wake up full of love and longing to see Annetta again.

He got into bed and fell asleep as soon as he put his head on the pillow.

CHAPTER

XV

But on waking he found himself with the same malaise. As he went over in his thoughts all the events of the night before, his revulsion grew. He disliked everything about the evening, from his first stolen embrace to that last greeting which he had answered by forcing himself to a pretense that had been an effort, however easy. He did not want to face up to the conclusion which he should evidently draw from this feeling; in spite of all his delight in possessing Annetta, he disliked the way he had won her. He did not believe Annetta loved him; she was bowing to the irrevocable.

Some time before, Macario had told him that he considered him incapable of fighting and seizing his prey; at that time he had gloried in this criticism as if it were praise. Now he had shown that Macario was mistaken.

He looked with quite different eyes at his little room, gay with a sunray, the only one of the day that penetrated it at that hour. He had spent some happy hours there! It had been a strange happiness, continuously finding sops to his pride by seeking weaknesses in others from which he was immune himself, by watching others struggling for money and honors while he remained calm, satisfied by the sense of talent burgeoning in his brain, by a sweeter emotion in his heart than falls to the lot of most human beings. He understood and pitied the weakness of others and felt all the prouder of his own superiority to them. When he entered the library or his own little room, he moved completely out of the struggle; no one contested his happiness, he asked nothing of anyone. Now, on the other hand, the struggling people whom he despised had drawn him into their midst and without putting up any resistance he had felt the same desires as they, adopted their weapons.

He wanted to combat his own disgust, which, when attributed to the reasons which he obstinately gave for it, was utterly unreasonable. As he dressed, he thought that if he had heard such a story about anyone else he would have laughed. He had entered the struggle because he had never allowed himself entirely to leave it; even the modest happiness he asked had never been accorded wholly. Oh come! Surely this victory of his did give him liberty! Even though his affection for Annetta was not what it should be—as in parenthesis he had already confessed—with this marriage his life was just beginning and he must surely be delighted at that.

Signora Lanucci, seeing him with knit brow, grew wor-

ried and, knowing he had come home late, asked if he
had spent the night gambling and lost. He laughed!
Yes, he had indeed gambled, but won.

During the morning, as he worked slowly and
stopped to dream, staring at a name or a set of figures,
the strange idea came to him that maybe by that time
Annetta's love had already ended and he would never
hear mention of it again. It was quite possible that a
love born so fast, the product of necessity and resignation, could die with the same speed as it had grown. He
felt no fear of that! If someone had told him it had already happened, he would have felt neither surprise nor sorrow, though no pleasure either. He would
have been liberated from doubts much graver than he
could bear. He knew that in that case Annetta would
not only cease to be his mistress but even his friend,
and that he would drop back among the mass of clerks
from which he stood out only by this relationship. But
before all else he wanted to have back his own peace
and calm.

A letter was awaiting him at home. It was from Annetta. He at once recognized her writing, the small
round strokes which he had got to know while working
on the novel with her. He opened it at once. Perhaps
that letter had the words which would free him from
his torture, either new pretenses of love, or labored excuses to free herself from him.

He was wrong! There was nothing false in the letter.

It was written to tell him something which he did
not yet know; and the first part concentrated on close-
knit explanation, with a few little remarks intended to
remove doubts or forestall opposition. Annetta began
with the statement, in a few simple but affectionate
words, that they now formed one single person in aims
and interests and so she expected him to trust her completely. In consequence, she would sometimes be tak-

ing action without telling him, which she knew he could not find agreeable. But now she needed his help. She intended to go to her father at once and tell him all. It would be a nasty scene, and that was not to be wondered at, because old Maller's surprise, even sorrow, might well be considerable, as he had hoped for something different for his daughter—quite wrongly, she hurriedly added. She could not promise to make her father change his mind at once; so Alfonso, for a short time, she was sure, might be exposed to rudeness and perhaps even to rough treatment. As she loved him, she would suffer for every unkind word said to him; so, for the sake of Maller's dignity she suggested that Alfonso should leave town for a time. She had already told her father that Francesca wanted to send him to the country on a mission for her, and Maller himself had promised to see he was offered leave. She asked him to accept it.

The letter ended there, but reopened with a postscript, two more, closely written pages. She wanted to see him again just once more before his departure, and asked him to be by the public library on the evening of that same day, on the slope toward Villa Necker, where she had seen him at other times. She did not want him to come to her home because she did not wish to be alone with him before their engagement. He must not dislike this. She had shown herself weak a first time, when so many considerations and fears should have held her back; so she knew that she would give way just as soon a second time, when such considerations no longer existed.

The letter closed definitely with a phrase with which Annetta tried to explain and excuse her fall: "You know, my dear, it was love that made me yield so easily, not your courage, great though it was. I have loved you for a long time and you knew it. When I abandoned myself to your caresses, I was just as much to blame as you. With you I have always yielded, but you did not always want what I did."

This letter, marked all over with strong affection, moved Alfonso, but in a completely different sense than Annetta might have hoped. In his eyes it seemed pointless to make all that effort to appear glad and not just resigned, and to make him believe that, if that step had not already been taken, she was ready to take it again when in full possession of her senses. No, she had fallen, and was acting like a person on the lookout for the most dignified posture to fall in, after forgetting to stretch out her arms to protect her head. That little head, always borne so proudly on its neck, had hit the ground with a bang, and Annetta now renounced ever raising it again. That letter, it seemed to him, showed that where sensuality stopped, reasoned necessity began.

Only now did he begin to understand why, after reaching the goal he had been aiming toward for so long, he felt restless and disgusted instead of happy. This was not how he would have liked to achieve riches, even if he eventually resigned himself to receiving them from Annetta. He remembered his hopes of reaching the same goal by quite another route. Annetta was to have declared serenely that she loved him and realized she could not put her destiny into better hands than his. He had recognized a long time ago that this dream was unlikely to be realized, and he had gone on because he was drawn by sensuality, not by anything else. Annetta was the more to blame since the excuses he had found for himself did not exist for her. From beginning to end she had acted out of sensuality and vanity. He had always had an urge to sweeten their love affair by words and gestures; she had merely tolerated his love without showing she returned it. So, eventually, he had found his feelings getting similar to hers—ceasing, that is, when desire ceased.

Yet, what disturbed him more than any doubt was the compassion aroused in him by Annetta. She had been struck in her most vulnerable part, her pride, and sooner or later that would make her suffer horribly.

Never had he felt so unhappy at the bank as he did that day, though after receiving the letter he worked fast and well as if wanting to be of some use to Signor Maller in compensation for his action against him. He met him in the passage and bowed deeply to make a good impression. In the afternoon Santo suddenly called him in to see Signor Maller. He quivered. Maller very rarely needed to talk to him and, as he went, Alfonso thought that Annetta had spoken ahead of time, leaving him unprepared to cope with her father's anger. But it turned out to be a matter of business. He was in such a state of embarrassment that Signor Maller looked at him with curiosity, certainly thinking that literature did not help its cultivators to an easy bearing.

His last daydreams had been based on this very fear, of being called by Signor Maller. He imagined him more pained by having to marry off his daughter to Alfonso than by her dishonor, and shouting jeers and insults which did not stop even when Alfonso declared that though he had behaved badly the consequences need not be those drawn by Signor Maller, for if necessary he would withdraw and renounce Annetta while taking her secret to the grave. Ah, he could do very little to diminish the anger of Maller, who must blame him severely. But, however much he wanted to impose his own conditions—to reject arrangements made under pressure of necessity—he had had no liberty in the matter at all. He had to submit to the will of those in whose hands his destiny lay.

During the day he felt a burning need to confide in

someone. It cost him a lot not to mention it all to Ballina, in whose room he spent half that day so as to
avoid feeling so alone with his thoughts. He felt a need
to hear the opinion of someone not blinded by Uto-
pias, as, so often, he had been himself. An average person might perhaps see it quite differently; a friend's
words could have lightened his conscience, even if they
did not bring him to accept what did not suit him.

But he was able to control himself with Ballina.
White was leaving the bank the next day, and Alfonso
brought up the story, changing names and details. He
told him that a young man he knew had courted a girl
much richer than himself who really did not want him,
until she was caught in a pathological impulse, changed
her mind from necessity, and gave way. The young
man, on achieving his desire, was hesitant to profit by
his action and put himself in circumstances which he
foresaw would certainly not give him happiness.

White looked at him with his calm gaze, unused to
worrying about the troubles of others, and replied:
"One needs more details. If the young man loves
the girl, then it's all fine; if he doesn't, it's very bad
indeed."

He had put his finger right on the wound; now that
the dilemma was posed by others, Alfonso could not
bypass it without an answer, this dilemma which tortured him throughout that morning. He had loved her
but did not know if he still did. What had happened to
destroy his affection? For no, he did not love her! His
problem was solved, but he did not want to tell White
this.

"If he doesn't love her," continued White, "I advise
him to cut it off regardless of any sense of obligation,
because a marriage like that is always and in all circumstances inadvisable. I don't know if your man thinks so,
but there are still things which can't be sold."

He spoke in grave moved tones, but Alfonso realized that his emotion was not aroused by the query put to him. White's thoughts were elsewhere; obviously, he could not turn his whole mind to answering Alfonso.

White's farewell was very affectionate. Alfonso was so predisposed to emotion that anything was enough to move him to tears, and the other, usually so cold, seemed to be in the same state. He told Alfonso that he did not know exactly to what port in the Levant he was being sent, but anyway it was somewhere very very very far away, and at that repeated "very" his voice broke with emotion.

Alfonso, who still had half an hour after leaving the office and before his appointment, walked home with him.

"And the Signora . . . ?" he asked, pointing toward White's home.

"She's not coming with me . . . she doesn't want to."

To cut things short and forestall any other question from Alfonso, he changed the subject at once.

"Ah! I've been much happier in this town than in Paris, and having to leave it just to earn one's bread. Oh! *Maudit argent!*" The French words made his imprecation sound more sincere. "If you wait for me, I'll be down directly and we can walk together toward the station, where there's a family I must say good-bye to."

But Alfonso could not wait, because he was just in time to arrive in a proper manner shortly before the time arranged.

The two friends shook hands and looked each other in the eyes for a wordless instant, White's regular features very serious, his glasses almost sticking to his eyes. Then they both walked quickly away from each other, and Alfonso felt how important their separation was.

Two beings who, by chance, had met, known, and appreciated each other, were parting, never to meet again. The irrevocable leaving of a something or some one is always sad.

It was now close on dusk. Alfonso felt a deep melancholy. Now he was just beginning to realize how much he had lost in every respect by the night's adventure. White was leaving, and he felt as if he had seen the last of a very important person in his life. He felt alone. What would his life be like now, when, twenty-four hours after achieving the goal for which he had lived, he realized it did not give him happiness?

And yet he still desired Annetta. As the time came near when he was to see her again, he evoked her pretty face and examined with curiosity the impression it made. It was desire, but desire which took away none of his revulsions and seemed indeed to provide another reason to appreciate his own feelings. Now he could vaunt a hatred of his own misdeed, for in spite of desiring and loving Annetta, he still felt disgust at the way he had won her. And in his gloom he was swept by pity for Annetta, realizing that by the events he regretted she was losing much more than he. This, he felt, formed the major part of his disgust.

When he was close to the little square he began to run, fearing he had arrived late. Annetta was not there yet. According to what she had written, she was to be in front of the school by the Law Courts. That evening he did not want to stand still, for fear of indiscreet eyes, and twice went slowly up and down the little incline. As he was beginning to climb it once again, he heard himself called: "Signor Alfonso!"

It was Francesca, not Annetta. She came toward him, her face slightly flushed, and greeted him in her usual level voice that was apt to sound like a machine's.

"Up there," and she pointed toward Villa Necker.

"I've a carriage in which we could talk calmly, but I prefer to walk. Anyway, I'm unrecognizable."

Actually she was not, in spite of a thick veil covering her face, and Alfonso thought that even at a great distance he could have recognized that thin body with its virile movements in a flowing black dress.

"What about Annetta?" he asked at last, remembering to show disappointment.

She had begun to walk with small but quick steps toward Villa Necker up the slope where he had lost his breath once before. She was two steps ahead so as to make passers-by think she was not in his company. Only after the Law Courts did she wait for him and answer his question. Annetta could not come and asked him to excuse her; her father had by an unfortunate coincidence taken it into his head to remain with her at the very time of the appointment. Francesca handed him a note from Annetta, a few words written hurriedly at the last moment.

"I'll read it afterward," he said impatiently when she showed that she wanted him to open it at once.

"I don't know what you think of me," she said without blushes or hesitation, "but I've had the part of intermediary imposed on me; it's the best I can do now for Annetta. We must reach the desired result as soon as possible."

This desired result must be marriage; it was her only hint and in no way necessary.

"Annetta says. . ." went on Francesca, and the opening was enough to show that the message she had been charged to give would be followed by her own ideas and advice. Obviously Francesca had thought over all she wanted to tell him, and if she showed doubts or surprise later, that was because Alfonso's attitude was so different from the one foreseen.

Annetta had merely asked her to repeat what she had

written. To avoid his having to face affronts, she
wanted him to leave town for a while, until he could
find everything settled on his return. The only new fact
was that she had had occasion to talk to Cellani, who
would be giving him the required leave.

Francesca interrupted herself, noticing Alfonso's
silence, which she interpreted with her usual quickness.

"You're against this plan, are you?" And with calm
satisfaction she added: "Oh, I foresaw that!"

"No, I'm not against it," exclaimed Alfonso, hesitating. What worried him most was the fear that Francesca would notice that he was not as interested in the
whole matter as he should be. In a voice which tried to
sound sad, he added: "Will it be hard for Signorina
Annetta to take the steps you mention?"

"Why?"

"Oh well! She might have some harsh words said to
her?"

He sounded angry, because, to one pretending, it is
particularly annoying not to be understood at once.

"Annetta won't care a bit about any harsh words on
a matter so important to her, though it may not seem
so to you, Signor Alfonso."

Her voice lent itself to irony. He felt that she had no
suspicion how close she was to the truth in that rebuke,
but her irony offended him all the same.

"How important this matter is to me you can easily
imagine, but I don't like leaving Signorina Annetta
battling all alone here on my account!"

She gave him a careful look.

"So you don't want to leave, then?"

"I don't *want* anything, but I'm allowed, I hope, to
express what I like or don't like?"

She looked disappointed.

"Oh, so that's how it is? . . . Listen, I'll be frank. I
see no reason why you should leave. Annetta is mistress

at home, and at her first words, if she says them properly, any opposition will collapse. So neither Annetta nor you need fear any affronts." Then, seeing him hesitatant and surprised: "I don't know how to win your trust in so short a time, but I need to. You are about to do something silly, and I want to prevent it. So listen to me, follow my advice, don't leave." She told him how fond she was of him, how she always remembered his village and the year she had spent there and his mother, whom she had so loved, all in her gentle calm cold voice that was incapable of pretense. "So trust me, don't leave." And she went on talking. She told him that, because it was he, she had been pleased to learn that Annetta loved him, but had Annetta given herself like that to anyone else, she would never have forgiven herself, as it could only have happened because she had not had the courage to ask Maller to intervene and cut short a flirtation which she knew had started. "I made a mistake, but if the result of my mistake is to be your marriage to Annetta, I can't say I regret it. I'll find myself rewarded for my own mistake."

They were at the top of the slope. Instead of looking where they were going, they had their attention all on each other. Almost instinctively, Alfonso made to cross the square, because if they went straight on they would be going through a busy street, but she made him turn aside.

"The carriage is waiting for me there."

"But why should I act against Annetta's express wishes?"

"Well, as you yourself have said, a man doesn't leave his post like that." She was accepting an argument whose flimsiness she would have destroyed a short time ago. "And what is more, it would not be wise to."

So she was advising him to remain in case of any danger to a match which she had already shown was much wanted by herself. For the second time she was giving advice, becoming worse than an accomplice, an instigator. He felt turned to ice.

"I can never oppose Signorina Annetta's wishes. I shall obey her orders or desires most scrupulously."

He spoke in the tone of someone wanting to cut short the conversation. He brought up no arguments himself; he had made up his mind and did not bother to think where the passive obedience of which he spoke would get him.

She looked at him in astonishment, not quite sure of having heard properly. Then she spoke again, and for the first time Alfonso heard her voice angry; it was still faint, but was now broken by panting, and when it rose lost all sweetness.

"But suppose that by following Annetta's advice you expose to great danger the happiness you're so sure of? What sort of love do you think you've inspired in her, that of the ladies of old which resisted all obstacles and lasted forever?" And she gave a forced laugh. "You're confident enough to leave her here, exposed to her father and her relatives' advice, are you? Do go if you want to, and return after only a week. You'll find yourself just a little quill-driver at the Maller bank again, and Annetta won't even remember she ever knew you." The words came from her mouth compact as a cry. She went on more calmly: "I know what the Mallers are like. Do you think that when Annetta is told what she has forgotten today, just for one day, do you think she'll still remain faithful?"

"I do!" said Alfonso calmly.

This was a solution he had not thought of during that long day, but as soon as Francesca brought it up, he realized it to be likeliest and best. Was it not almost certain in fact that Annetta's ambition, forgotten for a short time, would soon regain the place it had always occupied till then? It was a good solution because, while before he had feared being forced into the part of betrayer, now all of a sudden he became the betrayed, with no other obligation than granting a generous pardon, which was easy and agreeable to do.

"Then all is lost for you!" said Francesca in a voice calm for an instant to make her words more serious. "I don't understand your reasons for acting like this, and I don't care to; if you leave town even for a few days, you'll never see Annetta again."

"I must leave if Annetta orders me to."

"What I'm telling you is so obvious that either you don't care about Annetta at all or you have suddenly lost the use of your reason."

She spoke at random, without reflecting much on what she said, and Alfonso sensed that, but it did not make him forget to answer words which had struck a raw nerve.

"Annetta is as important to me as the light in my own eyes." He was pleased with the phrase. "But I don't want to steal her love; I want it to be given spontaneously." Then he managed to find the right intonation and words: "A love which could cease in a week would be no use to me, and now that you've brought up the doubt, if Annetta hadn't suggested this journey, I would have myself."

She laughed contemptuously.

"You've found a way of calling your own coldness 'dignity'."

She was right again; she had hit by chance on the word which most offended him, and to give herself the satisfaction of offending him again, insisted on it blindly.

He remained utterly calm. Only once did he become agitated, when, tired of seeing the argument always repeating itself, he made the mistake of declaring that discussion between them was useless because if he did not leave he would have to find good reasons to convince Annetta. In one breath she suggested ten. Alfonso was alarmed, as the possibility flashed into his mind that he could be forced to stay; he recognized his error and, without losing himself in refuting Francesca's suggestions, went on protesting, with an obstinacy like that of people with few ideas, such as peasants, that he would just carry out Annetta's wishes without probing into whether she was right or not. He was making a marriage of love—he repeated in order to go on talking longer—he was making a marriage of love and did not want to be shrewd about it like someone acting from self-interest.

She was walking two steps ahead of him again and seemed to have given up trying to convince him. Suddenly she slowed down, wondering again if he distrusted her. It was not a reasonable supposition, but she had been thrown off balance by the shock of having to leave him without obtaining what had seemed to her so easy. She acted without consideration, following her first impulse.

She began to explain why she was taking such an interest in his fate, and her calm voice must have hidden the great inner agitation that had brought her to such a confession.

"It's quite true that I'm fond of her and her family," she began, with a coldness which made her phrase sound ironic. "But it's not only my affection that makes me act. This marriage might have such consequences for me that my life's happiness could depend on it. Have you understood, or do you still wonder if my advice was given in good faith?"

He could no longer doubt it; he had understood. In the delirium of the night, Annetta had confessed that it was she herself who had opposed Maller's marriage,

and she had also hinted that by accepting him as a husband she could no longer persist in that opposition. So
Francesca had a great stake in this marriage and her
fury was understandable at finding, when she was so
close to her goal, something new, unforeseen, and
unreasonable arising to put her victory in doubt.

So shaken was he by this confession that he deviated
once more from his method of defense; he wanted to
convince her that his departure could not be such a
great danger to his relations with Annetta. Annetta
loved him, she had repeated it to him in every tone,
given proof. Why then should he be so offensive as to
doubt the seriousness of her affection?

She was the first to give up the struggle. She walked
another ten steps or so beyond the carriage, whose
coachman was keeping the door open; not replying to
Alfonso's long speeches, perhaps not following them.
Suddenly she looked at him, raising her head with a
quick movement.

"Either you don't love Annetta or you're afraid of
her father."

He thought it more dignified not to reply.

As she returned to the carriage, she muttered:
"Never have I seen such a thing."

Before leaving, she turned to him and put her small
cold hand in his, ready to shake it with the friendship
which she would otherwise have been unable to show,
saying: "Anyway, I shall do all I can to spare you the
misfortune you deserve. I'm sorry."

She jumped into the carriage and helped the hesitant
coachman shut the door.

He was free at last. No one could any longer try to
change his mind; he would leave knowing that by that
step he was renouncing Annetta. Francesca had convinced him; departure was equivalent to renunciation.
He felt calm and happy. If what Francesca foresaw

took place, he was free from all doubt and remorse. She had said that if Annetta abandoned him he would go back to being a wretched quill-pusher at the Maller bank. No! He would be superior even to the position that Annetta wanted to give him, a superiority shown precisely by his renunciation.

Next day at the bank he felt better. He worked willingly because, knowing nothing unexpected could happen to him, he felt calm, free from the fears which had torn at him the day before; the need he had felt to confide in someone for advice or support amazed him. Now he had tucked his secret away, and it merely seemed like an interesting episode in his life.

Cellani was to talk to him, not he to Cellani, so he did not even fear that interview. Finding he was not called by midday, he had but one fear, which was that Francesca, unable to convince him of the need to stay, had managed to convince Annetta that it was better not to let him leave. He would be in their hands, have to put up with rebukes from Maller that he deserved, and then, what was much worse, assume the part of an amorous lover.

At midday little Giacomo came to tell him that the assistant manager was waiting to see him in his room. Alfonso lost a little of his calm because he had doubted whether he would be called, and the unexpected always agitated him.

Signor Cellani was alone and had his desk clear of papers. Over that desk passed all the innumerable papers of the bank, not to leave it until they were signed by him; reading incoming and outgoing letters must have meant a vast amount of work.

Cellani was easily embarrassed, and so Alfonso was more at ease with him than with Maller. At first the assistant manager asked him how he was; then, in hesitating words, as usual, he observed with some wit that he usually only granted leave of absence when it was asked and this was the first time he found himself having to offer it.

As the matter was being treated so lightly, obviously he had not been told the reason why this leave was being asked. Alfonso felt so calm that he also made an effort at wit in order to help the assistant manager out of the embarrassing position he had mentioned.

"May I ask for the leave of absence which you can't offer?"

"Granted!" said Cellani laughing. "I don't know quite what it's all about, but it seems very important to Signorina Francesca, and even a little to Signorina Annetta, who asked me to let you go at once. I'm sure you'll not abuse this leave and that we'll see you back here in a fortnight." He asked him to warn Sanneo and arrange with him about his work; perhaps it would also be necessary for him to work longer than usual that day. "Finally, if Signor Maller asks you why you 'want' this leave, give him some good, watertight reason. Say, for example, that your mother is very ill; you can't do any harm by saying that," and he bid him a warm good-bye. "Have a good time, now!"

Sanneo was still hard at work, bent over a sheet of paper filled with his big writing, muttering words as he wrote them down. Alfonso entered and waited respectfully.

"Yes?" he asked without raising his head.

Alfonso began to speak, saying without remorse that his mother was ill and that Signor Cellani had granted him a fortnight's leave. He noticed Sanneo was going on writing and muttering eagerly over what he was writing; it must be some dispute—all on account of Maller & Company—and in his ardor he had heard nothing said to him. Alfonso became impatient and eventually said in a changed voice: "I'm leaving tomorrow."

"What's that, what's that?" asked Sanneo in surprise, raising his head at last. "Leaving?"

Alfonso repeated all that he had said, and Sanneo looked annoyed. Now the matter had all his attention, and he put his pen down to get away from other ideas. The day before, he had ordered Alfonso to take on some new work, checking computations for liquidation, which he had done himself since Miceni's departure from the correspondence department. It was work that prolonged his hours considerably, and after deciding to hand it over to Alfonso he was alarmed to find it falling back on himself. It had been an effort to hand over the work and teach Alfonso, and that was now all wasted labor.

"If Signor Cellani gave you leave," he would willingly have put that in doubt, "you're free to go. Were you called by telegram?"

"Yes," replied Alfonso, annoyed at having to give details.

"Oh! Then there's no objection!" said Sanneo. "Although in such a case I myself would not leave at once but wait for confirmation of news which is sometimes given by relatives too easily alarmed."

But seeing that Alfonso did not reply to this veiled suggestion, Sanneo suddenly became a courteous friend bidding farewell. He warmly hoped Alfonso would find his mother in good health and, wanting to cancel any bad effect that might have been left by his hesitation, added, laughing; "Even if you find your mother in perfect health, don't give up any of the leave you've got. We'll see you again in a fortnight, then."

Maller was no longer there, and Alfonso had to return in the afternoon to say good-bye to him. He found him alone in his office, working hard at some notes in a pocket notebook. Alfonso was about to say the lie suggested by Cellani, but Maller interrupted: "A good journey to you, Signor Nitti, a good journey!"

Alfonso bowed himself out; he was annoyed. Maller's cold bearing disturbed him, however little he cared, for the moment, about being liked; he had even calculated on Maller's decisive opposition to free him of his obligations with Annetta.

The only employees he said good-bye to, apart from his colleagues in the correspondence department, were Miceni and Starringer, the dispatch clerk. He also said a word to Marlucci, but only because he found him in Miceni's room. The Tuscan was cold, realizing why Alfonso remembered him.

Miceni behaved better than anyone else. Starringer had asked for all details, and what illness his mother was suffering from and for how long and whyever he could have known nothing about it till now. Then, showing that he was incapable of putting himself in the position of a son receiving news of his mother's danger, he said: "Lucky beggar, you, going home," and a shadow passed over his wide face. Ah! He was only thinking of himself, of the long holiday he had taken the month before, which cancelled any right to more for another two years. Ballina, after warm consolations, had a doubt: "Is your journey money being advanced by Signor Maller?"

Miceni, who obviously knew the ways of the world better, very sincerely hoped he would find his mother in good health. Then he exonerated him from bothering to bid good-bye to all the other clerks and promised to make his excuses to them. Alfonso told him of Maller's cold greeting, and Miceni was able to soothe him by describing the reasons for his chief's ill-humor.

"He's a man with many worries, and just at the

moment he's had a misfortune and a financial disaster in the family to cope with."

These were Fumigi's madness and the failure of his business, which was inevitable. Miceni told how Maller, from affection for his nephew, had taken on the responsibility of winding up this business, and only then realized that it was in debt for speculations of Fumigi's, which had failed in the last two months. Miceni said that the disaster was due to the weakening of Fumigi's intellect. As to the reasons for the illness itself, he supposed these lay in overwork.

"I know this summer he was working ten hours a day in the office and more at home afterward, on mathematical problems. His weak constitution couldn't stand the strain."

Alfonso thought he knew more about the cause of this illness. It must have been due to grief at Annetta's refusal. Had Fumigi succeeded in his suit, he would have enjoyed his good fortune very much more than Alfonso himself, who now felt another twinge of remorse at not profiting from it.

He was very worried about finding a good lie to explain his sudden departure to the Lanuccis. He did not want to say that he was leaving due to his mother's illness, or he would be asked for too many details.

"I'm going away!" he said, turning to Signora Lanucci, whom he found sitting at the table with the old man. Lucia was always out strolling with Gralli at suppertime.

"How long will you be gone?" asked old Lanucci, raising his nose from his plate in great alarm.

"A fortnight!" said Alfonso quickly to calm him. He had understood the reason for the alarm. "I'm leaving on business. . ." He had not yet decided on any particular motive from the selection at his disposal, but none of them seemed likely enough to be believed without hesitation. It suddenly ocurred to him that his mother had wanted to sell their house for a long time. "We're selling our house, which is too big and too far from the village for my mother."

The old man again stopped eating and straightened his spectacles, a sure sign that he wanted to talk business.

"So that's why you're leaving, is it? Leaving your job for a fortnight, if that's enough!"

Alfonso replied that Signor Maller had granted him leave quite willingly, and so he was losing nothing by his absence. But Lanucci did not give up so soon. He rebuked him for wanting to carry through such an important business deal all alone, being too young to know how to set about it.

"Our notary Mascotti will help me," replied Alfonso shortly.

One of Lanucci's many jobs was also that of real-estate agent. He suggested that Alfonso, instead of leaving, give him a description of the house and an idea of the price, to look around for a purchaser in town.

Alfonso did not accept this suggestion and laughed to himself at the thought that he ran the risk of selling the house without intending to, and without having explained his departure.

That evening Signora Lanucci helped him pack the things he was to take with him. During this operation, as she moved around the room with his shirts on her arm and spent a long time bent over the trunk straining to shut it, she talked to him about the happiness awaiting Lucia. That day Gralli had been to visit the Lanuccis three times, once for a few minutes, as his work did not allow him to stay longer. He had walked for a whole hour just to see the face of his beloved. At that moment they were next door, in the living room, chatting. "I wonder what about?" asked Signora Lanucci, raising her eyes from the trunk key, which she was trying to turn. And as she threw herself with all her weight on the trunk, she added, laughing: "They're talking about something which I no longer know and you don't yet know."

Before going to bed, Alfonso went into the living room, where he found Lucia half stretched on the sofa and Gralli sitting cross-kneed on the ground, admiring her. Even after catching sight of Alfonso she stayed in her position, while Gralli, with a twist of his muscular body, rose to his feet.

"You're leaving tomorrow? A good journey to you!" said Lucia and, without moving, held out her hand in a ladylike gesture.

Since her engagement, she had lost her shyness with others because she had been told to; she had lost her respectfulness to Alfonso for her own reasons. She had let herself be ill-treated and taken no revenge for so long that now she wanted to make him feel she was independent, expected nothing from him, and did not like him. She was being particularly offhand in order to make him forget the time when her behavior might have made him think she loved him. Alfonso had so many other things on his mind that he had not even realized what efforts Lucia was making to offend him, and when he could not avoid noticing her coldness, he thought her quite right to be so.

It was past ten o'clock when Santo brought him another letter from Annetta. She told him that Francesca had made her doubt the wisdom of his journey; but she left him free to do what he preferred and still wanted him safe from any possible offense. Anyway, she could not quite see how he could remain after having received the bank's permission to leave. In case he did leave, she sent her greetings, and was sorry not to have seen him before he went.

He had no hesitation before replying. He wanted to leave, and the doubts which Francesca had aroused in Annetta did not seem worth his attention. Why, even Annetta herself was still inclined to think he should leave!

Santo was standing by his desk when he wrote the reply; Alfonso kept his face calm with an effort, lest he show the other that this was anything but a routine reply. He had to cover his letter with another sheet of paper because he saw that Santo had calmly got to his feet and was reading over his shoulder. On seeing he was noticed, Santo was not at all confused and sat down smiling.

"I didn't look at your letter at all."

Alfonso, frankly and unhesitatingly, had opened his letter with "Darling wife-to-be." Then, "I'm leaving!" he wrote in the exclamatory tone of one decided on a sacrifice. He was leaving, he went on, because, though with such a prize reserved for him he was beyond being offended by any insults from her father, "who is right to hate me" (what objective indifference that phrase showed!)—he did not want such insults to be suffered also by her.

He felt pleased with this pair of phrases but, on re-reading Annetta's letter, realized that he had simply forgotten to answer it. Annetta, in fact, was telling him that she left him free to leave or not, and he was replying that he was leaving because she imposed it, and very much against his will. He would have to be more careful and astute in his reply, or it would eventually make her think him stupid or indifferent in spite of his melodramatic phrases. Like this, it was pointless or mistaken. If Annetta still cared enough to study his letters, she was clever enough to realize soon that Alfonso was pretending and not even taking much trouble about his pretense. This should have worried him a lot because he had tried to make her think he was the betrayed, but such was his indifference that he could easily console himself. Annetta would not pore over that note of his for long.

He was wakened by old Lanucci, who wanted to accompany him to the station. Lanucci always got up at that hour and, from what he said, slept a very small part of the few hours he spent in bed.

It must have been almost the same time as he had left Annetta's room two nights before, and that dim light of dawn, those deserted streets in which their steps resounded, reminded him of his walk home in a daze, not only at the adventure that had happened to him but at his own strange sensations. It was right that one walk should remind him of the other; this was the consequence of that. The sky did not promise a good day. A black cloud weighed over the city, and the tepid air showed signs of sirocco.

Old Lanucci, as he went along, was advising him on how to set about selling his house. He was first to pretend that he was in no hurry and had not come to the village on purpose for that, or he would be cheated; the rumor that he wanted to sell the house should be scattered artfully about. Whoever made the first offer should be made to believe that the offer was being listened to from pure curiosity. Then, depending on the offer, he must either pretend that it had seduced him into selling or hint that the offer was not worth considering but might be if improved on. All this was to be done with an air not of asking favors but of granting them.

But Alfonso was not listening to that vain chatter. Crossing Via dei Forni, he looked at the Maller house, brown and glum like all the others in the dawn color, under a cloudy sky. In the empty gray street it had a lordly look, with its two floors and wide windows, and its stucco work here and there, though rather graceless nevertheless. He was escaping because of the storm about to break over it. Gladder than ever to get away, he tried to excuse his own egotism and did so with a reason dictated by egotism personified; it was not worth suffering for something he did not want.

When he was alone in a third-class carriage and no longer saw old Lanucci's glum face, he stopped reasoning and felt no more need to make excuses for himself. He was free at last. For only a fortnight, but during it he did not even want to remember the town where he had suffered so much. He wanted to forget his own rather shabby behavior, his own and others' misfortunes. He was fleeing from Annetta, the girl who had given herself to him from adolescent curiosity and who was persecuting him with her artificial love; but he breathed freely also at leaving all the people, bad or unlucky, among whom he had been forced to live. Francesca, who had yielded to Maller because he was rich, and, astute simulator that she was, hid an iron will and scheming cleverness under a submissive air in order to better herself; that dreary Lanucci home where he felt so wretched amid all their troubles, with that girl already in love with the man she was marrying from self-interest. Oh! what dreary squalid people! The railway line running along the flat dikes seemed to be bearing him to a point from which he could judge all those people rushing after goals that were stupid and unreachable. And he went on to ask himself: "Why don't they live more serenely?"

He leaned out of the window. The town with its white houses in a big semicircle on the shore was hugging the sea; its shape might have been given it by a huge wave pushed back in the middle. It looked gray and sad, and an ever denser haze overhead seemed to come from a union with its own mists, only trace of its vitality. Inside, in that beehive, people were panting about after money; and Alfonso, who had known life there and thought it was like that nowhere else, breathed freely as he fled that cowl of cloud.

CHAPTER

XVI

In the last days' agitation he had quite forgotten that his journey would bring not only the pleasure of escaping from places he hated but the joy of revisiting his home village.

On evoking this, all his bitterness vanished at once. It was purest delight to think of the unexpected pleasure he would bring his mother.

This village of his was a group of houses scattered in a fold of a vast green valley crossed diagonally by the railway. The station lay a stone's throw from the village. It was a roadmender's hut, raised to the dignity of station as a result of pressure by the local parliamentary deputy. Before that, one had to leave the train at the station before and reach the village by cart. "Poor but happy!" thought Alfonso, remembering the villagers' joy when they got their station. And what a fine road they had made to join the new station to the village! Straight as on a map and wide enough for three carts at the same time.

The Nittis' house was as far from the station as it was from the village. Alfonso's father, wanting a shorter route to it, had improved an existing lane which passed his land and rejoined the main road halfway across. Alfonso remembered his father as a sort of man who must have lived in cities at one time; and yet he had been simple enough to be pleased when the locals called this lane of his Via Nitti.

Alfonso remembered the existence of this lane, to take him faster now to his mother's arms.

In front of the station hut, leaning on a thick stick, watching the train pass, stood Mascotti the notary. He was dressed in a black velvet jacket, light-colored trousers, and very high boots. Thickset and fat, but rather bent by age, with a sunburned face fringed by a short gray beard, he looked like a retired soldier.

"Here already?" he asked Alfonso in surprise.

Just as surprised, Alfonso asked in return: "Is she expecting me?"

"No no!" exclaimed the notary, slowly putting his forefinger to his nostrils and rubbing it up to an eye. The gesture, which Alfonso remembered, made him realize that the notary was thinking hard. With a naturalness which deceived Alfonso, he then added: "I'm surprised to see you, that's all! I wasn't expecting you."

They came down from the embankment and passed by a roadmender's shack, his wife and two half-naked children staring wide-eyed at Alfonso as if he had dropped from the sky. One of the children, aged about six, in a shirt and trousers reaching his knees, was holding the other, who could not have been more than two, dressed only in a shirt fastened around the middle by a band from which hung more shirt. They made up a tangle of thin dark limbs, even the one who could not yet walk by himself burned black by the sun.

Alfonso did not realize at once how odd Mascotti's bearing was; all intent on the first sensations at seeing his village again, he had no time to observe him.

Autumn had already stripped the valley, which in its bareness looked very close to the stony region nearby. The countryside had not the brownness of damp fertile earth, and was scattered with white stones, which became dominating a few miles farther on. Nearby fields were also scattered with little stones mingling with the soil, left so that the borea wind which raged there would not sweep off loose earth; a few rocks broke the regularity of furrows or stunted the growth of scraggy trees.

The houses of the village were scarcely visible in the slight mist covering the valley; but the wide road off which lay the Nittis' house, which went straight on to become the main street of the village, was visible as a gleaming streak. The landscape held no surprises for him; he remembered its smallest details. From beyond the village he could see the white tip of a hillock of stones, a regular-shaped dome without houses or vegetation, and on its right a small copse of young pine trees planted against encroachment by stones. But the copse had made little progress since he left.

There was one surprise. He had expected his home to be nearer the village; wanting his mother to be less isolated, in his imagination he had moved their home and now looked for it where it was not. In fact, it lay quote a distance off, all on its own in the midst of fields, although old Nitti had hoped that the area, being in the most fertile part of the valley, would soon be built over.

Alfonso hastened his step impatiently. Now he saw one side of the house, the color of terra cotta. The front faced the village and was the only side with windows worthy of the name; the other side had only a couple of holes bored by the old doctor himself to help air to circulate. He came to the alley leading up to the house. It must be little used, because it merged for stretches into a field from which it had never really detached itself.

Mascotti had been silent for a long time and, after waiting in vain to be questioned, spoke first.

"Please, I'm sixty-five, and if you hurry so, I won't reach your home at the same time as you!" He leaned against a tree to rest. Then, with an air of indifference, and staring at the white felt cap he had taken from his head, he said: "Your mother is not very well."

Alfonso glanced at him closely, hesitating. Was Mascotti's air of indifference sincere? Moved, he asked: "What's wrong with her?"

"Some little thing to do with her heart, it hasn't a regular beat, so the doctor says," replied Mascotti, thinking he had found the simplest way of defining the illness.

"You were waiting at the station; was I sent a telegram?" asked Alfonso, who remembered Mascotti's initial surprise at seeing him.

"Yes, but thank heaven . . ."

Alfonso heard no more than the "Yes."

"See you at home," he said and, bag in one hand and stick in the other, he began to run, taking no more notice of Mascotti, who followed him for a time, shouting some word which he did not understand.

The unexpected news had made his heart beat fast.

Things must be very serious if they'd had to call him back so urgently. Though soon tired from running and from emotion, he raced on, as it seemed that his mother's life partly depended on the result of his effort.

As he ran, he suddenly thought with horror that he might be running to embrace a corpse; could that be the announcement Mascotti had tried to shout after him?

Oh, it was so long since he had thought of this woman who was dying! She had not written for three weeks and, all intent on hanging around Annetta, he had not even noticed. He should have understood, should he not, that only something really serious could have made her interrupt her usual regular flow of letters?

Finally he reached the kitchen garden in front of the house. A tall strong old woman was gathering vegetables.

"What do you want?" she asked him, straightening to her full length.

Her face was quite new to him. The skin on it, only recognizable as a woman's by its hairlessness, was like parchment from the sun, and her whole expression concentrated in a pair of lively black rat's eyes in their wooden frame.

"How's my mother?" asked Alfonso impatiently.

"Oh! Signor Alfonso! You were right to come," said the old woman slowly, coming toward him. "The Signora's better, so the doctor says."

She was better, and he had thought her dead! Anyway, he was being granted time to kiss her and show the immense affection welling in his heart. Fate was treating him better than he deserved.

"Go on in! Go on in!" said the old woman to him, looking longingly at her vegetables.

He did not want to and asked her to go in first to

prepare the sick woman. Then, seeing her hesitate, he explained that she was first to warn his mother that there was someone there, then say it was someone she would be surprised to see again, finally someone she would love to see again, her own son.

He entered the house with her. The only two rooms that the Nittis had used in the relatively large building were on the ground floor. They were the only two with sufficient light, and in vain had the defunct doctor attempted to accustom himself to a third as a study. It lacked light and had been too big for the old doctor, with his few pieces of furniture and books, and he had felt lonely in it; the room remained as a library in intention, but the doctor never studied any more.

The entrance room was empty, with only a truckle bed in a corner; when Alfonso lived in it, everything good the Nittis possessed had been put there. The walls had been hung with the few pictures which the little family owned and with many reproductions of famous pictures, some by Horace Vernet, of camels with huge bodies and calm patient faces, beasts more attractive than the men leading them.

In the other room had lived Doctor Nitti and his wife. It was full of big old pieces of simple wooden furniture which looked well in that big room and dressed it up. Between the two windows was a modern pendulum clock, the last object brought home by old Nitti. During the month of the old doctor's last illness his family had dined in that room to keep him company, and the table was set in the middle; it should still be there, from what Signorina Carolina had written Alfonso.

The sadness which assailed him in that first room, where he waited to be called and which he recognized in spite of the fact that there was no object in it to help his memories, was not entirely due to finding his mother ill. He felt he was about to face one of the major disasters of his life. The death of his father had been big enough! Everywhere since leaving the train, in the village and the house and that first room, he had felt accompanied by memory. What a lovely childhood he had spent there! How calm and protected! The family must certainly have been through some bad patches of which he had known nothing, either during his early youth in the village or later in town, where for some time old Nitti had tried in vain to establish a practice. What goodness, what resignation! Never once had the old man complained; the father's experiences had not stolen the son's illusions. "It's only right!" he had said one day when Alfonso brought a good report card home with him on vacation. "The luck I've never had will come to you." And Alfonso had believed him because he saw that his parents, who were old and experienced, believed it themselves.

Now his mother called him with a cry in which he recognized both joy and weakness.

He wanted to fling himself in her arms but, on taking a step into the room, found himself in complete darkness and did not dare move forward.

He felt himself taken roughly by an arm and pulled to the right. His mother was in that bed, he realized. From there she was asking with a stutter: "Is that you, Alfonso?"

"Are you better, Mother?"

"Yes yes, much. Open the window, Giuseppina, so that I can see him."

The old woman threw open first the window farthest from the bed, and in the half darkness he recognized his mother's face, which seemed little changed. She was lying supine, looking at him and murmuring words in a low voice. Thinking her to be delirious, he was alarmed and called her.

"I'm religious," she said with a start. "I'd lost hope of seeing you again, and I thank God who made you get here so soon." And she drew him to her with a smile.

He recognized that voice and manner, that gravity so ready to merge into sweetness and jesting. He saw once more the physiognomy of his father, who had thought and spoken in just that way, never so near to smiling as when his face looked very serious and his words sounded deeply moved. During the long years she had lived with him, she had assimilated his mannerisms.

Giuseppina opened the other window too, flinging it wide with one blow, noisily.

Not even then did Alfonso realize how much his mother's face had changed. He kissed her on the forehead, almost calmed.

"You're looking fine."

"I'm quite plump, eh?"

Roughly Giuseppina's grating, low voice intervened.

"Yes, indeed! I always say she looks fine and that the doctor who makes her stay in bed is an idiot."

Signora Carolina had drawn Alfonso to her again and was passing her hand over his brown hair.

"You're better looking, too; Rosina would never have thought it possible," she said looking at him closely. "We were wrong to part. I'd surely be in the same state, but would have been happier till now!"

At that distance Alfonso now realized what made his mother look so fat. She was swollen, one cheek much more than the other, and on the swelling was reproduced the pattern of rough material and of irregular marks of sewing on the pillowcase. Her face, which had been oval, now looked round. Such white hair as she still had made a crown around a face like a baby's.

She realized what a painful impression that swelling must make on him and tried to attenuate it.

"Oh, it doesn't hurt me here!" and she touched her cheek with a contemptuous finger.

This produced a livid cavity, which remained even when she took her finger away. That was nothing, she explained; it did not hurt her. Where she was suffering was in her lungs, and she did not have enough air. Probably it was from that she would die. Finding herself so close to death, she was beginning to study its mystery.

He tried to prove she was wrong, which should have been easy, with her vague notions about her own illness, but he could not concentrate on deceiving her. She was dying, that was the painful thing, not her knowing it. He had realized there was no longer any remedy. He asked about other symptoms, always hoping to find indications of health. In vain; her whole organism was in decay. For years she had suffered from disturbances in which an expert eye could have recognized the organic disease which was their cause. Even when she noticed that her feet were slightly swollen, she had not called in a doctor, partly from ignorance and mainly from economy. When she finally did consult one, he made her stay in bed; she never got up again, saying she felt better than when up and that she hated dressing and seeing her body disfigured like that. Now she could no longer move. What had not been done by illness had been completed by inertia and lack of fresh air. The room was suffocating. When for an instant the windows had been opened, the breath of outside air that reached Alfonso was balsam compared to the air in the room.

"As you're here, I'll get back to the garden. If you need me, just knock on the window," said Giuseppina and went out.

"What about this nurse?" asked Alfonso. "Does she usually leave you as much alone as I found you a short time ago?"

His mother explained that she had only had her in the house for a month, partly to take over the little jobs that needed seeing to.

"I found her living in such squalor. She seemed so good and attentive."

He noticed the past tense, which suggested a present one in which her opinion about Giuseppina must have changed; and it was so obvious that his mother was surrounded by carelessness and utter indifference out of all proportion to the gravity of the illness from which she was dying that he could not restrain himself and burst into tears.

She understood why he was crying, and with tears in her own eyes at once hugged him in thanks for this sign of affection, to which she must have been little used.

"Now you're here and I need nothing else."

To soothe her he produced another reason for his outburst of grief, and lamented his not having been told before or he would have brought with him some competent doctor from town who would have cured her quicker and saved her a great deal of suffering. But these words only touched her the more. She wept, and her poor half-lifeless body lay motionless as if nailed there; only her head drooped over the sheets to be nearer to him.

Alarmed by the state he had thrown her into, he assured her that very soon, with the help of the doctor he intended calling that very day, she would be cured. For, unable to resign himself to the situation being desperate, however little hope there was, he wanted to ask Prarchi to come and tend her.

But she had a stronger mind than her son. She forbade him to call in other doctors because she had enough of the one who came already. She wanted to die in peace, and taking one of Alfonso's hands between hers brought it to her cheek so as to lean her head against it, jerking herself to one side with an immense effort to do so. Then she wept silently without a sob, hiding her eyes with a hand.

She was utterly finished. What miracle could ever again set to rights that body which that movement had shown to be all misshapen?

As it was no longer a question of saving her, he made an effort to distract her. He asked her what medicines she had been given, as if he thought it important.

"I'm supposed to take that one," she replied, "but I don't want to because it does me harm. After taking it, I not only have difficulty in breathing but feel my head going round . . . even convulsions sometimes."

Her eyes were not yet free of tears before she raised her head and asked in a lively voice, with an arch smile: "Will you soon be boss? How are things at the bank?"

At that moment the notary came in, saying he was exhausted by the race Alfonso had made him run. The good man was actually breathing quite calmly, and there was no trace of sweat on his low, wrinkled forehead.

He rebuked Alfonso almost sharply for making Signora Carolina cry.

"You're intelligent enough to realize it might do her harm."

"I cried, but it wasn't he who made me cry," said Signora Carolina.

But Mascotti did not hear and repeated the same phrases, maybe pleased at a chance of showing zeal, while Alfonso suffered at his making as much thoughtless noise in that room as if he were in a public square.

With a determination of which he would not have

thought her capable, Signora Carolina interrupted his shouts by declaring in a loud voice that she was quite well, and pressed the pulse of Alfonso's left hand; his right was still beneath her head.

Alfonso longed to reprove Mascotti for not having sent a warning before, and to make him realize he was not satisfied with the way the poor sick woman had been treated, but could not for the moment. He felt a certain satisfaction at noticing that Mascotti himself must be feeling to blame, since he tried to excuse himself. Before anyone questioned him on the reasons which had induced him to leave Alfonso in ignorance of Signora Carolina's illness, he said that it had seemed pointless to warn him since she had always been in good hands, and he repeated this phrase as if to silence anyone who asserted the contrary. Every day he paid her a visit, as he was only too pleased to, of course, and Giuseppina, whom he had put with her, was a good nurse.

This, which was perhaps true, seemed so little to Alfonso that he could not contain himself, and reproved him in front of his mother: "You should have warned me!" And he looked at him angrily to make him realize that he had other more serious things to complain of.

"And what about your career?" asked Mascotti. "I, as your guardian, had to see you didn't interrupt it."

Signora Carolina was not listening to this conversation.

"Now I understand." She seemed to have been studying Alfonso in silence for a long time. "Now I understand why you look so changed. You're dressed quite differently. You're in the fashion." And she laughed with pleasure at finding her son looking like a gentleman. She admired each garment, from his stiff straw hat to the cut of his trousers, and so interrupted the discussion between Mascotti and Alfonso. "But not given up," thought Alfonso, who needed someone on whom to take his revenge.

Shortly after, in came Doctor Frontini, a handsome, smartly dressed young man with an oval face, too regular features, and a thick brown mustache with gleams of gold. He was courteous to the sick woman, but Alfonso sensed her antipathy to the doctor and realized that she feared him. She swore she had taken his potion twice that day, while to Alfonso she had confessed not touchisg it since the night before.

As Alfonso learned later, Doctor Frontini was a young man who had started in a big city where, maybe for lack of patients, he had been unable to build up a sufficient practice and had fallen back on the wretched job of working for the Health Department; so he considered himself a misfit and disliked his patients.

After declaring that he found some improvement in the sick woman's condition and recommending that she take the medicine regularly, he left.

Alfonso ran after him and reached him in the garden. He wanted to hear his frank opinion.

Doctor Frontini declared that the illness was very serious indeed, but he did not exclude a possibility of the heart returning to regular activity; that often happened. He had noticed the immense anguish on Alfonso's face and added the second phrase from pity. Seeing that the doctor was looking at him attentively, Alfonso, with his usual quick perception, realized that the diagnosis had been modified to spare his feelings. He could not complain of that. He knew as well as the doctor did himself how serious the illness was, and the doctor's opinion could not soothe him, but as the doctor had been so kind to him, he felt he must be deceived about him. Certainly, at that instant at least, Doctor Frontini was taking an interest in the patient.

Perhaps that was an advantage derived by Signora Carolina from Alfonso's arrival, for a person's life seems precious mainly because of the value others put on it.

Alfonso spent the rest of the day by his mother's bedside. He suffered at being unable to go to the village and greet his friends, see some of his old haunts again, satisfy his yearning. But he could not move away.

When he entered the room again, Signora Carolina soon expressed a wish to sleep; her eyes were closing with drowsiness. He threw himself on his father's bed to watch her fall asleep. But it was more difficult for Signora Carolina than she seemed to suppose. Just when she was about to drop off to sleep, she came to with a violent start. Sometimes the start was so violent that she jerked her arms like a person losing his balance.

"I can't!" she sighed, and already resigned, asked him to talk so as to dissipate the drowsiness which she could not satisfy. Readily he rose and sat by her bed. Instead of talking to her of other things as she wanted, he tried to persuade her to make another effort to sleep. She closed her eyes to please him, and he sat still, looking at her. When by an almost imperceptible movement of her arm he saw that she was about to give another start, incapable of remaining a passive spectator he seized her hand in his and held it firmly. Seeing the sick woman grow quieter, he gripped her other hand, too. With surprise and happiness he saw her fall into a quiet, restorative sleep; but even then, if he relaxed his grip, she at once seemed less secure.

So he could still be of some help to her, and this made him so happy that for a time he forgot the doctor's bad prognostication and his own despair. It was long since he had felt a joy so intense and pure! He thought with contempt of his sorrows in town. What importance could they have in comparison with the feelings sweeping over him by the poor dying woman's bed? He remembered with pleasure Francesca's remark that his leaving town would mean breaking off his relations with Annetta once and for all. Now, beside this bed, he felt neither remorse nor regret. His love for Annetta and his repugnance for her both seemed colorless. The whole affair lacked importance, except that it had chanced to bring him faster to his post, beside his mother.

In the long hours which he spent there inert, he tried once more to reason out the motives which had induced him to leave Annetta; but, as always, his reasoning was nothing but dressed-up emotion. His revulsion to Annetta, he said to himself, was explicable, indeed natural. There was nothing in common between him and a silly woman whom he had come to know as closely as if he had been able to watch her every action, hear her every word, know her every thought since birth. Her chief motive when she spoke was a desire to please; when she wrote she was vain, vain and sensual when she loved. He compared her with the poor woman whose sleep he was watching. Even in that state, Signora Carolina betrayed how much and in what manner she had loved her husband; so humbly that she still kept as a living memory, and unconsciously imitated, his gestures and ways, even something of his physiognomy.

It would have been torture for him to live with Annetta. She would have made him rich and held to her right to enslave him; the vanity and sensuality which had flung her in his arms might lead to her doing the same with others.

"Aren't you very bored?" asked Signora Carolina, opening her eyes toward evening. In the weak light of dusk, those eyes were gleaming with laughter. She had not slept so well for a long time, and as she said this she gave a grateful kiss on Alfonso's hands, which he could then withdraw.

"Who knows, maybe I'll still live!" To talk like that, she must be feeling much better, and it was enough to rouse Alfonso's hopes. He gave her a long kiss on the forehead and said they would always be together for the rest of their lives, identifying his own condition with his mother's to strengthen her illusions. She did not have any great hopes even then. She declared that she'd given up any idea of even running or jumping again, of ever leaving the house perhaps; she might be in bed, but she wanted to live.

While she had supper with him, he looked at her ecstatically, amazed at watching the desire to live awakening in her so promptly. He tried not to see that the hunger suddenly aroused in his mother was merely the natural reaction of a weakened organism making a last effort. The haste with which she swallowed the small amount of food showed how much she wanted to delude herself, to make quick use of the truce granted her. Very soon she pushed the tray away with disgust. She stretched out on the bed, and it was difficult to know if she was really pleased to say: "It's ages since I've eaten such a lot!"

Guiseppina announced a visit from the doctor, which disturbed Signora Nitti. Surprised and annoyed, she said that this was the first time he had felt a need to come to see her twice in one day. Alfonso laughingly asked her if she wanted to criticize him for coming twice that day or only once on others. She replied disdainfully that he understood nothing about her illness and would have done better not to have come at all.

Then she agreed to the visit, unable or not bothering to hide that it annoyed her. The doctor was attentive, asked her for news, gave her advice, but in reply had only monosyllables, and found his advice received with silence interrupted by an unenthusiastic exclamation or two: "Yes . . . yes . . . I'll try this, too, if you want me to."

Alfonso tried to make up for his mother's rudeness by giving, himself, the answers the doctor wanted from the sick woman, but he saw by the doctor's pallor and embarrassment, and by the sudden interruption of the visit, that his intentions had not succeeded. Alarmed by the anger which he thought must be hidden beneath the pretense of coldness, he ran after the doctor and with the frankness which he thought his best policy asked if his mother's behavior had distressed him. He awaited the reply with real anxiety. As there were no other doctors in the neighborhood, he was anxious to keep this one. The young doctor made the mistake of hesitating for a second and then the even greater one of saying contemptuously, as he smoothed his big mustache affectionately with a hand: "Oh! These old people lose their heads, particularly when they're ill!" Then he did not reply to Alfonso's promise that he would induce his mother to be more respectful toward those who deserved it. The young doctor was offended and obviously intended to show it.

On returning to Signora Carolina, Alfonso tried to convince her that Doctor Frontini was worth treating better.

"Yes, yes," she replied, bored. "I'll treat him better; but not twice a day," and she forgot the doctor at once.

She had no wish to sleep any more, and they spent half the night making plans for the future. She would come and live with him in the city. To lure her into hoping and make her believe in the sincerity of his own hopes, he described life in town and even tried to embellish it. Then he found himself telling her most of his own adventures there and, since it was the most important, could not wholly avoid the one with Annetta. He described his friendship with old Signor Maller, with Marcario, and then how he spent his evenings writing the novel with Annetta. This girl Annetta was immediately suspected by Signora Nitti, and he told her she was very ugly and, what was more, engaged to a cousin; he could not have better assumed a tone of indifference.

In town they would both live happily and comfortably; the money from selling the house and garden would help. They would not go to the Lanuccis, who were too gloomy: they would keep to themselves because they wanted to live happily. Perhaps the hopes of neither of the two were sincere, but they were listening to lovely music. His words sounded almost reasonable. Why, in leaving town, should she not leave her illness behind, too?

Soon they were recalled to sad reality. For a quarter of an hour Signora Carolina succeeded in hiding that she was in pain. To questions by Alfonso, who had noticed her restlessness, she replied that she was well, though agitated. She pressed Alfonso's hand as if seeking relief in that grip, and kept her eyes closed, indicating that she wanted to sleep. But this resistance lasted only a short time, and she sat up with a cry of pain.

"I can't bear any more!" she muttered dully. Her breathing was fast and short. "Here," she said, pointing to her chest, "the air doesn't reach beyond here." Only from this did he realize what she felt.

He helped her to get out of bed as she asked, and sit on a comfortable armchair in which old Nitti had spent idle hours in the open air and which now was next to the bed, ready for the sick woman's worst hours. He covered her, as she let her head fall back in a cold sweat: apparently she did not see what he was doing. From time to time she gave a cry in an altered voice, or with a supreme effort brought out some complaint or curse.

She did not find so much voice to speak to him as to complain. Twice he did not understand what she was asking. She wanted air, she wanted him to open the window; after he had understood, and hesitated for fear of her catching cold, she murmured with a glance of exasperated resentment: "I'll open it."

She did not do so because she could not manage to get out of the chair.

From the window which he had thrown open, air now entered in abundance. In spite of his mortal agitation, he felt it enter his thirsty lungs, with relief. His mother continued to breathe hurriedly and in shallow breaths.

He remembered he might need Giuseppina. He ran into the room next door and found her sleeping, with the covers up to her chin. He called her with a cry, but in vain; then impatiently decided to shake her by an arm.

"What's up?" she muttered, obviously still half asleep and struggling to go on sleeping because she was trying to get free of his hand and was huddling up against the wall.

"Mother's bad. Get up and light the fire."

"What's the use? It's got to pass by itself."

She was certainly nearly awake, but used the little capacity for reason so far acquired to show him he would do better to leave her in bed.

"Get up!" replied Alfonso imperiously, but had to rush back at a shout from his mother.

Signora Carolina had got back into bed alone and was pressing her mouth on the pillow. She now asked him to close the window, as the warmth might do her

good, and soon after, made him reopen it again, always
surprised that she got no relief from so many efforts.

"I'll have the fire lit. Would you like some tea? It
may soothe you."

"Yes, yes," she cried with delight as if he had suggested her being well.

Giuseppina was still in bed, and asleep again. Furious,
he pulled violently at an arm dangling out of the bed; it
was the only part of her which had obeyed his first call.
Giuseppina, annoyed now and so wide awake, began
shouting that it was a shame that she was not allowed to
sleep after such a hard day's work. Then she became
alarmed.

"Are you mad?" she asked in a whisper, seeing him
rush about the room and fling her skirt at her.

"Go and make some tea at once!" he yelled furiously. "Or I'll throw you out of that door!"

Without another word, she began getting up.

His mother's terrible panting had lessened; she was
still breathing fast but no longer complained. A little
color had returned to her face. Supine like that, with
arms inert, she seemed to be sleeping. He shut the
window, taking care to make no noise. When Giuseppina came with the tea, he tried to prevent her from
going up to the bed, but Signora Carolina called her.
She drank some spoonfuls of tea without opening her
eyes, and Giuseppina, seeing her calm, said harshly:
"So it wasn't so serious!"

"Out with you!" yelled Alfonso, furious at seeing her
so indifferent.

"Why do you get so angry?" asked Signora Carolina
when Giuseppina had gone out. "It's no use! She
doesn't understand."

So she, too, had suffered from the woman's idiocy
and indifference.

For another half hour she did not move, but just

when he was hoping she had fallen asleep, he heard her speak. It was a thought aloud.

"I didn't say anything," she replied to his question. Then, without his asking anything more, she added: "I was thinking how silly it was to make plans for the future when I'm in this state."

He tried to encourage her and for lack of better arguments spoke of the medicine prescribed by the doctor. That should make her well, and as she had never taken it as regularly as she should, she must try. He was the first to be convinced of his own words. His chief duty in fact, what others had neglected, was to convince her to follow the treatment. If salvation was still possible, it could come only from that.

He put a spoonful of the potion to her lips before she had agreed. Shrugging her shoulders, she let herself be convinced.

An hour later, she felt better.

"Yes, yes," she said to calm Alfonso's enthusiasm. "Last month, too, the medicine helped me the first time I took it, but then it only did me harm."

He stretched out, fully dressed, on his father's bed, intending not to fall asleep. But sleep overcame him, and he awoke in broad daylight.

"How are you?" he asked his mother, who had been looking at him as he slept.

"Better, better!" she replied with a smile of gratitude. "I took another spoonful of the medicine and feel slight relief."

Then she asked him if he did not want to see the village and greet old friends. She assured him that she could remain alone for an hour or two.

He told Giuseppina, whom he found busy again among the vegetables, to look after his mother, and she promised. He spoke gently. Alarmed at the sight of him, the peasant woman hurriedly told him she was gathering herbs for dinner. She was not a moron, but preferred working on the land to tending a sick woman, and whoever made her a nurse was really to blame.

One side of the house looked out over the main road and was connected to it by a path made by the feet of passers-by.

The country was still white with the frost which the autumn sun had not yet melted. Seen from there, the village looked much more insignificant than it really was; it seemed only a couple of plain rows of houses. A bend of the main road hid the less regular but more populated part. On the valley side was another street, half the length of the main street, to which it was parallel, and next to that a disordered tangle of dirty shacks, where the poorest of the population lived. In its small way, the village contained, in embryo, every district of a city.

Alfonso felt excited and hastened his step on seeing, at a window, the black head of Rosina, his first love. He no longer loved her, that was certain, but it gave him a joyous sensation to see her again!

She looked after an old relative with whom she lived, but had so little to do in the house that she lived like a lady, better than any other girl in the village. Alfonso had danced with her at a *festa* and chosen her from all the others because he thought her pretty and also because her culture and clothes seemed superior. Then a friendship had developed between them; they exchanged a few words daily, she at the window and he on the road. Some evenings they would chat just beyond the houses and out of the village, but even in the complete darkness he had not risked kissing her hand. He had paid her exaggerated compliments on her beauty, but had not even told her he loved her. Rosina was not the realization of his ideal, and at the time he had not given up the chance of meeting it.

So he had never intended the matter to go further; while it was said in the village, so Signora Carolina had written to Alfonso a number of times, that Rosina had been very downcast at his departure.

He went closer, surprised she had not recognized him at once, though she had seen him.

"Signorina, don't you recognize me?"

"Oh, Signor Alfonso!" said Rosina with calm surprise, and she gave him a slight hesitant bow, either because she really had not recognized him or because she had decided not to.

"Won't you even give me your hand?"

"Here."

But she did not give it to him yet. Before leaning out of the window, she looked right and left to make sure no one saw her.

"How's Signora Carolina?" she asked, withdrawing her hand, which she had left, inert, for only a second in Alfonso's.

"Bad! Very bad!" said Alfonso, oddly moved by those black eyes and the smooth hair over her temples and ears. What she lacked in dress and speech gave her a coldness which made so much more desirable the friendly smile with which she had been lavish at other times.

"Are you still staying here?"

"No!" replied Alfonso. "Only as long as Mother can't move because of her illness; then we're settling in town."

"I'm engaged," she said with simplicity.

As she had not been asked for this information, it was obvious she was giving it to warn him that she cared very little about his leaving the village.

He almost forgot to ask her who the happy bridegroom was.

"Gianni."

Gianni was the son of Creglingi the grocer; a good-looking young man who looked after his father's land, as his father could not leave the shop where he made the money. Rosina was making a good match, certainly better than if she had married Alfonso.

"Congratulations!" said Alfonso, rather too late for them to be thought sincere.

"Remember me to Signora Carolina!" exclaimed Rosina and suddenly withdrew.

He soon saw the reasons for her flight. From a turn of the street Mascotti the notary had appeared, accompanied by Faldelli, owner of one of the two taverns in the place. He was an old man, with dirty clothes hanging from skinny limbs. He must have been cold because his hands were plunged into the sleeves of his jacket.

They greeted him, and he went up to them. Faldelli raised an arm, stretched his hand out of the sleeve, and shook Alfonso's in a strong short grip; then he put his hand back into the sleeve. He was not polite and, when Mascotti asked Alfonso after his mother, drew aside and looked around.

Mascotti's courteous question made Alfonso think that now was the chance to reprove him for taking so little care of Signora Carolina.

He began very seriously to describe his bad night and fright; then, in a very bitter, angry tone, spoke of the behavior of Giuseppina, to whom his mother's life had been entrusted.

Mascotti must have realized that it was himself Alfonso wanted to indict. He said airily but firmly: "Oh, we're all a bit lazy here. Giuseppina must have been taking it easy, now you're here, as there's no need for four people around a sick bed!"

It was not how he had defended himself the day before, and this surprised Alfonso. Now he saw that

Mascotti was obviously prepared for an attack, for he had understood and rejected the criticism at once. He no longer denied that little care had been taken of Signora Carolina but treated the whole matter as of little importance. He was the executor, but could it be proved that this made it his duty to look after Signora Carolina's health? Alfonso feared that if he spoke harshly to him, as he had planned during the night, in his anger at Giuseppina, Mascotti might give a sharp answer. But he was silent.

The notary now told him that Faldelli had saved some capital and intended to buy land. This communication seemed to be the start of something that could be more important for Alfonso. Faldelli interrupted to bid good-bye. He said to Mascotti, as he shook his hand: "There's no hurry, you know, Notary!"

He hurried off toward his tavern, which faced Creglingi's shop in the triangular piazza.

"Are you taking a stroll to see your childhood haunts?" asked Mascotti good-humoredly. "I'll come with you as long as you don't run."

It was a jesting allusion to the moment when Alfonso had lost his head at the announcement of his mother's condition.

Every house on the main street had remained unaltered, with colors unchanged because they could not fade any more, the same shopsigns, some windows always shut, others always open. To Alfonso the village seemed as old as some object in a museum which is only touched for repairs necessary to keep it as it was. The inhabitants' activity was all outside the village, in the fields.

Only one house had been changed by adding a floor, and the new part could be distinguished by the blackened lime that covered the old one. It was now inhabited by Silini the baker, but the house was still called Carli's, after the family who had owned it before.

In his mind's eye Alfonso easily saw this house again before the alteration, smaller, black, and sad, a house of misfortune in which every member of the family except one had died within a few days of each other; two boys with whom Alfonso had played, a child of three, and her father, who was a close friend of old Nitti, neat and always dressed in such a clean white smock that it never showed the flour scattered over it. Alfonso remembered all the details of that disaster, which had left an indelible mark on his youth. The fact of all those strong and healthy people being created and destroyed uselessly had given him his first religious doubts.

One evening old Nitti had come home later than usual and told him that Guido Carli, the younger of the sons, had such a serious case of typhus that the doctor thought he would not pull through. The day before, Alfonso had spoken to the boy who was now dying. The Nittis lived opposite the Carlis, and often during the night Alfonso went to the window to look at the dark brown house in which only one room was lit, the one in which a struggle was taking place with death.

A few days later, the boy died, and while Alfonso was wondering how to show his sympathy to his surviving friend, to console him for the loss of his brother as well as console himself, he was told that his friend, too, and his sister and father had been struck by the same terrible disease. Every day a coffin left the house; the first held the girl's body, the second the father's, while the building remained mute and indifferent as if some merchandise had gone.

Only when there was no bedside left to tend was a window finally opened behind the coffin of the last son, and there, held back by two men whom he had never seen, appeared the mother, shouting that she wanted to jump out of the window to join her family. She was still a young woman. She asked them to leave her alone and seemed amazed they would hold her back. Alfonso felt the same way, loathing these two violent men who were preventing her from dying.

The house was put up for sale, but no one wanted to buy it after such a tragedy had taken place, and eventually it was sold for very little to the Selinis, who had just come to settle in the village. Even Signora Carolina would not hear of buying it, although it would have made more sense for the Nittis to buy that house instead of the larger one so far from the village.

Certainly the notary, too, as he passed in front of the house, thought of the contract for that building, because, ingenuously making Alfonso think of the similarity between the two real-estate deals, he said to him: "Faldelli tells me he'd be willing to buy your house."

Alfonso started. "It's not for sale!" he said shortly.

"What do you want to do with it then?"

The notary's tactlessness made Alfonso realize how much more the man had been influenced by his long sojourn among peasants than by his university studies.

"What about my mother?"

The notary had been on another train of thought and was obviously surprised that Signorina Carolina should still be considered as alive. With good grace he resigned himself to this fiction.

"Your mother told me she intended to go and live with you!"

"I'll think it over!" said Alfonso sadly. The night spent at his mother's bedside had destroyed all his hopes, and Mascotti's words had made him turn his thoughts to the inevitable. What, indeed, would he do with the house when she was gone?

"Is old Signora Doritti still alive?"

This local character, a hard-working woman who always worked in the fields or at home, where she did everything rather than call in help from outside, so that it was said in the village that she even sat on eggs with broody hens to hatch chickens quicker, lived, Alfonso remembered, in a little colored house; it was greenish around the windows, with dirty gray on walls, crumbled here and there. It was said that the hut did not fall down only because it could not decide which side to tip, but its foundations were solid, if a bit out of line with other houses.

On the ground floor of that house, Doritti, the old woman's husband, had for many years kept a grocery shop and was said to have made a heap of money. Then Creglingi had arrived and, with his better-stocked shop in the center of the village, had taken away his customers. Doritti could not believe at first that he could be allowed to be ruined in that way; beside himself with rage, he quarreled with half the village, with Creglingi and with the customers whom he surprised in the act of betraying him, that is, making purchases in his rival's shop, where he would often stand outside to catch them. Then he calmed down. He waited without impatience for the two or three customers he still had, to consume the last provisions in his shop, then shut the doors and took down the sign. The two old folk had lived on for another few years together, without talking to a soul, because the wrong done made them hate all the inhabitants of the village. The old man died without seeing a doctor, and from then on, his widow only left the house on Sundays to go to Mass, dressed in black silk covered with twirls of black embroidery which made the stuff look very heavy. As this was a weekday, she was sure to be behind a window knitting or weaving. She was

an old body, just like her home, small, bent, but
vigorous.

Alfonso had forgotten those two old creatures and,
on remembering them, was surprised as at something
new.

"They must have led happy lives, though."

When he left the village in that direction there was
another mile or so of patchy green, then a stone hillock
announcing the region of stones.

The cemetery was behind the village, on a height.
Gay, fresh, all bright green interspersed at rare intervals
with white stones. There at least the dead slept very
close to the living and death seemed less of a separation.

Mascotti wanted to come with him to see how his
mother was, then stopped at the door of the house.

"It's too depressing," he asserted. When Alfonso
came out to tell him that his mother was worse, he said:
"Poor boy," seeing him so overwhelmed. But in spite
of emotion, he went leaping off to warm himself and
reaching the main road skipped along it like a young
man.

Signora Carolina was in fact worse, and Alfonso
reproved himself for having left her alone for a whole
hour.

Feeling relief after taking the medicine given by
Alfonso, she had naturally attributed the improvement
to it and taken another spoonful half an hour later,
according to the medical prescription. But she was
assailed by a feeling very different from what she had
had in the night but no less agonizing. This was utter
exhaustion, the feeling that every one of her organs
was rejecting life. Her forehead was pouring with sweat
as during a heart attack, but her eye, instead of being
dull, was shining and dilated with anguish. She could
give Alfonso no explanations, but his words of sympathy
made her cry.

"That cursed medicine!" he muttered, forgetting the benefits it had brought her.

It was a very bad day, as it had been a bad night. She never declared herself any better because toward evening she was again overcome by panting, which lasted almost the whole night.

From then on, there were no more improvements, not even slight ones. The worse the sick woman became, the more she wanted life, and it was always easy to persuade her to take the medicine, which, according to the doctor, was her only chance of life. Her suffering was constant, either from the illness or from the remedy. Another sign of her increased affection for life was her polite attitude to Doctor Frontini. Her state was such that it had broken down all her resistance and she forgot all her antipathies. She had been told that salvation could come from Doctor Frontini, and she believed it.

So the doctor came more often, and stayed for hours, chatting to Alfonso, usually about something other than Signora Carolina's illness. He had been unable to display his knowledge on her and tried to show it by talking of other subjects. Alfonso was glad to see him stay for long periods in the sick woman's room; if during that time Signora Carolina felt worse, even though Frontini could scarcely help her at all, it was better.

Mascotti often came, but stopped at the door, called out some word of encouragement, and did not come in. The sick woman noticed his repugnance to enter and asked Alfonso: "Do I stink such a lot that he avoids me so?"

The atmosphere in that room was becoming heavier and heavier, and even Alfonso felt relieved to go out in the open for half an hour. The room could no longer be ventilated; in the last few days there had been a snowfall and the temperature had fallen so that the window panes were covered with a streaky film of ice. Even when she felt her breath failing, the sick woman no longer asked for the window to be opened, for once, when she had hoped for relief in fresh air, she had been nearly killed by the cutting cold.

It was a strange life he led in that room, busy all day either convincing the sick woman that her sickness was not serious or trying to alleviate it. One day was so like the other that he could not tell how long he had been in the country. How far away was the time of his love-making to Annetta!

One day Marco the postman brought him two letters. One, according to Marco, who, on his long rounds, amused himself studying the handwriting on addresses, must be from a woman. On receiving it, Alfonso had an unpleasant sensation. So not everyone considered that enough time had passed for persons and events to be forgotten!

The other was from a man, in the characteristic writing of Sanneo, but signed by Cellani. This was really a letter from the Maller bank in its contents, too. In the cold and measured formula used by the bank in business communications with its clients, it informed him that the managers had learned of the seriousness of his mother's illness from the telegram sent to him signed Mascotti, and so they were spontaneously extending the leave granted him from a fortnight to a month. The bureaucratic style of this, signed by Cellani with the signature he used for notes to cashiers, did not surprise Alfonso. He was grateful for the month's leave and at once read out the letter to Signora Carolina, who, being in a moment of desperation, muttered dully: "A month's enough!"

The other letter was from Francesca.

"What I foresaw has already happened or is about to. I am not sure exactly what point negotiations have

reached between father and daughter, but they are going on daily, and the proof of their being already quite
advanced is that Annetta says nothing to me. I suppose
that secretly she already agrees with her father, but as
she was still genuinely yours until a few days ago, maybe
she is ashamed of having entirely forgotten you so soon.

"Immediately after your departure she had a long
talk with Signor Maller; according to Santo, who was
listening at the keyhole, he shouted a lot, so much that
Annetta cried, for the first time in her life, I think.
Then, finding she did not open her mouth to me, I
looked at her with an air of reproof which cost me a
great effort, as does everything that I do to help you.
Annetta told me that she still loved you, but would
have a big struggle with her father to get his consent to
your union. So she asked me to write and tell you to
find some excuse to stay in the country longer.

"I warn you, Alfonso, her not wanting to write directly is a bad sign. I agreed to do what she asked but
did not write, hoping to find you arrive unannounced
today when your leave is up; I know how you must be
counting the days. But you have not come! You're pil-
ing mistake on mistake and you'll ruin yourself. I am
writing to you with a last warning. By leaving at once,
you may still be in time, for nothing is lost yet. Annetta
is hesitating, struggling between her wish to please her
father, who is ranting away, and her love for you, because she *has* loved you. Now I can guarantee nothing,
and on your arrival you might be told she's engaged to
Macario. I don't know if this letter of mine will achieve
the aim with which it was written. I've done far more
than my duty for you. If you hesitate to leave in spite
of this warning, it'll be quite useless for you to reply or
write to Annetta. I expect no words or excuses from
you. They would be quite useless. Only your presence
here can save you, save us."

What she called a warning looked to him very much like a plea for help, and it shook him. Of course he could not even think of leaving the country and abandoning his dying mother; so he was saved from all doubt and, however much Francesca warned and called, he could not listen to her. But it was very sad that, by an act which had seemed natural and necessary to him but would have seemed unreasonable to any other man, he had set out on the road that Francesca was so energetically pursuing. Instead of finding him an ally in the struggle which she should win in the name of honesty and justice, he had blocked her way. Maller had seduced her, and it was right that he should marry her. This was Alfonso's only remorse. He regretted betraying not Annetta but Francesca.

For an hour he sat by his mother's bedside, absorbed in his thoughts.

"Does that letter worry you a lot?" asked Signora Carolina, who had been watching him a long time.

She spoke little because it was an effort for her, and the few words which she said sometimes came out a long time after she thought them. Perhaps she had been watching his face from the moment in which he had abandoned himself to reflection.

He started.

"No!" he replied. "It's a man I know, gossiping about things that make me laugh."

She asked nothing more. It cost her a great deal of effort to turn her attention to outside matters, and deceiving her was easy.

Francesca's letter did bring some good news, though. As she had foreseen, his departure from town was equivalent to renouncing Annetta. Now he was sure that the one jilted would be himself, and this role pleased him much more than a betrayer's. He guessed that Annetta would hate being the jilted party, and be far

more pleased to leave him first. So he had no regrets in
that direction.

Settling down to write the answer he must give to
Francesca, although she had not asked for one, he realized that, to make it effective and not attract Francesca's hatred, too, his main difficulty was to convince
her that his mother was really seriously ill. The two
women seemed to have had no news about this from
the bank. Eventually he found the right note. Avoiding all artifice, he was brief, like someone giving true
facts without bothering to adduce proof of their truth.
He said that his mother was in danger of her life and
that for the moment he could think of nothing else.
He ended with a phrase which seemed a real inspira-
tion. He pretended not to believe that his presence in
town could be as necessary as Francesca asserted.

"Annetta loves me, as you confirm in your letter.
Then, why should she leave me? Anyway, I'm only doing my duty here."

After sending the letter, he felt relieved, a relief, if
slighter, like the one he had felt at his departure from
town. After a plunge back into urban intrigues, he was
out in the country again, and the sight of his mother's
corpselike face could not quite rob him of the joy of
being safe from them.

That evening, during an instant of peace after a day
of terrible suffering, she asked him: "Have you written
to your girl? Don't deny it now, you'd be wrong if
you didn't."

But a gleam of jealousy passed in her dull eyes.

He did not deny it. Knowing himself apt to feel bitter regrets, he had been careful during all those days to
behave so that he would never have to reprove himself
for any brusque word toward the dying woman. He
must show confidence, satisfy her curiosity, but not tell
her lies, because he might be sorry for those, too. He

did not tell her the whole truth, out of regard for the secrets of others, or so at least he excused himself. He told her he had loved a girl, but found she was such a flirt that he wanted to cut her out of his heart, which he was managing to do without great difficulty.

"Is it Signorina Lanucci?" asked Signora Carolina with a forced smile.

"No!" he replied, as serious as if he were in the confessional. "It's a rich girl you don't know."

"Very rich?"

"Mm! Richer than me, anyway!"

He did not want to confess that by leaving the girl whom he had declared a flirt he was also rejecting a fortune, for had she known that, his mother would have thought him in the wrong.

That evening she spoke no more of it, but she must have reflected a long time about his words.

"You obviously don't love her," she said to him next day, "or you'd never have been so quick to realize she was a flirt or to forgive her when you did."

After an attack of coughing in which she seemed about to suffocate at any moment, in her gratitude at his help, she said: "Don't love her, don't love any of them. Women aren't worth it."

Although he had thought himself quite indifferent to the intrigues in town, after receiving Francesca's letter he found his thoughts dwelling on them for hours longer than on his mother. If, as Francesca told him in a tone which admitted of no doubt, Annetta was leaving him and marrying her cousin, what would her feelings for him be? Hatred, surely. If the memory of Annetta's fall disgusted even him, what effect could it produce in the mind of an Annetta married to another? Shame and hatred; maybe, for fear that the secret might be divulged, active hatred; she would get him thrust out of the Maller bank and try to make life

in town impossible for him. How should he react when
faced with such hatred? Defend himself? But he had no
right to, it seemed to him. He imagined all sorts of
persecutions and was shaken by imagined disasters
ahead.

His mother saw he had tears in his eyes. "Why are
you crying?"

"My eyes are smarting, I'm not crying!"

She was silent and thought he was crying at seeing
her suffer, while his tears were flowing at the thought of
being thrust out of the bank, with Maller and Cellani
cursing him out, at seeing himself leaving with head
bowed under a weight of guilt, though not of the guilt
that would be publicly held against him.

Often, when she needed him, she must have called
him a number of times before he heard.

The poor woman had constant need of help because
she could no longer turn around in bed by herself. Bed
sores had formed in a number of places, and the pain
of pressure on those parts of her body made her perpetu-
ally long to change position. Alfonso found an ingenious way of making the difficult change. He would bend
halfway down the bed, and she would then grip his
neck with both hands; then he moved over in the direction she would lean toward after turning; and the
sick woman made the evolution thus suspended, then
just withdrew one hand from his neck. The only time
she felt great relief was when, suspended on Alfonso's
neck, nothing but her feet rested on the bed. While
she hung there, he tore himself from his daydreams.
But when he was merely sustaining her while she cried
and sobbed as she made initial efforts to raise herself,
he was again dreaming of Maller, Cellani, and Annetta.

Very soon, however, Signora Carolina's sufferings increased so that they no longer left him time to dream,

for she had not a second's respite and needed him continuously, both for his strength to sustain her and for his brain to find new ways of helping her in her distress. He could no longer dream, could not even reflect, because the imminence of the event nearing its climax beneath his eyes hampered his every faculty.

Signora Carolina's most painful disturbances came from dislocations of her nervous system. The mattress seemed to the sick woman to be leaning over on one side and sliding her out of bed, and though level it had to be raised on that side with pillows underneath. Of course every effort only proved to the sick woman that her organism itself was wrong and not any objects that offended her. To the right of her bed was a window, which she wanted covered with a sheet because light from that direction hurt her. Then the whiteness of the sheet bothered her, and even when Alfonso put a black cloth over the sheet she had no peace.

"I see, yes, I see!" she groaned and asked for no other changes, but even when she had turned her back she went on feeling an indefinable malaise on that side.

Only one other time did Alfonso find her calm enough to enable him to go out. He did not want to stay too long away from the sick woman and longed at least to go as far as the village. So he was annoyed, as he left the house, to run into young Creglingi, Rosina's future husband, on his way, with two peasants, to his fields just beyond Alfonso's house, spread over half of the most fertile part of the valley.

Alfonso could not quite hide the fact that he had not wanted the meeting, but he noticed that Creglingi did not seem very friendly either; in fact, if Alfonso, ashamed of passing by an old friend without even greeting him, had not moved toward him first, Creglingi would have given no sign of noticing him.

"Am I really so put out to find he's engaged to Rosina?" Alfonso asked himself, surprised at his own
hatred and not at the man's.

"How are you?" asked Creglingi, a sturdy young man
with coarse features, sunburned skin, and little sly eyes
in a round face. He gave signs of some embarrassment,
which Alfonso attributed to jealousy over Rosina.

"Congratulations!" said Alfonso at once, and shook
his hand so as to leave no doubts about the sincerity
of his good wishes.

But even on receiving these congratulations Creglingi seemed no happier with his old friend and moved
off, saying he had to get home by a certain hour after
cutting the hay in a field which was still a long way off.

Their friendship went back to early childhood and
had lasted till Alfonso's departure, although as they
grew older the difference between the two young men
increased more and more. Creglingi's brain had developed little or, rather, had been suffocated by manual
labor. Alfonso would never have cut off their relationship, as he had a superstitious cult for memories of his
early youth. But he felt a stab of bitterness at finding
himself the one rejected. Creglingi had no more than
two or three ideas in his whole head and they had to
serve him all his life; but, in spite of that, Alfonso had
always felt a certain sympathy for his strength and determination.

He had the impression that the three men were having a quiet laugh at him. Blood rushed to his head; he
turned and was just about to shout some insult when
he found they were walking quietly along beside each
other, Creglingi in the middle with head bowed. He
doubted whether he had misheard. Then he realized
that what had provoked the peasants' laughter was his
doffing his hat to them as people do in towns.

"Idiots," he thought to calm himself. "When the

chance comes up, I'll explain what that gesture means."

His month's leave was now up; on the last day he remembered to ask for an extension and wrote a friendly letter direct to Cellani in which he thanked him for the patience shown till then and asked outright for another month. He had an intuition that a fortnight would be enough, but since he could hope for no improvement in Signora Carolina, to put too short a term in writing would have seemed as if he wanted to see her life shortened. Instead, he wrote of his hopes for her complete recovery and added from scruple that he might need to ask for yet another extension.

In the last week Signora Carolina's physical suffering had lessened, true sign of the approach of the great pacifier. Her organism had even become incapable of pain.

One morning, after a sleepless night during which the sick woman was often not only in delirium but obviously weakening in her senses, Alfonso found her voice changed, its tone deeper and less sonorous, interrupted by quick irregular breathing, though that did not seem to make the sick woman suffer. In a second of lucidity she said in a voice of anguish that she was dying; that the walls seemed to be folding in and threatened to fall in on her; that a storm was raging outside; once, beside herself, she asked him to send someone to the village to see if it was still standing. Then she wanted to describe what she felt and tried in vain for hours to find the right words. It was strange and terrible, she said, because she felt herself being martyred but felt no pain.

Toward nightfall she lost consciousness. Alfonso thought her dead and began sobbing unrestrainedly. That long day of new sufferings, the feeling of his own vast impotence, revealed surprising things that he had not known existed. The disease overwhelming his mother's wretched organism seemed now to be taking on an existence of its own. He had seen it strike at intervals, deride all efforts made against it, then struggle with someone who it knew could not escape, grant illusory truces, now, finally, kill.

Giuseppina touched her mistress's body, found it cold, and had the ingenious idea of reanimating it by warming the bed artificially. Once more, Signora Carolina opened her eyes and looked supplicatingly around. She was imploring grace from someone.

Giuseppina began vaunting her own miracle, but it did not last long. Perhaps the sick woman felt the nearness of death because, raising her head as if wanting to greet it courteously, she murmured: "This I've never felt."

They were her last words. The panting changed to a rattle. Alfonso thought that she had been granted some peace at last and that the lungs were returning to their regular work; he tried to hold one of her hands to support her and found it stiff.

That very moment Doctor Frontini happened to arrive. He confirmed death after a careful examination, as if it was still a question of remedies.

"It's all over," Alfonso said to spare him the trouble.

He had to repeat these words to Mascotti, who had hurried up, called by Giuseppina. He first refused to believe in the death, and then tried to comfort Alfonso by a speech to show that Signora Carolina was better dead. But Alfonso needed no comfort. He felt no emotion, did not shout; his voice was firm and calm. He was surprised by the speed with which that pain, that horrible panting, had ceased. The dead woman was laid out on the bed which would no longer make her suffer, from which she would never slide again. Her mouth was agape, but not to shout. It seemed open for a long yawn.

On seeing Alfonso so calm, Mascotti was soon at ease; for he had entered this house fearful of finding Alfonso in a state. He now wanted to stay and even asked Frontini to keep Alfonso company. Giuseppina, without being told, brought a table from the dead woman's room into her own, set chairs around, and put out some wine.

As soon as they had sat down, Mascotti suggested that Alfonso should come and stay at his home.

Alfonso refused, saying that he would remain in this house until he left the village. He said it calmly but firmly, and Mascotti did not insist.

Both Mascotti and Frontini tried to change the subject; they spoke of the wine they were drinking, the position of the house, the heavy fall of snow the day before, and the harsh temperature that day, and then they fell to talking again about the event which had reunited them in that room.

Giuseppina described how helpful her nursing had been to Signora Carolina. If she had not been there, the poor woman would have died half an hour before.

Mascotti sat listening with curiosity.

"Strange! So life was nothing but some warmth!"

He spoke like a peasant, while Frontini asserted that if the patient had come around, it could not have been due only to the little warmth supplied her by Giuseppina.

The doctor then assured them that all the resources of science had been lavished on the sick woman, but that from the very start of her illness he had realized that there was no remedy, and said so to Mascotti.

"Wasn't that true?"

Mascotti confirmed it.

Alfonso sat listening, understanding half, bothered by their voices. He did not drink at all and spoke little, only when forced to answer a direct question. He felt no emotion but seemed deep in thought; actually, he was prostrated by exhaustion in limbs and head. Mascotti must be thinking him a heartless son.

There were no beds in the house apart from his father's, and that would have to be dismantled in order to get it out of the dead woman's room. Mascotti renewed his suggestion that Alfonso should sleep at his house for a couple of nights, and Frontini, with slightly more energy because it cost him nothing, supported this. Alfonso, tired, agreed with whatever cost less words and accepted. Giuseppina promised to watch over the body. Never had she been so ready and active. She had informed the priest and busied herself around the dead woman, in whose hands she had put a crucifix; and she set two candles on either side of her.

Before leaving the house, Alfonso wanted to kiss his mother, and seeing Mascotti and Frontini were taking no notice of him, he tried to enter the room unseen. Mascotti prevented him, saying that he could give his last greeting to the dead woman next day. The poor man was still afraid of scenes. Frontini agreed with Mascotti, and Giuseppina in her new zeal took Alfonso by the jacket and pulled him back. But Alfonso insisted and eventually forced his way in. Tears came to his eyes as he struggled. Was he to leave his mother as if escaping from her?

The features were no longer those he had loved, and he turned pale at kissing a forehead that was already ice-cold. He had kissed a thing and not a person.

Then he was docile and did what Mascotti wanted. He left the house without giving Giuseppina any instructions; he was leaving so little in her custody. He walked along between the two men with bowed head.

They too were silent because, after seeing those few tears torn from him by the violence of their condolences, his wordless sorrow touched them.

The ice-covered snow crackled beneath their feet, and the full moon in a clear sky was bathing the white valley with its rays, dazzling on that cold night. The tip of the stone hillock beyond the village seemed afire, surrounded by pale motionless flames. In the village petty attempts had been made to sweep away the snow, and the terrible white uniformity was at last broken by some darker patches of bare earth.

The houses were silent and dark; only from two windows of a ground-floor room in Faldelli's tavern came strips of bright light and a sound of loud voices.

They stopped in front of Mascotti's house, next to the tavern. Frontini bid Alfonso farewell with some word which he did not hear; more sympathy, it must have been.

The notary's daughter, an ugly little old spinster, opened the door, and although she already knew of Alfonso's tragedy, as soon as she had shaken his hand in sign of condolence, she produced a phrase prepared long before, which she was unable to renounce though it was now quite out of place.

"You've never even found time to pay me a visit; not in a whole month!"

He tried to excuse himself, but Mascotti interrupted him by brusquely ordering his daughter to go and prepare a bed for Alfonso. She obeyed, after saying she was surprised not to have been warned beforehand of the hospitality suddenly demanded of her. Alfonso would have left that house, overcoming his utter exhaustion, had she not made her retort more polite by saying that as she had not been forewarned he would be very uncomfortable in the only room and bed which she could offer him.

In fact, when they left him alone in a tiny room with one window, he felt wretched. He had to open the window at once because the air was damper than outside. A strong smell of must increased his misery. Everything around him seemed to be rotting. The room was on the ground floor and the window gave on the main street. When he drew back from the window, the smell of the room was just as strong as if the air had not been changed in it. He nearly escaped by jumping out into the street, afraid of being unable to sleep that night even though he longed for the relief of sleep; he yearned to be free for an hour or two at least from the sadness which it seemed would never leave him again.

If he could only sleep! He felt utterly weary; his head would no longer keep straight on his neck. Had he left the house, he would never have reached his home but would have fallen asleep in the snow.

In bed he felt wretched. The sheet was of coarse stuff and, what was more, the bed seemed damp; immediately after he shut the window of the room, it began to stink strongly, the smell emanating from the walls, the old furniture. He did not feel the slow approach of restorative sleep. His misery, which he still attributed to the smell and lack of air, increased. Again he decided to get up and leave the house; so determined was he to do this that he began thinking up excuses for Mascotti next day. He seemed to have been on the point of putting his project into execution and even raised the sash; but actually he could not remember lying down again and realized only that he was in the same bed, pressing his aching head against the pillow.

Suddenly he felt better, more comfortable in bed, without pain. He lay motionless, fearing to lose his well-being. He was certainly not asleep but pleasantly reposing.

He never remembered how the change took place,

but he suddenly saw himself in quite another place and in a very different state of mind.

He was lying in bed, at home, in a big airy room with summer sun entering through an open window. He was convalescing from a long illness and so weak that he could not succeed in moving the covers pressing on his chest. But this was his only worry, for, apart from that, he felt gay and happy. He stared at the sunbeam lighting up innumerable specks suspended in the air, a faint mist found by the sun in the purest of atmospheres. He was glad because he knew that a few days hence he would be allowed to go out into the sun and air, glad because in the kitchen next door he could hear his mother, still young, and humming as she worked for him. A monotonous thud reached him of his mother pounding meat with a knife, but there was another monotonous sound, a gentle buzz, a continuous note in his ears which made him doze off.

Someone must have entered the little passage because he could hear the sound of a small foot on the stone floor and the rustle of a dress. From just in front of the door came the gentle voice of a woman: "How is Alfonso?" Then that voice, though gentle, became disagreeable because it seemed to echo and resound in all the empty spaces of the big house. Whose was it, that it sounded so familiar? He compared it with all the women's voices that he knew, and it matched none of them. "Ah yes, Francesca's!" And a sense of deep discomfort swept over him, and he thought: "If she's settled in the village, she'll destroy the quiet of all its inhabitants."

The door had opened and at once the room was invaded by loud sounds of carts in the streets and prolonged shouts of carters. Instinctively he shut his eyes to isolate himself. It was his mother. Before she reached his bed, he saw her and her pleased smile at finding

him so quiet. She bent down and kissed him, but on
the cavity of his ear. He felt a sharp pain as if something inside had burst, and woke up.

Light entering the window dazzled him. Day already?
His surprise was the greater because he still felt tired as
if he had slept at most an hour.

By his bed stood Mascotti and Frontini; they did not
seem to have noticed that he had opened his eyes.

"How long can it last?" asked Mascotti, looking worried and stroking his nose with his forefinger.

"Who can tell? Maybe a fortnight. It's probably ty-
phoid fever."

"Typhus?" asked Alfonso.

"He understands, you see, so must be feeling better,"
cried Mascotti, pleased.

"He has a temperature, but it's slight," said Frontini
turning to Alfonso, "and probably due to exhaustion
and grief. I guarantee it's nothing serious. He's much
better now, it seems."

So he was ill, and surprised not to have noticed it
before. He had a fever which still sent quivers up his
spine, made his body hot and dry, gave him a tendency
to laugh. It was not unpleasant, as the dreams it gave
him had not been either.

"So you're better, eh?" asked Mascotti, and bent
over him as if wanting Frontini not to hear. Alfonso
never forgot either that dream or what he heard then.
"I'd be quite willing to have you here, but there's no
one who can look after you as you need. Giuseppina
can act as nurse, as she's trained."

"Yes, yes, home!" cried Alfonso, whose fever did not
prevent him from seeing this poor man's fear of having
to keep a sick man in his house.

He heard Mascotti turn to Frontini and say that Alfonso himself wanted to return home.

He dozed off again but did not fall fast asleep. He

was struggling with fever and dominating it every now and again. He heard his mother's voice asking him how he was and, soon after, glimpsed the blond gleams of Frontini's mustache. Frontini was assiduous. Every time Alfonso opened his eyes, he saw him by the bed, taking his pulse or putting bits of ice on his head. He must be a good person, and Alfonso, in his fever, was touched by the poor man whom he had so hated.

Then his fever increased again, and with it came a violent headache. He panted in agony.

"Oh! Poor mother!" he thought, remembering that other panting he had watched, which must have been so much more agonizing than his own.

He must have lost the notion of time because, re-opening his eyes, he found it was dark. A night light was glimmering next to the bed, and Giuseppina, half asleep, was lying under the window on a sofa parallel to his bed. So they had called her rather than put him out of the house! Mascotti was a good person, too.

He felt very thirsty and put a foot out of bed to go and drink a bottle of water which he had noticed because it reflected the tiny night light.

"Now, will you stay in bed?" cried Giuseppina, suddenly coming toward him threateningly.

He drew his leg back in terror.

"I only wanted some water!" he said in excuse.

"Ah! He's come around," said Giuseppina, at her ease, thinking aloud. "Sorry," she added, in her coarse man's voice that was not used to apologizing. "They told me to be very careful with you!" She gave him as much water as he wanted.

He must have spent many days in that state because often, opening his eyes, he would be surprised to find daylight after shutting them in the dark.

Once when he opened his eyes he was surprised to find himself in the street in front of Mascotti's house, being supported by Frontini and Giuseppina. Uncertain whether it was a dream, he showed no surprise and asked for no explanations. He was put into a cart, which moved off at once, slowly but not avoiding a shaking like whiplashes on irregular cobbles. He was glad to find this vision driven out by others, and when that journey came back to him during the night it seemed the fruit of delirium.

But in the morning, calm now as if after a long rest, with a mind quiet and somewhat torpid, though turned only on what had preceded his illness, he realized that journey had not been a vision. There was his room at home in exact detail, its old furniture, the pendulum clock, which was ticking and showing eight o'clock, two beds. There was his mother's bed, too. The body had been taken away, and it had been remade as if the person who had left it intended to lie down again that night. The pillow was the same; he recognized it by a large coffee stain made by the dead woman when she pushed away a cup offered her in a moment of intense suffering.

That was enough for him to evoke all the terrible events at which he had been present during the last fortnight. Tears came to his eyes, sweet ones of compassion. It was not sorrow at feeling himself all alone in the world that made him weep. He wept for the poor old woman who had died loving a life which she had long known was to abandon her. He himself was still living, and life was sweet when the flow of the blood, the mechanism responsible for its regularity, could not be felt and there was only the calm and certainty of living, the sense of lasting forever.

At seeing Giuseppina, he began to laugh, because he remembered her already at work as a nurse.

"So the old man put me out of his house, did he?"

Giuseppina protested: "He had you brought here comfortably in a carriage."

From Giuseppina he learned that he had been taken from Mascotti's house because of Mascotti's fear, which Frontini had been unable to dispel, that it was a case of typhus. The notary's daughter had been most insistent and violent in demanding his departure, and one day, terrified by a headache she had had for some hours, she gave her father an ultimatum in front of Frontini.

"Either he goes or I do."

Frontini had asked for two days' grace; the third day, when he arrived, he found Alfonso already being carried onto the stairs, so he had been unable to do anything but help move him and see that it was done with care. Every detail which Alfonso had thought a dream was a reality. He had put up some weak resistance on the stairs, but after the first breath of fresh air had calmed down, looked around with an air of surprise and without a word let himself be laid in the cart, to the great joy of Mascotti, who cried: "Why, he's all right, he could even be taken as far as the city without danger!"

"Swine!" muttered Alfonso in indignation, thinking that for over three years that person had been his mother's only protector.

Shortly afterward, Frontini came and was much surprised to find him in his right mind and to hear he had been so for some hours—though the doctor asserted shortly afterward that it was a natural development and he had foreseen it. He was a doctor who must have been used to making mistakes because he did not seem surprised to find facts not bearing out his opinions.

But he had behaved well during the illness, and Alfonso thanked him with tears in his eyes, thankful, too, for the pleasure which he saw shining in the other's face at his words.

In the afternoon Mascotti came and seemed unwilling to speak of the journey which he had made Alfonso take during his illness. Alfonso tried to be distant, which Mascotti at once noticed because he had seen him angry and knew how he looked then. He explained that he had wanted him moved because the room in his home was in no way suitable for a sick man. Then, seeing that Alfonso's expression did not change, he grew confused and said that it had really been Lina his daughter who had wanted him out of the house. Alfonso was still silent, and eventually Mascotti became indignant.

"We may be old," he replied, "but we want to live another few years."

This remark was enough to make Alfonso gentle and friendly.

Mascotti at once changed the subject. He talked of the sale of the house, which was now necessary. Creglingi, Rosina's future husband, was offering ten thousand francs, including everything, even the furniture.

"It doesn't seem a bad offer to me," said Mascotti. Shortly afterward, he left.

Alone again, for the first time Alfonso thought over that adventure of his in the city. Illness had rested his brain, and the thought of Annetta seemed almost new to him. He could not feel passionate about things that had happened so long before, although he considered himself almost responsible for them. Now he was a new man who knew what he wanted. The other person, the one who had seduced Annetta, was an ailing boy with whom he had nothing in common. It was not the first time he thought he had left boyhood behind.

If, on his return, he found Annetta still loved him, he would marry her because he knew his duty. But he would warn her and try to show her what a huge mistake they would make by their union. He would say: "I'm like this and you're like that, but if I were to become your legal master I'd use every means at my disposal to change you, your tastes and your habits." And also: "Of course I love you but not enough to love and tolerate your faults. When I first knew you, I despised you for a long time, sometimes even when I was showing love."

He felt these thoughts stir his blood, making his forehead sweat and his sight dim. The struggle in which he was about to engage was serious, and coming immediately after that period of sweet fever which had made him live among dear ghosts of the past, he felt its harshness all the more.

But if, on the other hand, Annetta no longer loved him and was already engaged to another, as Francesca had foreseen, then he would withdraw into solitude and live calmly and happily. The affair's only consequence would be to destroy his chances of advancement in the Maller bank. That was no great disaster because his pay was adequate as it was. Anyway, he did not have enough aptitude for commerce to give him any right to much advancement, and he lost very little by spoiling his chance of getting it for other reasons.

He smiled at the ghost of his mother, who seemed to approve his propositions. His conscience was calm. He was doing what was right according to a definite moral code, for on the one hand he declared himself ready to carry out his obligations toward Annetta, although he regretted having assumed them, and on the other he was renouncing riches because he did not want them if stolen.

If Annetta no longer loved him, he would opt out of life, lose all interest in it, and, in the contemplative life to which he intended to dedicate himself, would have no need to flatter or pretend, and run no risk of one fine day finding himself involved in another love affair born of vanity or cupidity. He would live with desires that were simple, sincere, and thus lasting.

That evening the doctor found he still had a slight temperature and expressed a fear that it might rise again. Alfonso was not afraid of this because he knew the causes of the relapse better than the doctor, and in fact after a long dreamless sleep he found his head free and himself so much stronger that he could spend all day sitting up in bed.

On the last day which he spent in bed he received a visit from Creglingi about the sale of the house. By chance, Mascotti had come half an hour before to warn him hurriedly that Faldelli was making a better offer than Creglingi. Faldelli wanted to open another tavern and would use the upper rooms of the house as granaries and the lower ones, two of which were very big, as cellars. He was offering twelve thousand francs. Creglingi's visit was unexpected because Mascotti had promised to warn him that they were not prepared to sign a contract on the terms of his offer. But Alfonso would have been sorry to see his father's house turned into a tavern and asked Mascotti to get Creglingi to increase his offer. On first seeing him, Alfonso thought Creglingi had had a word with Mascotti, but instead found him surprised and angry to hear himself asked to increase his offer. Alfonso explained that Faldelli had offered more and so he could not give him preference although he wanted to. He was quite sincere. Had he not feared Mascotti's derision, he would have accepted Creglingi's offer without more ado. He would have liked to hand his house over to pretty Rosina, and indeed what most induced him to prefer Greglingi was the fear that Creglingi would think him an enemy because he was marrying an old love of Alfonso's. The difference of two thousand francs seemed insignificant. When Alfonso mentioned his wish to favor him, an ironical smile passed over Creglingi's face. Alfonso was deeply wounded.

"Even if I wanted to," he shouted, "my trustee wouldn't let me accept your offer."

"Maybe!" said Creglingi insolently. "But before deciding to increase my offer, I want a word with Faldelli."

He did not even pretend he believed Alfonso.

"Listen," said Alfonso, whose weakness had made the blood rush violently to his head from anger, "once you leave this room, I warn you, I'll consider all dealings between us at an end."

Greglingi lost his temper and said that he did not believe in personal considerations in business and would not cede to pressure.

"Business matters can't just be arranged like this on the spot!"

Faldelli, who came alone, found Alfonso still angry. Without reading the contract which Faldelli had brought, Alfonso signed it at once, although he had not been asked to do so in such a hurry. Some clauses were to be filled in later, and finding the other so ready to accept the contract, Faldelli lowered his offer. The furniture was older than he had thought, he said.

Although Creglingi had heard that the contract was already signed, he came to visit Alfonso once again, this time obviously to hurt him. He said two or three times that if he had been given time to reflect he would have paid very much more. This assertion left Alfonso calm, and he smiled contemptuously; but Creglingi interrupted this contempt in a way Alfonso did not mean.

"Yes," he muttered bitterly, seeing that the question of money did not affect Alfonso, "what you really care about is harming me."

Alfonso did not defend himself because he realized
that however he behaved this man's enmity would find
some reason for increasing. They parted brusquely,
never to see each other again.

He did see Rosina again and felt a sense of repulsion
as if he had met Creglingi himself. He made an effort
to control himself; he did not want to identify her with
her future husband, and gave her a smiling greeting,
even raising his hat to add to his courtesy. Rosina's
big black eyes widened with surprise, and she gave him
a hesitant "good day." Obviously Alfonso's form of
greeting would never become familiar in the village.

Some days before his departure, Mascotti asked him
to pay a farewell visit to his daughter, but Alfonso did
not go, although he promised to do so. He felt no rancor but found it a bother to have to hear her gossip or
backbiting. Mascotti became very cold toward him, and
only on the last day did he grow warmer.

That day Faldelli brought him all the money, one
franc atop the other, as he had said. Mascotti wanted
to leave, but Faldelli, who had arrived unexpectedly,
asked him to stay and witness the exchange of docu-
ments. Instead of twelve thousand francs, he paid nine
thousand only, and to cover the gap handed over a receipt from Mascotti with various items. In his first surprise Alfonso, somewhat offended, asked Mascotti why
he had not waited to be paid the money due him. Mascotti, confused, declared that he had acted thus to avoid
bother for him, and Alfonso had time enough to convince himself that it would be indecorous to make a
single word of complaint about the large amount sub-
tracted and did not examine the items till he was alone.

These were mainly chemist's bills, although they did
not come to more than a few hundred francs altogether,
then a receipt from Giuseppina for a sum which Al-

fonso did not find higher than she deserved, and a receipt from Frontini for an amount which would have made the most wretched doctor in town smile with contempt. Finally, there was a little note from Mascotti to justify the missing part, over half. On it were two words in pencil, of which Alfonso could only decipher one, "Trusteeship," and then the sum.

Alfonso's behavior seemed to have pleased Mascotti, for without being asked he suggested accompanying him on the visit which Alfonso made to the cemetery before his departure.

"Leave you alone there with your sorrow? I wouldn't have the conscience!"

His presence helped to lessen Alfonso's emotion. He had expected to feel sorrow and was surprised when it did not seize him. He stood there motionless in front of the little heap of bare earth, his mother's tomb, still without the headstone which had been commissioned, and felt so cold that he tried to make excuses to himself. What lay beneath? A decayed body which no longer bore even traces of "who" had lived in it. That "who," soul or occult force, faith of philosophers, was not in that tomb.

The cemetery was arranged like any other field, surrounded by a wall. The tombs, mostly furnished with little stone crosses, were arranged regularly one behind the other, with inscriptions facing the main road, which ran by the shorter side of the cemetery. It looked like an oblong field on which a hoe had made long, regular furrows. A single alley divided it and led to a small chapel opposite the entrance.

Old Nitti's tomb was near the entrance, but two rows away from the dividing alley. To reach it, Alfonso had to walk over those tombs. He came opposite a raised stone with his father's name and the years of his birth and death. How many tears Alfonso had shed on that tomb! How simple and how strong had been his feelings at his father's death!

The night before his departure, Giuseppina told him that Faldelli had hired her and told her what changes he intended to make in the house. The new owner would be putting the building to better use than the Nittis had been able to. Meanwhile, the part most useful to him would be that completely abandoned by the Nittis. "In the hands of those people," he had told Giuseppina, "it was so much dead capital." Like all ambitious men, he liked chatting about his plans.

Alfonso was almost turned out of the house. He was wakened up in the morning at four by Faldelli in person and told that he could go on sleeping and that he, Faldelli, had only come to ask if he could put all the furniture in the house into that room. Alfonso got up and, before leaving for the station, stood for half an hour looking at workmen carrying into that room pieces of furniture whose existence he had forgotten.

"Would you like this?" asked Faldelli, proffering a long wooden pipe with a meerschaum bowl.

He recognized it. His father had not used it in the last years of his life, so it was a memory of the loveliest years, when his parents had been healthy and he in his first youth in that house. Pride kept him from accepting it, but he wanted to show his gratitude to Faldelli and shook his hand affectionately when he said good-bye. Faldelli was kind but distracted, and suddenly let out a curse and kicked a peasant who in moving a table had broken a door panel. Alfonso smiled, noticing how tight Faldelli's clothes stretched at this; usually they were all wrinkled around him.

During the journey, Alfonso was all alone in his third-class carriage.

At an intermediate station he heard quarreling voices.

He looked out of the window and saw a very shabbily dressed individual jumping out of a carriage with a single leap. He had been thrown out: the inspector told Alfonso he had not paid his fare and that it was only from goodness that he had not been arrested.

As the train moved off, the poor devil was still standing in the same place, cleaning on his sleeve a filthy hat which had fallen as he jumped. He was looking after the train with intense longing. Whatever would he do in that village where he had happened by chance and knew no one?

CHAPTER

XVII

Arrival in town was dreary. Out in the country, gay white snowflakes had swirled, but here a sirocco was blowing from the sea and there was a monotonous drizzle over the city. Alfonso had a sad feeling that this weather would never change. There were no separate clouds in the sky, but one single layer of dirty gray as far as the horizon.

He was just leaving the station when he was stopped by Prarchi, who came running up and in his hurry forgot to shut his umbrella, though he was under cover.

"Have you seen Fumigi?"

"No, I have not!"

"Could he have arrived already?" and he left Alfonso to go and speak to the stationmaster.

He returned to Alfonso, who did not understand how the stationmaster could have given news of a single passenger so soon.

"He's not arriving today! And what may you be doing around here?"

"I've just arrived this minute myself," replied Alfonso, amazed the other did not know of his long absence.

"Oh, really!" Then he was sorry, in turn, at showing such ignorance about Alfonso's doings, and tried to correct himself. "I'm so absentminded! Of course I knew you were away! Macario and Maller told me."

They set off walking across the square and into Via Ghega, which from there plunged, compact and narrow, deep into the city. After a few paces they had reached the main streets.

"Are you in mourning?" asked Prarchi, with a surprise that he thought legitimate.

"Yes, for my mother."

Prarchi gave his condolences, then, put out at being unable to talk normally, tried to say good-bye. But Alfonso was eager to hear news of the Mallers as soon as possible and offered to accompany him in whatever direction he was going.

Then, finding Prarchi still mute, he told him that he had been away from town for over a month and no one had bothered to write him anything; and he asked for news of each and every member of the Wednesday Club. He managed to hint that there was one particular bit of news he wanted, and that a word about it from Prarchi would satisfy all his other curiosity.

But Prarchi did not say it and spoke of Fumigi. He repeated, partly, what Alfonso already knew. Fumigi, after the forced liquidation of his business, had shown

symptoms of an illness which Prarchi had at once diagnosed as progressive paralysis, while others wavered between that and spinal meningitis. Prarchi's voice showed
no emotion except when he described how he had in
a veiled way hinted at a famous doctor's ignorance.
Fumigi's wretched fate had given the young doctor mo-
ments of great satisfaction, and he spoke of this more
than of Fumigi's fate. Prarchi had been correct in another assertion, confirmed by Maller's accountant. Fumigi's disease was not the consequence of his commer-
cial ruin but its cause; the first symptoms of illness had
shown in his business affairs themselves.

"Oh, it's tragic!" and here Prarchi became volubly
sympathetic. "The work of a lifetime lost due to some
little corrupted nerve! The silly man, though feeling ill,
was determined to go on working and in a few weeks
plunged into speculations which the care of a lifetime
couldn't compensate for. It's sometimes a great advantage to see a doctor in time."

Still fixed on one idea, Alfonso now found a way of
making Prarchi talk about Annetta.

"Didn't he contract his illness from love of Annetta?"

"I don't think so!" replied Prarchi. "Maybe that was
the drop that overfilled the cup, but such illnesses build
up slowly. It must have been undermining Fumigi's
constitution for years! He worked too hard and lived a
celibate life: no other explanations are needed, it seems
to me. Now we can follow the progress of his paralysis,
but it had surely been growing in him for a long time.
A symptom is that he's always staring at figures, even
now."

Both silent, they crossed Via dei Forni. The Maller
house, seen through that water-soaked atmosphere,
looked just as it had through the snow on the day of
his departure; gray, solemn, shut. The inhabitants of
the house, in spite of the late hour, were still asleep.

Prarchi had not looked in that direction. He was still thinking of Fumigi.

"Now he's been handed over to me," he said bitterly, "when the most interesting phase is already over. Not that I could have brought him any relief before, but now I'm watching the process with complete indifference because it's been described thousands of times in great detail already, while, before, it would have been interesting to watch the clouding of his mind when it was still firm enough to put up resistance."

Alfonso did not open his mouth, despairing now of learning any news of Annetta from Prarchi. Had his conscience been clear, he would have asked him outright, but did not dare to.

Only when saying good-bye did Prarchi touch on the subject. Beyond the bridge, shaking hands with Alfonso, he said, laughing at him point blank: "Let's hope Signorina Annetta hasn't made another victim!" And he stared at Alfonso. "It was obvious long ago that Macario would get her in the end. You're clever enough to have foreseen that, as I did."

Instead, though Alfonso had been forewarned, the news gave him two surprises. One, the fact itself, which he had not expected; and the other, a sudden sharp stab of jealousy. As usual, he was thinking up an attitude which could prevent Prarchi from noticing his emotion, and too much carelessness, he thought, might arouse suspicion.

"Really?" he asked with surprise, but pleasantly, so he thought. "Is it official?" Then, not wanting to show he doubted the truth of the news, he added, to explain his question: "Can one congratulate her at once?"

Suddenly it seemed that it could not be true.

Prarchi said it was not official and that he had not yet congratulated Macario, but it was certainly true. The Wednesday Club no longer existed, and Federico

had come from Paris for his sister's engagement cere-
mony.

"Maybe they'll go on to the wedding at once," added
Prarchi, laughing, "because Macario is said to be in a
great hurry, and even Annetta doesn't want things to
drag on."

That the Wednesday Club no longer existed and that
Federico had come unexpectedly from Paris were not
sufficient proof that Annetta was engaged; so Alfonso
soon persuaded himself that they proved the news
was wholly an invention.

Prarchi went off convinced he had been wrong about
Alfonso's feelings for Annetta, and Alfonso had the
satisfaction of having succeeded in making Prarchi believe in his indifference. This soothed him; he would
behave in the same way to everyone and deceive them
all, as he had Prarchi.

As soon as he was alone, he felt intuitively that Annetta was already engaged to Macario. There was nothing in that to surprise him. He had been warned it
would happen and found it strange that, on receiving
Francesca's letter, the one giving him that news, he had
not felt the stab at the heart which had almost made
him cry out in front of Prarchi. He found an explanation for that, too. There in the country, seen from afar,
such things lost their importance. He had been more
worried by Creglingi's hatred than by Francesca's
threats.

He crossed the piazza, lost in thought amid the din
of fruit and vegetable vendors. He found himself surrounded by groups of maidservants doing their shop-
ping. They looked serene and had the frank air to which
their hour of independenc gave them a right. An occasional housewife or young lady passed hurriedly by,
accompanied by her maid. He did not press, through,
but waited for a long time until the groups dissolved

and left the way free for a single fruit vendor, roughly dressed but wearing gleaming black boots, to move a big umbrella and let him pass. In Alfonso's state of mind he was only too glad to be forced to walk slowly.

But he had still been in town when Francesca warned him of what was about to happen, and the impression it made on him then had been weak. Yes, indeed! He had been right to leave, as he recognized even then, for he had not forgotten any of the reasons that had led to that step. So why this surprise, sorrow, and jealousy?

What did still surprise him was that the choice had fallen on Macario. Annetta had never shown any great sympathy for her cousin, and in his turn Macario had spoken of Annetta in a way which might show he loved and desired her, but not that he wanted to marry her. He had so disliked Annetta's mathematical faculties and her pretensions and caprices! It was reasonable of Alfonso to be displeased that Macario was to become Annetta's husband rather than another, for Macario was or had been his friend and this relationship made his own future bearing more difficult. He saw himself invited to the wedding or even chosen as Macario's best man! That might do nicely as a plot for a novel, but what a bore and pretense in reality!

It was not this that afflicted him. He could not lie to himself. He felt jealousy, a sharp pain, a deep bitterness; and that was very silly. He was suffering from the results of his own actions! Since it was he who had left Annetta, no consequences of a renunciation freely made by himself should have pained him, and his consciousness of being the renouncer, even if no one had known it, should have been enough to soothe his pride. Once on this road, he wanted to go farther. What was happening now did not concern him at all; knowing himself free of Annetta should have been enough for his happiness, too. He was free! He repeated the word again in a low voice. Free of that silly chit who had abandoned him as speedily as she had given herself to him.

When he left the piazza, he was walking with long marked tread, his tread of big decisions. He looked around in case he ran into Macario, as he wanted to congratulate him at once on the happy event. Happy? Poor Macario! He really was the one betrayed.

In spite of all this reasoning, Alfonso remained sad. Once more, so he told himself, it showed the silliness of life, and he was not thinking of any wrong on the part of Annetta or Macario but of the harm done by his own strange and unreasonable feelings.

Then at the Lanuccis' his gloom increased. Even the size of the little low rooms depressed him, because in the country he had again become used to a lot of space.

The family seemed more miserable than usual. Lucia, who was embroidering in the living room, scarcely greeted him; she looked wan and had greenish marks beneath her eyes. Old Lanucci had been in bed for a fortnight with rheumatism, from which he might never recover—a grave new disaster for the poor family. Gustavo was not at home.

Old Signora Lanucci seemed to remember Alfonso's misfortune only an hour later. Very tired, he had thrown himself on the bed, when she knocked on the door. He went to her with some irritation. He did not understand why she was openly weeping; sobs prevented her from speaking.

"What's the matter?" he asked in alarm.

"She died, poor thing, and suffered so much!"

He was calmed to hear that Signora Lanucci was only crying about his mother's death.

"Yes, she died and told me to say good-bye to you all."

He had tears in his eyes, but only because his eyes were so sensitive they filled with tears at seeing anyone cry. He had to tell her every detail of his mother's death, and then really was moved.

"And what have you done with the house?"

"Sold it," and he told her how much he had got.

The conversation became affecting. Signora Lanucci embraced him and placed two hot kisses on his cheeks.

"Now I'll be your mother, with all my heart."

Certainly she must have suffered a lot in that interval of time, for he had noticed from the very beginning that a new sadness had altered her features. He thought she was suffering because of her husband's illness. She smiled and laughed, wanting to console Alfonso after having been herself the cause of his agitation, but they were grimaces. Before he had left, her thin lips had never lacked a smile even in her saddest hours.

Then he understood. There was other news in that house apart from Lanucci's illness. For two weeks Gralli had no longer come to visit Lucia. He had made a formal withdrawal in a letter which Signora Lanucci now pulled, all crushed, from her pocket. It said that as work in the printer's where he had had a good position was suspended, he could no longer consider marriage.

Signora Lanucci looked at him attentively while he read, studying his face to see what impression this letter made on him. She was very pale and gnawing her nails.

"Is it such a disaster?" asked Alfonso, forcing himself to laugh in order to console her more easily.

He critized Gralli, a man whom he had never liked, with his taut skinny face and short stature, certainly a man violent and insincere.

"Oh, I'm not sorry about his desertion." She tried to laugh it off, but again her face took on that expression of forced gaiety, contorted like someone trying to do gymnastics.

It was painful. To escape, he asked to go and greet old Lanucci, but she replied that the sick man was asleep. He then made a decision which cost him a great effort, in spite of his looking as calm as if he had merely remembered a duty. He decided to go to the bank at once. It was something which he had to do sooner or later, so it was better to rid himself of that worry.

As he went, he tried to acquire calm and strength by picturing the very worst possibilities to which he was exposing himself. He saw only one. To be fired from his job. That was bad enough in itself, but the thought of all the hatred on the part of those firing him was so unpleasant that to avoid being disturbed by it he tried to imagine himself saved from this situation entirely. Francesca had written that Maller had been told everything, but she had not been present at the interview between father and daughter and might have been deceived by Annetta, who had reasons for doing so. He had only known for two hours of Annetta's jilting him, but that had been enough to become used to that idea; now, remembering some of his observations about Annetta's character, her forgetting him at once seemed so obvious that he did not even have to suppose Maller's intervention to explain it. Even before talking to her father, she had repented of her slip, and if there had been violent scenes at home, as Francesca had written, they had been about something quite different. Perhaps while Francesca had thought that Annetta was fighting for him, she was really fighting to marry her cousin, who would himself not be entirely satisfactory to old Maller because he was not rich. That would have been fine! Her affair would have left no consequences except in memory. And for him it need be no nasty memory, he had to admit now. Its consequences could become so, but in itself, cut off short like that, the affair had been only an enjoyable experience. In his later years, in that old age to which he looked forward, he would be able to describe having "lived" in the sense that word was used by others.

Santo, the first person he ran into in the corridor of the bank, greeted him in a most friendly way and told him that he had been much talked of during his absence. He was sorry to hear of his mother's death.

Alfonso thanked Santo very warmly, because this friendship shown him by Maller's personal servant could be an indication of the feelings Maller himself had for him.

Signor Maller was not in, and his absence also seemed a piece of good luck to Alfonso. The idea of facing his chief without knowing what the latter thought of him gave him goose flesh; in any case, it would be easier to go to him after some preparation and after studying what attitude to take.

The blow fell unexpectedly and came from Cellani, his best friend among his superiors, who greeted him very coldly indeed. He did not stop writing and did not raise his head, except once, to stare him blankly in the eye.

"Let me advise you to work hard," he said to the flustered Alfonso. "Try to make up for time lost." Alfonso had already opened the door to leave when he was called back. "Signor Nitti!" He re-entered full of hope, expecting from Cellani, with that gentle and expansive character, some friendly word of greeting or a polite one of sympathy. Instead, Cellani, after making sure Alfonso was standing in front of him again, told him, as coldly as ever, that he had been charged by Maller to give his condolences and say he need not visit the managing director as was usual after a long absence. His whole mind seemed to be concentrating on writing because his voice was modulated according to the movements of the pen. "Signor Maller is very busy!"

he added in an even tone, as if this explanation was really unnecessary.

Alfonso, realizing clearly what conclusions he must draw from Cellani's attitude, again felt a need to be alone and reflect. He left that office undecided; he should certainly have said something, he felt that, but did not know what. And as he closed Cellani's door, he had a second's regret. He could not turn back, and he had certainly not behaved as he should.

How he happened to be in the dispatch department, the office facing Cellani's, he did not know. Starringer, in his stolid, safe, but unpleasant voice, was giving his condolences on his mother's death and shook his hand till he nearly broke it off. Then, not knowing that he had just arrived that moment and not yet got to work, he asked: "Did you put this letter on my desk?"

"I've only been in the office five minutes," replied Alfonso.

Ballina stopped him in the little passage by his room.

"These things happen to all of us," he said. "It's sad but. . ." and he ended by shaking Alfonso's hand hard, perhaps for fear of saying something silly.

In his room he was alone for a few minutes. Then Alchieri came in to offer condolences. He also wanted to know how Signora Carolina's illness had developed and what were the symptoms; he had heard it said that she had died of a heart attack and, being very frightened of the same for himself, wanted to take advantage of this chance to gather information. Alfonso replied in monosyllables, and Alchieri attributed this laconicism to sorrow and repugnance to talking about that subject.

Alfonso, on the other hand, had one thought on his mind: to find out what could have made a once polite man like Cellani be so rude. Not distraction, and not sorrows of his own, for obviously that coldness and offhand manner were assumed.

He settled down at his desk, which looked unchanged, just as he had left it: in the middle drawer a sheet of paper, a botched letter which he had not sent off, to the right a calendar cancelled on that last day in the office when Cellani had offered him leave with such laughing courtesy.

He was hated by Maller and Cellani. Before jilting him, Annetta had denounced him to her father. Who knew in what terms she had described him! Annetta, when she decided to leave him and marry Macario, must have come to loathe him; he might well have really seemed to her a seducer, even a violator, for nothing is easier to cancel from the mind than a fault of one's own which has been neither spoken nor written about. He would have been represented as the only one to blame; Maller and Cellani must certainly think that he had taken Annetta by treachery.

How would he defend himself if he was allowed to speak? Simply describe sincerely all that had happened since Annetta first welcomed him so kindly into her home. He had loved her and in return had not been loved but tolerated; that had helped exasperate his senses. He would alter the truth only to avoid accusing Annetta, not to diminish his own blame, for it had actually been she, with her coquetry, who had made him lose his head and she who had first trod the path that led them astray.

Alchieri asked him if he had greeted Sanneo. He had forgotten to do so, and went to his superior's room at a run, terrified of suddenly meeting Maller or Cellani again. He had been afraid for an instant that Sanneo might treat him in the same way as Cellani. He was very soon disabused, for Sanneo greeted him with the exaggerated courtesy which he used in dealing with matters outside office routine. He gave him his condolences in a friendly tone, said he did not look at all well, and added that he hoped his health would soon recover with the quiet routine of work in the office. That was sincere; he had not said it to make his clerk work harder. Then, as soon as he went on to speak of work, his tone became colder. He had been waiting impatiently, he said. He wanted Alfonso to take on the work assigned to him in the last days before he left, that of assessments, and also some of the German correspondence.

Alfonso accepted. He knew it was too much, but he did not mind that. By his work he would make himself indispensable at the bank; into his mind flashed the hope of getting Maller to like him as a clerk since he loathed him as a man. Later he thought of this again. What had business to do with family matters? For, to Alfonso, his relations with Annetta were family matters.

Jassy had died the night before, after an illness of a few days, half of which he had spent in the office. The poor man had always thought himself indispensable and died with that conviction, for the illness had not even left him time to realize how little his absence mattered to Maller & Company. Marlucci the Tuscan gave Alfonso the news of the death, and asked him to contribute toward a funeral wreath with which all the clerks wanted to honor the memory of their old colleague.

Not all the clerks knew of Alfonso's month and a half of absence. When he told Marlucci that he knew nothing of Jassy's death, as he had been away, the other did not hide his surprise and, on hearing that Alfonso's mother had died during this time, he did not even remember to offer condolences. As he waited for Alfonso's signature to dry on the sheet of paper, taking his time to avoid blotching, he told Alfonso that Jassy's funeral would be taking place next day.

Shortly afterward, Sanneo came in, bringing a packet

of letters, all the pending ones which he had been unable to get through during Alfonso's absence.

"I'll get down to work at once," said Alfonso, but so hesitatingly that it was an obvious request to be left free that day. He had to get his room in order and, what was more important, wanted to deposit his money in another bank.

Sanneo agreed and said that there was no hurry about those pending letters, but looked rather put out, so that Alfonso quickly decided to get straight down to work. He was starting at once on his policy of ingratiation with his chiefs.

Miceni came to greet him and was the first to use the genuine tone of a condoling friend. He said that he felt Alfonso's grief deeply, as he had recently had the identical misfortune himself, and gave a touching description of his own mother's death.

Then he changed his tone and told Alfonso the town gossip, the same things told him by Prarchi. Fumigi was ill and Annetta engaged. He had no intention of making Alfonso jealous or paining him at all, and seemed to have quite forgotten that at one time he had considered Alfonso as an aspirant to Annetta's hand.

He said he thought Annetta's marriage to Macario an excellent thing, in view of the social position of the engaged pair, and ingenuously wanted Alfonso to agree.

"Oh, it's certainly an excellent marriage," said Alfonso, sounding convinced.

Laughing, Miceni added: "You'll have some bothers now. As a friend of the family, you'll have to pay congratulatory visits, perhaps make wedding gifts."

He left Alfonso more disturbed than ever. If nothing had been said to him directly, surely that meant they wanted him to behave in a way that aroused no suspicion, as if nothing had happened. So he should pay

one visit at least to the Mallers', which would be as embarrassing as his first one. When the chance came, he
would also have to go up to Macario and shake his
hand. All this froze his blood.

Work distracted him. He was in it up to his eyes. He
still knew the routine but was out of practice, so that to
make any headway he had to give all his attention to it.
When, toward evening, his pen finally began moving a
little faster, he felt almost grateful to the mechanical
work which had helped him to pass a day that he was
already considering one of the worst in his life. Even
when work stopped, he felt calmer than in the morning. He was able to present Sanneo with a big pile of
answered letters, for which he at least expected gratitude.

In fact, Sanneo was most polite. He made some comments on the drafting of one or two of the letters, but
explained gently and did not shout, interpolating words
of praise with the few of blame. For a second or two
Alfonso felt really happy; they were the first kind words
he had heard in the bank since his return.

When he was out in the open, at the spot where he
had often made a little effort of will to walk toward the
public library, the horror of his position suddenly struck
him fully. Of what importance was Sanneo's sympathy
compared to all the hatred there must be against him
higher up? His working hard and intelligently was not
enough to diminish that hatred. He said to himself that
the only way to get out of it all was to resign his job,
but he did not feel like doing that. It was the hatred
and contempt which dismayed him, not the fear of any
persecutions that could derive from it. Once more, he
was not being sincere with himself and did not reach a
clear realization of why he was not leaving his job. He
did not tell himself that his only hope was to attenuate
that hatred and get those who despised him to esteem

him, but he tried to convince himself that he was staying on at Maller's because he did not yet know if that
hatred would show or even if it really existed. Perhaps
another tacit renunciation such as he wanted to make
would be enough.

Just as he was about to enter the Lanuccis' door, he
heard himself called. It was Francesca, who had been
waiting for him in the street.

"I've been waiting half an hour for you." She called
him without moving, then walked only a little way toward him with her firm unhurried step.

"I am charged by Annetta to tell you to forget her;
she will do the same."

The brevity of the announcement had certainly been
thought out to give him most surprise and pain.

But he was prepared for the worst now, and greeted
almost joyfully someone who had finally come to give
him explanations.

"I'm resigned!" he replied and found nothing else to
say. Then he hesitated so long that Francesca began
moving away, but he stopped her; she was the only person from whom he could hope to have exact information on how they felt about him at the Mallers', and
once this chance of talking with her was lost, he knew
that he would not easily find another.

"But why, why?" he asked in a strangled voice. That
was not the question he had intended; he would have
liked to ask straight out what was required of him, but
thought it too abrupt.

"You must know the reason; I'd explained it more or
less before it even happened." Her voice was trembling
too now, but with anger. "You left as if you were escaping from a woman out to trap you, and Annetta was
quite right."

"But my mother died!" protested Alfonso. "Isn't that
enough to explain my absence?"

Francesca remained cold.

"You didn't know she was ill when you left, or you'd have told me. You were escaping from the consequences of your good luck, that is how I explained your flight."

Her small face was always composed, its pale features always the same, but she was growing more and more heated without making any gesture to show it. He could hear the anger in that voice; she was saying things that only anger could have made her confess so explicitly.

She considered the battle lost and was leaving the field. Her first great disaster, she realized, had been to have people like the Mallers to deal with; then it was Alfonso who had decided her fate.

"I'd be Maller's wife by this time if you hadn't suddenly turned up! I hope there aren't many of your kind around, you rat!"

He already knew that Francesca was Maller's mistress, and her revelations surprised him only because they came from her own lips, but that was enough to make him forget to draw from her the news he so much wanted. He stood listening to her with his mouth open, amazed at this vital woman, who in misfortune felt nothing but anger at her own failure.

She went on talking. She told him that a few days after his departure Annetta had regained her calm and probably had begun to influence her father against Francesca. She had realized this from a change in Maller's behavior, and had then written to Alfonso the letter which he had at once realized was a call for help.

"My chief consolation in my misery is knowing you're miserable, too."

With these words she left him, and he did not try to

retain her. It would have been useless to ask her anything apart from what was on her mind. Anyway, would she have had time to explain the Mallers' intentions toward him and what they expected his behavior to be? She had not come with any intention of bringing him comfort or calm; she had carried out with glee a mission from Annetta, hoping to hurt him, and added on her own what she thought would make it hurt more.

Yet this interview did give him some tranquillity. Of all Francesca's words, only the first ones remained impressed, Annetta's message. She was asking him to forget her! Then she wanted him to keep quiet, that was all. This was enough for him to decide to adopt the bearing which from the start had seemed to him most natural and which could in some way make his position easier. He would bother neither about Annetta nor about Macario; at least the bitterness caused by Miceni's words would vanish.

He returned to town, feeling an intense desire to reflect more. He had an unpleasant sensation of not having understood the situation completely even yet, and every new word he heard seemed to him to be changing it utterly.

He wasn't so badly off in his little job—he thought of that day spent at work—and would stay in it. If Annetta was asking for his silence, surely Maller himself would want no more and would be careful to take no step which might reveal to others why he hated his own employee.

He would keep calm amid this hatred, do his duty at the bank, and not expect any lessening of hatred to result from his work but rather from his bearing. He would behave in such a way that it would eventually be thought he had forgotten everything. That was more than he had been asked.

He had never really loved her; now he hated her for the disquiet she was causing. If he was asked just to forget her, he would certainly do that.

In the street he ran into Gustavo, who greeted him. "At last! I thought I'd never see you again! We've had no end of trouble since you left. Has mother told you? And have you seen father?"

Alfonso looked at him closely to see what impression those misfortunes had produced in him. He looked as usual, filthy, a cigarette in his mouth, hat tilted rakishly over the right eye. Only when he asked if his mother had told Alfonso of Gralli's desertion did he show a gleam of anger.

In the Lanuccis' living room there was utter gloom. A yellowish tablecloth, a few squalid napkins, and all those pale anemic faces around the table made it the picture of disconsolate misery.

"Curse," muttered Gustavo, "with all these long faces one can't digest even the little one eats." Then, turning to Alfonso: "I'd be the same as usual if it weren't for them. . ."

Alfonso, from his corner, tried to back his attempt to shake the two women out of their gloom.

"Yes, indeed," he said, "I can't understand either why they're so mute."

Signora Lanucci, who was taking a piece of boiled meat to her mouth, put it back on her plate; food revolted her. Lucia raised her eyes, swivelled them to force a smile and give Gustavo the lie, but the smile did not appear; she burst into tears, hid her face in her napkin, and, unable to control herself, slowly left the room, sobbing violently, to avoid everyone's eyes. Old Lanucci shouted uselessly after her not to move from the table while they were at supper because he would not tolerate it. Now he could not move he particularly disliked confusion; for, exaggerating a treatment prescribed by the doctor, he had his legs bound in heavy blankets under the table.

"It's all because of that Gralli business," said Signora Lanucci, in a voice suffocated by restrained tears. "You can understand a girl being unable to put up in cold blood with such treatment, with no reason, for it's sure she gave him none, poor girl. She loved him."

"I offered to go and break that little man's head, but they forbade me," yelled Gustavo. He wanted to show that he was not passive at his sister's disaster.

"Oh," said Signora Lanucci, "no extremes! He still might not desert her, and as long as there's been no violence things might still work out."

She explained to Alfonso that, although she had not liked Gralli at first, she was now supporting Lucia's hopes because the girl's gloom showed she was in love.

After that, on the old man's suggestion they did not talk of it again, but they did not talk of anything else either.

Lanucci was first to go to bed, and while he was walking slowly off, leaning on his wife's arm, he complained of various aches and pains, but she would not listen and urged him impatiently to move forward when he obviously wanted to stop and get his breath.

Exhausted, first by the journey and then by work and the day's agitations, it was a joy for Alfonso to stretch out in bed. He hurriedly put out the light and flung himself on his side with a deep breath of satisfaction, looking like a man tired after pleasure.

Then Gustavo came in after politely asking permission.

"You've already put the light out, have you? Are you very tired?"

"Yes, very."

Slowly and with an effort Alfonso told him how ill he had been and how his illness had left him very weak.

He thought that Gustavo must soon leave and was on the point of dozing off. Instead, Gustavo, from very close, talked on and on without asking for any reply. Alfonso understood all that was being said, but in his weariness the facts told him came as no surprise. He did not even feel stirred at the thought of his own relations with Annetta, which Gustavo's words recalled.

"Oh! Just a few words!" said Gustavo in a low voice. He declared that he did not in the least approve of Lucia's great sorrow on account of a man who did not deserve it. "There's something else beneath this," he said, again lowering his voice threateningly. "It's not natural for Lucia to get in such a state about a swine like that leaving her." He declared that he was talking to Alfonso like a brother. What he supposed was that Lucia had been overtrusting and given herself to Mario Gralli. "I'll kill him if I go to prison for it," he repeated in a louder voice, "I'll kill him if he's abused our confidence like that."

Alfonso understood, but his one desire was for Gustavo to leave him as soon as possible. He was still reasoning, however, and felt it his duty to protest in Lucia's name.

"Lucia's a decent girl and you're wrong," he said, without raising his head from the pillow.

"Decent?" shouted Gustavo. "She's a girl, so she's weak."

From the living room came a cry and the sound of noisy weeping. Alfonso heard Signora Lanucci's voice, first low, obviously trying to calm Lucia, then louder; she was calling Gustavo. He hurried out and closed the door behind him. Then Alfonso heard an excited discussion, one voice trying to talk the other down while both were accompanied by Lucia's weak and continuous sobs. Suddenly these ceased and Lucia spoke in a clear voice, accentuating the syllables, word by word;

she was swearing or promising. All that did not succeed in shaking Alfonso out of his torpor; he felt so weak and indifferent that all of it seemed like the emanations of a new attack of fever. Another time he thought that the door of his room had been opened and that Gustavo had called him in a low voice, apparently only to make sure that he was asleep.

He did not reply, incapable of coming to.

Alfonso rose refreshed from sleep. He now knew quite well that the night before he had overheard a real scene, but he had not grasped the details enough to understand how important he should consider the doubts so hurriedly told him by Gustavo. Certainly Lucia's voice had not sounded like one at fault, and Alfonso found that enough to believe in her complete innocence. As soon as he woke up, his own worries seized him again; he could not turn his whole mind to studying facts that did not concern him directly.

In the living room he found only Gustavo, sipping his coffee.

"Excuse me for not listening to you last night," he said frankly. "I was so tired that I fell asleep as you were talking and never understood a thing, even before falling asleep. What did you want to tell me?"

Gustavo raised his eyes from his saucer and glanced at him suspiciously.

"All the better," he said to him. "I was a bit drunk and don't know what I told you."

That he was drunk was not true, but Alfonso did not try to think out why he was being told a lie. Perhaps, and this was the kindest interpretation, Gustavo was lying to excuse himself for having said and thought things that were untrue.

CHAPTER

XVIII

In the bank, passing down the passage toward his room, Alfonso felt the same acute sensation of uneasiness as the day before. He met no one whom he did not want to meet, but was glad when he reached his little office. It was uncomfortable to be in a place where he might suddenly find himself face to face with Maller.

Alchieri greeted him in his usual brusque, joking manner. He told him that he had read through the file and had been amazed at the great number of letters of his in it.

"Take care not to work too hard, or you'll harm others!"

This observation pleased Alfonso. If Alchieri had noticed the great amount of work he had done, Maller would realize it all the more, since every letter came to him to sign.

Toward ten o'clock Alchieri prepared to go off to Jassy's funeral. He bemoaned the five francs he had been made to contribute.

"At least I'd like to attend the funeral and get out of the office for an hour."

Off he went, as if to a celebration.

Alfonso did not want to go because Maller would be sure to be there. He was saved from embarrassment by Sanneo, who asked him to stay at the bank, as everyone else in the correspondence department wanted to pay Jassy their last respects since they had been closely associated with him. Someone had to stay in the department because, although Signor Maller would probably go to the funeral too, he had not said so and might, if he stayed at the bank, need a letter or some information.

Alfonso gave such a start that Sanneo noticed it.

"Oh, he won't ask you much!" he said to soothe him. "At the worst, you'll have to buzz around the bank after a bit of paper."

So he ran the same risks by staying as by going to the funeral.

But how lovely it would be if he were always left so quiet! Usually, although the room was out of the way, from the passage and other offices came sounds which were often indistinct but always bothersome because continuous; but that day he could only hear the occasional step or voice of one person or so. The courtyard which the window of his room overlooked was always silent.

His solitude did not last long. There was a knock at the door, and he got up in alarm and called: "Come in!"

It was a woman, a seamstress by the look of her; she had a black veil on her fair hair, and her dress, though old, was decent and worn carefully and with good taste. She looked at him, waiting to be recognized.

"Don't you know me?" and she stood hesitatingly by the door, maybe already regretting having come. "Signor White introduced us."

"Ah! Signora White!" he cried in surprise, offering her a chair. Now he remembered the fair pale face which he had seen bent over a loom in White's home. He tried to come out of his embarrassment. "Do excuse me for not recognizing you, but I've not seen you in a veil before, it makes you look quite different."

She gave a smile which was forced and negligent at the same time; her mind was not ready to cope with him. She said that she was coming to him because he might know something about his friend White. She spoke the language perfectly.

"Don't you write to him?" asked Alfonso in great surprise.

He had remembered that on White's departure she had remained. A fine figure, this Frenchwoman. Tall, straight, firm; feminine lines on a virile body.

"The last letter I received was from Marseilles," she said flushing.

Completed by her blush, that phrase was a confession; it explained why White had no scruples in breaking off with her from one day to the next; it made their relationship seem very superficial.

He pretended not to understand.

"Perhaps he's not reached his destination!"

He knew quite well that White could have gone around the world in that time.

"Oh! I know he's arrived because I heard it from another source, his brother in London. Do you know where he is now?"

By his urge to show sympathy Alfonso betrayed how much he'd understood.

"I'm sorry I don't," he burst out, "for if I did, I'd tell you in spite of my friendship for him."

He was taking her side because he sensed some similarity between this woman's grief and Lucia's. White, with all his gentlemanly airs, was behaving worse than Gralli.

The woman's blue eyes filled with tears which did not well over; they vanished again, reabsorbed without drying off. She was not trying to be confidential but spoke as if Alfonso had already been told everything.

"He thought he was fulfilling all his obligations to me by pensioning me off." She raised her head proudly. "I hoped in a few months to earn enough to do without his help."

Alchieri entered singing, pleased with his outing. Finding a woman there, he was confused and excused himself.

The conversation so well under way was over.

Alfonso stopped her at the door a minute to advise her to ask Maller, who should know where White was. The woman's beauty and pride increased his desire to help her.

She replied that she had already been to Maller, who had declared he knew nothing.

"They're in league," she added contemptuously. Then, maybe humiliated at having aroused the pity that Alfonso showed, she added: "Anyway, I don't really know why I'm trying to get his address. I'd only use it to write him insults which would be useless because he must already know what I'd say if I could."

Alfonso would have remained moved by this odd

visitor if, on the departure of Signora White, as he kept on calling her, she had not bid him a cold good-bye, barely polite and enough to show how little she cared about any sympathy from him.

Sanneo called Alfonso to thank him and ask him if anything had happened during his absence.

As he was returning to his desk, he met Signor Maller for the first time. He could have avoided him since Maller, just back from the funeral, was walking ahead of him toward his room, but Alfonso thought he had been seen and did not want to give the impression of fearing this meeting. He hastened past Maller and gave him a bow; he was not sure, but thought Maller bowed his head in return. Before moving into the little passage to the left, he turned around and saw Maller about to enter his office. The managing director's face was deep red, and Alfonso was uncertain whether that redness was produced by the flurry of the sudden meeting or whether that was its usual color, which Alfonso had forgotten.

This meeting put him in a state of agitation the whole day long, an agitation which resulted in an increased output of work. His activity now was in direct ratio to his disquiet about his relations with Maller.

At midday he did not dare leave the office at once in case he should again see Signor Maller, who was in the habit of going to the Stock Exchange at that hour.

Ballina kept him back with his chatter. Alchieri had told Alfonso that Ballina's good humor had sadly deteriorated of late. The ex-officer had not grasped the exact nature of this change, but realized that it was a change for the worse. Ballina was still gay and laughed a lot, but more at other people's expense and with a touch of spite. His position had not worsened and no misfortune had struck him, but he declared himself tired of struggling against poverty.

"When I think what I thought, ten years ago, that I'd be at thirty-five and then consider what I actually am, it puts me into a cold sweat," he told Alfonso, who asked after his health. It was a fixed idea with him.

A short time before, a new clerk called Brovicci had entered the correspondence department; he was very young and knew nothing, but was so well recommended that he had been put on the payroll at once and with a higher salary than Alfonso. He dressed carelessly, often even dirtily, and made heavy weather of the copying work to which Sanneo had relegated him. He was not liked by his colleagues, and Ballina had a particular loathing for him.

"He has a hundred or two hundred thousand francs of his own and comes here to take the bread from the mouths of us poor people."

Alfonso did not believe him.

"Yes," said Ballina, "it's difficult to believe, and one never would if one didn't know that the more money people have the sillier they become."

Then, forgetting Brovicci, he had a return of his old, rancorless good humor and asserted that he himself was sillier with his money at the beginning of the month, as soon as he got his pay, than he was at the end; by the last days of each month he was spending only on bare necessities.

Alfonso's work at the bank was now satisfying to him because there was a great deal of it and he concentrated on it intensely, with the constant stimulus of some meeting with Maller or brusque nod from Cellani. In the evening he would leave the bank exhausted, calm, satisfied with work completed, and think of it with pleasure even outside the office. Surprised at himself, he would sometimes wonder whether he had not been wrong about his own qualities and whether such a life was not exactly the most suitable to his constitu-

tion. His old habit of daydreaming remained as megalomaniac as ever, but it evoked quite different fantasies.
Now in his daydreams he would attribute to himself
extraordinary diligence which simply had to be highly
praised by Sanneo and by his chiefs; and he imagined
this diligence of his saving the bank from ruin.

As a result of this activity, and for other reasons too,
he felt easier in his job. If it was not quite up to his
daydreams, Sanneo did praise him, which was a lot
compared to the way his superior usually treated his
clerks so as not to spoil them by praise. He consideration for Alfonso was quite unusual. His gave young
Giacomo orders to serve him and run errands for him
around the bank for any papers or files he needed. Alfonso was very grateful because he hated those long
searches, for which one got no credit.

Without the irritation of these useless searches, his
life grew calmer than ever before. During the day he
spoke little and always with the same people. In the
street he felt ill at ease and hurried along to reach his
office or home.

He was, he thought, very close to the ideal state he
dreamed of in his reading, the state of renunciation and
quiet. He no longer even felt enough agitation to work
up energy for more renunciation. No one ever offered
him anything: by his last renunciation he had saved
himself, he thought, from the depths to which he might
have been dragged by urge for enjoyment.

He did not want things different. Apart from fears
for the future and regret at the hatred of which he
knew himself to be the object, he was content, balanced in mind as an old man. Certainly, as he was well
aware, his peace was the result of the strange events of
the last months, which had thrown over him, as it were,
a leaden cloak preventing any deviation whatsoever; all
his mind was on those events, either admiring the

greatness of his own sacrifice or wondering how to avoid the dangers still threatening him. He was, anyway, calmer than in those discontented years he had spent at the bank before this, years of restless and ambitious living in accordance with the blind sensations of the moment. Now he had forgotten his dreams of grandeur and riches and could muse for hours without a woman's face appearing once among his ghosts.

He dreamed of this peace increasing even more, of remaining as he was and forgetting Annetta entirely and being forgotten by her and the others. He dreamed, too, of lessening Maller's hatred and being greeted by him once again as he had been that night in his office when he had been called in and encouraged so kindly. What about Macario? Did Macario know how many reasons he had to hate him?

An improvement of his position in the bank was not among his dreams. The income from his little capital, together with his salary, should suffice for him, and he expected nothing from his chiefs except to be left quiet in his place.

Around him in the bank battles went on, the savagery of which made him realize better the superiority of his own position above such struggles, petty as they were savage. In the lowest echelon they were battles among the messenger boys for jobs near the management, and extended as far up as a battle then going on for the post of manager of a branch about to be set up by the Maller bank in Venice.

For this post in Venice were battling two old men, Doctor Ciappi and Rultini, both persons with whom Alfonso had had little or nothing to do till then.

Doctor Ciappi had only been employed at the Maller bank for a short time. He had completed all the necessary legal studies, but being of a poor family and lacking sponsors, he had not succeeded in acquiring enough clients to make a living, and after long years of useless efforts had accepted a post offered him by Maller as manager of the legal department and lawyer to the bank. It was a post which did not give him the income he could hope for as manager of the branch in Venice.

Rultini had also entered Maller's when he was already an elderly man. He had been put in charge of receiverships more from deference for his white hairs than for his ability; but what was worse, as everyone knew, was that he felt himself not up to his job, due to his slowness and lack of practice in stock-exchange dealings. That was the chief reason why he was competing for the job of manager in Venice; for, as the new branch was to be entirely dependent on the main office, the post was a responsible but not a difficult one.

The four old men of the bank, Rultini, Ciappi, Jassy, and Marlucci had been close friends, linked by their ages, which cut them off from the young men invading the bank; but the friendship best known and admired had been between Rultini and Ciappi. Rultini, a first-class linguist, helped Ciappi when the legal office had to draft letters demanding great purity or clarity of style; and on settlement days Ciappi was often with Rultini to help him through the terrible complications of those days. But at the funeral of Jassy, who was the oldest of the four, for the first time the two white heads were seen apart. The Doctor (as Ciappi was called, out of respect) glanced secretly toward Rultini, waiting for the other to approach him; but the Professor (Rultini was somewhat ironically called Professor, due to his linguistic studies) was looking elsewhere—with a hard, stubborn expression. From then on, they did not exchange another word, which aroused general surprise because the matter of the Venice job had already lasted a long time and at the beginning the two old men had pretended to be even closer friends than usual.

Ciappi said there had been a dispute which he never thought Rultini would consider so important; it had broken out in the tavern for some futile reason, a light word from him, spoken without malice. One day in Alfonso's room he showed signs of wanting to talk about his relations with Rultini. Alfonso realized this to be an astute but mistaken diplomatic move; Ciappi thought he was still a friend of the Mallers and hoped to win his sympathy and influence Maller through him.

"Rultini still hates me, that's the reason why a simple discussion, of which we've had a number already, could degenerate in such a way. He thinks I've betrayed him, but even for a friend like him I couldn't sacrifice the biggest job I could ever aspire to. I tried to remain his friend and limit our rivalry to that matter only. But he lost his head in a most improper way."

Ciappi's indignation was all very well, and human; but it was said at the bank that he had the greater chance of victory, and in fact, with his legal knowledge, he seemed more suitable for a manager's post than did the other with his languages; so Alfonso, though agreeing with him, thought that in Rultini's place Ciappi would not have been calm and reasonable either.

He also happened to hear the other side. He had gone into the counting office to look for a file and stopped to talk to Miceni, while Rultini was having an excited discussion in a low voice with Marlucci. Miceni signed to Alfonso to be quiet, and both stood stock still but in an attitude of talking, so that the other two, who were getting more and more excited, did not notice they were being overheard.

Rultini raised his voice first.

"He knows how essential that job is to me because

my position here is unbearable, while the change would bring little advantage to him. So this is treachery on his part."

Marlucci also raised his voice to make himself heard, but calmly, like one who finds it easy to see the matter objectively. He said no one could be expected to renounce such a chance out of friendship, and he considered wrong whoever had first turned a business rivalry into a private quarrel. It was Rultini's duty to make peace with Ciappi as soon as possible.

Rultini cried that he was ready to do anything, even renounce the post voluntarily, but not make peace. His hatred, he asserted, did not only spring from their rivalry in business but because at the tavern, in front of other people and without any consideration, he had been blamed for a mistake at the last liquidation proceeding.

"He's clever, he is! He pretends to be indifferent, but meanwhile is working quietly on the sly, stealing from me the little respect I still have."

On his fat face, still free of lines, was a look of pained surprise that one so wretched as himself should also be considered in the wrong, and Alfonso felt a twinge of pity for him.

When Rultini left, Marlucci, with a nasty little laugh, turned to Miceni.

"I told him my opinion."

The unexpected happened. Maller gave the position of manager of the Venice branch to Rultini. The Venice branch was only to take a passive part in movements of stocks and shares, that is, accept and transmit orders to the main office, and perhaps one reason Maller took this decision was actually because he wanted to rid himself of an incapable receiver.

The first announcement of this choice showed in the bearing of the two old men. They seemed to have

changed heads by magic. Rultini, who had been
brusque and glum for years, became gay and friendly.
He was constantly festive; warmly shaking the hands
proffered in congratulation, worried when he saw sad
faces. One day he stopped Alfonso, with whom till
then he had only exchanged a few words, and asked
him the reason for his gloom. Alfonso started and tried
to think of some reply, but Rultini in his restless joy
had no time to wait. He went off crying: "Never worry;
that's the most important maxim for happiness." Actually he cared very little about anyone else's sadness, but
it surprised him. "What! Still someone complaining?"

There were others in the bank besides Alfonso with
sorrows. Ciappi came back to the office five days later;
for those five days he had pleaded illness. The first day
he only stayed an hour or so in the office and left because of glances from his colleagues, who knew that the
news was a surprise to him and wondered how he
would take it—which was with some dignity, as all recognized after a few days. When he began to work, he
did not seem too sad, and worked as precisely as ever.
He even spoke to Rultini on business matters, though
before his success Rultini had avoided coming into contact with him even on those. Rultini, to complete his
happiness, wanted only to make peace with his old
friend and kept on giving him friendly glances, but Ciappi was dumb and treated him coldly. Even when he
had to talk to him about business, he did not look him
in the face.

"Oh! So it's like that, is it? Now he's killed me off, he
wants my friendship, does he?"

Rultini confessed to Marlucci that he regretted having quarreled with Ciappi but that his own anger had
been justifiable, for it would have been an obvious injustice if Ciappi had been appointed. Ciappi had no
right to bear a grudge.

"If he hands over to me his job here and his pay, and of course his knowledge too, so that I can feel up to his job and happy at it, I'd be very ready to let him go to Venice in my place."

These remarks were repeated to Ciappi.

"Pass my knowledge on to him? If he hadn't always been such an ass, he'd have got it for himself. I guarantee that however little is asked of him in that job it will always be too much, and if Maller doesn't change his mind he'll learn one day that his branch has taken an independent decision; it'll go bankrupt on its own."

Maller heard of this hatred, thought it bigger than it actually was, and out of prudence made Rultini leave a week before the appointed time.

Rultini went to the station in the triumphant company of the oldest employees, including Marlucci and Sanneo. Marlucci then said that he would greatly miss Rultini, his oldest friend in the bank.

"I can't understand how Ciappi could have behaved like this."

Alfonso, before whom Marlucci said this, thought the Tuscan must have a habit of always being on the winning side.

One of the most indomitable fighters was Giacomo, the little boy with pink cheeks whom Alfonso had been so fond of. The lad had grown, got thinner, and entirely lost the color he had brought from his native Friuli; his face, as it lengthened, had become nothing but bone structure, large and evenly shaped.

The messenger boys of the bank were considered as clerks and attached each to a department—the countinghouse, the receiving and correspondence departments; their immediate superiors were the managers of these various offices. But in time a custom had grown up, begun by Maller himself, of senior executives having a messenger boy of their own and making him partly into a servant, paying him separately. The jobs for their bosses made up the office boys' day, which was only partly filled by other office duties.

Cellani had chosen an ex-stableboy, Antonio, and though he was carelessly served put up with him for years. Out of kindness, one day he suggested that Antonio get Giacomo to help him; Antonio accepted gratefully and made the mistake of taking advantage of the help offered. From that day it was Giacomo who cleaned Cellani's room and put back the books consulted during the day; often Antonio would even assign to Giacomo the job of taking Cellani his tea twice a day. The lad quickly realized the use he could make of this situation and was most zealous in Cellani's service, to the detriment of the bank, which he could not help.

On New Year's Eve Cellani, in spite of his good nature, forgot Antonio, whom he scarcely ever saw, and gave a tip to Giacomo. This was a surprise to Antonio, who had not calculated the natural consequences of his inertia. He did not dare complain, but tried to change the arrangement and forbade Giacomo to work for Cellani any longer. He then set himself to carry on his job alone so as to reap full benefit from it.

But it was too late. The very next day Cellani noticed the change because he was now used to better service. He called Giacomo to complain that his desk had been left dirty. In came Giacomo and quickly blurted out the words which he had been turning over in his mind since Antonio had forbidden him to set foot in Cellani's room; he had calculated all the consequences and was not taken by surprise.

"You know, it wasn't I who cleaned the office today, it was Antonio. I'd started on it and he sent me away."

It was the second of January and the tips had been distributed on the first, so that Cellani found it easy to connect Antonio's new zeal with that. He understood and was touched. He gave Antonio money, but could not take his side entirely and asked him to let Giacomo do his room. His comfort had become precious to him.

This dismissal was a disaster to Antonio, for it meant a lessening of pay without any perceptible lessening of work. The countinghouse clerks for whom he worked had given him little to do out of regard for Cellani, but now he was again made to rush around town, drawing out and depositing money. What was more, knowing he had only the countinghouse job now, when the other offices needed more messengers they often asked the chief cashier for permission to make use of Antonio.

He himself told Alfonso his sorrows. Sanneo wanted the paper reserve, which had till then been kept in the countinghouse, taken to the correspondence department, and Antonio, Santo, and Giacomo were told to carry it over. But Santo and Giacomo were soon taken off the job because they were summoned by the electric bell in the passage. They did not return, and for two hours Antonio puffed and panted at the bundles of paper as heavy as, in his own words, lead.

"Aren't you in Signor Cellani's service any longer?" Alfonso asked him.

"What, you didn't know?" asked Antonio, amazed that everyone didn't know of his misfortune. "I upset a cup of tea, and Signor Cellani wouldn't forgive me." He did not confess that he had lost his job because he was so slow at it, since he did not want to spare Giacomo the rebuke which the boy actually deserved. "If it hadn't been for that darned boy who pushed himself forward and spoke ill of me to Signor Cellani, I'd still be in my job at this very hour."

Giacomo told Alfonso clearly and frankly how the whole matter had happened. Alfonso took him by

the chin and looked him seriously in his still-childish
eyes. "Did you really take Antonio's job away?"

"Me?" cried Giacomo with a satisfied grin. "The fool
was doing nothing. He's blind and lazy; so he wasn't
good enough for Signor Cellani."

Alfonso left him, surprised at his lack of sympathy
for the vanquished.

"I'd never let him touch my neck if I'd any gold in
my throat." Now that he knew what he himself lacked
compared to others he felt calm and content. He was
not inferior as he had so long thought. He could judge
them from a detached, serene position, because he had
been through the struggle, too, and knew what it was
like. And he pitied both victor and vanquished.

So convinced was he of the justice of his own feelings
that sometimes it seemed almost easy to convince others.

One evening he happened to be alone in the living
room with Lucia. She was truly a poor girl in need of
sympathy. Grief had changed her expression and habits.
Now that she no longer concentrated on the mend-
ing and embellishing of her clothes, the poor material
showed wear and tear which had been cleverly hidden
before, her skirt hung on her thin ungainly body as if
from a hanger, her waist had no shape; yet, though thin,
she was not really ugly. Lucia often sobbed, sometimes
only when her mother reminded her of her grief by
some reproof for her dreary slovenly appearance. The
girl made no secret of the cause of her sorrow; she had
never spoken in front of Alfonso but had the courage
to protest when others did.

Could nothing console the poor girl? He felt like
trying. He sat down next to her and spoke very sweetly
and sincerely, and was very soon touched to notice that
she seemed to be following him onto the heights where

he was trying to lead her, and that her ascent was being
made easier for her by his own feelings.

He talked to her about his observations on life over
the years and how silly he had come to find both our
joys and our sorrows. He reminded her of the teachings
she must have had from priests and teachers. The value
in life consisted in something quite different from what
people usually loved life for. Priests put this truth too
coldly and so were apt not to be believed, but it was
true, profoundly true. It had been a big surprise for him
to realize this, he told her; that it was not the rhetoric
of priests and schoolteachers, but truth! A balanced
life, a hard-working existence with modest aims, was
worth more than all the pleasures that riches and love
could give. The most important element in happiness
was peace of mind. She must not think that this man
who had deceived her could ever enjoy great happiness,
for remorse, lack of self-respect, was the worst of all misfortunes. But even if he lived as happily as he could,
that should not matter to her, should not hurt her.
Why did she think of herself as so unfortunate? Could
she not live calmly with her mother, show her the affection which the old woman needed so much? Was
that not enough? Simplicity of habits was happiness,
goodness was happiness, peace was happiness. And
nothing else.

She had not quite understood all this, and certainly
the little she did understand had not convinced her,
but she admired his conviction and was touched by his
ideas, while the vast amount excluded in his peroration
left her agape. For him, on the other hand, that speech
of his had been of greater importance than he could
have foreseen; he had convinced himself. Never had he
been so clearly conscious of feelings long burgeoning
in his mind. Surprise at the discovery of his own serenity prevented any regrets at his not achieving better

results with Lucia. And she had given him a look which meant anything but renunciation; it was dangerous to talk to that girl too warmly.

Now he knew why he had renounced Annetta. He had nothing to blame himself for, because he had acted according to his own nature, which he had not recognized then. It was good to know at last the motivating forces in his own organism, which brought him new surprises every day. By knowing them, he could now avoid other deviations from the road his nature imposed on him; a pleasant, easy road without a goal.

He tried to resign himself to the false positions in which he still often found himself. Though he did not consider himself justly punished, he found some comfort in the thought that it would very soon all be forgotten; then, as far as he was concerned, he would never compromise his peace again.

Prarchi wanted him to see Fumigi, and asked him to accompany him one morning to the café at the railway station where the poor man spent his time copying out newspapers. He showed him one of Fumigi's writings, a fragment which he carried about with him. It was a margin torn from some newspaper, filled with pencil marks so strongly made that they tore the paper. Some of the letters were printed upside down, others in italics, which were odd-shaped, while the printed ones were copied exactly.

He felt he must really make up his mind to go and see the sick man. Prarchi was as eager about the visit as if the illness had been his own creation, and Fumigi a creature raised by himself. Alfonso was afraid of offending him by showing how little interest he took in it.

When one fine morning he was walking along toward the café with Prarchi, Prarchi told him that Macario, who visited his cousin every day, would probably be there. Such a meeting seemed yet another step to-

ward peace of mind, Alfonso felt; now it would not be
long before he knew what to expect from Marcario. It
was unpleasant not to be prepared for this meeting,
and while Prarchi continued to talk to him about Fumigi, he was wondering how to behave with Macario.
It would be easy to show the sympathy he had before,
listen all ears when Macario spoke, and finally congratulate him on his engagement to Annetta, which, according to Prarchi, had been official for the last few days.
He did not hate Macario, and the fiction should not be
any great effort.

This was how circumstances dictated that he behave.
Probably Macario knew nothing and his attitude would
not reveal anything to Alfonso, but even if Annetta
had told him all, as was her duty, Macario would be
careful to hide it; though it might make him suffer, he
would try to imitate Alfonso's bearing, for which he
would surely be grateful. During the short walk, though,
he found himself imagining Macario swept by hatred
at the sight of him, and insulting him publicly. It was
possible: Macario might well have forgiven Annetta to
satisfy his own self-interested love, yet find he could
not endure the sight of the man whom he considered
chiefly to blame.

Prarchi, meanwhile, was criticizing the Mallers. They
were giving some money to Fumigi, but very little.
They let him go about with a male nurse, whereas they
should have him accompanied by one of the family.

"By that idiot Federico, for instance."

Annetta's brother had returned to town two months
before and was doing nothing but walk around the
main streets dressed up in the latest Paris fashions, with
a short jacket and tight trousers, flaunting his spindly
legs. Alfonso had not yet seen him.

They went through the front part of the café, a fine
room with rather gaudy curtains in bright colors not

yet faded by time; then, through a little door hidden by a green curtain, entered another oblong room reserved for billiards and cards.

No one was there except Fumigi, sitting by a window and reading a newspaper so attentively that he did not notice them. Only when Prarchi touched his shoulder did he turn slowly and look over first Prarchi and then Alfonso for a long while, with a smile that seemed doltish only because it never let up and was prompted by nothing, while Fumigi's usual smile was rather flabby and inert. His face was thinner, more haggard, but, sitting up as he was, his body seemed not to have lost any of its straightness. Alfonso thought that he seemed to be chewing on something in his mouth; he seemed at first sight to want to talk, but soon forgot their presence and began reading again with convulsive eagerness.

"Signor Fumigi!" said Prarchi aloud, shaking him. "Don't you recognize this man?"

Fumigi looked at Alfonso for a long time and, thinking he recognized him, gave a little cry of surprise; then he changed his mind, and decided he didn't.

"How are you?"

Obviously he was making no more effort at recognition; he had lost his memory but not his courtesy.

"Very well, thank you, and you?" asked Alfonso, touched.

"Well . . . well. . ."

Then he pointed to the newspaper and chewed out some unintelligible words, wanting to describe what he had read. Although the two young men made no move, Fumigi realized they did not understand him. He repeated a phrase in a shout, then abbreviated it to pronounce it more carefully. Finally he gave up the idea and contented himself with hissing the syllables of a name. It was that of a politician who had been much in the news a few months before. He plunged back into his reading after an instant's hesitation while he glanced at his two companions, with the questioning look of a dog for a master who has forbidden it to touch some meat.

"Is he always like this, never violent?" asked Alfonso in a whisper.

"You can talk aloud," replied Prarchi, and made him move closer.

Fumigi was declaiming as he read, pausing with pleasure at certain words with clearer sounds. Then he seemed to grow angry, shouted, chewed up his syllables, and repeated them.

Alfonso got between the light and the newspaper. The poor man raised his head after an instant's surprise at seeing a shadow projected on the newspaper. When the shadow vanished, he went calmly back to work again.

Someone had entered the room, and even before hearing the voice, Alfonso realized it was Macario. In his embarrassment he tried to put off this meeting and began looking at Fumigi with close attention, pretending not to notice Macario even when he heard him greet Prarchi.

They went up to Fumigi and thus to him.

"How are you?" asked Macario, clapping a hand on the sick man's shoulder.

He was so much at ease that he might not have seen Alfonso. When he did see him, no change came over him, he remained impassive; then he gave an indifferent nod, as if they had met a few days before. Alfonso had done well not to tell Prarchi that he would be seeing Macario for the first time since his return, or Prarchi would have been surprised by Macario's behavior.

"Congratulations!" muttered Alfonso, holding out a hand, which Macario shook with a bow that was polite but certainly not friendly.

Then they said no more.

Prarchi had given some paper and a pencil to Fumigi, who, though he had not asked for it, as soon as he got it began writing with care as if painting.

"Are you coming along?" Macario asked Prarchi. "There's something I want to tell you."

"What are *you* doing?" Prarchi addressed Alfonso, not asking him along on purpose because Macario had shown sufficiently clearly that he wanted to be alone with him.

"I have to pay a visit nearby," said Alfonso and went out after shaking Prarchi's hand but not Macario's, though the other seemed to hold it out mechanically.

He was annoyed. Now he had put up with Macario's bearing, it seemed both disagreeable and unjust; either way, it should have been different; colder still if Annetta had told him everything, friendly as usual otherwise. He had expected violent anger or glacial indifference, but never contempt. Macario was treating him almost as Annetta had at the beginning, as a little clerk at Maller & Co.'s bank, and Alfonso had been ready for persecution but not contempt. He could resign himself to being thought a dangerous enemy, an evil creature to be feared, but not someone who could be ignored.

Soon he had to laugh at himself, seeing the obvious contrast between his intentions and his feelings. Did he still care so much about Macario's friendship to be as sorry as that for having lost it? He should have liked that calm coldness. Presumably Annetta had told her future husband a part of what had happened, just enough to find an excuse to keep Alfonso out of her home forever, and Macario's coldness had been merely gentlemanly affectation toward an inferior, increased by a reasonable antipathy toward a person who, though with negative results, had tried to win Annetta's love and perhaps given him a few unpleasant minutes of jealousy. For other reasons, too, he would have preferred ill-treatment from Macario. He might have had scruples of conscience for the trick Annetta was playing on Macario with his help, and now his own fault was diminished by the fact that he was no longer betraying a friend but betraying an enemy.

His feelings remained the same in spite of all reasoning. He could not be grateful to Macario for, without a motive he could see, cutting off his friendship so soon.

That day he felt less happy than usual at the bank; the struggle to remain quietly at work revolted him. The desire to revenge himself on Macario made him have strange fantasies. He imagined his position if the idyll begun with Annetta had come to another end. In that case, Macario would surely have treated him as an equal, and for an instant that seemed incalculable happiness.

CHAPTER

XIX

It was a most disturbing evening. On reaching home, Alfonso did not immediately notice that something was seriously amiss with the Lanuccis; he was too preoccupied on his own account. Neither Lucia nor Gustavo was in the living room, and Signora Lanucci was sitting there, on a chair away from the table and set in an odd position, lost in thought, her eyes red with tears. The only person in his usual place was old Lanucci, his legs wrapped up in blankets.

Alfonso had to turn all his attention on them as they did not say a word or answer his questions, and finally he asked impatiently: "What on earth's the matter with you all?" It cost a great effort to tear himself from his own thoughts.

Signora Lanucci did not seem to want to answer, but when she finally did she said a lot in a few words.

"Oh! Nothing much! We've only had to put up with poverty so far, now we have dishonor too." The old man protested and told her to keep quiet, but she shouted that it was something everyone would know sooner or later and there was no point in hiding it from Alfonso. She blurted out crudely: "I'm to be a grandmother."

Alfonso pretended to be greatly surprised by this news, which no one had yet told him explicitly. He had had his suspicions because of some words dropped by Gustavo the night of his arrival; but then they had been denied, and he had not stopped to examine whether Gustavo was to be trusted when he blurted them out or when he denied them.

He was told of an incident which had just happened and which had made Lucia betray herself. Apparently she had realized her condition only that day, and in desperation rushed off to Gralli to tell him all and ask for his help. Gralli had rejected her, saying that he could not take on the responsibility and was sorry but had to leave her to her own devices. He offered her a monthly sum on the condition that he would be allowed free access to her in the Lanucci home. The wretched girl lost her head, rushed to her mother, and told her everything.

"She'd be better off dead! That would have been less of a grief, I assure you."

With this excited account Signora Lanucci had relieved her feelings and acquired sufficient calm to try to save by words the family honor compromised in Alfonso's eyes by facts.

From her room Lucia heard these last words, which had been shouted, and began to sob aloud, invoking her mother and asking her forgiveness.

"It's too late for weeping, you should have thought of it before," shouted Signora Lanucci pitilessly.

Lucia, poor girl, could not determine how much pretense there was in her mother's words, as Alfonso could —and she sobbed louder than ever without saying another word; perhaps she, too, thought herself worthy of death. Only for her did Alfonso feel any sympathy; Signora Lanucci's cries dazed and bothered him.

Old Lanucci imitated his wife.

"If I were a fit man," he cried, "I'd go to the seducer, take him by the scruff of the neck, and force him to restore the honor he's stolen from my daughter. But now I'd have to be carried to him in a chair."

"Gustavo went to Gralli!" said Signora Lanucci proudly, and when Alfonso said, unimpressed and somewhat irritated, that he should have been stopped in case a second disaster follow the first, she cried that they could not be made to accept the offense quietly and that it would be a good thing if Gustavo killed the betrayer; she would not regret his action even though it cost him twenty years in jail.

But soon after, Gustavo reappeared safe and sound and more or less calm. He said he had been running around town in search of Gralli for two hours without being able to find him; he had just managed to discover where he'd be in half an hour—at a tavern not far away.

"I'm headed there!" and he made the words ring with a threat. He then asked his mother details about the day's events. At first, when he had rushed off to find Gralli whatever the cost, he was under the impression that his sister had been ill-treated when she went to him and asked him to marry her. He was relieved to

hear that was not true, and asked if he could eat something before leaving. Turning to Alfonso, he then said:
"What do you think of it all?"

Alfonso recommended that he not be rough with
Gralli; things might still just possibly be settled, and it
would be a nuisance to have offended a future member
of the family.

Then Gustavo did get angry, apparently with
Alfonso; red in the face, he cried: "I'll not be rough
with him. I'll just say; 'Will you marry my sister, or
won't you?' If he replies 'Yes,' I'll hug him and call him
brother; if 'No,' I'll take him by the throat and he can
start thinking of his soul, as I'll not leave him much
time."

His grateful mother threw her arms around his neck
and kissed him. But she told him that she forbade him
to commit murder, whatever happened, because Gralli
was not worth going to jail for. The poor woman was
afraid of risking too much if she let this heroic play-act-
ing go too far. But Gustavo, encouraged by her caresses, did not reply, looking like a man who had made
up his mind and was not prepared to listen to others.
Alfonso offered to go with him to see Gralli. He
refused but quite gently. Alfonso was really one of the
family, though not everyone knew it.

Shortly after Gustavo left, Signora Lanucci was
seized by impatience and went to the window, where
she stayed for about an hour in spite of the intense
cold. The old man went to bed declaring that he knew
he would not sleep but needed the warmth of bed for
his ills. Alfonso began reading. The old clock grunted
away every quarter of an hour; it was no longer ringing
because Gustavo had taken out the chime.

"This delay seems a good sign, for if something
awful had happened, we'd know it by now," said

Signora Lanucci, drawing back from the window and looking at Alfonso in the hope of his agreeing. He told her that was how he explained the delay, too.

From the street the sound of a quarrel rose. Both rushed to the window. Slowly, with long stops, five men were coming up the slope in heated discussion. At intervals, it could now be seen, two of them would face each other and be kept apart by force. One was Gustavo's height and the other Gralli's, or so it seemed. They stopped just under the window, and only then did Alfonso and Signora Lanucci realize that neither Gustavo nor Gralli was in the group. They breathed again and glanced at each other with relief.

Even so, the sight of this quarrel seemed to have cast a gloom over Signora Lanucci. She confessed she had lost all hope and felt sure already of the fate reserved for her daughter. She knew what sort of man Gralli was. She had not paid close attention before, but now she recalled details of his behavior which should have put her on her guard and made her suspect his sincerity.

"When one's good oneself, it's so difficult to suspect evil in others."

She praised Alfonso; he was good and she felt it, knew he was revolted by evil. "It's so nice to be with someone one can really trust." Then, going over in her mind all the pains she had taken to bring up that only daughter of hers, she asked herself if there was any justice in this world, when all her efforts had come to such an end. She remembered bitterly that the engagement to Gralli had been a grief in itself. "I'd hoped for better for Lucia. Not riches or noble blood, but brains. Wasn't there ever a chance of your falling in love with Lucia yourself?"

It was the second time that she confessed this hope

so frankly. This time, too, it came from deep emotion; the shame that made her so melodramatic a short time before had vanished, and now she felt only grief at her daughter's fate, not at the loss of family honor.

He was embarrassed and quoted some words said to him in anger by Lucia which he considered to be proof that she had never loved him.

"She did love you!" said Signora Lanucci with conviction. "She never told me; but I realized it and was surprised that you who think you know the human heart did not realize it, too. Think of all the sorrows that would have been avoided!" So she thought it was by a mere misunderstanding that he had not loved Lucia and was mourning her poor daughter's being so ill-treated by fate. Then she came out with a blunder: "How wonderful, though, to tell Gralli, if he does ask to marry Lucia as a result of Gustavo's exhortations: 'Go to hell; we've got someone better and you don't deserve her!'"

Alfonso did not open his mouth. She was suggesting he should marry Lucia. It was appalling, but he tried to understand and excuse this. He understood how this poor mother could lull herself with the hope of saving her daughter from dishonor and at the same time avenging herself on the person who had wounded the girl's deepest affection. He himself, when he felt at his most wretched, took refuge in unrealizable dreams! She was asking him to sacrifice himself, for she could not think he really wanted to marry Lucia; she had a high enough opinion of him to think him capable of such goodness! Why should he be offended? Since he had adopted his own ideas, this was the first time he met anyone actually putting them into practice. True, rather than use them herself, Signora Lanucci wanted to impose them on others, but since she had spoken quite without artifice, as if it was the most natural thing in the world, she must be convinced that, had she been in his shoes, she would herself have acted as she was advising him to.

In his desire to help in some way, he offered to go in search of Gustavo and bring back news. Signora Lanucci thanked him, already cooler.

When he reached Via degli Artisti, a small street very dark at that hour, the tavern seemed shut; he knocked and was pleased at hearing someone coming to open up after a long hesitation. The place was oddly shaped; to form it, one or two dividing walls must have been pulled down, traces of which were still to be seen in the middle of the terrace.

There were only two people there, sitting at a round table in a corner. One was Gustavo, whom Alfonso recognized in spite of his having his back turned; he had his forehead in one hand, apparently in deep meditation. The other was Gralli, who greeted Alfonso.

Seeing them seated in such friendly fashion next to each other, with empty glasses in front of them, Alfonso thought they must have come to an agreement and held out his hand to Gralli, who shook it at once and ordered the innkeeper to bring another glass. A glance at Gustavo, who was laughing and told him to drink as much as he could because it was all paid for, showed that this youth sent from home on such a serious mission had allowed himself to get drunk.

"We're real good friends, we two!" shouted Gustavo and looked at Gralli affectionately. "I came intending to give him a hiding, but found him so nice that it would be a crime to hurt him. You talk to him and see. He's really decent, and Lucia will be very happy with him."

He burst into a roar of laughter.

He demanded more wine, and Gralli ordered it, turning to Alfonso with a sly smile. "Have as much wine as you want."

"Enough wine," intimated Alfonso. "Drink water."

"Water is for washing," replied Gustavo wittily and drained a whole glass. After a long silence he began laughing again and cried that someone was tickling his brain. "I know no one can get in there, but someone seems to want to." And he burst out laughing again.

Alfonso said that his mother was waiting for him at the window and had sent him to the tavern to bring Gustavo home.

"Mother's waiting for me?" asked Gustavo laughing, "Well, I'll go now because I've talked to Gralli long enough. And to think I wanted to hit him! Poor devil! With that little dark face of his."

It did seem impossible that this little man, almost lost behind the table, was a seducer whom old Signora Lanucci hoped to see dead.

"I'm just going to tell Mother I've settled things; then I'll be back. It's only right the poor thing shouldn't be worried."

He went off, apparently intending to return at once, but was not seen again.

Gralli roared with laughter.

"He came here breathing fire and sword, and within half an hour I'd got him into the state you saw him. For the last two hours we've been just as good friends as ever before."

"And how did you settle things?" asked Alfonso, put out at finding himself treated as an accomplice, but incapable of sharpness.

"Well, I can't marry her!" said Gralli very calmly. "But I've no idea of leaving her; I'll help her as long as I can. The family are bound to give way and let her come and live with me. My boss has a woman like that;

he doesn't want to tie himself up for life either. Marriage is too serious a matter. So why do it?"

The wine must have gone to his head too, although the effect was not as obvious as in Gustavo.

"But you seduced her, didn't you?" observed Alfonso, very timidly.

"Seduced her! Never! I'm not that kind! They kept on leaving us alone together! I'd never thought of anything else, and she thought of it the whole time."

"But why don't you want to marry her?" asked Alfonso, already despairing of being able to overcome such logic and hoping to bring the matter on to another plane.

"For lack of this!" replied Gralli, raising his right hand and rubbing his thumb and forefinger as if counting money.

"You can't lack it altogether!" replied Alfonso.

It occurred to him that by sacrificing a small sum of money for Lucia's happiness he would show Signora Lanucci that he was not wholly indifferent to Lucia's fate.

At his first offer of a thousand lire, Gralli looked at him in surprise but refused.

"I can't see what it's got to do with you!"

Alfonso flushed scarlet because he realized what Gralli's first suspicion must be, and explained that he had been a close friend of the family for years and wanted to do his best to save it from disaster. So, though dealing with an inferior, he became embarrassed and found no other way out of this embarrassment than to double and triple his offer, as if not wanting to leave Gralli time to reflect.

Gralli soon changed his tune, hesitated, was about to give way. Alfonso noticed it. Then Gralli refused again.

"I'm not marrying her, I can't marry her. I've a mother to think of and can't take on such an expense."

With repugnance Alfonso went back to reasoning. He had not yet understood the real reason for Gralli's hesitation and thought he could convince him in the end. He said that it would take very little extra to keep Lucia because food for two was nearly the same as for three and the dowry he was offering would cover most of their expenses.

But this was a workman who knew his sums. As Alfonso had said that the expense of keeping Lucia was insignificant, Gralli now demonstrated that the interest from the sum offered was not enough to cover more than a fifth of this expense.

"So you want to live on interest now, do you?" exclaimed Alfonso indignantly.

Gralli was making an act of reparation depend on selfish calculation, and that stirred him.

"No, I'm not thinking of myself but of whoever wants to live on me," replied Gralli brutally. He stopped the argument. "If Lucia had a dowry of seven thousand lire, I'd marry her."

Alfonso tried to get him to lower this demand, having already decided to give way if the other resisted, and Gralli was immovable.

"You'll get your seven thousand lire," said Alfonso, getting to his feet.

Gralli went as far as the Lanuccis' door with him.

"Your word's enough, just your word before a notary." Having so ably looked after his own interests, he now wanted to cut a good figure as well. He said that Alfonso's money would be far from enough for Lucia's needs, but he was also thinking both of his affection for her and of his feelings as a father, aroused, so he assured Alfonso, the moment he knew he was to become a father.

"Yes," he added seriously, "I'm convinced it's much better for the child to be born legitimate."

These amiable remarks from Gralli were so incompatible with his bearing till then that Alfonso thought he was quoting verbatim from someone else. But he was pleased that Gralli was making an effort to seem disinterestedly in love, since this lessened his worry that Gralli would suspect an impure motive for his own interest in the Lanuccis.

Gralli seemed to guess what his benefactor was expecting of him. He said, looking moved: "You love Lucia's parents as if you were their own son."

He could not have expressed himself more delicately. They agreed that next day Gralli would go to old Lanucci and ask for his daughter's hand.

Signora Lanucci ran to meet him on the stairs.

"So everything's settled, is it?"

"Who told you that?"

"Gustavo! He was in such a state, though, that I doubted if he was telling the truth! Dear son, I wronged him!"

She threw kisses in the air and leaped up the stairs like a little girl.

She left him alone without saying good night, and while on his way to bed, Alfonso heard her waking her husband to give him the good news. Then he heard her again in Lucia's room, and the sound of resounding kisses. The girl was sobbing from joy.

Finally everyone in the house was at rest except himself. He had done well not to throw his charity into Signora Lanucci's face, for it would have lessened her joy. She would know it sooner or later. He did not want to be an unknown benefactor, nor seem to be seeking gratitude either. He went to sleep happy, at that expected gratitude. It was some days before he realized what a great sacrifice he had made and how much he had worsened his situation by that huge decrease of his capital.

Next day, after wandering a long time around the streets, he reached home very late and missed Gralli, who must have been there some hours. He did not learn what had been talked of because no one bothered to tell him, but it was obvious from their attitude that they had no idea it was he who had saved Lucia.

Soon after his arrival, the girl left the house, giving him only a reserved bow. Signora Lanucci said it had all been a misunderstanding, their ideas about Lucia. This remark, which excluded him from their confidence, was said coldly, on purpose, because Signora Lanucci was clever enough to realize he would not believe her; its only purpose must therefore be to hurt him. When alone with Gustavo, he found to his great surprise that the brother also believed Lucia's salvation to be due to his own action. He boasted of it.

"A reasonable word at the right time, what!"

Alfonso left him with that opinion for the moment.

Not even next day did anyone breathe a word about Alfonso's generosity, and he felt no need to mention it. He did not want to admit it, but he was keeping silent because he enjoyed increasing his own generosity; every cold word from the Lanuccis gave him a little stab of satisfaction because as soon as they realized how unjustly they had treated him, their gratitude would be all the greater. He felt like laughing when Lucia, who hated him because she had offered him her love twice, turned her back on him to show her contempt, which was, however, no greater than old Signora Lanucci's, now that she had given up all hope of his marrying Lucia. He smiled as he confessed to himself that he liked the idea of their gratitude so much that he was even acting a part in order to let it grow. His actions, he still kept on finding, were in contradiction to his theories. That intense desire to be thanked and admired was quite unlike genuine renunciation. He was still vain.

Next day at supper old Lanucci waited gravely for Alfonso to be seated; then he told them dryly that for reasons which he had been told but forgotten Gralli would not be coming that day. Then he turned to Alfonso and went on: "I did not know he had been promised seven thousand lire of dowry. He asked me about it and I said I knew nothing. Is it true you want to give him that?"

"Yes," replied Alfonso. "It's no use to me."

There was a chorus of thanks, not all equally lively. Signora Lanucci could not have enjoyed passing suddenly from hatred to gratitude. She held out her hand to Alfonso and, trying to make up in the firm brevity of her thanks what they lacked in intensity, said: "My thanks to you!"

She smiled at her daughter, whose eyes were full of tears, and said to her: "Why are you crying? Silly girl! At least it means you'll have some money!"

Lucia thanked him amid sobs. The thought of Gralli returning to her from love alone had flattered her, and the pain of learning the contrary was greater than her gratitude. She cried and cried, then withdrew to her room, after saying good night to Alfonso with thanks which sounded fervent because of repetition.

"What I don't understand," said Alfonso, talking to avoid the embarrassment he found those thanks gave him. "What I don't understand is the connection all this has with Gralli's absence."

Lanucci said he thought Gralli had said something to excuse himself but he could not remember what.

That evening as he left the office, Alfonso easily guessed the excuse Gralli had given Lanucci and he had been silent about. On the Corso he was stopped by

Gralli, who must have been waiting for him on purpose but did not want it to seem so. He was very friendly, but obviously his thoughts were elsewhere and he was looking for a way of saying something difficult.

"How are you?"

Apart from what was so close to Gralli's heart, they had nothing to talk about. After giving the question a dry answer and waiting unsuccessfully for the other to begin explaining why he was waiting for him, Alfonso, impatient and irritated at having to walk the Corso in his company, asked what he wanted. Gralli had no chance to prepare his little speech as he'd have liked; he asked him to follow him away from the crowds, and they went toward a fountain. The sirocco had made the weather milder, and warm air had called many people out of doors.

"I spoke to old Lanucci today, and he told me he knew nothing about the promised dowry . . ." He was talking slowly to give the other time to get used to his distrust, but in those few words he had already expressed everything.

"Why should old Lanucci know about it? I've promised it and that's enough!" cried Alfonso, quite capable, in his fury, of letting Gralli believe he had wanted the Lanuccis to know nothing of his gift.

"I never had any doubts!" cried Gralli.

That must be true, because Alfonso knew that Gralli had acted on his promise alone. He told Alfonso in a tone of sincerity that his mother had insisted he must not marry unless he had the dowry in hand first.

Alfonso began laughing contemptuosuly, pretending not to believe what he had already realized was true.

"So you think me a liar, do you? Well, I utterly refuse to hand over the money because I distrust you with better reason than you could have to distrust me."

Gralli looked desperate.

"If that's how things are, what shall we do? Mother sticks to what she says and declares she won't hear of it before seeing the money? She won't even accept your promise before a notary."

This, which seemed an insurmountable obstacle to Gralli, could have been used by Alfonso as an excuse to get out of his pledge. He had no wish to do so, and as he suggested a possible arrangement he felt his chest swell at his own generosity. He proposed they should go before a notary together next day and deposit the money, with a declaration that it was to be handed over to Gralli only on the day of his marriage to Lucia.

Gralli gratefully accepted this suggestion, which he approved of and he thought his mother would approve of too. Urged by Alfonso, who warned him that they were worried about his absence, he went straight to the Lanuccis'. Alfonso recommended that he say nothing of what had happened, because it would not help him with Lucia. Now that he knew there was no danger of the beneficiaries remaining in ignorance of his sacrifice, he felt he could act as if he had wanted to hide it.

Gralli the egotist, as Alfonso called him, was franker than he was himself.

"I don't care what Lucia thinks," he said simply. "The others, if they're not stupid, must realize I could do nothing else. Without this dowry I just couldn't marry her." Anyway he was going to the Lanuccis' with no fears, because the moment they saw him enter, their faces would clear, whatever they had against him.

"They're so fond of me," he said slyly.

But they could not have been very pleasant to him that evening, for when Alfonso arrived, he found Gralli already gone and the whole family in bed, sign of great ill-humor. Alfonso felt a pang of disappointment that not even on the very day when the Lanuccis heard of his generosity had they felt grateful enough to wait up for him.

Lucia did, but in her own room, so she did not realize he was home. Just as he was leaving the living room on his way to bed, the girl appeared at her door.

"May I?" she asked with a shyness unusual for her, and essaying a smile. "I've come to thank you. Mother knows I've come; I must thank you in her name, too, in fact."

She broke off and burst into tears. They seemed the continuation of tears suppressed a short while ago, for they came gushing out.

Touched and embarrassed, he asked her to calm herself. He felt an unpleasant sensation, almost a remorse at suffocating this poor family under a weight of gratitude. He told her that he had done nothing but his duty. She went on sobbing, holding the handkerchief to her mouth and standing on the threshold but not leaning against the door.

"There's nothing to thank me for or to cry about. You'll be happy now, that's all."

At this, Lucia at once began talking.

"Happy? Never!" Then, interrupted from time to time by tears, she told how that same evening she had asked Gralli to renounce the dowry and he had refused. "Now I don't love him any more," and she began crying again. She was a child really, and Alfonso felt more revolted than ever at the thought of Gralli's betrayal. "I've never really loved him! They told me I had to marry him and I realized it too, but I'd never imagined he'd be so horrid."

Alfonso tried to convince her that Gralli was better than she thought and that he wanted money only in order to enjoy it with her. He could find no other arguments. And he realized he was making no real effort to turn away a new and gentle affection for himself born in the girl's heart and see that it was directed at Gralli.

She tried to kiss his hand and he did not let her, but drew her to him and kissed her on the forehead, while the girl trembled in his arms. Slowly, with dignity, talking to her and telling her not to cry, he led her back into the living room and finally to the door of her room.

Thinking over his own behavior with Gralli, whose admiration he had not scrupled to arouse, and with Lucia, whose gratitude he had managed to increase, Alfonso repeated to himself the question: "Is this how a philosopher should behave?"

Once again he had to smile at himself for being so pleased at old Lanucci's gratitude. The latter would bow before him as to a superior being, listen with reverent attention whenever he spoke.

"Never have I seen such a thing in all my life!" he exclaimed when he was present at the consignment of the money to the notary.

"You're very kind!" Gustavo said to him. "How much money have you got left now?"

On hearing Alfonso's reply, he refused to believe it was true. And Alfonso was weak enough to spend a long time persuading him.

CHAPTER

XX

The yearly balance sheet had been made up for a fortnight, and still no one at the bank knew anything about the bonuses annually distributed among employees on that occasion.

"Do you think they mean to do away with them?" asked Ballina, worried. The sum he hoped for was already earmarked to pay debts and, as he said, it would mean bankruptcy for him if nothing was forthcoming. His remarks now became more biting than ever. "If it's his fault, that old redskin ought to be strung up." Old redskin meant Maller.

Alchieri acted the buffoon, though also worried at the long delay in getting money on which he was relying; he jeered at Ballina and urged him on. He arranged with Santo to call each clerk, except Ballina, one by one and make them all pretend that they had received a hundred or two or three hundred francs apiece. Ballina went wild, saying he was going to complain to Maller, and listing his services to the bank, the hours which he had worked overtime. To Alfonso, who had agreed to pretend he had received three hundred francs, he said: "Of course you're favored, we all know that, you go to Signorina Maller and give her lessons! It's a scandal, this bank is!"

Hurriedly Alfonso revealed the joke, red in the face and thoroughly regretting he had provoked Ballina.

One Sunday Santo came to call Bravicci in Maller's name. Bravicci warned Ballina before going, but the latter went on calmly writing.

"My dear fellow, you can pull my leg once but not twice!" When Bravicci returned and showed him two notes of a hundred francs each, Ballina had doubts, and when he, too, was called, he went off to Maller with his springiest tread. "If you're deceiving me, it'll be all the worst for you." He was almost content when he came out. "It's enough, I can't complain. I'm fated never to be quite free of debt."

Starringer and Alchieri were the most pleased; both received more than they had hoped.

Miceni came in for mutual congratulations and to tell what his luck was. He was not discontented; he had been praised but told that he was not charged with as much responsibility now that he was in the counting-house, and so he was not to expect a lot from his superiors.

"I'm still looking out for another job, and one of these days I hope to cut and run."

The only one not yet called was Alfonso; Santo, who was acting as messenger that day, eventually came up to him instead of shouting his name out and whispered a few words which Alfonso did not quite catch but supposed to be the call to see Maller.

From the moment Bravicci was called, Alfonso had been in a great state of agitation. Now after all this time he was about to speak to Maller again; he was disturbed by the idea that Maller might have to exercise self-control to treat him in calm office tones. Alfonso had now persuaded himself that he could hope for an increase of pay and a big bonus; a few days before, he had actually feared the possibility of overpayment as a bribe for silence. Now that he needed money, he would try to enjoy what was given him, remembering that he had done work enough to deserve any bonus.

Disappointed in anticipation, he was about to enter Maller's room when Santo stopped him with an ironic smile.

"Not in there! It's Signor Cellani who's calling you in!"

Santo thought he had not been called in for a bonus. Alfonso went purple in the face; this was even worse than he had expected. Even on that occasion Maller did not want to see him.

He went to Cellani, who was bent as usual over his desk and did not see him at once.

"Signor Maller was suddenly called out of the office and told me to give you this!" and with ill grace he put two bank notes on the table. Alfonso took them glumly, murmured scarcely intelligible thanks, and went out.

In the passage he had another proof of the contempt with which he was being treated. Maller was in his office! His red head peering outside his room, he was shouting, calling for Santo. He was in such a rage that he did not see Alfonso. Alfonso, in his first flush of anger, could not restrain himself; he wanted to be seen. Without bowing or greeting Maller, he called to him: "I'll get Santo if you like."

Maller looked at him with some surprise.

"All right!" he said shortly, and shut the door in his face.

Alfonso returned to his room without bothering to look for Santo. He was asked how much he had received and what Maller had said to him, and replied that there had been the usual words and showed the two bank notes. Everyone thought the money was too little. Alfonso reminded Ballina of his words a few days ago.

"Do you think I'm favored now?"

He left with a firm step, after hesitating an instant in front of Sanneo's door. The custom was to go to the department head and thank him for the bonus. But no, Sanneo did not deserve that! His recommendations must have been very weak if that was all the result they had.

Reaching the open air, he remembered how, when he was at school, his parents came to town at the end of the scholastic year and accompanied him to school to get his certificate. They would wait for him in the public gardens opposite the school, and he would hurry triumphantly over to receive his father's praises and his mother's warm embrace when he knew he had deserved them. One year his certificate was spoiled by a bad mark. Alfonso had hesitated a long time before entering the garden, then finally had made up his mind, and had gone up to his father and handed over the certificate without saying a word, not answering Signorina Carolina's affectionate words of encouragement. His father pointed at the bad mark very seriously and,

when his wife made excuses for their son, doubted if
the mark was deserved and suggested it might be
attributed to the antipathy of some teacher, he replied
that he did not believe it and that whoever does his
duty banishes all evil. How wrong his father was!
Even at that young age Alfonso already knew from
experience that none of his efforts could lessen a hatred
roused through no fault of his own.

At that very moment he met Annetta for the first
time since his return. Her figure looked majestic in a
heavy black cloak; beside her trotted Francesca, insignificant as a servant. It seemed impossible that he had
ever possessed such a splendid creature. It must have
been a dream. No trace of his kisses remained on that
beautiful pure white face. How calm and regal she was,
as if she had never sinned with him and not been
about to deceive and dishonor another man.

He greeted her humbly, feeling he looked at her as
if asking her pardon. Francesca did not answer his
greeting, as if she had not seen him; Annetta nodded
after a slight hesitation, as if just remembering she had
known him.

Turning around to look, he saw her talking to
Francesca; her face seemed very pale. He tried to assure
himself about this and hope he had not been deceived;
it would have been a comfort if she had been flustered.
He followed her slowly but could no longer see her
face, as he did not dare walk any faster. The distance
between them increased, and when Annetta vanished
into the milling midday crowd on the Corso, he felt
more alone and unhappy than ever. How far away from
her he was! There was no way open for his return; he
would stay poor and abandoned when he could have
been rich and beloved. Perhaps it was his own fault.

That evening, when he entered the living room, he
heard himself called from Lucia's room.

"Mother forgot," said the girl in a voice which seemed to be trembling with emotion. "Do please close my door."

Her flustered tone made him think that door had been left open on purpose. He glanced into the little room and saw a sheet gleaming in a ray of light from the window. He had to struggle with himself not to enter. Though he did not desire Lucia, it seemed to him that a kiss from her might cancel the effect of Maller's behavior; why spend the night alone in such a state of agitation? Actually he needed no kiss to calm himself; a small effort at self-control was enough. "One more renunciation!" he said to himself with a smile, and the word recalled the state he had been in a few days before. It had taken so little to get him out of it! Maller had now shown openly the antipathy he had given signs of before; nothing else new had happened!

He went to bed quite surprised to find he could achieve quiet by cold reasoning, slept soundly and had a fantastic dream of a kind he had not had since childhood, about riding through the air on a wooden plank, walking dryshod over water, and lording it over a great city.

But next day something happened for which no reasoning could console him, a disaster that showed he really was being persecuted.

Early that morning he went as usual to Sanneo to ask for instructions about letters arrived the day before. Sanneo greeted him with an embarrassed smile, holding the packet of letters in front of him and staring at them, which was obviously to gain time to think. Then he politely asked that Alfonso, before receiving instructions, go in to see Cellani, who wanted to talk to him.

"Do you know what he wants to say?" asked Alfonso,

to prepare himself for Cellani's communication, which he already guessed to be very important.

"I don't know," replied Sanneo, "but they seem to have gone off their heads in there."

But he obviously knew quite well what it was, for in the offhand way he dealt with everything not strictly business, he asked Alfonso to give the bundle of letters in his hand to Bravicci. He was polite but obviously wanted to waste no time. So Alfonso expected the worst. Dismissal.

Cellani was not in his office but hurried in as soon as he heard Alfonso enter. He looked very serious, but as he was at last using complete sentences, Alfonso found him politer than usual.

"I have something to tell you which you may be glad to hear." He obviously doubted this, and in spite of his serious air the phrase sounded ironical. "In the countinghouse they need an expert clerk for the central desk, and Signor Maller has decided this clerk is to be you."

It was an order, not a suggestion, though transfers to the countinghouse were usually made by agreement with the particular clerk, on the basis of a suggestion.

"So I'm to leave the correspondence department, am I?" asked Alfonso, to prolong the interview. He was undecided whether to protest, react against what he realized to be a punishment, or resign himself with good grace. But anger won. Was Cellani jeering at him by trying to pass off such a humiliation as advancement? "What have I done to be kicked out of the correspondence department like this?"

Cellani looked at him in surprise. He moved toward his chair with an impatient shrug, incapable of more pretense.

"Ask Signor Maller; I know nothing about it myself."

He puffed out his cheeks and began writing and signing nervously.

"All right," said Alfonso resolutely, "I'll go and ask Signor Maller!"

He went out. But already in that brief interval he had calculated the risk of going to Maller. He could always take that step later, after he had had time for reflection. He went straight to his own room and handed the letters to Bravicci as Sanneo had told him to. Bravicci said he'd known the day before that he was to take over Alfonso's work. Alfonso, who had been told nothing, brusquely handed over his other pending letters. For a moment he hated the other man.

"So you're being sent to the countinghouse, are you?" asked Ballina, seeing Alfonso leave his room with overcoat, hat, and a bundle of papers. "You're the second one! Sanneo is gradually shoving the lot of us in there!"

Alfonso did not excuse Sanneo; in fact, Ballina's observation suggested a reply to give all those who asked him the reason for his transfer.

In his new office he found his old colleague Miceni, who greeted him gaily and congratulated him on having finally left the correspondence department. It was worth the lower pay, he asserted; they were much better off in the countinghouse and, what was more, had the privilege of not seeing Sanneo.

Marlucci was less warm, but only because he was sorry that the room in which there had till then been two would now have to accommodate three. It was not very big, and not quite square because one corner, that of the building itself, was rounded. Alfonso's desk had not been brought in yet and there was no gas jet.

Miceni explained to him what his work would be, so briefly that Alfonso understood little or nothing. He was merely to look after the central desk, which Miceni had taken care of with others till then.

"I never asked for an assistant," said Miceni, laughing because other people's misfortunes always put him in a good humor. "The only reason why they could have sent you here was because Sanneo wanted to get rid of you." He asked Alfonso what had caused the quarrel, but Alfonso felt incapable of making up a story.

"Don't let's talk of it," he said, the blood rushing to his face as if at a gust of rage.

He would soon adapt himself to this new situation too, he thought, and remembered how at one time he had even wanted to move to this section for its cool calm. The clerks called it "Siberia" because people such as Miceni were sent there from other sections for punishment or because they had failed at other jobs; but advance was possible in the countinghouse too, and in fact Cellani himself had been head of it before becoming assistant manager. In that quiet, only reached by the faint sounds of business, he could work calm and happy. His pay and the money he still had should be enough to live on for some time; there was no reason to make hasty decisions.

So he reasoned, though still agitated; a first day of long dull unsuccessful work was enough to unsettle him. He had been shown how to draw up the day's accounts and enter them in the master ledger, a long but easy job of copying. But every night he was to add up the sums registered that day and balance the debit against the credit columns. His first attempt did not work out, and both Miceni and Marlucci, after spending some time helping him look for errors, had given up trying to make the figures tally and had gone off. Before leaving, Miceni, sorry at wasting so much time, exclaimed: "I wonder what mistakes you've managed to think up today!"

Alfonso went on comparing columns for some time still but did not find a single one of the errors which must be there: he realized the work had got on top of him and that he could not concentrate enough to compare the two sets of figures properly. Then he remembered telling Cellani that he wanted to go to Maller and complain of the injustice done him. He had not given up this idea; now he told himself that he had not gone to Maller at once in order to avoid disturbing him during working hours, but that he had never thought of taking the injustice done him without a protest. The ineffable boredom of his day had an effect. Rather than go home with his worries about unfinished work, he turned his thoughts on the idea of Maller at that hour calmly congratulating himself on disposing of Alfonso; this made the blood go to Alfonso's head, and he entered Maller's room intending to show his anger. Once inside, he had a second's panic; Maller might reply by telling him frankly the reasons for his hatred! But he controlled his agitation. If that happened, which seemed very unlikely, he would have less regard for Maller and he would speak of Annetta as if he were not talking to her father, insulting him; after taking his revenge, he would leave the bank with head high. A satisfaction like that was worth anything; the loss of his job was nothing in comparison.

Maller was lounging on a sofa reading a newspaper which hid half his face. He raised his head to speak to Alfonso and during the interview often let it drop back, either from weariness or to hide the expression on his face. In spite of the warning which Alfonso had given Cellani, Maller did not seem prepared for the interview. His bearing was uncertain, first cold and severe like that of a superior who considers he is being kind to reply at all, then restless and changeable.

"Signor Cellani told me that I was transferred from

the correspondence department to the countinghouse by your order," began Alfonso, stuttering. "I'd like to know if that's to punish me for some failure."

"No!" exclaimed Maller. "We needed a clerk in the countinghouse and could spare one in the correspondence department. That was all!"

He bent his head down behind the newspaper for the first time, obviously thinking the interview was over.

Maller's coldness made Alfonso calm; his tone was very far from the frank one he had feared. The matter was represented as being purely office routine. In a coolheaded moment he realized that he must not behave in a way that would force Maller to dismiss him, yet possibly say all he had in his heart. But he was now in a battling mood, conscious of being so and more resolved to fight than he had ever been in his life.

He had worked hard in the correspondence department, he said, and was sorry to lose, through no fault of his own, a place won with so much effort. In the correspondence department he knew he could be useful to the bank and expect quick advancement, while in the countinghouse he would be just another employee.

"It's just for the time being," said Maller, with a look of surprise at finding him so bold, and also with some curiosity about what was in the back of Alfonso's mind.

"Forever!" insisted Alfonso.

The resolute phrase gave him back the calm nearly swept away by Maller's glance. In a voice no longer uncertain he said that he was not a person who could live among figures alone; his brain needed to use words and sentences because it was used to studies, which Signor Maller knew something about. He tried to smile because this last observation was intended as a joke.

Maller's face went the color of his mottled hair; that

must be his form of pallor. The smile froze on Alfonso's lips; on that face there was no trace of good humor. What had alarmed Maller, he realized, was his allusion to studies which his chief could have known nothing about if they had not been connected with Annetta.

"Well, what do you want?"

Alfonso had looked so fierce that Maller had become calm; then, as soon as the other grew calm, he attacked in his turn.

The question annoyed Alfonso: was this a flat refusal?

"What I want!" he exclaimed angrily. "I demand to be put back in the correspondence department. I need a chance of advancement," and he gave a candid account of his financial difficulties.

"But people get on in the countinghouse, too," said Maller. He seemed very impatient.

Alfonso, firmly intending to put up an energetic defense and to answer every remark, was now in a great state of agitation due to the intense effort he had been making. So he was more and more at the mercy of his first fears. Usually he was hesitant and silent when faced by the unexpected, not carrying through his intentions and eventually regretting his own lack of resolve. This time his regret was quite different. Maller was being brusque, and he wanted to be, too.

He repeated that his transfer to the countinghouse must be a punishment; the clerks called the countinghouse the Siberia of the bank.

"I don't see why you're doing me this wrong!"

If Maller lost patience and gave a frank explanation, then the battle was lost; otherwise, this way it was won.

Maller dryly observed that he was not used to reversing his decisions and would be glad if Alfonso accepted them, otherwise . . . and he completed the phrase with a gesture which clearly meant that, even if Alfonso left the bank, he would not be happy.

"All right!" shouted Alfonso. "I'll leave." He felt strengthened at the thought that the worst that could happen to him was to be left jobless. He went on more calmly, but with a wish to hurt and offend: "I can't stay in a job where I'm persecuted with no reason . . . or no reason *I* can see."

This last addition gave him relief; he had had his say. For an instant he was undecided still, unwilling to leave before he was certain of having said his all; then he gave a bow and moved toward the door.

At his last remark Maller had made a slight movement which did not escape Alfonso; then he raised his head from the newspaper.

"Don't make a serious decision like that on the spot," he said in a gentle voice, almost begging, which surprised Alfonso because its tone was quite different from that of his replies till then. "I'll see if I can get you back to the correspondence department some day."

It was obvious! The great man was worried.

For a moment, quite dazzled by the unexpected victory, Alfonso did not find this enough.

"Till then, am I to go on working in the counting-house?"

The day's boredom was too oppressive for him not to bring this up, too.

"I'll see you're helped with your work there," said Maller, giving way at once.

Alfonso left without any thanks after a slight bow.

This interview left him in a ghastly state of agitation. Once outside Maller's room he was dissatisfied, felt that the victory obtained was not the desired one because he had not succeeded in destroying the management's disdain for him. He was keeping his job—that was about all! The honest Cellani would continue to treat

him coldly and contemptuously! Oh, if he could speak
to him, tell him how much his affair with Annetta was
due to her flirtatiousness, which had aroused in him
an emotion maybe ignoble or impure but irresistible.
Then he would no longer be considered by Cellani
merely a person who had insinuated himself into the
Maller home in order to grab a dowry by dishonest
wiles.

Every detail of that interview worried him as he went
off, and he tried in vain to think of a word in it which
he could remember with any pleasure. Maller's every
word had been stamped with antipathy or offhanded-
ness when he did not betray fear; and he himself had
made the mistake of gearing each word of his so that
he might keep his position and improve it, none at
making Maller friendlier. What put him in despair, in
fact, was that he had won the battle only by alluding to
recondite reasons for his ill-treatment in the bank. Had
he made a threat which alarmed Maller?

Then he must be thought a blackmailer! That was
why he was feared! He did not want to let such an
accusal stand. No voice would be raised in his defense
if he did not act. Maller knew too little not to be suspicious of him, and Annetta's memory of him must
have been twisted by hatred into that of a mere
adventurer.

He would ask for another interview with Maller next
day, hand in his resignation, and tell him frankly his
reasons for this action. He did not want to keep even
for a day what he was allowed only for fear of vengeance. "You hate me," he would say to him. "You're
boss, why keep me on? It's an insult not to dismiss
me!"

This idea should bring him some calm, he felt. He
went home and flung himself on his bed half dressed,
still feeling a need to find relief in dreams. He had

made up his mind! He would be without a job; what would he do with his life? He could not live by studies even if they were much better than his were; and it would be very difficult to find another job. Which of his contacts in town would be of use to him except those made at the Mallers', and on one of these, the most important, he could not count. He saw himself abandoned, poor, starving maybe; and hunger, he knew too well, he could not endure. Eventually he would even hold out a hand to the Mallers for their charity or perhaps reach the point of threatening them to make them help him. In his long soliloquy tears often came to his eyes. He must try to keep his job at the Maller bank as long as he could.

Then he thought of one possible way of giving necessary explanations without losing his job; by giving them to Annetta herself! He knew her to be vain and selfish, but not heartless; she had often forgiven him out of compassion, that compassion which had made her forget her fear of compromising herself. He would turn to her. After all, he was asking nothing but to be left in peace, and he was asking it of those who should have even greater interest than he had himself in silence being kept. Surely Annetta would grant his request?

His first idea had been to wait for a chance to talk to Annetta, maybe to stop her on the street; then he felt he could not bear to live in such a state of agitation and longed to get rid of it at once. Next day he would write to Annetta and ask her to grant him an interview.

Eventually he did it there and then; the activity would help restore his calm, he thought. He jumped out of bed and lit the lamp. It was a long time since he had written at that table; the rusty nib resisted, the ink refused to flow and had to be diluted.

He began with an opening which seemed dignified

and humble: *"Illustrissima Signorina,"* then asked for the interview in a few words, saying that he had something to tell her of great importance to himself and, he thought, to her too. If she granted this interview, as he did not doubt she would, he asked her to be on the mole closest to Via dei Forni between eight and nine o'clock next evening. Then he added a touch of ingenuous regret: "I no longer know how to treat you, Annetta, now you may hate me," and one of equally ingenuous irony: "I'm signing both my Christian name and my surname, as you may not recognize my Christian name alone."

He did not sleep, but the depression which often brought tears to his eyes ceased. Now his agitation was of quite another kind, and he traced this back to those two gentler phrases, like an excited lover's, addressed to Annetta. How pleasantly he was lulled by the thought that he would see her again next day! There, once again, at the thought of that face which had once blushed and paled for love of him, he had forgotten the hostile faces surrounding him. For love of him, not of Macario; he knew that from Macario himself, who had denied that passion could ever throw a shadow over her face.

Now his purpose in asking for that interview no longer mattered; his main wish was to re-establish himself in her eyes, to make her feel he was not the adventurer that she supposed. Not that this would mean the end of her projected match with Macario; but affectionate gratitude and friendship for him remaining in the heart of the woman he had loved would be enough.

He began imagining what he would say to her. He would not apologize for seducing her, that would be an error in tactics; he had done it in passion and could not regret an action which had brought him the greatest happiness of his life. He knew from his reading that women always forgive a homage to their beauty in any, even criminal, form. He would waste few words about himself, just assure her that he would die rather than say a word about the secret uniting them. Maybe she should be able to guess that from his bearing without his lowering himself to say so. Though he would have liked just to tell her he loved her, he would not say a word about love to her. In his misery now he no longer depised that love. Even the thought of it had comforted him in his gloom! To let out any hint of it to Annetta would be dangerous because a man in love cannot be trusted, however honest and benevolent he may appear; so he must be very careful to hide this new affection of his. He must appear as a lover with no rancor at being abandoned, one whose love has turned into sweet fraternal friendship. He would ask her affectionately if she was happy and make a great show of joy if, as she probably would, she assured him that she loved Macario. On the other hand, she might possibly confess that she was not happy and confide in him freely. If that happened, there would be no more difficulties for him, and he need not spend time on what attitude to assume.

Santo willingly agreed to deliver the letter.

For the first time Alfonso was able to put to use his observations on character. Assuming an air of importance, he asked mysteriously whether Signorina Annetta had told him she was expecting that letter. Then he warned him that it was a matter of giving a surprise to a member of the Maller family.

Santo, delighted to be in on a secret concerning Signorina Annetta, put the note in his pocket. He promised to be very cautious and was offended at Alfonso's so often telling him to keep the secret. Then he went further and complained that Alfonso never showed his face at the Mallers' any more. Was he offended with someone? He gave the impression that if Alfonso was he would avenge him.

Alfonso replied boldly: "I was there at the end of last month!"

Santo, who knew nothing of that, gave a gesture of surprise.

"Ah, really! But even so, you don't come as often as you did before."

The note was sent. At midday Alfonso delightedly watched Santo leave the bank. Every minute that brought him closer to the time of his interview with Annetta gave him joy. His only fear was that Maller might take some step before this interview took place. No! If he had to accept any improvements in his position at the bank, he did not want them prompted by fear. Even rejecting his silly dreams of the night before, he still believed this interview would dispel all misunderstanding. At the worst, he would succeed in convincing Annetta that if they had loved each other and no longer did, this was no reason for mutual hatred.

He could not put down a single figure in his ledger, or even try to spot the mistakes which had caused so much trouble the day before. By evening his impatience was such that it made him leave the office and sent him wandering around the bank in search of people to talk with to pass the remaining hour of waiting.

He went to Ballina and asked for news of the correspondence department; it seemed years since he had left it. Ballina, as usual, was having his supper at the bank, and that evening he cooked eggs on an oil lamp, and ate them with bread and butter washed down by a glass of wine. He explained to Alfonso how little that succulent supper cost; scarcely seventy *centesime*.

Alfonso envied him. Ballina was preoccupied, he

saw, by his own health, and was very successfully coping with quite unfavorable circumstances. He slept, so he said, calm as a baby, tired out after copying those endless names; his only worry was some Hungarian or Slav name with many consonants.

When Ballina left, Alfonso went to Starringer to waste another half hour in the dispatch department, which was humming with work. He ran into old Antonio, who was in charge of taking letters to the post office. The poor old man was walking along, cursing against the directors who signed letters so late. This was the dispatch department's usual complaint. Even Starringer brought it out, and Alfonso pretended to listen to him, though not taking in a word in his impatience.

He did not leave the bank yet. Next he brushed his trousers and cleaned his shoes carefully with Miceni's equipment; that was also something to do.

It was a little past a quarter to eight when he left the bank, and he began to run, fearing to arrive at the rendezvous late. What would he do in that case? Such a delay might be fatal.

The sirocco still persisted, but no rain had fallen during the whole day. Until nightfall the city had been covered with a slight mist, but that had also gone and the sky was clear, strewn with stars, moonless. A thin but unending slime covered the paving stones.

At ten minutes past eight Alfonso had his first doubt whether Annetta would turn up. It was quite likely she wouldn't. Without confessing it to himself, he had acted until then as if he were sure she loved him still; otherwise he could not hope that a girl who was engaged should take such a step. He realized he had written her a poor letter. He should have merely told Annetta he wanted to talk to her and awaited an indication of when and where from her. But it was too late to correct that now. He would wait until nine; and he leaned against a parapet, patient and resigned.

He noticed a young man passing him for the second time and giving him a curious stare: he had already seen that oblong face, with its fair mustache and penetrating look, and that long thin body. He looked after him; it was Federico Maller; he recognized him by his narrow trousers. Was this a coincidence, or had Annetta given her brother a message for him? He had never liked young Maller and was sorry to have him to deal with, but now he must try to facilitate whatever duty the brother had taken on out of affection for his sister.

Feeling Federico draw closer again, he turned to greet him, but got a shove which nearly flung him to the ground.

"Apologize, you swine!" young Maller yelled at him, raising a hand which in the darkness Alfonso thought was armed.

Did they want to kill him? He flung himself on the thin figure, held the upraised threatening hand, and seized young Maller by the throat. The other moved back toward the sea in an effort to break free. Alfonso was panting and using much more force than was necessary.

"I'll throw you in the sea!" he threatened, giving him a push, but not hard enough.

"What manners people have in this town!" said young Maller disdainfully, putting a hand up to straighten his neckband.

"I thought you were trying to pick my pocket," replied Alfonso indignantly.

He accepted Maller's visiting card and proffered his own. His own seconds would call on Maller at twelve o'clock next day, he promised. It was a surprise to be behaving so correctly all at once.

So this was the appointment which Annetta had

granted! She had made a quick decision, had an easy means to hand, and sent off her brother to kill him. Annetta, too, hated him, which grieved him; she did not think herself safe from him, and thought he must be eliminated so as not to have to fear him any more. Oh, she did not know him! In all the time he had loved her she had not realized how open and honest was his nature. That was the sad part, not that Federico would probably kill him!

He walked along faster and faster toward home. On the Corso he stopped an instant, thinking Macario had passed him. It was not he, but Alfonso wondered if it would be any satisfaction to take revenge on Macario by giving him a full description of his affair with Annetta. No! His only possible satisfaction would be to convince Annetta that she was mistaken about him. He would write her a letter, a dying man's farewell.

Then he found himself sitting at his desk, pen in hand, but could not manage to put down a single word. Never in his daydreamer's life had he been so completely possessed by a dream. He dropped his pen and put his head in his hands, longing to reflect but dreaming obsessively. Annetta wanted him dead! He longed for her to get her wish and then regret it. He imagined her rekindling her love for him one day, and her visiting his grave to scatter tears on it. Oh! How sweet and calm it would be in that cemetery, which he thought of as green and warmed by the sun!

When he opened his eyes, he was surprised to find himself facing a piece of writing paper.

He was to fight Federico Maller in an unequal duel, his adversary having the advantages of both hatred and capacity. What had he himself to hope for? Only one way was open to him of escaping a duel in which he would play a wretched and ridiculous part: suicide. Suicide would give him back Annetta's affection. Never had he loved her as he did at that moment. It was no longer a matter of self-interest or his senses. The farther he saw her moving away from him, the more he loved her; now that he had definitely lost all hope of reconquering her smile, her affectionate word, life seemed colorless, null. Once he had vanished, Annetta would no longer feel disgust born of fear at the thought of him, and that was all that he could hope for. He did not want to live on and appear to her as a contemptible enemy whom she suspected of trying to harm her and make her pay a high price for the favors she had granted him.

Till then he had thought of suicide only as others with their prejudices saw it. Now he accepted it not with resignation but with joy. Liberation! He reminded himself that, until a short time before, he had thought differently. He tried to calm himself, to see if that feeling of joy were not a mere product of some fever possessing him. No! He was quite lucid. He lined up in his mind all the arguments against suicide, from the moral ones given by preachers to those of modern philosophers. They made him smile! They were not arguments but expressions of a wish, the wish to live.

He, though, felt incapable of living. Some feeling which he had often tried and failed to understand made it an unbearable agony to him. He knew neither how to love nor how to enjoy; he had suffered in the best of circumstances more than did others in the most painful ones. He was leaving life without regret. It was the one way to become superior to the suspicions and hatreds of others. That was the renunciation of which he had dreamed. He must destroy this organism of his which knew no peace; while it was alive, it would continue to drag him into the struggle because that was what it was there for. He would not write to Annetta. Even the bother and possible danger of such a letter he would spare her.

N———, October 23, 18———

Signor Luigi Mascotti:

In reply to your letter of the 21st instant, we would inform you that the reasons for the suicide of our clerk Signor Alfonso Nitti are quite unknown. He was found dead in his room on the 16th instant, at four in the morning, by Signor Gustavo Lanucci, who, on returning home at that hour, had his suspicions aroused by a strong smell of gas diffused throughout the whole apartment. Signor Nitti left a letter addressed to Signora Lanucci in which he named her his heir. Your question about the sum of money found with Signor Nitti should therefore be referred to the above mentioned.

The funeral took place on the 18th instant in the presence of colleagues and management.

We remain,

Yours faithfully,
Maller & Co.

A NOTE ON THE TYPE

THIS BOOK is set in ELECTRA, a Linotype face designed by W. A. Dwiggins (1880-1956). This face cannot be classified as either modern or old-style. It is not based on any historical model, nor does it echo any particular period or style. It avoids the extreme contrasts between thick and thin elements that mark most modern faces, and attempts to give a feeling of fluidity, power, and speed.

Composed, printed, and bound by
H. Wolff, New York.
Typography and binding design by
VINCENT TORRE